My thanks go to my partner and co-author, David Colane. Without his inspiration, advice and encouragement, this book would not have been written!

Jan Mount

To Lo,

Best wishes,

Jan

x

FAME AND MISFORTUNE

JAN MOUNT

Ӝ

Copyright ©Penskills Publishing 2015

Printed and bound in Great Britain by
Clays Ltd, St Ives plc

ISBN-13   978-0-9933295-1-7

Front cover illustration by
Rob Francis www.ink-corporated.co.uk

First published 2015

PEN
SKILLS
PUBLISHING

ABOUT THE AUTHOR

Jan Mount worked in the City of London as a Chairman's PA for various commercial and financial companies over a period of almost thirty years.

During that time Jan was appointed as Editor of the House Magazine for three of those companies. She was able to combine her talent as a photographer with her literary skills - and her nose for a good story!

In the late nineties she was invited to help run a newly formed Sports Management Agency alongside Olympic swimming gold medallist, Duncan Goodhew, MBE. The agency office was situated near London Bridge, with a wide ranging client list of sporting celebrities, notably cricketer Sir Ian Botham, OBE.

Jan moved from London to a village in Lincolnshire in 2002. Now retired, she realised her long ambition to write and drew on her love and knowledge of sport for this, her first novel.

FAME AND MISFORTUNE

PROLOGUE

Minutes before one o'clock on a cold, January morning, two glamorous young women giggled noisily as their taxi cab pulled up outside a magnificent mansion. Kathie and Melanie were returning from a girls' night out with a few of their fellow footballers' wives and girlfriends, and both were a little tipsy.

Kathie, trying to maintain some modicum of dignity, was tugging at the hemline of her flimsy designer evening dress, in a vain attempt to avoid flashing the tops of her thighs to a gawping driver, as she opened her door and swung out her long shapely legs. She could see he was craning his neck to get a good eyeful in his mirror.

Melanie was laughing as she tumbled out of the car on the other side and took in the scene. 'Don't worry Kathie – he's seen it all before! Oops!' Melanie slightly stumbled as she moved away from the taxi, still giggling.

'Not mine he hasn't!' retorted Kathie.

She fished in her evening bag and handed a fifty pound note to the driver. 'Keep the change', she said as she turned and began to walk towards the house.

'Thanks ladies!' The driver smiled widely, as he eagerly grabbed the note. 'Any time – it's been a pleasure.'

Kathie pulled a face. 'Not for us! Yuk! Dirty old man!'

'Well, you can't blame him, Kathie. I think he got a good look at your knickers! Just as well you put them on tonight!' Melanie held her hand over her mouth to stifle a loud guffaw, and Kathie began to laugh.

'Shut up, you silly bitch. Let's get in, it's bloody freezing,' she said, as she fumbled with the door key, finally managing to turn the lock and push open the heavy oak door. The two girls stepped into the vast hallway of Kathie and Max Rawlings' palatial house. Kathie bowed dramatically to Melanie.

'Here we are – home at last,' she said in a high, accentuated posh voice. 'Welcome to my humble abode, chez "Rangers Lodge" - named, of course, after England's famous football team, which we all love and cherish!' She kicked off her six inch high heels with a sigh of relief. 'Phew, that's better. They were killing me.' Looking at the antique grandfather clock at the far end of the hall, as it struck one, Kathie giggled.

'Good Lord Mel — it's one o'clock. Ooh, I say — we'll turn into pumpkins!'

Melanie, who was sitting on a velvet chaise longue near the hall table, was trying to undo the ankle straps of her own break neck heels. Finally, she had the shoes off, and stood up, lost her balance, and nearly fell over. They both laughed uncontrollably as she began to make exaggerated tiptoe steps across the hall, with her finger to her lips. 'Shh!', she was hissing, which made Kathie laugh even more.

'Don't worry Melanie my dear, Max won't be asleep yet. If I know him, he's probably playing the re-run of today's game in the TV lounge for the third time and making notes!', she said, as she walked unsteadily towards one of the several rooms leading off the huge vestibule. 'And anyway, it makes a change for me to be out. It was a good night though wasn't it — it's not a bad place.'

Melanie nodded and replied, with heavy sarcasm, 'Yeah, Leeds' answer to Stringfellows! That's got nothing on our *Stroke of Midnight* dive!'

'Dive! How very dare you! I think it's okay as nightclubs go. We should have more GNO's, don't you think? I enjoyed tonight - it was a good laugh!'

'Too right!', agreed Melanie.'

Kathie scanned the television lounge. 'Ooer, he's not in here, but he's left the TV on, stupid devil.' She frowned. 'That's not like him though!' She crossed the room to turn off the TV. 'That's weird,' she said to herself, 'it's on freeze - and it has been for over an hour. He must have gone out for a pee or something and then got distracted by his phone. Idiot!' She tutted and switched off the television.

Coming back into the hall, she began to open doors to the dining room, into the kitchen, then traced her steps back to the library, which led off through the main lounge into a fully stocked games room. She switched on the light and glanced at the leather Chesterfield armchair near the bar, thinking Max may have dozed off in his favourite seat. The vast room was illuminated by numerous wall lights, highlighting Max's many trophies, cups, photos and framed football shirts. She looked towards the full sized snooker table which graced the centre of the room, brightly lit by its own overhead green shaded lights. Still giggling, she crossed to the table and peered under. 'He's not under here either!' She tutted. 'He must be upstairs. Don't tell me he's actually gone to bed, and it's only ...' she checked her gold Rolex watch, 'just gone five past one!'

Having checked every downstairs room in the massive house, she walked back into the hall. Melanie was in the kitchen, taking two mugs from the dresser.

Kathie went upstairs to the master bedroom. He wasn't in there, and the bed was undisturbed. She hurried along the long landing and opened the door to the nursery. She went immediately to the little four poster bed with its pink frilly drapes and "Barbie" design duvet. Blowing out a sigh of relief, she saw that Becky, their five year old daughter, was sound asleep. She leaned over and kissed her lightly on the head. But where was Max? She was feeling uneasy now. Surely he wouldn't go out and leave Becky on her own! 'Ah, the pool – I forgot that. I bet he's having a ruddy night time swim!' She was becoming more and more concerned as she fairly ran down the stairs, through the games room and into the huge gymnasium that housed the indoor pool. The main lights were off, but the small spot lights dotted around the walls glowed dimly. He wasn't in the pool, so she checked each of the six changing rooms to make sure he wasn't in one of them. Alarm bells were ringing in her head now as she hurried back towards the kitchen, where Melanie was leaning back against the central oasis, watching the kettle boil.

'Mel, I can't find him anywhere! Where on earth can he be? He promised faithfully he would keep an eye on Becky all night. I'm getting really worried now - it's not like him is it!'

Melanie shrugged.

'Don't panic Kathie, he must be here somewhere. Anyone can get lost in this flipping great house!

Perhaps he went out into the garden - have you checked there? Try his mobile.'

'What? At this time of night? I could ring him though. Good idea!'

Melanie wrinkled her nose and sniffed, looking all around her. 'Can you smell anything – like gas fumes or something?'

'What?' Kathie sniffed a few times. 'Yes, vaguely. She looked puzzled. 'That's mad, we're all electric!' The two women walked back out into the entrance hall, where they stood in silence, looking at each other, wondering what to do next.

'Listen,' whispered Melanie.

'What?'

'Listen,' she said again. 'Can you hear a car?' They both rushed to the front door and each looked through one of the two small bubbled panes of glass. There was no car outside.

'It's coming from the garage!', exclaimed Kathie, eyes and mouth open. 'What's the silly bugger doing in there at this time of night?' She walked towards a door halfway along on the left-hand side of the hall. 'That's strange as well,' she said. 'It's not locked - look the key is still in. We always take the key out when we lock up at night, so he must be in the garage.' Suddenly feeling very sober, and with an increasing sense of panic and bewilderment, Kathie pushed open the heavy fireproof door. The smell of fumes knocked her back, but she could just about make out the nearest car, a Porsche, through the acrid haze and she could hear that the engine was running. Putting her hand over her mouth, she ran to the driver's seat. The sight that met her eyes made her almost faint. She let out a piercing scream and tried to pull the car door open.

A tube was fastened to the exhaust pipe, running along the side of the car and into the rear window, which was opened just enough to prevent the pipe from falling out. In the front seat a young man was slumped, head on chest, his thick fair hair pressed against the window. A small trickle of saliva was dripping from his mouth, down the window and onto his collar.

'Oh no, hell, it's locked! Mel, Mel, Oh, my God! What's happened? Call an ambulance, quick, call an ambulance!', Kathie shouted hysterically between loud sobs, as she yanked the tube out of the back window of the car with both hands and then began pulling at the driver's door.

Melanie, who was standing holding the heavy door open, didn't wait to be asked twice. She grabbed a small rug and used it wedge it under the door to prevent it from closing. She ran towards the telephone on the marble table near the staircase and dialled 999.

'Ambulance please and hurry, it's an emergency.'

A few seconds passed. 'Hello, yes that's right, it's my friend's husband. No, there's no blood, no, no, not an injury - I don't think so anyway, but he's locked in a car with the engine running – yes, exhaust fumes and he's unconscious. Er – post code - LD16, don't know the rest, sorry, but it's Ranger's Lodge in Willoughby Avenue - yes that's right, it's his house. Thanks. Please, please hurry!'

Melanie was white and shaking as she pressed a button near the front door to release the electric gates for the ambulance. She hurried back to the garage, where Kathie was frantically running around the car trying all the doors. They were all locked. Kathie began to bang on the window of the driver's side where she could see her husband was slumped, his face pressed up against the glass. She was screaming hysterically, 'Max, Max!'

Melanie took her by the shoulders and turned her around. 'Kathie, Kathie – calm down. Where are the keys to the Porsche? Is there another set anywhere?'

Kathie stared at Mel, trying to get her head straight. 'Keys, keys! Yes – Mel – yes – on the key hooks in the kitchen - the utility. They're on a black and silver fob, in a white cupboard. Quick Mel – get them.'

Melanie rushed off to the kitchen and came back with the keys in her hand. Kathie, hands shaking, opened the driver's door. As she did so, Max, slumped over towards her. She pushed him back so that she could lean across and turn off the ignition.

Between them, the two women pulled Max, heavy and lifeless, from the car, dragging him across the garage floor towards the heavy, self closing fire door, which Melanie had wedged open. Once they had Max in the hall, Kathie fell to her knees beside him, and saw for the first time that he was blue. She put her face close to his mouth and nose. She screamed. 'Oh my God, Mel! He's not breathing! He looks dead, look at him, he's dead! What's happened to him – what's he done?' She kneeled over him and took him in her arms, shaking him, screaming hysterically, 'Wake up Max, wake up, darling!'

Melanie pulled her gently away. 'Let me see Kathie – perhaps we can try to resuscitate him – I know how to do CPR.' She kneeled down beside Max and felt his pulse. She gasped and bit her lip. Hoisting up her dress she kneeled either side of his lower chest. 'Let me think, heel of right hand on the chest, other hand on top, lock fingers. Whew!', she whispered as she began to press down repeatedly. Kathie, stricken with shock, was sitting on her haunches, motionless, by his side.

At last they heard the welcome sound of a siren coming down the drive.

Melanie looked at her dazed friend and said sharply, 'Kathie! Get the door, quickly!'

Kathie got up and hurried to the door to let the paramedics in. Two men walked quickly towards Max. The older of the two addressed the women.

'Hello ladies, my name's Mike, and this is Levi'. He motioned to his colleague, a young black man who looked no more than twenty.

Melanie and Kathie nodded in acknowledgement.

'How long have you been administering CPR?', he asked Melanie.

'Oh, I'm not sure, about five minutes I think. I couldn't find a pulse though,' she added quietly.

'Well done, well done.' He offered his hand to help Melanie to her feet, then sank down beside Max, feeling for his pulse. He gave a small shake of his head but continued with CPR for another five minutes.

Levi was asking the two women questions to ascertain details of the incident. Melanie was answering, as Kathie was still in a state of shock, standing a few feet away from Mike, who was now using a defibrillator. She was deathly white, standing stock still and staring at her lifeless husband, not able to open her mouth to speak.

'Which one of you is his wife?', Levi was asking as he looked at Kathie. He obviously recognised her, but the question had to be asked.

Melanie pointed to Kathie. 'This is his wife – her name's Kathie.'

He nodded. He had seen that beautiful face many times on television and in newspapers, and he was a great fan of the famous footballer, Max Rawlings.

'And your name?'

'Melanie Peguy.'

Levi smiled. 'Thank you, you must be Anton's wife - Rangers' goalkeeper?'

Melanie nodded. 'We came home from a night out and found him in his car in the garage. The engine was running and there was a tube fixed to the exhaust. It was terrible!' She burst into tears and sobbed as the young man put his hand on her shoulder. He was also feeling shocked and horror struck at the sight of his football hero lying lifeless on the floor, and he felt close to tears himself.

'I'm so sorry. I can imagine. What a shocking thing to happen. Have you called the police by the way?'

Melanie wiped tears away with her hand and looked at him, shocked. She realised the implications of what had happened here tonight. She shook her head. 'Oh, no – the police! No, no, we haven't. Our first thought was the ambulance.'

'Don't worry, I'm onto it - just to check. They should have automatically been alerted anyway when you called us.' Levi was already dialling.

'Oh, God – the papers are going to have a field day when this gets out!', sighed Melanie.

Kathie was looking at Melanie and Levi in horror, but still didn't utter a sound. The tragic scene before her seemed to be unfolding in surreal slow motion.

'I know, love', Levi shook his head, 'but everyone in the world knows Max Rawlings, and there won't be any way of keeping this lot quiet.' Levi looked down at the lifeless body and was certain that Max was dead.

Mike looked up, wiping his brow. 'I'm so sorry Mrs. Rawlings – there's nothing more we can do. I'm afraid he's gone - quite some time before we arrived I'd say. I tried everything. I can't tell you how sorry I am.'

Kathie fell to the floor on her knees, wailing uncontrollably, then threw herself across Max. 'No, no, no! Max, oh Max! What am I going to do now?' She looked up at Melanie. 'I can't live without him, Mel. What am I going to do?'

Melanie pulled Kathie to her feet and held her close as the doorbell rang. Levi secured the security chain and opened the door a few inches. He saw it was a man in his early fifties, a plain clothes detective he guessed, accompanied by a young uniformed policewoman.

'Police,' said the man, showing his identification.

Levi let the two officers in.

The detective shot a glance at the body on the floor and then addressed Kathie, recognising her immediately.

'Mrs. Rawlings, I'm Detective Inspector Hackett and this is Constable Lambert.' He indicated the young policewoman at his side. 'Firstly may I offer you my heartfelt condolences. This is a terrible tragedy and no mistake.' He shook his head, then knelt down briefly to look closely at the body, avoiding any contact.

'I know this sounds strange, but I must ask you to confirm that this is your husband Mrs. Rawlings - Max.'

Kathie nodded and managed to whisper, 'Yes, it is.'

D.I. Hackett got to his feet and Mike quickly explained the situation to the two officers, as Melanie was still hugging Kathie tightly. Mike confirmed that it appeared Max had been dead for some time before they arrived. He began to pack away his equipment.

'Constable Lambert here will take a statement from you both.' D.I. Hackett nodded to the policewoman, who signalled to the two paramedics to follow her a few yards away while she took out her notebook. He turned to Kathie. 'Mrs. Rawlings, can we sit down somewhere?'

'Of course, shall we go into the kitchen. I was just making some tea,' suggested Melanie.

'Good idea,' he replied.

Melanie was guiding Kathie towards the kitchen when the doorbell rang again.

P.C. Lambert opened it to face three people clad in white plastic. The older man confirmed that he was the pathologist, with his assistant and a police photographer.

Kathie turned and gasped as they walked through the door.

D.I. Hackett walked up to the three men and spoke quietly to them. As they walked towards the body, he gently pulled Kathie away and nodded towards the kitchen.

'I have to ask you some questions Mrs. Rawlings. Shall we sit down and have a cup of tea?'

Kathie just stared at him, unable to speak. Melanie took her arm gently and together they followed the detective into the kitchen. He pulled out a chair for Kathie, while Melanie made the tea. When they were all seated, he took out his note book and addressed both women, looking from one to the other.

'Who discovered Mr. Rawlings?'

'We both did,' said Melanie in a little, trembling voice. 'Max was nowhere to be found in the house - Kathie looked everywhere.' Tears were falling down her face.

'Okay, take it slowly.' D.I. Hackett put a reassuring hand on her arm. 'I understand how distressing this is for you both.'

Melanie wiped her eyes with a tissue, took a deep breath, and continued. 'It was only when we smelt the fumes that we looked in the garage.'

Kathie ran In and saw Max in the front seat. She eventually pulled the tube out and tried to open the car door, but it was locked. I managed to get the car keys from the kitchen.' She bit her lip hard, trying to stop herself from crying.

'Go on, love,' D.I. Hackett said gently, 'you're doing really well.'

'Well - she unlocked the car door, and turned off the ignition, and we managed to drag Max out between us and got him into the hall.'

'When did you call the ambulance?'

'I did that as soon as we realised what had happened - while Kathie was pulling on the tube. It was really hard - the window had been wound up so tight.'

'Has anyone else been in the house tonight?

Melanie looked at Kathie, who was shaking her head. 'No, I don't think he was expecting anyone.'

P.C. Lambert joined them. 'Can the paras go now Guv? I've got their statements.'

'Yes, well done Lambert. Thanks lads, you can go now.'

The two paramedics said 'goodnight' to everyone. Turning to Kathie as he reached the front door, Levi said quietly, 'so sorry Mrs. Rawlings. I can't believe it - I'm so sorry.'

Kathie nodded.

'What about the CC system?' D.I. Hackett looked towards the door, where he could see a screen, adjacent to the small black box housing the recorder, just above head height on the wall to the right of the door.

The two women looked up towards the screen.

'Oh yes, of course,' said Melanie. 'There are three cameras. One on the front door and one on the electric gates - and one at the rear of the house. We can look at that.'

'No, I can't allow anyone to touch it I'm afraid,' D.I. Hackett said quickly, as he moved closer and examined the system. 'I'll have to remove the tape, so that it can be thoroughly examined by our forensic experts. If anyone has tampered with it, we need to be aware. There'll be finger prints on it, other than yours and your husband's,' he said to Kathie. 'We have to rule out any foul play.'

The distraught Kathie looked at him and spluttered, tearfully, 'foul play? What else can it be? Max would never, ever, commit suicide! Why would he? He just wouldn't do this to me and Becky. No! No way, Inspector. Someone has done this to him, for the life of me I can't think why. You've got to find out who did this to him!'

'Of course, there will be a full investigation', he said. 'Please be assured of that.'

Kathie was now sobbing loudly, her words almost incoherent. 'Someone has killed my Max. He'd never take his own life, never in a million years! Oh, my dear God - what about Becky? How am I going to tell her that her daddy is dead?'

Tears were now streaming down her face as she buried her face in her hands, crying desperately. 'And his parents. Oh, no, poor devils. This is going to destroy them.'

'Where is your daughter, Mrs. Rawlings? Is she here, in bed?' The Inspector looked overly concerned.

Kathie, trying to wipe away her tears, whispered, 'Yes. I checked on her when I came in. She's fine. She was fast asleep.'

'That's one good thing', Hackett said. 'Look, this is what has got to happen. The forensic team will be here very soon, and will have to go over the whole house. I'm afraid you will not be able to stay here until forensic have done their job. P.C. Lambert here will take a statement from you and then stay with you to answer any questions. She will go with you, wherever you decide, preferably with a friend, or a relative for a few days. Are the car keys still in the ignition? If someone did do this, there might be fingerprints, unless they wiped it clean, or wore gloves.'

Melanie answered. 'Yes, they are still in the car, and of course, Kathie and Becky can stay with me.'

'That's good. Can you help her pack a few things, and I'm afraid you'll have to wake your little girl Mrs. Rawlings.'

'Hang on!' Kathie looked at the detective. 'When I came in, the TV was on, and it was on freeze. So doesn't that tell you Max was interrupted? He must have got up to answer the door to someone - surely!'

'Not necessarily, Mrs. Rawlings. Who knows what goes on in someone else's mind? You'd be surprised what people do when they are depressed, and the last person to know is nearly always their nearest and dearest. You may remember there was a famous football manager a year or two ago? His wife came home in the morning and opened the door to find him hanging from the banisters.'

Kathie looked at him in utter despair.

'That's different!' Melanie retorted. 'She'd obviously been out all night, I read about it. Something was definitely wrong there! The papers said she had been having an affair. But Kathie and Max were very happy, believe me. He was never depressed, was he Kathie?'

Kathie shook her head. 'Of course not!'

'Well - as I said, who knows what goes on behind closed doors? I've been in the job for many years, and nothing surprises me anymore. But you can rest assured we will do everything in our power to get to the bottom of this,' Hackett said.

'Well, I can tell you something,' Kathie sobbed. 'No way did Max kill himself, no way. Why would he? He had everything to live for, and he loved me and Becky so much. Why on earth would he do such a thing. It doesn't make sense!'

'I'm so sorry, Mrs. Rawlings, so sorry. This is so distressing for you, I appreciate that.'

The pathologist finished his examination, stood up and addressed the two police officers. 'Carbon monoxide poisoning, as I thought. Time of death over an hour ago. There will have to be a full PM of course.' He turned to face Kathie. 'You have my deepest sympathy, Mrs. Rawlings. I am so very sorry.'

Kathie just nodded slightly through her tears

When the pathologist and his assistant had gone, D.I. Hackett spoke to the photographer, who had joined them to confirm his work was done.

'The forensic team will be carrying out their meticulous examination of the whole house very shortly', he explained. 'Meanwhile, the house will have to be vacated.'

D.I. Hackett walked with the pathologist, his assistant and the police photographer to the door and let them out. Kathie and Melanie watched as he searched the pocket of his overcoat, then reached up to the CC central console to remove the tape with a cloth, before placing it in a plastic bag.

'Good evening ladies', I will be in touch as soon as possible. PC Lambert will stay with you while you pack your things and then she will accompany you to your destination.'

Melanie let the Inspector out, then put her arm around Kathie. 'Come on my love, let's get little Becky and pack your bags.'

'I can't leave him!' Kathie wailed, as she moved towards Max.

P.C. Lambert caught hold of her arm, gently but firmly. 'I'm afraid you must, Mrs. Rawlings, this is a potential crime scene. The forensic team will be here shortly, and as soon as they are finished they will arrange for your husband to be taken to the pathology mortuary. It's best that you go with your friend now. There's nothing more you can do.'

Melanie put her arm around the loudly weeping Kathie and began to lead her upstairs.

CHAPTER ONE

Young Max

'Aw, please, dad – just another ten minutes'. Ten year old Max Rawlings was lining up his football to take a corner.

'Your mum'll kill us, Max!', called his father from the other side of the pitch, looking at his watch. 'Do you know it's nearly seven o'clock? It's getting dark – and I've got half an hour's drive yet. Come on son, play the game!'

'That's what I'm trying to do!', Max said cheekily.

Brian smiled. He was so proud of his young son. Max was a good looking lad, tall and well built. His deep blue eyes, thick blonde hair, and ready smile was destined to set many a female's heart fluttering.

From an early age, Max had inherited his father's obsession with football. Brian Rawlings had been a useful non-league player in his youth and had even had a trial with one or two of the London second division clubs. An injury with a resulting torn ligament in his knee had kept him out of the game for six months. The recurring problem with the damaged knee, when he was only nineteen, had determined the end of a promising career as a professional footballer and Brian resigned himself to the fact that he would have to settle for sticking to his trade as a self employed carpenter. He made a good living for himself and his wife Pauline, and by the time their son, Max, was born, they were able to afford the move to a more desirable, rural area in Hertfordshire. Although Brian was a Londoner, born in Hackney in London's East End, he had, since his schooldays, been an avid fan of Leeds' Premier League team, Redthorn Rangers FC, like his father and grandfather before him, who had both been born and raised in Leeds.

Brian passed on his hopes and aspirations as a young player to Max, along with his passion as a 'Rangers' fan. For years Redthorn Rangers FC had remained in the top four of the Premier League, and was a household name, highly revered worldwide as one of England's finest teams. Whenever possible, Brian and Max went to see Rangers playing an away game against a London club, or occasionally they travelled up to Leeds to watch their idols play a home game.

For over five years, Brian had become a referee of some notoriety for local non-league clubs, and sometimes young Max went with him to watch the match his father was refereeing. Often, after the game, when all the players and supporters had left, father and son stayed behind so that Max could put in a few hours practising on a full sized pitch, perfecting his technique. Brian, regularly acting as surrogate goal keeper, was truly amazed at the boy's skill. It was uncanny how Max could drill the ball in the net from near impossible positions and distance. As a ten year old, his corners and dead-ball kicks were powerful and accurate, putting some adult players to shame. Max would practice his shots over and over again.

It was on such an occasion that Brian was watching Max take the corner kick. It landed just two meters in front of the net. 'Well done Max! Just right for the striker to put one in!', he shouted. 'Come on, we're going now.'

Max picked up the ball and ran swiftly across the field to his father. 'We're playing Witham tomorrow' he said, as he walked along juggling the ball from his knees to his head, perfecting his 'keepy uppy' technique.

'Yeah, I know. You watch that big bully defender - Stockbridge. He'll kick you to death if he gets a chance!'

Max grinned cheekily. 'He'll have to catch me first!'

At the age of nine, Max had been selected to play for his local team, Hartley Rovers, in the Essex District League, with matches being played on Sundays. The young hopefuls practised every Tuesday night on Hartley Secondary School's football pitch, which served as their training field. They played their league home games on one of the many pitches at Hackney Marshes,

East London, the launching pad for many a successful footballer.

There had been over forty youngsters entered in the open trials for Hartley Rovers, in Woodford, Essex. Max was an obvious choice, along with twelve others making up the squad. His friend from school, Chris Faraday, was also selected. Max and Chris were both in their school team and both boys spent every minute possible kicking a football around in their local park. Chris was a great little player. He was fast, strong and fearless in tackles, despite being shorter than average, and acknowledged as the undisputed best defender in their team.

Max, however, was something else - a unique talent, with a passion to win and an overriding dedication, seldom seen in one so young. As a midfielder, with a natural ability in distribution and assist, he often overlapped on the right wing. His accurate crosses and free kicks, were, in the main, the reason that Hartley Rovers won every single match they played. Also, as the team's leading scorer, Max ensured that Hartley Rovers ended up an amazing seventy goals ahead of their nearest rival in their league.

Brian revelled in his boy's talent and went to every Rovers' match, shouting encouragement and cheering loudly from the sidelines. After three years, Max had proved himself to be the most outstanding player. At the end of each season, he was always the boy chosen to hoist the winner's trophy.

Max was eleven when he was spotted by a London first division club's scout. For the next six months he trained twice a week at the Brompton FC Youth Academy, but he remained loyal Hartley Rovers and played in every game.

He was already making a name for himself, but the best was yet to come.

Doug Masters had been an outstanding, exceptionally talented player for Redthorn Rangers and England, back in the seventies. He was now a renowned, very successful manager of a Championship League club. He was as popular and well loved as ever as the nation's favourite veteran, revered as an outstanding player in his time, and presently as a manager and dedicated patron of the game.

Doug made a surprise appearance during the half time commercial break of a match being televised. He announced that he was keen to promote opportunities for promising young players and intended to organise and finance a football skills tournament for under 13's. The winning boy would spend two weeks training in Milan, rubbing shoulders with many famous footballers, and would gain automatic entry into Redthorn Rangers' Youth Training Academy. News of his tournament venture went viral, aided by huge publicity from the media and social networks. Televised sports and children's programmes in particular gave the forthcoming competition profuse air time.

'You're never too young to get into football,' he enthused on Saturday night's 'Soccer Highlights'. 'We should be seeking out and encouraging our home grown young talent and building on it.'

Never one to mince his words, Doug added, animatedly, 'there are far too many top players in the game being bought from other countries today! It's no wonder we can't put together a decent English team! Think about it - 1966 was the last time we won the World Cup, thanks to the likes of Geoff Hurst and Bobbie Charlton - and not, please note, someone with a name ending in vich! I for one long to see our clubs demonstrating patriotism for a change. Let's concentrate on promoting English players and dominating what, let's face it, is our game!'

Doug was banking on the fact that any suggestion of controversy would invite some provocative headlines on the following day's back pages and the next edition of 'Goal' magazine.

Brian couldn't believe his eyes as he watched, agog, the unexpected appearance of his idol of many years. Max was asleep in bed, but Brian couldn't resist racing up the stairs to wake him.

'Max, Max! Wake up son; you'll never believe what old Douggie is doing!' He was gently shaking Max, who opened his eyes and blinked at his father in the half light.

'Blimey dad, what's up? I was fast asleep!'

'It's Doug Masters, Max - he's only running a ruddy tournament for under 13's, and the winner gets to go to Milan for a fortnight to train with some of the top young players in their Youth Academy! How do'ya like that? This is your chance to show what you can do! You could end up getting into the Rangers' first team, like you've always dreamed of!', he enthused, hugging Max. 'You'll walk it, son, I'm telling you — well run it really, I should say!', he said, laughing.

Max had sat up and was staring at his father sleepily, then turned to look at his mother, who had hurried upstairs to see what all the commotion was about.

'Pauline, this could be his first foot on the ladder — and the final's gonna be held at Rangers' ground, would you believe — before a home match!' Brian grabbed Max's hands and was jumping up and down in excitement. Max was being bounced in his bed, dumbfounded. Suddenly he was wide awake. His father was right, all his dreams **could** come true!

'Wow, that's really cool, dad', he said, grinning from ear to ear. 'When does it all start? Hey, I must tell Chris! He'll want to have a go as well.'

'God, I can't believe this!' Brian was still fit to burst. 'Max, son, do you realise that if this all works out, you could be training with Rangers within a year? I just can't believe it!'

No-one could get much sleep in the Rawlings' household that night. Brian had already got on the internet to download the application form.

For months, before the final to be held in November, Max trained harder than ever, putting in every minute he could. Brian and Max's trainer, Bob Collins, at Hartley Rovers, were with him every step of the way, encouraging him and praising him before each of the three elimination legs of the tournament, which took place at the end of each month. Max easily made it into the last hundred. His only disappointment was that Chris didn't make it with him into the final.

On the day of the tournament, Max, Brian and Pauline were up early and heading up the MI in Brian's old Ford Estate in a state of nerves and excitement. Brian and Pauline were nervous, Max was just excited. The contest was to be begin at 1 o'clock, before a Rangers' home match, which kicked off at 3 pm, and Brian was paranoid about getting to the ground early to avoid the traffic, or any hold ups that might delay them. With hours to spare Brian parked up and they made their way to 'Parkside', Rangers' stadium. Brian and Pauline were still too nervous to eat, and just got themselves a drink,   but Max was as cool as a cucumber.

'Don't worry, dad, I can do it, no danger!', he said calmly, munching into his beef burger.

In later years, Max was to reflect in an interview, on a television chat show, that standing on Rangers' famous pitch for the first time, as a boy of eleven, was the most exciting thing that had ever happened to him – a feeling he would never forget.

Max was up against the best young players in the country. Hundreds of boys, from the various Youth Football Schools all over the country, had entered. Having gone through the preliminary rounds, he found himself one of the ten finalists. He had to go through several skill tests, kick a ball at goal from the edge of the penalty area, take a corner, demonstrate his skill by dribbling the ball through a series of cones, then at keeping the ball in the air, using his feet, knees, shoulders and head – something he had been doing since he was seven!

He won the tournament hands down, and savoured his first experience of being cheered by sixty thousand fans on the terraces.

Brian, proudly watching from a privileged position in the stands, was overcome with excitement and had made himself hoarse from cheering his son on. Pauline was in tears. They drove home in a state of euphoria.

Max was sitting in the back seat of the car, gripping his certificate tightly. He just couldn't stop looking at it.

'Dad, do you really think Doug Masters will call me personally?', he wondered.

Brian looked in his rear view mirror. 'I wouldn't be surprised son,' he said with a smile.

Max was in seventh heaven. Three months later he spent two memorable weeks in Milan, meeting many of his professional footballing heroes, and then a month after, he commenced his training at Redthorn Rangers' Youth Academy. He put his heart and soul into his training and it was obvious to his coach, and to George Wallis, manager of the Rangers' first team, that young Max Rawlings was destined to become an outstanding, gifted player.

For the first time in his life, Max had to leave the family home to live in the Academy's halls of residence. He soon settled in and became popular with the other boys straight away. It came as no big surprise to anyone involved in the game, particularly the media and television pundits, when Max, just turned sixteen, was selected to join Rangers' Under 19 team and then a year later, for the Under 21's team.

At eighteen years of age, Max Rawlings finally realised his childhood dream to play for Rangers in the Premier League. Within a year he got his first cap for England.

It was in the early stages of the qualifying rounds of the European Cup when Max, the youngest player in the team, became an overnight hero, gracing every headline in the newspapers next morning. He scored a memorable, nigh impossible goal from an acute angle on the left wing, from yards behind the penalty area, curving the ball high over every player's head. Millions of fans all over the world, in the stadium and sitting in front of their television sets, watched in wonder as the ball travelled majestically through the air, as if in slow motion, to drop out of the diving keeper's reach into the left hand corner of the net. Wembley Stadium erupted. The crowd were celebrating wildly on the terraces, while Max was being unceremoniously jumped on and hugged by every player in the English team. Men, women and children were cheering and jumping up and down in pubs, clubs and homes all over the country, many with tears in their eyes.

In later years, George Wallis soaked up much of the credit for the English team's success at that time, since, as he often pointed out, he was the manager of Redthorn Rangers and it was his signing of this wonder boy, after all, who had made the difference to England's hitherto lackluster side!

George gushed to television commentators and newspaper reporters that he had recognised Max's potential years ago, proudly boasting that it was all down to him that England at last had a player to match the great players of yesteryear, such as Stanley Matthews, George Best and Bobby Charlton - even Pele, he ventured.

At the same time as Max's meteoric rise to fame, Chris Faraday was also making his mark, echoing Max's success with Rangers via his own signing to London's Stampford United Youth Academy. Although, to the dismay of millions of his fans, he was never picked to play for England, Chris became a well loved and respected player for Stampford's United's first team. He was reputed to be one of the best backs in the game, along with an unbeaten record of yellow card awards!

Ironically, the lifelong friends were playing for the two biggest rival football teams in the Premier League. Neither of these two young men could guess that their chosen football careers would be inextricably and disastrously linked in the years to come.

CHAPTER TWO

Young Kathie

Kathie Neilson added the final touches of makeup and surveyed her reflection in the mirror on her dressing table. She liked what she saw, but she guessed that her mother would have quite the opposite opinion! At almost seventeen, Kathie was already a stunning looking young woman. She had inherited her beautiful features from her mother and her unusual colouring from her father. Her pale complexion was accentuated by emerald green eyes and deep titian hair, which fell long and thick, below her shoulders.

Kathie heard the front door bell ring and knew that it would be Melanie, her best friend. She hadn't the faintest idea who this boy was that Melanie was raving about – 'Max' somebody. Apparently he had film star good looks and was a fantastic football player.

Melanie had recently started to go out with another famous player, Chris Faraday, who played for a top London club. She was determined to do some matchmaking for her best friend, although Kathie really needed no help in that direction. She was a beautiful, smart girl, and already had a string of young male admirers. None of them 'impressed her much', she would casually quote, from the popular song.

Melanie had briefed Kathie about the match they were about to watch. Today was the first of the two Under 21's League semi final matches between Stampford United and the top northern club, Redthorn Rangers. As the first game was being played at Stampford's ground in London, Chris had given two VIP tickets to Melanie for herself and a friend. Against her better judgment – she had no interest in football and cared even less – Kathie had been persuaded by Melanie to come along to the match. The carrot being dangled by her friend was hard to resist: the prospect of meeting the incredibly hot Max Rawlings.

After several changes, Kathie had finally settled on tight jeans and a figure hugging white crop top, which accentuated her slim, curvaceous figure. A short, faux fur jacket completed the ensemble, the front edges of which scarcely met, allowing a purposeful, tantalising glimpse of her bare midriff and curves. She stood and turned this way and that, checking out her outfit in the mirror, finally satisfied that it was the perfect choice.

'That'll have to do!', she murmured, putting in her gold hoop earrings. 'It's only a stupid football match anyway'. She was, in truth, secretly excited to be meeting some hunky young footballers and keen to make an impression, particularly with the famous Max.

'Kathie!', her mother, Margaret, was calling from the kitchen, where Melanie was perched on a stall having accepted a quick cup of coffee. 'Mel's here.'

'I know, mum, I heard the door. Just coming.' Kathie pulled on her knee length suede boots, grabbed her imitation designer handbag, and skipped downstairs. 'Hi Mel. Wow, get you – I like the fashionable scarf!'

Melanie's hand went to her throat, and touched the bright green and yellow scarf round her neck. Chris had given her a supporters' scarf in Stampford's colours. 'Yeah, awesome isn't it! She fluttered her eyelids in an exaggerated manner and waved her hand in front of her face like a prima donna.

'More like gruesome', laughed Kathie.

'I promised I'd wear it, but it's not exactly haute couture is it!'

They both laughed, and Margaret, looking on, tutted and shook her head.

Melanie looked Kathie up and down approvingly. 'You look ab fab, Kathie,' she said, 'as always!'

'Do you think so? Wasn't sure what the smart young thing wears at football matches these days!'

Margaret had been sipping her coffee listening to the banter between the two girls. As expected, she looked disapprovingly at her daughter and remarked, 'I don't know why you want to put all that muck on your face, girl! You don't need it. You're pretty enough -

and you're only sixteen for goodness sake. That outfit doesn't leave much to the imagination either! Do you want to be going out looking like a tart?'

Kathie was embarrassed as she glanced over at Melanie and noted that her friend had far more make up on than herself, and in fact, she noticed, Mel was wearing false eyelashes!

'Nearly seventeen mum – sorry to shock you, but I'm an adult now.' Kathie gave Margaret a little hug. 'Don't be so old fashioned, mum. The whole world wears make up now, even men!'

'More's the pity!' came the reply. 'What's the world coming to?'

Kathie took Melanie's cup from her hand and took a mouthful of the coffee. 'Come on then Mel, let's get this over with.'

'Charming – there's gratitude for you! I hope you realise we are very privileged to have these tickets – **and** we are sitting in the VIP visitors' area.' She got up and playfully pushed Kathie on the arm. 'Bye Mrs. Neilson. Thanks for the coffee. Don't worry about Kathie – I'll look after your little girl!'

'Ha, ha, funeee! Like I need it!', Kathie retorted.

The two girls hurried out of the front door, avoiding more confrontation about make-up and tight clothes.

Once outside, they both giggled. Kathie looked heavenwards. 'What is she like?'

'I know, isn't she quaint. She's so, so – Irish!' She looked at her watch. 'We'd better look sharpish, we've got a bus and a tube to catch.' They quickened their pace and hurried down the road towards the bus stop.

Kathie had become friends with Melanie when she and Margaret first moved into their rented council house in Enfield, North London. Melanie lived two doors away with her parents and two younger brothers. She had taken Kathie under her wing, feeling sorry for her when she found out that Kathie's dad had recently died. Kathie had just moved into her first year at secondary school. Melanie was in the year above. The two girls caught the bus together every morning and evening and started chatting to each other, soon becoming firm friends. Melanie was an out and out extravert, whereas Kathie was more reserved. They complemented each other perfectly.

Melanie was a sweet girl with a sunny disposition and a lively wit. She had naturally fair, curly hair, which she spent most of her time trying to straighten, an attractive, open face with soft hazel eyes, a generous mouth and a captivating smile. She didn't have Kathie's exquisite beauty, but she had a sensual air about her and a voluptuous body. 'A real man magnet!', Margaret was prone to mention, disapprovingly.

The two girls drew admiring glances wherever they went, from men and women alike.

Margaret stood at the window of her lounge, wiping her hands on the tea towel she was holding, as she watched the two girls disappear from view.

'She's a good girl,' Margaret thought. She knew that she could be over protective. 'But what mother wouldn't worry about a gorgeous teenage daughter who could pass for twenty any day of the week!', she reasoned.

There was no denying that Kathie was the spitting image of her mother, both in looks and temperament. But that copper coloured hair and those green eyes were so much like Patrick's, Margaret thought. A constant reminder of the sadness she felt at losing her beloved husband much too soon. She missed him every minute of every single day.

But life's swinging pendulum had brought her such joy in her beautiful daughter. Margaret was so proud of Kathie and loved her beyond words. As she stood at the window, she sighed as she reflected on her own childhood. How different it had been to the privileged lifestyle Kathie and her peers enjoyed.

CHAPTER THREE

Mother and Daughter

Margaret Hanrahan was born in Cork, Southern Ireland, the eldest of a Catholic family of five boys and two girls. Being the only female child, until the birth of a new baby sister when she turned fourteen, it had always been Margaret's lot to be treated as a second mother. She accepted the role without question or complaint and carried out a good deal of the household chores and care for her younger siblings.

Money was always short. Margaret's father, like most men of his ilk, worked as a poorly paid labourer. He gave precious little housekeeping money to his long suffering wife, spending more than he should on the black stuff and smokes, and the odd illegal wager.

There was no television in the small, terraced house, but they did have an old radio, which the children would be allowed to listen to in the evening, if they had behaved themselves during the day.

Often, Margaret would read to her younger siblings before she tucked them up, three to a bed. They loved to listen to the stories Margaret read over and over again, not minding how many times they'd heard them before.

Margaret, along with her brothers, did not enjoy the pleasure of having new clothes, much less toys or books. She couldn't recall ever being taken out to a shop to buy anything new to wear. Her wardrobe consisted of simple clothes, made by her mother or herself, or hand-me-downs from one of her cousins. Occasionally a pretty dress, or coat, or even shoes, came Margaret's way from Mrs. O'Brien, whose daughter, Clodah, was the same age as Margaret. As wife of the local butcher, Mrs. O'Brien was one of the better off women in the community. Margaret's mother would do an extra hour's unpaid cleaning for her in return for the clothes. Unfortunately, Clodah was an inch or two shorter than the object of her mother's benevolence. Consequently, Margaret spent many an evening taking down the hems of such garments, pressing them repeatedly with a hot iron and a damp cloth in a vain attempt to disguise the crease of the original hemline.

Margaret was considered the local beauty, with her dark hair, blue eyes and flawless complexion; envied by the girls and lusted after by the boys. She was a serious, intelligent girl and paid little heed to comments made about her looks. She preferred to concentrate on her learning, vowing to make something of herself and get a job with a decent wage when the time came. An avid reader, she borrowed books wherever possible, aside from those she read In class. She always asked that her one and only birthday or Christmas present be a book of her choice.

Margaret's dogged determination paid off. To the enormous pride and admiration of her family, she was employed as a junior clerical assistant in a local accountants' firm when she left school.

She was little over fifteen, enjoying her newly found independence and wearing a brand new, shop bought, dress, when Margaret first caught sight of Patrick Neilson. She was at a birthday party being held for a cousin of her friend, Mary. A young man, a year or so older than herself she judged, was holding court across the room. With a glass of beer in one hand and smoking a cigarette, he was laughing and joking loudly with a crowd of teenagers, mostly girls. He was outstandingly good looking, with a shock of bright auburn hair. 'Far too long!', she thought. 'Not very tall, though.' Margaret was sizing him up. She guessed that he could only be about two inches taller than herself. She nudged her friend Mary and nodded in the young man's direction.

'Who's that?'

Mary followed her gaze. 'Oh him! That's Paddy Neilson. You don't want to be knowing him Maggie! He's nothing but trouble.'

Intrigued, Margaret asked, 'What do you mean?'

'Surely you've heard of him girl! He's always in fights, and he's got an awful family, Maggie! His father is a drunkard. He's never done an honest day's work in his life – and his mother's no better than she should be!'

Margaret giggled at her friend's graphic description of what sounded like a family from hell. 'Well, I've seen him around, but I didn't know who he was,' she said. 'Anyway, it's not his fault, he can't help his family. He looks really nice to me.'

'By *nice* you mean he looks like a frigging film star!' Mary grinned and tapped Margaret's arm in mock reproach.

'Well, yes', Margaret admitted, laughing. 'He is quite a looker! How old do you think he is?'

'About seventeen or eighteen, I think. Looks like you'll have to join the queue!' Mary looked over again in the lad's direction.

As they were giggling together, a young man approached them. 'Will you have a dance with me, Margaret?', he asked, holding out his hand.

She smiled. 'Sorry, I'm sitting this one out. I'm sure Mary would like a dance.'

He turned to her friend. 'Mary?'

Mary raised her eyebrows at Margaret, and then with a resigned sigh and pulling a face at being second choice, she took Michael's hand and followed him to a few feet away, where they began to jive to the music blaring out from an old record player.

Margaret headed towards an empty chair near a table bursting with glasses and bottles, and sat down, grateful for a rest. She was never short of admirers – young men competing to get hold of her, and she had been dancing for most of the evening.

She was reaching to put her glass of orange juice and lemonade on the table, when she heard a deep voice from above her.

'Hello, and who might you be?'

Margaret looked up into a pair of the greenest eyes she had ever seen. 'Who wants to know?', she asked.

'Me name's Patrick Neilson – Paddy to me friends – as I think you well know already! I saw you and young Mary looking at me a while back.' He was smiling widely as he winked at her.

Margaret felt her cheeks going hot. She bent down and fiddled with her shoe, then picked up her handbag and took out a hanky, hoping he hadn't noticed her blushes.

'Well you might have!' she retorted, 'But we weren't looking at **you**, we were looking at Kellie actually!,' she lied.

Patrick threw his head back and laughed loudly, and Margaret knew he didn't believe her for a second. 'So, what do they call you then?', he asked again.

'Margaret Flanahan, and my friends call me Margaret'.

Patrick laughed again. 'You're a rum one and no mistake. Would you care to have a dance with me Miss la-di-dah Margaret Flanahan?'

Margaret had to smile. She shrugged, and trying to sound nonchalant, replied, 'why not?' She got to her feet, and Patrick took hold of her hand. The music was now playing a slow ballad as he put his arms around her, pulling her close. Margaret was surprised to feel an exciting little sensual shiver go through her body, as he pressed against her and they began to move slowly together in time to the music. Until now, she had had little time for members of the opposite sex. She considered that, in the main, boys of her age were unintelligent, uninteresting and quite over rated. There was not one lad that she had ever been remotely interested in. But at this moment, she didn't want the dance to end, already smitten with this handsome, over confident and charismatic young man.

Margaret could not help feeling very pleased that the physical attraction appeared to be mutual. Patrick was visibly very taken with her.

'I think you are very beautiful, Maggie,' he whispered in her ear as he put his hand lower down her back and pulled her even closer so that she could feel him grinding his hardening groin against her.

Margaret was shocked, but thrilled, and so relieved that Patrick couldn't see the little smile of pleasure on her face, as she looked over his shoulder. They moved against each other and she experienced a quickening arousal. 'My name's Margaret, not Maggie, thank you very much,' she replied, hoping that he wasn't aware of the effect he was having on her.

'You'll always be Maggie to me.' Patrick pulled away slightly and looked at her squarely. 'Will you be my girl?'

Margaret was taken aback, and just stared at him. 'What do you mean? I don't even know you.'

'Course you do! You're dancing with me aren't you – and I'm sure mischief making Mary has filled you in, if I know her! But don't believe everything she tells you.'

'You know what I mean, Patrick.' Margaret said his name with deliberate emphasis. 'We've only just met.'

'I noticed you the minute you came in Maggie. I knew right away that you were a cut above the rest. I have a feeling that we're gonna get along real fine!'

Margaret pulled away from his gaze, putting her head on his shoulder as they continued to dance in silence. Patrick stuck by his new conquest all evening, not letting another lad have a look in. They talked, danced and laughed together. Margaret caught Mary's disapproving look several times, but she just smiled back and shrugged, as if to say, 'can you blame me?'

Already she felt herself hopelessly in thrall of Patrick. From that night on, they were inseparable until the day he died.

Margaret was eighteen and Patrick twenty-one when they married in their little village church. She had dismissed warnings from her parents and friends that Paddy was no good, and that she would rue the day she wed such a 'lowlife', as her father would repeatedly call him. But she was deeply in love with Patrick, and she never had cause to regret a single day of their life together.

In turn, Patrick worshipped Margaret, and she blossomed into full womanhood under his care and adoration of her. She found her handsome young husband to be kind, hardworking, and, as she discovered on their wedding night and to her constant delight thereafter, he was a wonderful, sensual lover. Any sexual inhibitions that Margaret may have had took flight from that very night. Their physical and emotional union continued to be complete in every way. The happy newlyweds rented a small terraced house, which they moved into straight away, with the minimum of secondhand furniture which they had managed to buy or had been given by family and friends.

After a year labouring for a local builder, Patrick was offered the opportunity to become an apprentice bricklayer, which he readily embraced. He became accomplished at his newly acquired skill and the couple were immensely grateful for the extra cash. Life was good, but short lived. Work became scarce and there were weeks when there was none at all. Margaret was still employed at the accountants' firm, which kept the wolf from the door, but Patrick hated it – it made him feel inadequate and went against every atom of Irish manly pride in his body.

When Margaret found she was pregnant, they were both delighted, despite the hard times they were going through. They sat in their tiny kitchen one evening, Patrick with a small glass of Guinness in front of him, Margaret with a cup of tea.

'I've been thinking Maggie.' Patrick took a swig from his drink and wiped the back of his hand across his mouth. 'Y'know me cousin Joseph in England works for Fitzgerald's. Last time I spoke to him, he told me they have got a big contract for a new housing estate in North London and they're looking for good brickies.'

Margaret looked shocked. 'Oh no, Patrick, don't even think about it. I'll not leave Ireland, you must know that. All my family and friends are here. And what about the baby? Surely you don't want the poor mite to be born in England!'

Patrick sighed. 'Well, we can't go on like this me darling girl! You won't be able to work in a few months time, and you know full well there's not much going for me around here – or anywhere for that matter. I think I'll have a word with Joseph. Sorry Maggie, me mind's made up! You won't be sorry, I promise. And if it doesn't work out, well now, we can always come back, can't we!'

Joseph was pleasantly surprised to get the phone call from his cousin, asking him if there were still jobs going for qualified bricklayers. 'Are you kidding Paddy! Get yourself and that gorgeous woman of yours over here man! You can stay with me and Elizabeth while you're looking for a place to live. It'll be good to have you here, and you won't regret it I tell ya! The wages are fantastic.'

Margaret was sad and apprehensive about moving, but she had no choice but to go with Patrick to England. She knew deep down that it was the answer to their problems, and she told herself that as long as they were together, she was sure she could be happy. Then there was the excitement of a new baby on the way, which would hopefully take the edge off any homesickness she might feel.

By the time their baby girl, whom they named Kathleen, was born, they were settled in a rented house in Enfield, North London.

Margaret's pregnancy had been dogged with problems from the very early stages. She suffered with severe morning sickness until her seventh month, high blood pressure and painful, swollen ankles. The birth itself turned out to be a trauma. The baby had the cord around its neck, and an emergency caesarian section was necessary. Margaret lost a lot of blood and was very weak. Patrick was beside himself with worry, and sat by her bedside trying to stifle his tears, holding her hand. Margaret had to have a blood transfusion, but was doing well within a day or two. Their baby girl was beautiful. She already had a shock of titian coloured hair.

'Just like her father!', the young nurses would remark, as they smiled coquettishly at the good looking young man. Margaret looked on with amusement, knowing that Paddy was causing a few paces to quicken when he grinned broadly and winked at them.

The proud parents waited to see whether their little girl's eyes would turn from baby blue to green. To their delight, they did, and Kathleen was destined to become an extraordinarily beautiful child.

For no reason that anyone could fathom, Margaret never became pregnant again. She and Patrick were devastated to think they might not have more children, and sought medical advice. For a few years they each underwent various tests, but no obvious faults on either side were diagnosed, although one pediatrician, at a loss to give the couple a tangible medical reason, suggested that Margaret's caesarian section operation could possibly be the cause. Margaret knew Patrick yearned for a son, although he never ever said so, but she suffered huge pangs of guilt for years. Nothing anyone could say would convince her that it was not her fault.

Patrick, however, was philosophical and simply said it was God's will, and they should be thankful to have Kathie, as the little girl had become known. They agreed not to broach the painful subject again, but would just wait and hope that they would be blessed with another child. Although unspoken, it was heartbreaking to both Patrick and Margaret to contemplate that they might never have a large family. They did their best to put it behind them and concentrated on saving to buy a house. When Kathie reached school age, Margaret found a part time job as an administrator with a local solicitor, which allowed her to meet her daughter from school.

Within a year Margaret and Patrick had saved enough for a deposit, and they took out a mortgage on a three bed-roomed semi detached house on the new housing estate he'd helped to build. Margaret kept walking around the house in an excited daze, hardly able to believe it.

'It's so beautiful Patrick,' she said. 'I can't believe we've done it at last.'

Patrick thought his heart would burst with pride as he put his arms around Margaret and picked up little Kathie, giving her a kiss on the cheek. 'It's no more than you deserve, me darling girl,' he said, beaming from ear to ear. 'I told you it would work out now, didn't I!'

Kathie had just turned eleven when Patrick became ill. He brushed Margaret's concerns aside and said he was just tired. Long hours and hard work had been the order of the day for Patrick since they moved to England. He drank rarely, just the odd Guinness, but he smoked heavily. Margaret knew instinctively there was something dreadfully wrong with her husband. Suddenly his appetite had waned and he lost weight. He was always tired and became quiet and depressed. She pleaded with him constantly to see a doctor and at last he agreed. After blood tests, Patrick was immediately referred to hospital for scans. The couple sat in shock, horror and disbelief when the specialist oncology consultant gravely advised them that Patrick had lung cancer and that his condition was irreversible.

Patrick took the harrowing news like the man he was. His concern was not for himself but for his wife and child. He knew that life would be a struggle for them when he died. They had a small life insurance plan, but funeral costs would take care of that. Margaret insisted he mustn't worry and repeatedly told him that they would be fine. That was the least of her worries. She just wanted Patrick not to leave them, and, out of sight, when he was sleeping, she shed a river of bitter tears.

When Patrick passed away, at the untimely young age of thirty-four, Margaret and Kathie were inconsolable. Both lives, which had revolved around a cherished husband and father, had suddenly been torn apart. Their shared grief was intense and unrelenting. Margaret was unable to function fully for months, and Kathie, despite her own heartbreak, had to grow up very quickly. She was a strength and comfort beyond her years to Margaret. They clung to each other for solace and became more than just mother and daughter. They became totally dependent on each other's love and togetherness.

The house had to go, Margaret knew that. She mustered all her mental strength to set things in motion. Less than a year later they had sold the house and moved into a rented council house in the same area of Enfield in North London. Margaret had insisted that Kathie should continue at the same school, since she was doing so well there. Always an intelligent and hard working student, Kathie had shown a marked ability and leaning towards art.

Margaret was astonished when she attended a PTA meeting as Kathie turned fourteen, and marvelled at the graphic designs, drawings and paintings she was shown by Miss Peters, Kathie's young arts and crafts mistress.

'I think Kathie should seriously consider a career in this direction', she advised Margaret.

'I can see how good she is,' conceded Margaret. 'I knew she could draw, but I had no idea she was this clever! But art as a career? That's a bit risky, and not very lucrative, surely!', she said.

Miss Peters smiled. 'Not just art per se, Mrs. Neilson. I think she could do very well as a designer. She has a very creative talent and her needlework is exceptional. She has the ability to get good A level results in all her academic course work - I've discussed it with her other teachers. She's a very intelligent girl - I'm sure I don't have to tell you that - above average in most subjects. And she has the work ethic and personality needed to do really well!'

Margaret looked up from Kathie's various designs the teacher had given her to look through. She was surprised and very impressed. 'I know that, of course, but I obviously haven't given her the credit she deserves for this sort of thing,' she replied.

Miss Peters nodded. 'I appreciate that, but it's not unusual. Teenagers are not known for discussing their school work with their parents! May I speak frankly Mrs. Neilson?'

Margaret noticed the teacher looked slightly uncomfortable and wondered what was coming next.

'Of course.'

'I have discussed Kathie's further education with her recently. She has expressed an interest in interior design and I think that would be an excellent choice. She would almost certainly achieve the necessary 'A' levels to go to university, and then as a post graduate she would be eligible to do a specialised course at the RCA.'

'RCA?'

'Sorry - Royal College of Art.' Miss Peters went slightly pink as she continued. 'Kathie thinks university would be out of the question though, given your financial circumstances. I understand you are a one parent family.'

'Yes, my husband died when Kathie was eleven.'

'I'm so sorry. But I am afraid that the cost of going to uni these days is becoming very difficult for a lot of families, not to say prohibitive in some cases. Students graduate with an immediate debt of thousands of pounds, poor things. It's shameful I think.' She looked at Margaret's crestfallen expression and smiled. 'But it's not all gloom and doom. There is an Academy of Interior Design in London. You can look it up on the internet. They do an eight month course of Saturday tutorials to achieve a Higher National Certificate. The good thing about this is, if Kathie is able to find a company willing to take her on as a junior - an apprentice - she could earn enough to pay for the course. It's around two thousand pounds. She's really keen on that prospect!'

Margaret was feeling embarrassed, and not a little hurt, that all this was obviously news to her, the girl's mother! She got up to leave and shook the teacher's hand. 'Thank you very much, Miss Peters. I appreciate everything you are doing for Kathie. Obviously I will talk to her tonight. I'm surprised she hasn't discussed any of this with me.' She tried not to sound too peeved.

'Good evening, thank you for coming. Don't worry, I am sure Kathie will be successful, whatever she chooses to do,' Miss Peters replied.

Later that evening, Margaret and Kathie were washing up after dinner, when Margaret broached the subject, and told her about her conversation with Miss Peters.

'I know, mum. It's what I really want to do, but I wasn't sure how you would take it. I know you've got high expectations of me!' Kathie looked anxiously at her mother to gauge her reaction.

'Well, I think it's just grand, Kathie. If that's what you really want, and I can see you are really talented, then you should go for it.'

'Oh, mum, I'm, so pleased you said that'. Kathie gave Margaret a big hug, and with a smile said, 'I'm not cut out to be a solicitor I'm afraid!'

Margaret smiled. She had to admit that she had always hoped her bright young daughter would go to university and become a doctor or a lawyer, but she couldn't argue with the practicalities put so patently by Miss Peters.

For the next few years, Kathie applied herself even more with her studies, determined to do well with the forthcoming final exams. She was academically as well as creatively gifted and left school with six good grade A levels.

Kathie hugged Margaret excitedly as they studied a brochure together. She had enrolled for a course at the London Academy of Interior Design, due to commence in September, and had received the details of the syllabus.

'I can't wait to get started, mum. It looks great doesn't it. The tutorials cover so many aspects of interior design - I had no idea it was so involved.'

'It's wonderful, love. I know you'll do really well. All you have to do now is find yourself a job.'

Kathie had already been contemplating the idea.

'Mmm, I know! My careers teacher has a few contacts and might come up with something and I will start looking in earnest myself. Meanwhile, if all else fails, I can always work in MacDonald's for a year. Free burgers - yay!'

Margaret chuckled. 'I don't think so!'

'We'll see. Roll on September.'

CHAPTER FOUR

George Wallis

Billy and Irene Wallis's son George, named after the baby's grandfather, wanted for nothing from the day he was born. Two sisters followed his entry into the world, but George was always the apple of his father's eye. Although Billy could well have afforded to have George privately educated, he would have none of it. 'No son of mine is going to a poncey, private school!' he would crow. 'Local comprehensive was good enough for me, and it'll be good enough for him. What do the likes of him want to learn Latin and stuff for? Fucking senseless in my opinion! He'll take over my business one day anyway. No danger!'

Thus, George grew up in his father's image. He inherited his looks and bearing, his arrogance, violent nature and, above all, his short temper. On the plus side, George was reasonably good looking, of above average intelligence and sharp as a tack, with a certain irresistible charisma. He actually believed his father's publicity and thought he was superior to the rest of his classmates and neighbours. His impressive build, aggressive nature and overbearing confidence, combined with his father's reputation, ensured that

George was well respected, even feared, by his peers, and no-one went out of their way to upset the belligerent youngster.

George resisted any form of discipline, particularly from his teachers, whom he dismissed publicly as 'a bunch of wankers'. He bunked off school as often as possible and by the time he reached adolescence, he was out of control. He was fast becoming a young thug, and it was evident to most of his peers' parents and his teachers that his future looked decidedly dubious, just like his father, who was known to be less than honest. Not yet fifteen, George would often stay out late at night, and come home smelling of alcohol and cigarettes. Then he would refuse to get up to go to school in the morning.

George's mother, Irene, born and raised in London's East End, was no shrinking violet, but she had become wary of her husband's violent temper over the years and knew when to keep her mouth shut. She had felt the force of his fist on many occasions - but by way of compensation from Billy, she possessed an enviable collection of expensive jewellery that he'd given her as a half hearted apology when he had calmed down.

Irene was deeply concerned about her son George, but was powerless to do anything about it. She could see the way he was heading and despaired of trying to talk to him about his behaviour, only getting a stream of abuse for her trouble. She'd given up trying to turn to her husband for a solution. Billy would just dismiss it with a wave of the hand and say, 'boys will be boys, gal. He'll grow out of it. Leave him alone, he's alright! Look Irene, it's tough out there, and he's got to learn to stand on his own two feet, like I did.'

George's salvation came in the form of one Barry Williams, his games teacher. Williams despaired of George and secretly loathed him, longing for the not far off day when the unruly miscreant left school forever! George's one and only redeeming feature, however, was that he was a natural athlete and was a very useful team player on the football pitch. George was a surprisingly dedicated player, committed to winning, and his enthusiasm encouraged the rest of his team to be the same. Astoundingly, he turned into a normal human being on the pitch, plus he was an exceptional player.

One afternoon, as class was dismissed, George, as usual, was elbowing his way to the front of the queue of boys, noisily jostling and punching each other in an attempt to be the first out of class and on their way home.

'George!', called Mr. Williams.

George, in the act of grabbing the collar of the boy in front of him, dropped his hand and looked round.

'Yeah?', he grunted, without the courtesy of a 'sir'.

'Can you come back here for a minute please?'

George didn't move, but just stared at his teacher with a surly look on his face. 'I ain't done nothing – sir,' he added as an afterthought.

'No, no – nothing wrong. Just want a quick word,' assured Mr. Williams.

All the boys looked on, hoping George was going to get detention, thus lessening the chance of getting a thump on the way home.

'Off you go, you lot!', Williams called out loudly, waving towards the door. They shuffled out, muttering to each other about what it could be about.

'Come and sit down George.'

'What's up, sir?' George was wary.

'Did you enjoy the game yesterday, George?'

Their team had beaten Hornsby Comprehensive's team 4-0 in the Under 15's league. George had scored two of the goals and taken out Hornsby's striker, leaving him injured enough to be taken off.

'Not half!', came George's response. 'We gave 'em what for alright! Hammered 'em!'

'Quite!' agreed Williams – but elbowing an opponent in the throat is not a good practice! And I don't know how you got away with that blatant foul tackle, personally.'

'You have to box clever, sir!' George smirked proudly. 'Make sure the ref is looking the other way!'

Williams sighed and shook his head. 'You've got to lose that attitude George! You know, you have a raw talent for the game – real potential. Your enthusiasm is admirable, but you must have discipline!'

'It's only a game though! They give as good as they get, given half a chance. Is that what you called me back for, to give me a bollocking? Aw, sorry, sir, that just slipped out!'

Williams tutted. 'No George, I've long since given up on that line of admonishment. Look!', he said, as patiently as he could. 'You'll be leaving school next term. Have you thought about what you are going to do – as a career I mean?'

'Probably work for me old man I suppose,' George mumbled, becoming bored with what he considered a pointless conversation. He looked pointedly at his watch to indicate his lack of interest.

Williams persisted, although it had crossed his mind that he was probably wasting his time and energy on the ungrateful lout. 'Have you considered football? I mean, trying to get into a Football Youth Academy?'

George looked perplexed. 'Are you kidding sir? Blimey – no, can't say I have. Never give it a thought.'

'Well go home and think about it, that's my advice! I'm sure your father can pull a few strings.' Williams was looking at George earnestly. 'George, you could be a really good player if you put your mind to it – you know, become a professional - even get into one of the top division clubs.'

George began to look interested, which encouraged Williams to press on. 'And, George, to use your vernacular, you could earn loadsamoney!' Williams felt pleased with himself that he seemed to be getting through to the objectionable boy.

'Okay, sir, thanks. I'll talk to my old man when I get home.'

'Good – that's all then. Off you go – and let me know what your parents say.'

'Cool – see you tomorrow,' adding under his breath, 'if you're lucky!' George took his cue to get out and quickly left. He nipped smartly through the school gates, disappointed to see that all his classmates had disappeared. 'Shit,' he cussed. 'Fucking little jessies!'

Later that evening, George was sitting in the television room of their Chigwell mansion with his father, watching England playing a friendly game against Holland.

'Jesus Christ,' groaned Billy. 'What a load of tossers! What the fuck are they all doing, poncing around like a load of girls? There's no-one up their own end to take a shot – no wonder we never bloody win anything anymore! Grievesey would've been through that lot like a dose of salts and put the ball in the back of the net, and taken the keeper with him!'

George was amused at his dad's rantings. It was always the same, whether it was England or the club he supported, Stampford United, playing. They could never do anything right by him.

'Dad, you'll never guess what old Baz did today.'

'No?'

'He called me back after the bell went.'

Billy didn't take his eyes off the screen. 'What you done now, you little sod?' He managed the curt response, in between a lot of cussing and swearing at the referee.

'Charming! Nothing actually, mon papa!' George retorted, grinning widely at what he thought was wit. 'Trust you to think the worst! As it happens, he thinks I could be a super-star footballer.'

Billy swung round in his leather chair to face George. 'Do what!!'

'Well, what he actually said was, with proper training and stuff I could get into an academy and then pro football. That shook ya, didn't it!'

'Did he now?' Billy raised his eyebrows. 'Bleeding hell, that's a turn up! Who'd have thought it?'

'Well, if you'd ever bothered to come and watch me play and support our team, you might have a clue,' George retorted. 'The other dads manage it.'

'Yeah, well, perhaps I am too busy earning the dosh to keep my blood-sucking family in a manner to which they have become bleeding well accustomed! Most of those layabouts you're talking about are on the dole and haven't got anything better to do!'

'Yeah, yeah, same old record!', scoffed George.

'Okay, I'll do a deal with you. When you're as famous as Jimmy Grieves or one of the Charlton boys, or your hero, Kevin Keegan, come to that, I'll deffo come and see you!'

Billy noticed the disappointment on his son's face and realised he was being a bit harsh. 'Look son, I'm just giving you some sound advice - don't get your hopes up. You'll never be a bloody pro footballer as long as you've got a hole in your arse! 'Sides, you know I've got plans for you in the business. I've been meaning to talk to you about it as a matter of fact.'

George shot his father a look of disgust. 'And what 'business' would that be then dad? Don't tell me, I know, behind the counter of one of your poxy betting shops. I don't think so!'

Billy glared at George, gritting his teeth, as he felt his hackles rising. 'No, as a matter of fact, not in a shop. Course not! I know some influential people who can set you up in their organisation. I think you'll fit in very nicely!'

'Please dad, save your breath. Do you really think I'm that stupid? I know all about your 'connections', same as everyone else does at school. No, whatever I do, it will be **my** choice. Yeah, I may even be a Grievesey, as you call him, one day. Although I'd rather be another Kevin Keegan. He's the dogs bollocks!'

George was stung. He resented his old man's lack of faith in him. What did he know anyway? The nearest he ever got to a football match was from his armchair. He stomped out of the door. 'I'm going to bed!'

Billy took a swig of his whisky. He was stunned by the whole conversation, especially George's reaction. The exchange of words had turned, seemingly, in the boy's favour. 'He's certainly growing up', he thought, smiling to himself. 'He's got some bottle, I'll say that. Chip off the old block! Oh no, I don't believe it - that was a yellow card without a doubt. That fucking ref's on the take without a doubt!'

When Billy got into bed later, he began to tell his wife about his conversation with George. 'What do you make of this, Irene? George's games teacher thinks he could become a pro footballer. Who'd have Adam and Eved it?'

Irene was half asleep and didn't stir. 'That's nice love – talk about it in the morning.'

'Bloody typical! Stupid mare!', he grunted. 'Like talking to a brick wall.' Billy pondered on what George had told him and regretted that he hadn't given the boy a bit more credit. What if his son did become a Premier League footballer? He might even play for

England! Christ, that would make some of his cronies sit up! Billy fell asleep vowing to talk to George about it the next day. He might even go and have a yarn with Williams himself.

In his room, George too was reflecting on what Mr. Williams had said. He had to admit, football was the only thing in his life he found remotely stimulating. He hated school with a vengeance, had no real friends, thought his dad was an arrogant twat, and as for his mum, she didn't know what day it was! Apart from the punch ups he loved to get involved in, more often than not instigating, and terrorising the girls at school, life was one long yawn. He thought about another of his heroes, Georgie Best. Same name! What a star and what an amazing life that player had. Tons of money, gorgeous girls, fast cars. 'Blimey, I could do with some of that! Yeah, perhaps I will talk to old Baz tomorrow. That'll show my old man! He can stick his poxy job where the sun don't shine!'

By the time George left school, his footballing skills, coupled with his father's connections, saw him gain easy entry into the Stampford Youth Football Academy, where he showed himself to be a talented mid field player. To the amazement of everyone who knew the deplorable boy, George emerged as an impressive game player. He could be relied on to set up a shot for one of the strikers, as well as pulling off many successful goals himself. His strength and stamina made him a ferocious opponent. George Wallis had found his vocation, and the precocious bully-boy was turning into a decent young man. At the end of his training, he was selected and transferred into the Stampford's Under 21's. He was a fearless, exciting and thinking player, respected by his team mates, and loved by the fans.

Mr. Williams followed George's career avidly, and boasted proudly that it was he who had put George on the right road! Billy, too, was immensely proud of his son, and gained a good deal of kudos from his circle of friends and contacts, mostly of the criminal persuasion, who saw having a famous footballer in the fraternity as being very useful in years to come.

As a matter of course, and no surprise to anyone connected with football, George Wallis became a prominent player for Stampford United and within a few months he was one of the well known faces in the game.

Sadly, like so many of his contemporaries, over the following years George became a victim of his own success.

His excessive lifestyle of drinking and hellraising, along with his sexual obsession for bedding as many women as possible, became a serious concern for his coach and manager. The media revelled in his newsworthiness and hounded him relentlessly, which frustrated and angered him to boiling pitch.

One evening, over an after match beer with his father, George was bemoaning the fact that being besieged by journalists was giving him grief on a daily basis. 'A total pain in the arse!', he said angrily.

Billy asked casually, 'is there anyone in particular you want taken care of?'

Even George was shocked. 'Leave it out dad! Christ almighty – who do you think you are, Al Capone? It's the same for all us famous players, it just gets on your tits that's all. Not enough to have anyone bumped off, if that's what you have in mind!' The very thought that his father was serious made him laugh out loud.

As a result of his enormously high salary, George enjoyed a fantastic lifestyle beyond his wildest dreams. At the age of 23, he'd already had his fill of everything money could buy, including property, cars and women by the score.

He was, however, enormously unselfish in regard to material things. It gave him a genuine kick and boosted his ego to share with those less fortunate than himself the outrageous remuneration that came with being a talented, high profile, professional footballer. He was lavishly generous to his siblings and friends, who happily benefited from George's newly gained wealth. His circle of new 'friends' grew rapidly.

George met the girl he was to marry at a swimming pool party, held by a fellow player at his mansion in the Cotswolds.

Ruthie was an exotically beautiful, olive skinned young woman with huge brown eyes and lustrous black hair. She deluded herself into believing she could be another Naomi Campbell, destined to become a super-model. Despite her amazing looks, however, Ruthie's ample curves would certainly have precluded her from the fashion catwalks graced only by stick thin models.

When George first set eyes on Ruthie she was lying seductively on a sun lounger by the pool, displaying her voluptuous body in a miniscule bikini. All eyes were on her that day, and George fell in lust, then love, for the first time in his life. He made a move on the gorgeous girl within minutes, and continued to shower her with adoration and affection from thence on, much to the surprise and amusement of his peers.

George and Ruthie were married within six months. Ruthie still hankered after a modelling career, but George convinced his new bride that she didn't need a career, as she was now a famous footballer's wife who would want for nothing for the rest of her life. Ruthie didn't argue!

Apart from a few lapses and one night stands on George's side, he and Ruthie shared a very happy, sexually charged and compatible marriage, which lasted until her untimely death when she was just forty-nine.

It came as a terrible shock to George when his lovely wife had a mild heart attack. Hospital tests confirmed that she had always had a defective heart and the second, massive coronary took her life.

George had continued to play for Stampford into his early thirties, despite several attempts by other Premier League clubs to buy him. His manager could not be tempted by huge transfer deal offers, and George himself had no wish to leave Stampford. He had also been selected to play for England for nearly a decade and, as Billy would proudly boast, ad nauseam, his son had over twenty caps.

George was 33 years old, during a crucial FA Cup semi final match, when he suffered a horrific injury from a violent two footed tackle from one of the opposing team's defenders, Robbie MacFarlane, a ferocious six foot, fourteen stone, Scot. With fifteen minutes to go until full time, United was one goal up and looking quite comfortable to win the match. The result of the outrageous foul was a red card for the offender, and a broken leg in two places for the victim. George was stretchered off to tumultuous booing from the crowd and a potential fight among some of the players of both teams and on the terraces. The referee finally managed to separate the players, and after ten minutes of mayhem, the two sides eventually calmed down and play recommenced. Stampford players had lost their momentum and were still stunned and seething from the loss of George, when the score went to one all. After extra time, Stampford lost 2-1. It was a sad day for all concerned. Full scale fights broke out amongst the fans, George was inconsolable and Billy was baying for blood.

George knew his days as a player were over even before he got to hospital. Had he been ten years younger, he would probably have recovered fully and got back on the field. As it was, he realised he would never be the same again, besides which, his verve for the game had gone. He took a long sabbatical, while he and Ruthie enjoyed a year of relaxation, holidaying in their house in the south of France, followed by a luxury Mediterranean cruise. The much needed rest gave him time to seriously contemplate his future.

It was while he was sunning himself on deck, scanning an English newspaper, that George read with horror the headlines: *'Robbie MacFarlane, one of Nottingham FC's powerful defenders, maimed in car crash.'* The article reported that the accident had been in mysterious circumstances, and investigations were taking place as to the condition of the car MacFarlane was driving. He had not been drinking, and the roads were dry. A witness had come forward to say that the car appeared to be going quite fast but for no apparent reason had swerved off the road and gone headlong into some iron railings. A young lady passenger was seriously injured and was still unconscious in hospital.

George went cold. 'Oh no, dad, please don't tell me you're behind this!', he said aloud to himself. He went to his cabin and threw himself on the bed. His head was spinning and he felt sick. He knew without a doubt that Billy had arranged for revenge to be wreaked on the player who had ended his son's career and lost United's chance of the FA Cup.

George could not explain to Ruthie why he was suddenly so ill, couldn't eat or sleep. He put it down to seasickness. He could not stop thinking about MacFarlane and the poor innocent girl in the car. He prayed that she would survive.

The young woman died two days later and George knew that this would haunt him for the rest of his life. MacFarlane was recovering in hospital, but was brain damaged. George was convinced Billy was implicated and could never forget, nor forgive him. He sent huge floral tributes to MacFarlane and the girl's family, which he knew was a pathetic gesture, but what else could he do? He felt helpless, and moreover, guilty. The sins of the father!

George was no saint, and normally just turned a blind eye to his father's dealings, sometimes even benefiting from them. The odd illegal wager, a fixed game – there was always a player willing to take a bribe, not to mention some bent referees. But murder! That was a whole new ball game.

He took his father to task at the first opportunity, but Billy didn't turn a hair and calmly said, 'listen son, I don't know what you're talking about. That had nothing to do with me! Don't talk such fucking rubbish! If your mouthing off gets to the wrong ears, you'll get us both in big trouble – and I'm not talking about a broken leg! Just forget the whole thing. It was a tragic accident, no more.'

George had no option but to reluctantly let it drop. He knew that even if Billy had been involved, he would never come clean in a million years. Police and forensic investigations revealed that the car had been tampered with, causing the brakes to fail, but, oddly, without any plausible explanation, the case was closed, as apparently there was no proof or line of investigation to charge anyone.

Six months later, when George was approached by a second division club to take over as manager, he thought about it long and hard, and eventually cautiously accepted. For one thing, it meant moving to the North of England. Ruthie, as ever, had been happy to go along with whatever he decided, and they moved to York.

Within five years, George had become a high profile, successful manager, having taken the first team he ever managed into the first division. He was, as ever, the well known colourful character, outspoken and voracious. He was hard on his players, but he got results. He stood no nonsense from anyone, and was often seen on the sidelines giving the referee and his assistants a mouthful of abuse. It was not uncommon for him to be thrown off the 'dugout' for his behaviour, having to endure the rest of the match from a safe distance in the stands.

George was fiercely loyal and refused all managerial offers from other clubs up and down the country. Even hugely gratuitous offers from famous foreign clubs could not entice him. Yet he never once denied that his heart would always remain with one particular Premier League club. Consequently, when he was offered the job as manager of the internationally famous and revered Redthorn Rangers FC, he had no hesitation in accepting. Managing the team he once played for was a dream come true.

Billy had mixed feelings. As a life time devotee of Stampford United, it was a bitter pill to swallow when he first learned that his sainted son was batting for the enemy! On the up side, he could not ignore that it was an enormous privilege and even higher profile opportunity for George, and, as his well known father, he would savour reflecting in his son's glory, milking it for all it was worth.

George became one of the game's finest and most controversial football managers for many years. The continued success of Rangers was legendary and George Wallis became a household name, often commanding media publicity to equal his players, albeit sometimes for all the wrong reasons.

One of George's most notable and successful signings was the young Max Rawlings. George recognised Max's talent within minutes of seeing him play, and wasted no time in securing him first for the Under 19's, then the Under 21's teams. Finally, despite his initial reservations, he was pressurised by his Board of Directors to elevate Max into the Premier League team, sooner rather than later, to the delight of Rangers' millions of fans. As a manager, George could not ignore that Max would be one of the greatest assets the team had ever seen, but his intuition warned him that the rising young star would surely become bigger than the game. He somehow knew that would inevitably mean grief for himself. Time was to prove him right!

Unfortunately, as George had predicted from the outset, Max, through no real fault of his own, was becoming a double edged sword, destined to cause his manager extreme frustration, sometimes rage. George deplored Max's 'nancy boy' image, as he referred to it, especially when Max became just as famous for his face and fashionista reputation than his performance as a player. Images of Max were soon appearing in magazines and newspapers on a daily basis, either lauding his latest performance on the pitch, or featuring him modelling hair gel, razors and jeans. His 'pop idol' status by the fans and media was becoming worldwide.

George was publicly frank about his disdain for Max's publicity, especially after Max's image, usually sporting another new hairstyle, had been splashed all over the newspapers' back pages the previous day. George's disparaging remarks were not appreciated by the press or the embittered Rangers' fans, who heralded Max as England's hero. George was the regular object of their insults and lampooning on social networks. The general consensus was that Max was a decent lad and couldn't put a foot wrong - either on or off the pitch! Men respected and revered him, women wanted to marry him and children adored him.

George had never been popular in his whole life. That suited him just fine!

CHAPTER FIVE

A perfect match!

Melanie enthused endlessly over her newly found passion for Chris - and football. Kathie was beginning to find it all a little tiresome, but she kindly disguised her indifference for the sake of their friendship. Then came the day of the match! It was a day which was to become an unexpected milestone and would dramatically change the rest of her life.

Kathie genuinely enjoyed the Rangers vs Stampford match. She found herself caught up in the frenzied atmosphere, cheering, clapping, singing, booing, along with the rest of the stadium's thousands of fans. She and Melanie jumped up and shouted excitedly when Chris's team went one goal ahead. Stampford's advantage was short lived, however, as Rangers went on to beat them 3-2.

Throughout the game, Kathie couldn't take her eyes off one of the players, who seemed to be all over the pitch at any given time and had taken an impressive free kick, resulting in the winning goal. 'Who's the one with the pony tail?', she had asked Melanie, a few minutes into the game.

Melanie shot her a look of utter disbelief.

'That's him Kathie! Max Rawlings! For goodness sake - that's who I have been telling you about. What are you like - where are you from, planet Zog? Drop dead gorgeous isn't he!'

'Mmm, he looks it from here, and he's a great player,' Kathie observed, suddenly feeling a little excited.

'Well aren't you the lucky one Kathie – as I told you, he happens to be Chris's bessie mate. That's who I've been going on about! Don't tell me you don't remember.' She eyed Kathie suspiciously. 'They've known each other since they were kids. They're blood brothers - can you believe it?' She giggled. 'You'll meet him soon when they all come into the players' lounge.'

As the game finished, Melanie and Kathie fought their way to the nearest exit among the milling fans, amused by the pathetic, sexist comments and chat up lines from some of the younger fans who were wolf whistling and ogling the two girls. They eventually found their way to the players' lounge. After a comfort visit, and the opportunity to touch up their make up in the Ladies Room, they made their way to a luxurious red leather sofa and waited expectantly for the arrival of the players. Kathie was feeling excited and nervous, really looking forward to meeting Max. She glanced down at her jeans and wished she'd worn something a little more glamorous. Melanie was chatting away to her, but all she could think of was the handsome lad with the blonde pony tail.

After what seemed an age to the two girls, the double doors swung open and the players, having bathed and changed into their fashionable casual clothes, began to come in. Melanie nudged Kathie and nodded towards the door.

'Here comes Chris,' she said excitedly. Kathie was thrilled to see that he was followed closely by Max. They walked towards the girls. Melanie jumped up and gave Chris a hug. 'You were brilliant! Weren't they Kathie?', she exclaimed, turning to her friend. 'It was really good - sorry you lost though.'

'Thanks Mel – glad you enjoyed it,' responded Chris, eyeing Kathie up and down. 'Rangers were jammy as usual!'

'Hi Max.' Melanie greeted Max. 'We thought your goal was totally magic!'

Max was looking at Kathie. 'It was nothing!', he said with mock modesty. 'And who is this?'

'Oh, sorry – this is Kathie, my best friend. I told Chris about her, didn't I!' She frowned at Chris. 'He said he would tell you we were coming today!'

Chris nodded, and grinned, clearly amused by Max's and Kathie's reaction to each other. 'Yes, of course I did. He's got a brain like a sieve! He can't cope with all this female adoration, obviously!'

Kathie had been staring back at Max, even more handsome up close, his damp hair now hanging loose about his shoulders.

'Pleased to meet you Kathie,' Max said, offering his hand, while examining her intently. He looked at Chris and asked, 'and did Mel mention how stunning her friend was?'

Kathie took his hand and felt a little thrill shoot through her body at his touch. He was smiling and searching her face for a reaction. Feeling slightly self conscious, she let go of his hand and found herself gabbling, 'hello Max, nice to meet you too. It was the first time I've ever been to watch a football match. I'm really surprised how much I enjoyed it.'

'Wow, a football virgin!', Max exclaimed. He and Chris laughed at his jibe, and a few other players nearby joined in the laughter. One of them called out, 'fuck me, that's a first!'

Kathie was annoyed as even Melanie started to laugh. She glared at Max. He sensed she was miffed and smiled at her, saying, 'only kidding Kathie! You'll soon learn that you have to be able to take a joke with our lot. Football players are renowned for their lack of respect - and foul language!'

'You'd better believe it!' added Chris.

Kathie managed to smile, still feeling a tad annoyed at being the butt of the hilarity.

'Okay then girls, what are you having to drink?', Chris asked. Melanie asked for a vodka and tonic, and Kathie said she would just like a diet coke. Max pointed to a table and led them over to it as Chris made his way to the bar. When he came back with a tray of drinks, peanuts and crisps, he said to Max, 'Guess who's at the bar? It's your manager's sidekick …. you know, Rangers' scout! Blimey, wonder what he's doing here?'

The two girls and Max looked over to where Chris was nodding and saw the man he was referring to. Sure enough, Tony Kyle was sharing a pint with one of the Stampford United's directors. Unknown to any of the youngsters, he was there at the behest of George Wallis to take a last look at the young player everyone was talking about, Max Rawlings, before confirming his recommendation that the player be signed up for Rangers' Premier League team. Kyle looked over at them and nodded at Max, then back at the director and continued his conversation.

'Very interesting!', Max mused, almost a hundred per cent sure that Kyle had been sent here to confirm back to George that their young protégé was ready for promotion. 'Watch this space, guys', he grinned. 'I'll be signed up for Rangers first team next week!'

'Cocky sod!', said Chris, knowing that Max had probably hit the nail on the head.

'Are we all up for the Moon River then?' Max looked directly at Kathie.

'What's that, a film?', she asked.

Max laughed. 'Are you for real? It's a nightclub, on the embankment - you know, by the river, hence the name!'

Kathie felt stupid once again and retorted indignantly, 'Oh – well I didn't know. I'm not dressed to go clubbing anyway.' She looked anxiously at her watch and turned to Melanie for support. ' I don't want to be too late home anyway. We've got quite a journey back to where we live.'

Melanie was shaking her head in frustration.

'We'll see you home safely, don't worry. You look great anyway,' Max assured her, with a wink. 'With your looks, no-one will even notice what you're wearing anyway!'

Kathie took the compliment with, 'thanks, but I'm not sure.' She looked at Melanie.

'He's right, Kathie. Come on, don't be a drag - you'll enjoy it.' Melanie patted Kathie's arm.

'Okay, but I can't be too late home.'

'I'll see you get home safe and sound,' said Max and put his arm round her shoulders, giving her a gentle squeeze. That exciting little thrill again!

They ate their snacks, drank up and jumped in a taxi to the Moon River night club. Kathie was dazzled by this new experience. As they entered the club, she noticed all the young women were parading the latest fashionable clothes and shoes.

'I'm so glad I didn't bother to dress up!', she remarked sarcastically.

'You knock spots off all of them!', Max whispered in her ear, which had the desired effect. Kathie smiled with smug satisfaction.

The bar of the Moon River nightclub was close to the entrance door.

'Stick with us you two, while we get the drinks,' Chris said to the girls. 'Then we can find a table somewhere.'

Several men, in their twenties and thirties, in smart suits, braces and loud ties, were standing around the bar, talking and laughing loudly. A couple of them noticed Max and Chris waiting to be served.

'Hello, hello, if it isn't Rangers' answer to Hitler's Youth!', one of the men shouted above the din. 'How's old Georgie, porgie, pudding and pie, Max?' They all roared with laughter.

'You twat, Greg!,' Max commented with distain.

The brokers all started to chant, 'Come on you blues! Wave your arms if you hate Rangers'

'Give it a rest, you tossers!', said Chris.

The man whom Max had addressed as Greg was still laughing. 'Come on you two, just pulling your plonkers!'

Max nodded and grinned. 'Yeah, I know!'

'You gonna join us for a drink?' Greg offered. 'Card's behind the bar – anything you want. Bottle of Bolly?'

He ran his eyes over Kathie and Melanie approvingly. 'Hello darlings! What are you two gorgeous creatures doing with these two 'erberts. They're still wet behind the ears! Are you sure you're old enough to be in here anyway?', he laughed as he looked at the two boys. The other men had turned round to survey the interchange and were laughing loudly, adding their own jibes. 'Yeah, come and have a drink with us, girls,' one of the younger ones offered.

'Knock it off!', Max retaliated. 'They wouldn't be interested in bloody old geezers like you lot. They know a bit of talent when they see it! What are you all doing here anyway? Not exactly your scene is it? I thought your normal watering hole was a wine bar in the City.'

Greg took it in good part. 'Oh, some bloody ball-aching seminar nearby. I fell asleep after an hour. How did you get on tonight, then?'

'They won, what did you expect?' Chris chimed in. 'Lucky goal by Max - and the first one was offside! I'm sure the ref's his uncle! Thanks Greg, we'll have a bottle of fizz with you, but if you don't mind we'll find a table for the girls.'

Max raised his eyebrows and opened his mouth in disbelief. 'What bollocks, of course it wasn't offside!

Your lot played like a load of wankers, mate! Pathetic! All that passing it back to the keeper, instead of getting up the field.' He turned to Greg. 'The only dribbling they can do is down their shirts when they're pissed!'

The girls joined in the laughter. Even the football virgin could see the joke. Greg ordered them a bottle of Bollinger, which they accepted graciously and began to move off into the gloom of the seating and dancing area.

'Enjoy yourselves kids,' shouted Greg, as he turned back to his group.

'Who were they?', Kathie wanted to know, looking back over her shoulder as they moved away from the bar.

'They're money brokers, from the City.' Max explained. 'More money than sense, but they work hard and play hard. They get absolutely enormous bonuses in return for a heart attack. Sod that for a game of soldiers. Give me football any day!'

Kathie was finding the banter very amusing and joined in. 'What, you mean get vastly overpaid in exchange for a broken leg?'.

The two boys gave a high pitched, 'Whooo!'

'Listen to her!', added Chris, as they cracked up laughing.

Kathie was puzzled. 'Why were they saying blues?', she asked Max. 'Your team are red and white.'

'They're Chelsea supporters dear – you know – blue strip? Proves my point! Shows you how fucking stupid they are!', Chris interjected, laughing raucously at his own joke, joined heartily by Max.

Kathie frowned disapprovingly at his language, and he said, 'Oh, pardon my French, I'm sure!'

They drank the champagne, which was quickly followed by another bottle. Chris's and Max's loud repartee over the music was hilarious, and soon Kathie was feeling deliciously high spirited as her first taste of champagne began to take effect. She was giggling incessantly and responding to Max's flirting with her. 'If mum could only see me now!', she thought, 'she'd have a blue fit.'

Kathie had never had such an exciting time, enjoying every minute of her new adventure and wallowing in Max's attention. It was gone midnight when the boys hailed a taxi and insisted on accompanying Kathie and Melanie all the way to their homes. Max sat next to Kathie with his arm around her, which caused exciting, sensual tingles to race downwards through her body, butterflying around her tummy and beyond. She was grateful for the subdued light in the taxi as she felt her cheeks beginning to burn. The girl was now enjoying the sexual awakenings of a woman, as Max ran his hand seductively up and down her back and then, pulling her long hair to one side, he nuzzled her neck.

His warm breath and moist lips made the little hairs on the nape of her neck stand up - and then his hand was fondling her breast. Max felt her body stiffen slightly with apprehension as to what was coming next. He pulled away from her slightly and dropped his hand. He gave her a gentle, reassuring squeeze, still keeping his arm around her, while Kathie took a deep breath and regained her composure.

Max had become highly aroused, but he had the good sense not to push things at this stage. Kathie was clearly becoming responsive and excited, but he sensed she was inexperienced and nervous. It was patently obvious that the sexual vibes between them already promised something special to come. He would just have to wait!

They continued the journey chatting together like old friends, in between kissing and cuddling. It was the first opportunity they had had to speak to each other properly since they had met earlier in the day. They both appreciated for the first time that evening that the other was really intelligent and interesting, as well as being breathtakingly gorgeous and sexy! They were so preoccupied with each other, they hardly noticed that Chris and Melanie were all over each other on the opposite seat.

Kathie began to tell Max about college and her new job and how she hoped to become a successful interior designer one day, while Max explained enthusiastically that he was expecting to be selected to join Rangers' first team. 'That's my ultimate goal', he told her, grinning. 'No pun intended - in the Premier League', he added, realising that Kathie hadn't a clue what the first team was. 'That's why old Kylie was there tonight'.

'Kylie Minogue?' Kathie gawped at Max.

'No, you twit - that's just our nickname for Tony Kyle. He's Rangers' scout.'

She giggled. 'Sorry, I'm still a bit squiffy.'

'I'll put money on it that he was there just to check up on me today. Don't know why though. He's seen me play hundreds of times! But he has to convince old Wallis. He's the problem. I don't think he likes me for some reason. Although, I guess he could have been checking Chris out, or one of the other players. That's a thought!'

'I know you're in Rangers' Under 21's, but that's up North isn't it? Why wouldn't you want to play for a London club?', she queried. 'What's wrong with Stampford's proper team?

Max laughed out loud. 'Proper team! You're so cute! There's nothing wrong with Stampford at all!

Chris looked up at the mention of his team and Max, still laughing, winked at him. 'They are one of the top teams in the country. Most young players would give their right arm to get into their first team – or proper team,' he teased. 'It's a long story, but next time we meet, I'll explain.'

Satisfied at Max's explanation, Chris resumed groping Melanie, who was still writhing expectantly under his grasp.

'You're taking it for granted we'll see each other again then', Kathie said, secretly praying that he was going to ask her out for a date.

'You bet! Give me your number. I'll give you a bell next week. He pulled her close and caressed her back again as he gave her a gentle, sensuous kiss.

Kathie's whole body shuddered with excitement. She closed her eyes and thought this was the closest thing to ecstasy she could imagine!

'You okay?', Max asked.

'Yes, just a bit cold', she lied.

The taxi drew up outside Kathie's house. Melanie extricated herself from Chris's clutches and adjusted her clothing, while Kathie was overwhelmed to receive a full lingering kiss on the lips and a huge hug from Max, before they both climbed out of the taxi and said their 'Goodnights'.

Kathie went into the darkened house as quietly as possible and crept upstairs to her room. She was still in a state of rapture thinking about Max, how unbelievably good looking he was – and his kiss - and when he touched her! She shivered as she thought of the sensual feelings she'd had as he'd caressed her in the taxi. She relived the whole day over and over again in her mind before finally falling asleep. She didn't know if there was such a thing as love at first sight, but if the way she felt about Max and the physical effect he had on her was anything to go by, it must be true, she thought dreamily.

Kathie was also pondering whether or not to admit to her mother that she had spent the evening in a night club, drinking champagne, which she had no right to do at her age. She decided to stay on the safe side and, if questioned, she would say they'd had a quick drink in Stampford's guest lounge and gone to the cinema. She hated lying to her mother, but it would save a lot of hassle in the long run.

Early next morning Kathie's mobile phone signaled an incoming text. She grabbed it excitedly but was disappointed to see it was from Melanie.

'Great evening!! U & Max seemed to hit it off. R u seeing him again? xx'

Kathie texted back: *'Yes, it was totally awesome, and Max has taken my number! Wow, he's so nice, watch this space! xx'*

Kathie hoped and prayed that Max would call her. She couldn't wait to see him again. She was in love!

CHAPTER SIX

Max's dream

On the way home in the taxi, Max closed his eyes and leaned back, thinking of Kathie.

'What did you think of her then?', Chris's voice interrupted his thoughts. 'As if I didn't know! God, she's really hot! You seemed to be getting on like a house on fire!' He guffawed loudly at the unintentional pun.

'Yeah, she's a great girl. Not only beautiful, but clever too, and did you check out her figure? Wow, she's bloody gorgeous!', Max replied. 'But, she's not like the usual airheads we seem to attract! Skirts up their arses and boobs hanging out, most of them with a single brain cell!'

'Don't knock it mate!', Chris replied. 'Anyway, you gonna see her again?'

'Yup! I said I'd give her a call next week.'

Max was dozing as he heard Chris's dulcet tones. 'Fill your boots!'

Later, in bed, Max was thinking about Kathie again. He remembered now that Chris had mentioned Mel was bringing her friend along to the match. Both boys were looking forward to the needle match between their two teams and Chris had suggested that they take the girls out clubbing afterwards. Max was always besieged by girl fans wherever he went and the prospect of yet another under aged, over eager female was a bit of a pain in the rear end, but he had given in to Chris, as always, then thought no more about it.

Max was gaining a reputation as a real heart throb and was ribbed mercilessly by his team mates over it. His incredible good looks and physique, trendy clothes and hairstyles drew so much attention, it became the talking point of the media and his growing number of fans. This, and his popularity with women of all ages, unfortunately often overshadowed coverage of his talent as a player.

Max was surprised, therefore, that from the moment he had set eyes on Kathie, for the first time in his life he was totally attracted to this lovely girl. It was obvious to him straight away that she wasn't like the other young women who hung around the bars and clubs hoping to snare young players for husband material.

As the evening together had drawn on, Max reflected that Kathie was not only exceptionally glamorous and sexy, but she was smart and witty with a great sense of humour. He thought about their conversation during the journey home in the taxi, during which they had told each other briefly of their hopes and aspirations. Kathie was hugely ambitious - he liked that, and he had found her so easy to talk to, even though she knew nothing about football! 'Doesn't make you a bad person,' he smiled to himself. He had truly enjoyed the evening. 'Yes', he thought, 'she was refreshingly different'. He hadn't failed to notice the admiring glances she had drawn from men all evening in the club. He couldn't wait to see her again. He naturally couldn't help imagining what it would be like to have sex with her – no – make love to her. She was not the sort of girl you just had casual sex with, even if she was willing, and he had a good idea she wouldn't be!

He guessed Kathie was a virgin, since she had told him she'd had a pretty strict Irish Catholic upbringing. Everything about her aura and body language told him that she was a virtuous girl, prepared to save herself for the right man!

'I hope that man is me!', he thought, as he visualised taking off her clothes and caressing her lovely body, before making love to her in every position possible. He closed his eyes at the stirrings of arousal. He had studied her closely and unashamedly during their evening together, and now he could imagine her beautiful naked body under him, those lovely long legs wrapped round him - and God, her gorgeous boobs! At least he'd managed a brief feel in the taxi!

Quite absurdly, and unexpectedly, the thought of Tony Kyle being in the players' lounge came into Max's mind, intrusive and uninvited, expelling the sensual fantasies he had been enjoying for the last ten minutes.

'Wow, that had been a real turn up, seeing Kylie at Stampford!', he thought. 'He must have been there to eye me up, surely. He looked over and nodded. It has to be only a matter of time before I sign for the first team - can't think why it's taking so long!' He chuckled to himself. 'They know it makes sense!' All thoughts of Kathie had gone, and Max fell asleep, dreaming about scoring the winning goal for Rangers at the FA cup final.

Tucking into his breakfast next morning, Max was excitedly relating to his father, between mouthfuls, about Kylie being at yesterday's game, and then going into the players' lounge.

Brian was shaking his head knowingly and smiling, as if to say, 'what have I been telling you?'

'He looked over a few times and he nodded at me once', Max was enthusing, 'and I played really well, thank God. You should have seen my goal, dad, it was ace!'

'Of course I saw it Max, it was on the telly - just a small bit on the highlights - unusual for an Under 21's match. Great shot, nice and low, and right between the keeper's legs. A proper nutmeg! That first one wasn't offside by the way, the playback was quite clear.

I recorded it for you, knowing that you would be painting the town red after the game!'

'Yeah, we had a good evening. I met a really nice girl - Kathie.'

'Jees - not another one!'

'No, this one's different.' Max shook his head. 'She's a really lovely girl, dad. She's Catholic though, and a bit straight laced, but a real looker. I really like her.'

Brian frowned at the Catholic reference. 'Yeah, yeah. I know.'

Max was laughing. 'No, honest, dad. I mean it, she's really something special. We really hit it off.'

Brian tutted. 'Anyway - back to Tony Kyle. It's looking good! My son playing for the Reds! Can you believe it!'

'I thought I already did!' Max joked. 'But I know what you mean - me in the first team at 18! Rooney, eat your heart out! Anyway, fingers crossed. I've got a gut feeling they want me. They'd be mad not to!', he grinned cockily.

As the notorious and successful manager of Redthorn Rovers, George Wallis was well aware of the publicity already surrounding the high profile Max and it didn't sit well with him. In fact, he found it worrisome, casting doubt on what, to the rest of the sporting fraternity and fans, was a given. An exceptional talented young player like Max, already proving himself as an outstanding player in the Under 21's, would normally, without question, automatically be signed up for their first team.

George was discussing it with Martin Brownlow, Rangers' Under 21's manager, following the match against Stampford the previous day. Tony Kyle had been impressed with Max for some time and had already emphasised repeatedly that if they didn't sign Max up soon, another club would, without a doubt! Apart from that, he reminded George, Rangers' Board had already agreed they wanted Max in the first team as soon as possible and were concerned and very annoyed that George had deliberated for far too long.

'I can't believe you're even having to think about it!' Tony was exasperated. 'He's fantastic, George, and you bloody well know it. I've not seen anyone like him for years - an outstanding rare talent. His work ethic is unrivalled - he scores and creates more goals than any other player, and I can't name anyone who can kick a dead ball into the net like him! He's gonna be another one of the game's greats, mark my words. Another Lineker - or Beckham of course! What more do you want for Christ's sake?'

Rangers' coach, Harry Russington, was nodding emphatically. 'Couldn't agree more, Tony. He's outstanding to put it mildly. Such intensity - he plays like his life depends on it. George knows that as well as we do! I don't know what your problem is, man. Can you imagine Wenger or Mourinho wasting any time to sign up a player like Max?'

George was silent for a moment or two. Of course he knew damned well that his two colleagues were absolutely right. One hundred percent! A raw talent such as Max's was rare, but George was an astute man, with years of experience under his belt, and his instinct was warning him that although this young man was destined for fame and fortune, from which the club and George himself would benefit greatly, he could also turn out to be 'one huge pain in the arse'. He just prayed he wouldn't turn out to be another Georgie Best, whose sad, untimely demise was well known as being the result of him being a chronic alcoholic. No, Max was too smart for that, he reckoned, but George's intuition, and he was seldom wrong, was that young Max Rawlings would become not just another footballer, but a world renowned superstar, an icon. 'Too bloody big for his own boots - and probably the team!', he muttered.

'Okay,' George relented. 'I'll leave it to you to fix it up. But you're wrong about him going to another club, Martin. Young Rawlings is a Rangers player through and through. It's in his blood, just like his old man! Brian was a great player. Bloody shame that was!'

Max and Brian had spent a few anxious days waiting for 'the' call. Every time the phone rang one of them jumped up to answer it straightaway. It was three days after the Under 21's game against Stampford, when Brian answered the phone at 8 a.m. Max was still in bed on his free day.

'Max, it's for you,' Brian called up the stairs. Covering the phone with his hand, he added, grinning, 'someone called Mr. Kyle.'

Max leaped out of bed and almost fell down the stairs, to grab the phone from Brian. Taking a deep breath, he said, 'hello, this is Max.'

'Morning, Max, this is Tony. I enjoyed your game.'

'Thanks, Mr. Kyle.'

'Call me Tony, Max. I guess you'll be pleased to hear you will be joining the first team. That's if you want to of course!'

Max could hear Kyle was chuckling. 'Are you kidding Mr. - er, Tony! It's all I've ever dreamed of!'

'Glad to hear it, son. See you on Friday morning in George's office, after your training.'

'Absolutely brilliant. Thank you, I'll be there.'

'Okay, see you then.'

'Thanks, 'bye', Max was saying as he heard the receiver being put down at the other end. He put the 'phone back on its cradle and hugged Brian, who was patting him on the back, both of them near to tears.

Pauline came into the lounge from the kitchen. 'What's happening,' she asked, looking from one to the other.

'Nothing much Paul - just that our Max is going to sign with Redthorn Rangers' first team!', Brian shouted excitedly.

'Oh Max, that's wonderful!', she exclaimed, giving him a big hug. Then she turned to Brian. 'Does that mean he will be away in Leeds all the time now then?'

'Fraid so love, in fact all over the bloody world. But think of the up side, he'll be a millionaire soon', he beamed. 'He can buy us all a house in Leeds if he wants!'

'Well, congratulations darling. It's marvellous news,' Pauline said. 'But I hope that horrible George what's his name - Wallis - doesn't give you a hard time. From what I've seen on the telly, and read in the papers, he's a right piece of work!'

The two men laughed, and Max hugged Pauline. 'Don't worry, mum, I can look after myself,' he assured her. 'His bark's worse than his bite.'

'Hope so,' Pauline said. She didn't know why, but she felt very uneasy about Max's news, an awful sense of foreboding, or possibly just a woman's intuition. Of course she was thrilled that her son had become so successful, but she had a nagging feeling that from now on, life would never be the same again for any of them.

CHAPTER SEVEN

Billie Wallis

For centuries the area in London's East End, which is now the prestigious 'Docklands', was widely known as 'the Isle of Dogs'. Several theories abounded as to the source of the name, ranging from the fact that dead dogs were often washed up on the banks of the River Thames, which meanders round the 'island' on three sides, to the much preferred stories that it was the place where King Edward III kept his greyhounds. In later years it was also reputed to be the receptacle for the dogs of Henry VIII. Some historians lectured that it was a corruption of the 'Isle of Ducks', from ancient records of wild fowl inhabiting the whole area, which was originally simply known as Stepney Marsh.

Whatever its true origins, no-one who had ever lived on The Isle of Dogs as far back as 1588, when the name was first recorded, could ever have envisaged that in the twentieth century it would become a fashionable enclave for upwardly mobile city workers.

Numbers of these 'Yuppies' were moving into hugely expensive, luxury flats in high rise buildings and converted warehouses, whilst banks, broking houses and financial institutions were shifting their locations from the square mile of the City of London to the new Canary Wharf office complex in what was now 'The Docklands'.

Decades before this transformation took place, it was on the West Ferry Road, Millwall, on the Isle of Dogs that Billy Wallis's betting shop could be found. The premises were situated conveniently opposite 'The Weighed Anchor' pub, next to a small scrap of disused land, which served as a reminder of the German Luftwaffe's bombing raids on London's docks during World War II. This abandoned little area, now covered with weeds and litter, was used as a car park for the patrons of the pub and the betting shop.

Billy Wallis was born and bred on 'the island', growing up with his three older brothers in a two up, two down, terraced house, not a mile from the shop he was to own one day. Billy's father, George, was a giant of a man, working as a stevedore in the West India Docks. His reputation as a hard man afforded him much respect from his workmates and neighbours, more from fear than admiration. He was hard working, hard drinking and a fearless fighter.

Violet, Billy's mother, was a timid little woman, standing no taller than five feet, with a pretty face and a shock of black hair that fell to her waist when it was not tied up in a neat bun at the nape of her neck. She, too, worked hard, as a cleaner in what the locals termed 'The Anchor' every morning, and she did her level best to keep their small house clean and tidy and her family well fed and clothed, despite the meager remains of George's wages which came her way, after he had spent a good deal of it in the pub on Friday nights.

Billy was by far the brightest of the Wallis offspring. From an early age he was a real handful: cheeky and naughty, but with a lively, enquiring mind which helped to make him somewhat tolerable to most people and endeared him to his long-suffering mother. At school he was the class comic, and the most popular boy. He was a constant source of amusement to his mates with his quick wit and antics. To the despair of his teachers, he often disrupted classes and was on the receiving end of the cane most days.

Somehow, however, not yet fifteen, Billy left school with a decent education behind him. He had a good head for figures and had always been top of the class in arithmetic. He liked to read, and because there was never enough money for his parents to buy him books, he joined a library and devoured with relish boys' adventure stories, 'Just William' books and tales of brave explorers. He had an extraordinary vocabulary and, as his mother would often remark, could talk the hind leg off a donkey. Never lost for words, he was quick thinking and articulate. He didn't know it then, but these qualities, combined with his rugged good looks and charisma, were to become the cornerstone of his successful career and lifestyle.

Billy was a strong lad for his age. With his father's strapping build and his mother's features and thick dark hair, he was not text book handsome, but he had a 'Heathcliffe' broody look about him, which women found irresistible. Billy rebuffed, without a second's thought, his father's urges for him to work alongside him in the docks. The idea of getting up at six in the morning and grafting all day, coming home filthy and tired was abhorrent to him. 'I'd rather be kicked up the arse by the milkman's horse!', he said cockily.

It was fate that led him to the door of Jim Pascoe's house in Limehouse. He had met a girl, nearing sixteen, in a coffee bar in the Mile End Road. Joyce was with her friends, feeding the juke box and swooning over the latest Elvis Presley hit, when Billy spotted her. She was a small, pretty girl, with long brown hair and a voluptuous figure. He gave her the once over and, liking what he saw, decided to chat her up, egged on by his mates. She had already noticed him come into the café with his mates and was quite taken with the looks of this big lad.

'It was a piece of cake,' he told his mates afterwards. 'Never any doubt!' Meeting young Joyce was to be a turning point in his life.

It turned out that Joyce's father, Jim Pascoe, was a well known bookie, running his business from the front room of his semi detached house. When, a few weeks after going out with Billy, Joyce took him home, Jim was very impressed with the lad's confidence and intelligence.

By the same token, coming from a back street terraced house, Billy was blown away by Irene's posh home and enviable lifestyle.

'He's got a good head on his shoulders,' Jim said to his wife after Billy had left. 'I'm looking for a lad to become a runner now that Joe's gone into the army, and that boy could be just the ticket!'

'But he's under age, Jim', his wife pointed out.

'So what? Who's to know? Put him in a suit and he'd pass for eighteen any day of the week. Look at the size of him – he looks like bleeding Burt Lancaster - and he's got more clout than a barrow boy!'

Joyce was dispatched the very next morning to go and fetch Billy so that Jim could put his proposal to him. Billy was over the moon. What a result! He could go to all the dark and mysterious clubs and pubs in the East End, meet people, which he loved, and perhaps even mix with some famous 'faces' in gangland. His imagination was running wild. As Billy saw things, he would be learning a trade and finally earn some serious 'wonga' for himself, instead of having to ponce off his mum. He couldn't wait to give her a few quid out of his first week's wages. He accepted Jim's offer without a moment's hesitation.

Looking back, Billy often reflected that one of the highlights of his young life was walking into Burtons the tailors to get fitted out for his first three piece 'whistle'. Costing just two pounds, ten shillings, it was known as a fifty bob suit. Jim paid for the suit, and deducted two shillings out of Billy's wages every week until he'd paid off the debt. Billy wore it with pride as he carried out his duties as Jim's runner. On his first day of work, he paraded in front of his mum like a peacock.

'What do'ya think then mum? The dog's bollocks or what!'

Violet tutted at his language, but had to laugh. 'You look lovely, darling,' she said. 'A proper toff!'

Billy proved himself to be an indispensable asset to Jim. He was always punctual and anxious to please. Above all, he was honest and diligent and a quick learner. His rough charm and wit made him very popular with the punters. To Billy's eternal delight, he had dealings with several of the well known East End 'faces'.

These dubious characters took a liking to the lad, and more importantly, trusted him. Consequently, Billy often carried out special 'ask no questions' errands for them, and made a few pounds on the side.

'Lucky Jim Pascoe' also had a stand at the Walthamstow Dog Stadium in East London. Three nights a week Billy was there alongside Jim, looking out for him and doing a bit of running for those punters who couldn't be bothered to get off their backsides to place a bet.

By the time he was eighteen, Billy was well known all over the Isle of Dogs. He was earning good money and having the time of his life. Joyce had long since been replaced by a stream of young women, who fell for Billy's charm and looks but inevitably had their hearts broken. He loved the fairer sex, but his heart was set on his future and girls were nothing but titillation and sexual relief for him. He had ambition and raw determination. He saved every penny he could, which he knew he would need if he were to achieve his goal.

When Jim Pascoe opened one of the first legalised betting shops, located in the Mile End Road, Billy was employed on the tills. He missed his life as a runner, but that activity was now becoming redundant with the advent of the betting shops springing up all over the country. Billy took to the new concept like a duck to water and within a few months Joe knew his young protégé was ready to become a settler, taking bets, working out the odds and payments. There were no computerised tills back in the forties, so all calculations were made in Billy's head or with pencil and paper. It was only a matter of two years before Billy became the manager and took over the day to day running of the business. Jim was looking to retire within the next few years and knew he could safely leave it for Billy to step into his shoes.

Billy, however, had other ideas. He bided his time and worked tirelessly for long hours to turn the betting shop into a success until, at the age of 22, with a decent amount of cash behind him, he was ready to go it alone. He knew that a confectionery and newsagents shop in the West Ferry Road was becoming vacant and up for rent soon, so he made his move. The shop had a small flat above it and he moved into it with his current girlfriend. Irene, two years older than Billy, was intelligent as well as attractive. She was a good investment and he knew it. He reasoned that she would make a good wife and mother and was smart enough to help him run the business. Another bonus was, she was a good cook, had a great body and was a willing sexual partner. Billy wasn't big on romance, but had a hearty sexual appetite, and Irene never said 'no'. Marriage was a necessary evil he told himself with a resigned sigh.

Billy's three older brothers were beginning to build a reputation for themselves as 'hard nuts around the island'. No-one with any sense of self preservation messed with the Wallis ruffians. One of them had a fruit and vegetable stall in the local street market, while the other two worked in the docks, subsidising their income by doing a bit of protection work or fencing stolen goods from the ships. They all drank and gambled heavily, and had been banned from several pubs for fighting and smashing the place up on a Saturday night.

Billy was horrified and embarrassed on a regular basis to learn of his brothers' latest misdemeanors, distancing himself from them as best he could. He was earning a good living from the betting shop business, and being in the public eye, it was essential that he maintain his reputation of respectability. To those in the know, however, the honest bookmaker's sudden fortune came from his inscrutable dealings with various members of London's underworld. Among the favoured few - his intimate circle of equally dishonest chancers - Billy enjoyed the myth that he was a man of some status in his patch of gangland. He fancied himself as the local 'Godfather', although he was, in fact, an insignificant minnow in the world of crime prevalent in the East End. He would boast that he knew people – and could arrange to do a number on someone if they got out of line. He would often name-drop the Krays as if he knew them, although he'd never actually set eyes on any of the three brothers.

Billy's initial involvement with some of the local mobsters, could, in some part, be put down to Arnie Fellowes, a well known villain. Arnie approached Billy out of the blue, shortly after Billy opened his new shop. He wanted to place a huge bet on a horse, a rank outsider, but for reasons known only to himself, Arnie was confident that the horse would finish in the first three. He told Billy he wanted to put a monkey (five hundred pounds) each way on the horse, and take the odds, which were 20-1. Billy quickly reckoned Arnie would pick up thirteen and a half grand if the horse won and three grand if it came second or third. Arnie promised Billy his cut would be five hundred pounds if he could manage to lay the bet off for him.

In the normal way of things, a small betting shop would never take on such a wager without the common practice of laying it off to one of the national turf accountants such as William Hill or Ladbrokes, which is what Billy did. He saw his chance to make a quick small fortune, and went along with Arnie's proposition, adding his own hundred pounds to the bet. That was the small beginning of Billy's rapid rise in the world of corruption, dishonest dealings and subsequent wealth. His six bedroomed house in two acres of land in Chigwell, Essex, a chain of betting shops extending throughout the East End from Bethnal Green to Chingford, a race horse and two greyhounds, were testimony to his becoming a multi millionaire in a short space of time.

The icing on Billie's cake was when his son, George, was selected to play for Stampford United FC. Billy was ecstatic. His saw his own kudos going up by a mile and he wasted no time in becoming even more high profile by sponsoring Stampford to the tune of a million pounds annually. Having his betting shop logos on the players' strips gave him a huge buzz. Suddenly, Billy Wallis was elevated into the higher echelons of public respectability, whilst secretly becoming a more significant figure in the growing new era of mega rich, criminal fraternity in London's East End.

For many years, Billy enjoyed his new found status within the football circles, and attended almost every one of Stampford's matches. As he sat proudly in his personal designated seat in the VIP area, he relished the fact that his face might appear on television in the highlights of the game later that night.

Billy was sitting in his usual seat on the fateful day that George suffered the horrific attack by MacFarlane. As his injured son was stretchered off, Billy leaped from his seat, made his way to the tunnel, and ran puffing and panting to the medical room. He stared in horror as the doctor confirmed the leg was broken in two places and they had to get George to hospital as soon as possible.

As Billy sat in the ambulance with George, he swore to himself, 'that fucking Scots bastard won't get away with this!' He took his phone from his pocket and dialled a number.

CHAPTER EIGHT

Max's Proposition

After her intoxicating experience - in every sense of the word - on the previous Saturday, Kathie could not stop thinking about Max. She spent the next few days on tenterhooks, anxiously waiting to hear from him. Every time her mobile phone rang, or signalled an incoming text, she grabbed it excitedly, only to be bitterly disappointed that it wasn't from Max.

'Why am I not surprised?', she scolded herself. 'He must have dozens of girls throwing themselves at him. why would he bother with me?'

Margaret realised her daughter was not her usual chirpy self, and had noticed how she pounced on her phone every time it rang. 'Come on then Kathie, what's going on? You're like a cat on a hot tin roof these days', she said.

'But Elizabeth Taylor I'm not!', sighed Kathie.

'Ah! I know the signs. A boy is it? Anyway, you're just as beautiful as her, to be sure!'

Kathie sighed and looked at Margaret, pulling a wry face. 'Yes, you're right mum, as usual. I met this amazing boy - well young man - on Saturday. I don't expect you've heard of him, but he is quite a famous football player - Max Rawlings. He plays for Redthorn Rangers' Under 21's. You know I went with Mel to a match - well he is the friend of her boyfriend, Chris, and we all went out for a drink together after the match.'

Margaret was frowning. 'How could I forget? A drink? What sort of drink?'

'Well, it was champagne, and I didn't drink much. Anyway,' she went on hurriedly, realising she'd let the cat out of the bag. 'Max is just so cool! He's going to be a really famous footballer one day - well he is already I suppose. But it's only a matter of time before he plays for Rangers in the Premier League, and England no doubt, and then he will be known all over the world.'

Margaret was horrified. 'You don't want to be having anything to do with a footballer for goodness sake, child! They are nothing but trouble. You read about it every day. They never stay married for more than a couple of years, having affairs and suchlike, drinking and taking drugs, and most of them haven't got the brains they were born with!'

'Well, say it like it is mum! Anyway, they're not all like that, don't be silly! Max is nothing like that!', Kathie retorted defensively. 'He is very intelligent, and really kind and considerate. And no, he didn't try anything on,' she added, anticipating what Margaret was about to ask next.

'And did he promise to call you then?'

'Yes, but he did say he would be busy for the next few days as he was expecting to have a meeting with his manager.' Kathie was even convincing herself.

'Well, take my advice and steer well clear of him from now on. He'll only break your heart.'

'Thanks mum, that really helps!' Kathie was close to tears, and grabbing her phone, she turned and stomped out of the kitchen, leaving Margaret shaking her head.

'God willing, she'll get over it soon enough!'

Kathie sat on her bed. She knew her mother was right and was only saying what she herself had been thinking. But she couldn't help how she felt about Max. The mere mention of his name gave her butterflies in the stomach, and she yearned to see him again. It was agony. Agony and ecstasy! She had never understood what that meant until now. She phoned Melanie to have a chat. Mel always cheered her up.

'Blimey, Kathie, it's only been a couple of days!', exclaimed Melanie. 'What do you expect? He told you he would be busy. Ahh, you really like him don't you!', she mocked.

'I think I'm in lurve, Mel!', Kathie said dramatically.

'What, after one day? Leave it out - you hardly know him!' Melanie thought she heard a little sob from Kathie. 'Oh, love! Don't be upset. I'm sure he'll be in touch with you soon. He seemed to be very taken with you. Listen, Chris told me Max thought you were really something - his words.'

'Did he really?' Kathie wiped her eyes. 'I know, I'm being stupid, but I've never felt like this before - about anyone!'

'What if I come round tonight? We can have a chat.'

'Thanks Mel. You're a star. See you later then.'

Kathie was having lunch in the college canteen on the following day when her phone bleeped. When she saw that it was a text from Max, she nearly choked on her sandwich. She opened the message, her heart pounding.

'Hi Irish. Good news. Been selected for the proper team. LOL!! Hope you can help me celebrate. In London next Sunday. I'll call u. Bye for now gorgeous. Max xxx'

Kathie punched the air excitedly. 'Yes!', she exclaimed, not noticing that other students were looking at her. Grinning from ear to ear she said softly, 'result!' and quickly replied to his text.

Sunday couldn't come quickly enough for Kathie. She was wondering what to wear. Where would he take her? Would he ask her to go steady with him? Her stomach was in knots. The thought of being with Max again was just a dream.

Margaret was not so pleased.

'I warned you my girl. Be it on your own head! And don't come crying to me when he does the dirty on you,' she warned.

'Oh, mum, please, don't be like that. How can you say that when you haven't even met him?'

'I've seen him in the papers enough times! Do you think I have my head up my own backside Kathie? I do watch the news and read the newspapers you know!'

Kathie was surprised. She thought football was the last thing Margaret would know anything about. 'I know, mum. But you can't believe everything you read in the papers. Anyway, I hope you can meet him soon - that's if he wants to go out with me of course.'

Margaret looked heavenwards and tutted. She could see this all ending in tears. 'As long as it's not a one night stand! You know what I mean!', she said pointedly.

'Don't worry on that score, mum. That's not going to happen I can assure you. I'm not that naive.'

Kathie was out of bed, showered and dressed by ten o'clock on Sunday morning. She had spent an hour trying on different outfits, deciding at last on a black mini skirt, with her favourite sparkly emerald green top and long black knitted jacket, finished off with her favourite black suede, knee length boots. Next was the decision on her hair. Long and glam, or swept up to look more sophisticated? Long and glam, she decided.

She had shampooed and conditioned, blown dried and brushed till it shone. She tossed her head from side to side as she surveyed her reflection in the mirror. She looked great.

Lunchtime came and went and Kathie was beginning to fret, checking the clock every ten minutes. It was gone 2 pm when she finally got a call from Max, making her jump so excitedly she nearly dropped her phone.

'Hi, gorgeous. Shall I pick you up about seven?'

'Yes, that'll be fine. Where are you by the way - are you in London yet?'

'Yes, of course. I'm with mum and dad. I got here about midday and have just had one of mum's lovely roast dinners.'

Kathie could have kicked herself. How stupid of her! Of course he would want to stay with his parents. What was she thinking - that he would drive all the way from Leeds just to see her?

'Oh, that's good. I'll see you later then.'

'Okay. 'Bye'.

'Bye.'

Kathie was jumping up and down excitedly when Margaret walked into the room.

'No need to ask who that was!', she said, her lips tightening in disapproval.

'Yes, mum, it was Max. He's picking me up at seven. Do you want to meet him? Shall I ask him in?'

'I suppose so, it's only polite,' Margaret conceded grudgingly.

Kathie thought that the next few hours would never end. Finally, just before seven o'clock there was a ring at the door. She rushed to open it, and there stood Max, exuding a waft of Chanel, in designer jeans and shoes, an expensive leather jacket over one shoulder. He could have stepped out of a page of Vogue magazine.

Kathie's heart was pounding once more. She took a deep breath and somehow managed an outward appearance of calm. 'Hello Max. You're nice and early. Would you like to come in and meet my mum?', she asked nervously, in a voice she didn't recognise as her own. She gritted her teeth in annoyance.

'Sure, just quickly. Am I okay parked outside for a minute or two?'

'Yes, that's fine.' Kathie opened the door and he walked in.

Margaret had come into the hall, surveying the scene.

'Good evening Mrs. Neilson,' Max said politely and offered his hand.

Margaret shook his hand and said, 'Good evening. I hope you are going to take good care of my daughter here. She's a good girl. You know what I mean!'

'Mum!' Kathie glared at Margaret.

'I sure will,' said Max, winking at Kathie as she hurriedly grabbed her coat, which she had placed on the bottom of the banister in readiness for her departure.

'Bye then mum, see you later.' Kathie was already halfway through the door, followed by Max, who turned and said, 'Goodbye Mrs. N. Nice to have met you.'

Margaret closed the door behind them. 'Mrs. N if you like! Bloody cheek.'

Once in Max's brand new Jaguar sports car, Kathie, still smiling from ear to ear, gently chided him.

'I'm sorry about my mum. I can't believe you said that to her though - it was so funny. The look on her face!'

They both laughed.

'She's really nice though,' Max said. 'Quite beautiful actually. I bet she was a stunner when she was young - I can see where you get your looks from.'

'I know, she's great, but she worries about me too much.'

'Well, she won't need to from now on, gorgeous. I'm going to look after you.'

Kathie felt a thrill of excitement. She was falling for Max in a big way, and to hear those words was music to her ears. She shot a sideways look at his handsome profile and gave a sigh of utter contentment and happiness.

Max had already booked a table in an expensive restaurant in Soho. 'I hope you like Chinese.' He suddenly thought perhaps he should have asked her first.

'Love it!', Kathie replied.

They had a wonderful evening together. Kathie was high on adrenaline and excitement; Max couldn't take his eyes off this enchanting girl. He was beginning to realise he had feelings for her, a new experience for him.

This was to be the first of many dates. Over the next few months the young couple took every opportunity to spend time together, which was becoming more and more difficult. Max's football fixtures and training regime meant he could rarely get to London. Sometimes Kathie would catch a train to Leeds so they could spend a few precious hours together.

They were both becoming increasingly frustrated, emotionally and physically. It was on such an occasion, whilst they were enjoying lunch in a bistro near Rangers' ground, that Max took the bull by the horns.

'Kathie, you know how I feel about you don't you?'

'I think I do ... but you have never actually said it.'

'Well, I should have. I think I'm in love with you Kathie. I've never felt like this about anyone, honest.'

'Oh, Max, I'm sure you know I feel the same about you. I have since the first time we met I think.' Kathie blushed. She had blurted that out before she could stop herself.

'Well, I'm flattered.' Max took her hand across the table. 'I did have an inkling though! But I'm pleased to hear it in writing!'

They both laughed.

'But we, well I for one, can't really go on like this Kathie, if I'm honest. I don't know about you, but, well, it's not ..... how can I put this?'

'I know what you're saying, Max, she said quickly.'

Kathie averted her eyes from his gaze and looked down at the table and fidgeted with her serviette.

'It's because we haven't slept together', she almost whispered. 'Don't think it's easy for me either, but you know the score. To quote you, no pun intended.' She made a little face.

'Of course I do, and I respect you for it. That sounds like a cliché, but honestly, it's true.' Max lowered his voice and leaned closer towards her. 'It's not just sex, Kathie. But when do we ever get time to be alone together, I mean really alone? We are either at my parents' house, your mum's house, in a restaurant, in the cinema, at the matches ... you know what I'm saying. We have never, ever, been in a situation where we are completely alone, where we could, say, watch

TV, have a kiss and cuddle in private. It's bloody ridiculous.'

'I know, I know.' Kathie knew this moment would come. She had been worrying about it for the past few months, not sure how she would deal with it. Their most intimate moments so far had taken place in Max's car. Their mutual desire for each other was now reaching fever pitch. It took every fibre of Kathie's self-control to stop them going the whole way. It was agonisingly frustrating.

'Let's get out of here,' Max said. 'We need to talk about this in private.'

They walked to a nearby park and sat on a bench. Max put his arm around Kathie as she laid her head on his shoulder. For a while they sat in silence and watched a boy throwing a ball for his dog.

'Kathie, please don't be mad, but I have done something.'

Kathie looked up at him in alarm. 'What? What have you done Max?'

'Don't worry, nothing serious.' He smiled at the look on her face. 'Look, about what we were discussing. I think we need to get to know each other better, and that means spending some quality time together. '

Kathie was looking at him anxiously.

'Okay,' he hurried on, 'I understand your morals and religion, etcetera. I don't like it, I can't pretend I do, but I can't force you. What I have in mind is, we spend the rest of the day completely on our own,'

'Well, we are aren't we?'

'No, we're not Kathie. Look around you. We're in a public park, with people everywhere. And if we go for a meal tonight, we will be in a crowded restaurant. Christ, Kathie, I haven't even seen you with your kit off! I've imagined it a lot though!'

Kathie chuckled. 'Kit! What am I, one of your players? You're terrible! So, what have you done then?'

'I've booked a room at a hotel. Don't worry, it's nowhere near here - and it's a nice private one, tucked away off the main road.'

'A hotel!' Kathie was shocked. 'Blimey, you've done your homework! You crafty devil!'

'Yes, why not? You don't have to do anything you don't want to, I promise you that faithfully, but don't you see, we can just be ourselves, have a meal sent up, listen to music, just have some intimacy - and I don't mean sex,' he added quickly, 'unless you insist - as if! But just a kiss and cuddle, be on our own together, like any normal couple!'

Kathie could see Max was getting agitated. He did have a point, she had to agree. Besides, the mere thought of what he was saying sent her pulse racing. God, if only he knew, how she had managed to hold on to her virtue and not to beg him to make love to her before now, was nothing short of a miracle. She had often dreamed of the scenario.

'Okay Max, but like you said, no means no!'

Max jumped up and pulled her up towards him, wrapped his arms around her and gave her a huge hug and a lingering kiss.

'Come on then, what are we waiting for?'

CHAPTER NINE

Bernie Cummings

Another crucial witness to the incident of George's injury had been a young reporter, Bernard Cummings, who was covering the match for his paper, 'The Leeds Tribune'. Along with the thousands of fans watching the match, he was sickened at the horrific two-footed tackle from behind which had taken George out. George was lying on the pitch for ten minutes, in obvious agony. His trainer had signalled to the bench, and the crowd fell silent in anticipation, whilst the injured player, groaning in pain, was surrounded by his physio, the referee, stretcher bearers and a doctor.

Finally, as George was carried off, the reporter took out his portable recording machine and began talking into it, in preparation for the report he would be typing when he got back to the office. He knew this was a big story, marking a day which would go down in the game's history, as it was clear to all that George Wallis had sustained serious injuries and would be out of the game for months, if not forever.

Like most small boys, Bernard Cummings - Bernie as he became known - had dreamed of becoming a famous footballer when he grew up. The only team he would play for, he assured his mates, would be, undisputedly, Redthorn Rangers.

Although Bernie was the undisputed brainiest kid in his class, nicknamed 'clevercloggs', he was very popular amongst the boys and girls alike, with his commanding presence, and an endearing disposition. He was not only smart, he was tall and not bad looking, besides which he was a very good athlete. The boys vied for his friendship as he could be very useful when it came to helping them out with their homework, plus he was in the school football team, in itself worthy of respect. The girls just found him adorable.

Bernie was smart enough to realise that although he was a useful player, he was not naturally outstanding. He was tall and muscular, but a little on the gangly side and he lacked the all important pace and turn of speed. He was not blessed with the above average talent that he appreciated the professional footballers had, when he watched games on TV. At fifteen years of age, whilst discussing his future with his careers master, Bernie suggested that, realistically, he saw himself as a sports journalist, which would enable him to combine his literary talent and knowledge of all things sporting, especially football. His ambition, he had informed his teacher confidently, was to become a sports correspondent and eventually a television presenter or pundit.

The eloquent, rather pompous, teacher could add nothing to Bernie's statement of intent, other than to remark in his effeminate voice: 'I'm inclined to agree with you Bernard. You certainly have the required literary skills, and I have to admit that, from what I have observed, you appear to be a slightly above average soccer player, but whether you have the wherewithal to join the ranks of the immortal Stanley Mathews, is questionable!'

Bernie graduated from Oxford with a first class honours degree in English Language and Media Studies, but he was more proud of the fact that he had achieved a Blue for rugby and had rowed for his house.

He first met Veronica Hollingsworth, a vivacious and highly intelligent young woman, at university. Veronica was reading Business Studies and English Language and Literature, so they were often attending the same lectures. She was petite and slim, with short black hair framing a pretty heart shaped face. At 6ft 2ins, Bernie towered above Veronica. It was a source of constant amusement to him that someone of such diminutive size could have such a huge presence.

Veronica hailed from a wealthy family with an impressive pile in Surrey. As the only child, she had received a privileged upbringing, affording her a private education and her own pony. At eighteen she was presented with a brand new BMW sports car.

Her father, Maurice, had inherited his father's business and had run a lucrative luxury car main dealership in Putney for over twenty years. Her mother, Valerie, had been a struggling model when she met Maurice and was becoming reasonably successful as a photographic model. When she married and fell pregnant with Veronica, Valerie had been only too happy to become a suburban housewife and a lady who lunches.

'That's a name and a half!', Bernie smiled, when Veronica first introduced herself. 'Veronica Hollingsworth! I think I'll call you Vonnie Holly.'

She laughed loudly. 'Well Bernard, I think I'll just call you Bernie'.

Bernie was enchanted with Veronica from the moment he first set eyes on her. They chatted over coffee a few days into their induction period, and he was impressed with her vitality and ambition. She was cute and intelligent - and very sexy, he thought, as he pictured her voluptuous little body bereft of any clothing. Bernie had found it difficult not to stare at her firm, perky breasts, straining against a tight pink angora sweater, as he sat opposite her at the table they were sharing at lunch time.

Veronica had giggled and said, pointing to her face, 'the speaking part is up here!' Bernie nearly blushed for the first time in his life.

He mumbled unconvincingly, but with a grin, 'I was just admiring your fluffy jumper.'

Veronica could be very deep and serious sometimes, but she shared the same wicked sense of humour as Bernie and, like him, was fiercely ambitious. The one thing they didn't have in common was Bernie's passion for sport. Vonnie admitted that she had hated any form of gym or sport at school, and told him she would have to be drugged and bound to watch a football match! They found that their educational backgrounds were very similar, however. Veronica's father was a wealthy businessman and she had been privately educated at an expensive girls' public school, whilst Bernie had won a scholarship to his local grammar school. Bernie's father was a salesman and his mother was a part time librarian.

Very soon, Bernie and Veronica were hopelessly in love and spending every possible minute of their time together. Bernie was to be seen creeping out of her student's pad in the early hours most mornings after a long night of intellectual conversation and even longer sessions of varied and passionate sexual activity.

'Now you've had your wicked way with me, you'll have to marry me!', Bernie joked.

Vonnie sighed dramatically. 'Oh, no! What have I done?'

'I'll take that as a yes!'

They were married the year they left university and moved to Leeds, where they rented an apartment. Bernie had already landed a job there and Veronica was on the short list as a journalist for a weekly woman's magazine in London, writing a fashion and beauty column.

With his outstanding qualifications, easy manner and refreshing, youthful enthusiasm, Bernie had had no trouble securing his first job with the local newspaper. Tom Howard took to young Bernie straight away. Tom had been editor of 'The Leeds Herald', commonly known as 'The Herald', and its sister publication, 'The Advertiser', for forty years. The newspaper encompassed over a thirty mile radius around Leeds. Bernie was employed to cover all social and sporting events and part of his salary package was a slightly battered five year old Renault, which took him to every corner of his patch.

Bernie thought he'd died and gone to heaven. He loved his job. He got to attend all the sporting fixtures, particularly football, and quickly perfected his craft as a skilled sports reporter. To attend Leeds' Premier Division club Redthorn Rangers matches and be paid for it, was all he could ever have dreamed of. He soon became a well known figure in his area. He managed to lay bare every last detail from his interviews. His reports were brilliantly written, often controversial, always thought provoking, and eagerly looked forward to and commented on by the fans and often the players. Bernard Cummings was becoming a byword in media circles. He was regularly invited to appear on local television to give his unbiased view on an event, and he never disappointed. He was often the butt of irate callers on radio's Sports Night chat show.

Before he turned twenty five, Bernie was sub-editor of 'The Herald' and was also writing his own columns in the sports pages of a famous Sunday newspaper supplement.

Bernie always wrote prolifically about Redthorn Rangers' latest fortunes, in both 'The Herald' and his Sunday column. One particular scathing attack by Bernie on George Wallis's attitude towards his players, in particular Max Rawlings, gained him an enemy for life.

The article was picked up by a Sky Sports pundit - an ex famous footballer - and Bernie had appeared briefly on national TV being interviewed about his article. Bernie was garrulous, humorous and easy on the eye, plus his knowledge of the game was impressively vast. He was not afraid to voice his opinion, however controversial, and he was a natural on the small screen. Men and women viewers alike were impressed, for different reasons, and took notice of this charismatic young man.

This five minute TV appearance was to change Bernie's life. The reaction from the public was unprecedented, setting the studio phones and social networks alight. George Wallis was livid.

'Who is this young punk anyway?', he snarled as he threw the newspaper across his desk top. 'He knows fuck all about the game - just some posh, know it all, tosser, trying to make a few quid on the back of the likes of me!'

His secretary, quickly turned off the television which had been showing a re-run of the programme.

'Get me the editor of that fucking rag he writes for, Susan. He won't know what's hit him when I've finished with him!' Despite his best efforts, however, George's rantings and ravings at Tom Howard fell on deaf ears.

'Freedom of the press old boy!' Tom was leaning back in his chair smiling. He winked at Bernie, who was standing in the doorway of Tom's office.

'There was nothing slanderous in our article, Mr Wallis, and this paper is not responsible for what one of my reporters has to say on television. It's beyond my jurisdiction, you know that. I'm sure you've heard a lot worse!' He was loving it.

George was spluttering with rage. 'You haven't heard the last of this!', he spat, as he slammed down the phone.

Bernard Cummings was a name George would not forget for a long time.

Over the next twenty years, Bernie become a famous journalistic icon. His face was as familiar on television as those of the players and managers. He had taken over from Tom Howard, when he retired, as Editor of 'The Herald', and was then headhunted by a national red top newspaper, 'The Daily Tribune'. After a few years as Sports Editor, he decided to go freelance and never looked back.

To Bernie's huge disappointment and sadness, Veronica had made it very clear from the start of their relationship that she did not intend to have children and that her career was the most important thing in her life. 'Apart from you of course', she had added.

Bernie did not press the subject. He figured it was natural for her to think like that, as she was so young and embarking on an exciting career.

She had just accepted the job she was hoping for, as a journalist for a weekly woman's magazine. The publication was at the lower end of the market, with a limited distribution, but it was a start, and Veronica was full of enthusiasm and ideas.

Bernie guessed, and hoped, wrongly as it turned out, that after a few years his wife would become 'broody' and want a child.

Veronica was adamant, despite her husband's pleas.

'You can always go back to work - thousands of professional women do! In fact my mother did,' he argued.

At the same time as Bernie was making his mark in the media world, Veronica had become a senior journalist, heading up the fashion columns in 'Freemale!', a glossy magazine with a huge distribution, avidly read by women all over the UK. She had a massive input into the restructuring of the magazine. Sales figures soared and the magazine was extended into France, Italy and Spain. Ten years later, Veronica was largely instrumental in the takeover of a competitive publication. Her tremendous work ethic and contribution to the company's success was rewarded on her 40th birthday when she was appointed European Editor.

Veronica's huge work commitments and deadlines in London, as well as overseeing the European operations, meant that she only went home to the marital house in Leeds perhaps once a week and at weekends, often not at all. Bernie was by now appearing on television quite regularly as a football correspondent and pundit, as well as continuing his freelance journalism, and he was constantly travelling the world. After twenty years, their marriage inevitably began to crumble. It was a joint decision that they should have a trial separation. Veronica moved out and rented an apartment in

London. Before twelve months had passed, they both conceded that their marriage was in name only and that divorce seemed to be inevitable.

It was a huge blow to Bernie. He still loved his Vonnie, and for months after they divorced, he found it difficult to function. He lost some of his enthusiasm for work, and fell to drinking and smoking more. He often didn't bother to shave and his usual immaculate appearance began to wane. The decline in his general well being and attitude to work was becoming evident to his friends and colleagues.

Sitting in his study one morning in early January, Bernie was gazing absently through the window of his study, taking a long drag on a cigarette, as he watched the icy rain beginning to turn to snow. The flakes were landing softly on the window, sliding slowly down, to leave little patterns on the glass as he followed their path.

He jumped as the phone rang. It was a familiar voice, one of his regular snouts.

'I've got something for you, Bernie. This is big! Got to be worth a fifty!'

CHAPTER TEN

Commitment

Max and Kathie jumped out of the taxi cab in a small village on the outskirts of Leeds. They stood hand in hand looking up at a large, three story detached house, which stood at the end of a small row of similar houses. Six stone steps led up to its front door. 'Sandhills Hotel' welcomed guests by way of an ornate board sunk into the lawn in front of the house. Its wording offered *'Comfortable rooms, with friendly service and delicious home cooked meals'*.

Max put on his dark glasses and woollen bobble hat, which made Kathie giggle. 'That's the trouble with having a mug everyone recognises!', he moaned. 'I've booked in the name of Robinson by the way.'

'Oh, very original!', said Kathie sarcastically. 'But it's better than Smith I suppose!'

Max grabbed her hand. 'Come on then, let's bite the bullet.'

They were greeted by a friendly lady who introduced herself as Sally, and were shown to their room.

'No luggage?', she observed suspiciously, looking from one to the other.

Kathie responded quickly.

She held up a huge handbag in one hand and then in the other hand a large, exclusive boutique's bag, which contained a designer dress and jacket Max had bought her earlier.

'No, everything we need is in these', she replied, 'It's only for one night, and we like to travel light.'

Max looked impressed. He raised his eyebrows and winked at Kathie behind Sally's back.

'Oh, that's okay.' Sally seemed to be satisfied with Kathie's explanation. 'I was just making sure you hadn't left it downstairs.'

Once in the room, Kathie breathed a huge sigh of relief. Max threw his glasses and hat on a chair and bounced on the bed. 'Feels lovely', he said.

Kathie couldn't help thinking that Max was taking all this with a pinch of salt, and probably had done it before. It was a ghastly thought. She couldn't bear to think of him with anyone else, it turned her stomach.

He was patting the bed beside him. 'Come and sit down.'

Kathie put down her bags, took off her coat, slipped out of her shoes and sat down beside him, looking around the room. 'Oh look, there's a kettle and tea and coffee', she said, 'and biscuits!'

Max laughed. 'Of course, you numpty. Shall we have a drink?' He put his arms around her and gave her a little kiss.

Kathie leaped up, embarrassed that Max now knew she had never been in a hotel before. 'Yes, I'll make it.'

They drank their tea and laid down on the bed together. Max put his arms round her and pulled her towards him, kissing her gently.

'Old snooping Sally has probably got a glass to the wall now', he joked.

'Oh, don't say that. Do you think she suspects?'

Max laughed. 'Of course she does, but what can she do? We're both over the age of consent, and she's not likely to turn us away is she? It's not exactly over crowded with guests from what I can see. Anyway, she's kindly agreed to let us have our dinner in the room, and she's even got a bottle of Chardonnay chilling for us. I hope you'll like it. And we can slip out about nine and get back in time for you to catch your train back to London. Unless you decide to stay of course?'

'Steady tiger. You promised!'

'Okay, I know.'

Max turned to face Kathie and pulled her closer. 'You are so gorgeous. I can't stop looking at you. Mmm, you smell nice.' He caressed her gently as they kissed. He nuzzled into her neck, gently running his tongue along the tip of her ear lobe.

Kathie felt the sensual tingles running down her spine, to the tip of her toes.

She pushed him gently away and swung her legs to the floor. 'I'm just going to freshen up - I won't be long. How about you sorting out our dinner, my darling. I'm quite hungry.'

'Good idea. I'm on it.' Max picked up the phone.

They ate their meal and drank the wine with relish at a small table, chatting all the while. Kathie realised that what Max had pointed out was so true: they had never had any real quality, private, time together. She was thoroughly enjoying this impulsive, romantic little assignation with the man she adored so much. It gave her goose bumps just to be close to him.

They loaded the empty plates and cutlery on a tray, and Max took it downstairs, ensuring that Sally didn't have an excuse to knock their door. Kathie picked up her glass and put it on the bedside table, then laid down and closed her eyes. Soon Max was back, and, swigging back the last of his wine, laid down beside her.

'It's warm in here,' he said, sitting up and taking off his shirt. 'Come on, don't be shy. At least take off your top, love - we can get under the duvet. Shame to waste it!' He smiled mischievously. 'I'm not going to rape you!'

Kathie was feeling relaxed. A mixture of adrenalin and two glasses of wine was taking effect. She began to lose herself in a delicious haze of sensual arousal.

She so desperately wanted to lay as nature intended next to her gorgeous young man - to feel his strong, fit body against hers. Max leaned over and began to pull up her little crop top and she didn't resist. She held up her arms like a child as he pulled the garment over her head, threw it down and began kissing her neck and chest. He caressed her breasts and she shivered with the thrill of his touch as he moved his hands slowly down to her inner thigh, his gentle touch arousing every sense in her body as she returned his long, sensual kiss.

'I really want you, Kathie!' Max breathed heavily. 'I can't help it!'

'I know - I want you too. I can't believe I'm saying it! But it's true - I've never felt like this before.'

'You mean .....?' Max turned her face towards him and looked at her earnestly.

'Yes, I really do,' she whispered huskily. All thoughts of resistance, that she had carefully harboured and rehearsed, vanished as Max whispered, 'Kathie I adore you. I want you to be mine, really mine, forever.'

'I know. Of course I will be.'

Max gently removed the rest of Kathie's clothes and gazed down at her as he quickly stripped off his own. 'You are so beautiful Kathie. Even better than I'd imagined!'

'So are you! You should be a movie star!'

'Ha! Flattery will get you everywhere!' He kissed her tenderly as he held her arms above her head and began to move seductively against her yielding body. She gasped with sensual pleasure as she felt his hardness against her soft belly.

'I've fantasised about this moment so many times,' he whispered.'

'So have I!'

'Ever since we first met and went to the night club.'

'Me too!'

'I really do love you, Kathie. I don't want you to think ....'

'Shsh, I know, don't worry,' Kathie whispered, before he could finish his sentence. 'I love you so much too, Max,' I just can't imagine not being with you now.'

'This is your first time isn't it?' It was more of a statement than a question from Max.

'Of course! I thought you knew that.'

'I did, really, but I had to make sure. It's a big thing for a girl, I know that. I won't hurt you Kathie, I promise. I just want it to be special.'

Kathie drowned in sexual fulfillment and emotion as Max gently made love to her for the first of what would be many times. He too was experiencing a sensation he had never felt before. He had been intimate with girls, several in fact, but it was nothing like this. This was a new sexual experience - an all consuming feeling of combined passion and emotion that heightened the exquisite pleasure of making love. He now realised how desperately much in love he was with this exceptional girl. He felt quite emotional as they lay in each other's arms afterwards and Kathie said, 'why does love have to hurt so much?'

Max wiped away a tear which had begun to trickle down her cheek. 'And I thought I was really gentle!', he teased as he kissed her closed eyes.

'You know what I mean! I have this terrible ache inside me all the time. You know, real pain! It only goes away when we're together. Is it the same for you?'

'Yes, it is, lovely girl. It's called the agony and the ecstasy I believe.'

'Yes, exactly what I've been saying!', Kathie was surprised at how likeminded they were. 'And what just happened was ecstasy, Max, truly.'

'Wow, praise indeed!', Max said proudly. 'I have to admit I was a little nervous myself. I mean - I didn't want your first experience to be a letdown! Do you know, I think of you all the time, and worry that you'll meet someone else? I couldn't bear it Kathie. I couldn't cope with anyone else touching you.'

'No-one ever will, never.'

'You're not sorry are you, darling? I mean you're not going to regret it and have to make a confession - and then have to say a lot of Hail Marys, or whatever it is you do?'

Kathie smiled and shook her head. 'No, I'm not that religious - don't let my mum hear that! - and anyway, I'm not a bit sorry, honestly. In fact I'm so happy Max. I really feel that we are closer than ever now.' She gave him a reassuring hug. 'But I will have to change my name to Madonna,' she said seriously.

Max looked puzzled. 'Oh, no why?'

'You know! Think about it!'

He shook his head, so she began to sing, 'touched for the very first time.'

Max laughed. 'You idiot, you had me going there! Very funny!' He kissed the top of her head. 'I love your hair.' He furled a long, silky lock around his finger. 'Will you stay with me tonight ... please? I can ring mum and tell her we won't be home - make some excuse. I just want to wake up and see you lying there next to me.'

Kathie nodded without a moment's hesitation. Nothing mattered now she knew for sure that Max really did love her and they would be together for the rest of their lives. 'Mum knows I'm staying with your parents for the weekend, so she won't worry,' she said. 'Can you imagine it? She'd have the Metropolitan and Yorkshire Police out looking for me otherwise, with tracker dogs!'

Grinning at Kathie's quip, Max took out his phone to call his mother.

'When I buy my own house, will you come and live with me, Kathie?', he asked.

'I don't think so, my love. I think that will be going a bit too far.'

'You mean, unless we get married?'

Kathie blushed at the inference. 'Well, that's not what I meant. It's just a bit previous, isn't it? I want a career as well, Max. And you have your future to think of. You are going to be such a star! We have plenty of time - let's not rush into anything.'

Max pulled an exaggerated surprised expression.

'Don't tell you don't like the idea of being one of those WAGs!', he mocked. 'I don't believe it!'

'God no! Heaven forbid. If anything, that would put me off, big time!'

Okay, I know you're right, but I just want to be with you all the time. Not too much to ask!'

'Treat 'em mean, keep 'em keen! Kathie quipped.

'I couldn't be more keen, babes!'

CHAPTER ELEVEN

Heartbreak

Margaret took a sip of tea, as she studied her lovely daughter across the breakfast table. Kathie was flicking through a 'House and Garden' magazine, putting the occasional spoonful of low calorie cereal into her mouth. Margaret had noticed a definite change in Kathie over the last few months. She seemed to have become more sophisticated, more worldly wise and confident. She now had the aura of a woman - no longer a girl. Margaret realised that having a responsible job, mixing with professional people, was partly the cause of this new persona, but she had a good idea that it was more to do with a certain young man! The couple had been seeing each other for a year now, and Margaret was pretty sure that they had become lovers. She sighed. Kathie looked up.

'What's up, mum?'

'Nothing darling. Just thinking how grown up you are now. Not my little girl anymore.'

Kathie smiled. 'I'll always be your little girl, mum, don't be daft.' She reached across and patted Margaret's hand as she checked her watch. 'Oops, must dash. See you tonight. I might be a bit late, so don't panic. There's a meeting about a big contract we've just got from a famous lady; don't know who yet though.

She kissed her mother on the head as she left the room. 'Laters!'

'Bye, love - take care.'

Kathie had turned eighteen and was now employed in an exclusive interior design company in London's fashionable Islington. Her careers teacher had sourced **Bowens Interior Designs,** a flourishing up market company presently looking to take on an apprentice. The teacher had highly recommended Kathie.

Armed with some examples of her work, a nervous Kathie sat facing Josie Green, Bowens' Sales Director and Head of Furnishings, on the other side of a huge desk. Josie, an impeccably dressed and attractive forty-something, liked the look of the young hopeful straight away and was very impressed with her work. She reported to her MD later that the girl was 'an absolute peach'.

Thrilled beyond words, an astonished Kathie accepted without hesitation when Josie offered her the position as her trainee assistant.

'I particularly love this, Kathie,' Josie said, as she fondled an intricate miniature patchwork quilt. 'It's just exquisite - wonderful use of colours. All hand stitched. It must have taken you ages!'

'It did! But I enjoyed doing it - it's my hobby more than anything. I just love doing things like that.'

'Mmm - I can see a market for this. Food for thought. Well, it's been great to meet you, Kathie. I look forward to working with you. And you can believe the rumours that I'm a hard taskmaster. Be warned!' She smiled as she held out her hand. 'Good luck at college by the way, good choice! When you achieve your Higher Certificate, we will automatically give you a pay rise.'

Kathie was in seventh heaven. She was thrilled at the prospect of being part of such a glamorous, multifaceted profession and couldn't rush home quickly enough to tell Margaret. She couldn't believe how lucky she was!

Kathie was a keen and gifted student, eager to learn and improve her skills at college, whilst loving every minute of working at the prestigious design company. Her exceptional talent and fresh enthusiasm was appreciated by everyone at Bowens and it was within the year, at the end of her college tuition, that the newly qualified designer became a treasured member of the team. Josie relied on her young assistant more and more and began to take her along to clients' houses.

Kathie stared around her in wonderment at the sheer opulence of beautiful mansions belonging to the rich and famous. She would have a such a house with Max one day soon - she was certain of that.

At an inspiring meeting in the Board Room one Monday morning, everyone was excited to learn that the much awaited new contract was with Madeline Colbert, a popular singer, turned actress, who was presently starring in a West End musical.

The publicity for Bowens Designs promised to be unprecedented. Kathie couldn't wait to share the news with Margaret and Max. She would be helping Josie with the drapes and furniture in each of the fifteen rooms of Madeline's period house in Northampton.

Reaching home, Kathie hung up her coat, kicked off her shoes, and walked into the kitchen. Margaret was seated at the table, looking solemn. Kathie guessed something was wrong the minute she saw her mother's face. 'Hi, mum. You alright?', she asked anxiously, as she sat down.

Margaret quietly said, 'you obviously haven't seen the papers today.'

'No, course not. Where do I get time to read newspapers? It's been really hectic today. Why, what's happened? Someone died?'

'Not quite.'

Margaret pushed the red top tabloid towards her, open at a page with the glaring headlines: 'My Steamy Night With Sexy Max.'

Kathie turned white as a sheet. Her hands trembled as she looked at the picture of Max with his arm around a beautiful, young blonde, whose huge breasts were falling out of a dress cut to her navel. Rapidly scanning the article, Kathie learned that a notorious Page Three model had sold her 'kiss and tell' story to the paper, and there was promise of more to come the following day. Even more humiliating was a picture of Kathie and Max further down the page.

Kathie burst into tears. She was mortified. In just a few minutes she had gone from elated excitement to heartbreak. She stared, transfixed at the page, hardly able to believe her eyes. But there it was, in black and white. She would never have believed Max was capable of such treachery, had the hard evidence not been staring her in the face, for all the world to see.

Margaret leaped up and put her arms around the sobbing Kathie. 'I'm so sorry my darling. I'm so sorry. I can't believe he's done this to you. I don't know what to say.'

'Why, mum? Why would he do this? He loves me. We love each other. He wants to marry me!' She took a tissue from her bag, wiped her eyes and blew her nose. Taking a deep breath to calm herself, she said, 'There must be some mistake. That's it. Perhaps it was a publicity photo and that little trollop has made it all up to make a lot of money. They do that you know.'

'Maybe. I don't know, love. You'll have to speak to Max won't you.'

The phone rang, making them both jump.

'Oh God, if that's him, what do I say?' Kathie, numbed with shock, couldn't think straight. Her mind had gone blank, her mouth was dry and she felt slightly dizzy. 'You answer it, mum.'

Margaret picked up the phone. 'It's Mel,' she said, handing it over to Kathie.

'Kathie, I'm so sorry. It's shocking. Are you alright, love?'

'I can't speak now Mel, I'm still trying to take it all in. I'll call you later.' Kathie was still shaking as she put down the phone.

'The disgusting, rotten bastard!', she screamed, hurling the newspaper across the room. 'I'll never forgive him for this, never! Not in a million years! I hate him .... he's ruined my life!' She held her hand to her mouth and shot a look at her mother, hoping Margaret hadn't realised what she meant by the last few words. But Margaret already knew. And Kathie's outburst was enough to dispel any doubt.

Kathie ran out of the kitchen and upstairs to her room, where she threw herself down on her bed, her whole body convulsing as she wept.

Earlier in the day, several players had gathered around Max to take a look at the newspaper, which

Laurence Morrissey, the sub goalkeeper, had brought into the changing room. Max was reeling with shock as he read the headlines heralding the girl's account of their steamy night together.

The graphic photo of him and the girl was bad enough, but further on there was a small picture of him, coming out of a restaurant with Kathie, with the caption, 'Max and his glamorous girlfriend, Kathie Neilson, before the break up.'

'What break up?', he shouted angrily. 'Where do they get this shit from? We haven't broken up. She won't even know about this until she gets home from work. It's total bollocks.'

'You'll be lucky if you have any left when she finds out!', he heard someone shout, followed by hoots of laughter.

Most of his fellow players, however, commiserated with the woeful Max, knowing full well it was a case of 'there but for the grace of God'. A few thought it was hugely amusing and were coming out with all the usual chauvinistic comments.

'You lucky little git.'

'Look at the lamps on that!'

'Wouldn't mind a go at it myself!'

'Jees, Max, don't you get enough with that horny little bird you're going out with?' .... etc. etc.

The jibes and laughter went on and on.

Anton Peguy was genuinely sad and sorry for his young friend. He did his best to console Max, who was by now frantic with worry.

'What on earth is Kathie gonna do when she sees this lot?', he groaned. 'Christ, and my parents! They'll go apeshit! And my fans! They think I'm squeaky clean!'

'Just keep your head down,' Anton advised. It'll all blow over. Tomorrow will be some other poor devil's turn. Everyone knows what the gutter press is like! What is it you English say? Tomorrow it will be at the foot of a bird cage.' This caused an outburst of laughter. Even Max had to smile.

His coach was not amused. He was visibly devastated and angry beyond words. 'Oh for God's sake! What a fucking disaster!', he spluttered. 'You'll be the death of me, Rawlings! George is gonna love this!'

He threw down the paper and stormed out.

Over the next few days, both Max and Kathie had to contend with the paparazzi camping outside her house, Max's parents' house, Rangers FC grounds, even Bowens, her workplace, causing Kathie especially yet more hurt and humiliation. She dreaded going to work, but her colleagues were kind and sympathetic.

Josie gave Kathie a big hug. 'You'll get over it, poppet. Better now than later eh? You are so young, and very beautiful. That man must be out of his mind. He doesn't deserve you!'

The reporters who had found their way to Bowens, got short shrift from every member of staff, although the Managing Director was secretly quite pleased about the publicity coming his company's way.

Kathie stubbornly refused to answer any of Max's calls or texts, other than one, which advised him that if he ever tried to go near her again, she would call the police. He turned up at her house at the first opportunity, but could not get past Margaret at the door. She couldn't help feeling sorry for the devastated young man, who was pleading with her to let him at least talk to Kathie. 'Just leave her alone, Max, take my advice. Maybe she'll come round.,' she advised.

Max couldn't believe that Kathie wouldn't even give him a chance to explain, and he too became very angry and increasingly frustrated. Somehow he managed to turn the whole thing round in his mind so that he wasn't the only one to blame for their break up, as 'she was being totally unreasonable!'. It softened the blow, but he was heartbroken that he'd lost his lovely Kathie. I'll get her back if it's the last thing I do!', he resolved.

In the following months after the break up, Max tried desperately to dispel the hurt and anger boiling inside him by focusing on his game. He stepped up his team practice and gym training with gusto, determined to improve his already near perfect performance on the pitch. He became stronger, fitter and even more skillful.

Already the undisputed darling of the press and his millions of fans, Max Rawlings was becoming more famous, more revered, more iconic, by the day.

Kathie also threw herself into her work over the coming year, in a concerted effort to put the painful breakup behind her and move on with her life. She still loved Max with all her heart, there was no denying. She ached for him every day and cried endless tears.

The agony without the ecstasy.

CHAPTER TWELVE

Chance encounter

Bowens Designs was abuzz with preparations for their stand at the forthcoming Ideal Home Exhibition. Kathie was thrilled and honoured to have been given the task of producing a full size version of the miniature patchwork that Josie Green had so admired. The theme for Bowen's stand this year was 'Rustic Splendour'. Plans were well in place for a scaled down version of Madeline Colbert's master bedroom to be replicated, which had recently been completed. Madeline had willingly endorsed the project and agreed to visit Earls Court one day to sign autographs.

With a week to go before the exhibition, a final meeting took place at Bowens. To gasps of admiration, Kathie proudly produced the finished article which she had been working on for months. It was a breathtakingly beautiful, hand sewn, patchwork quilt, based on the original 'Grandma's Garden' design. Each flower was made up of twelve outer and six inner hexagonal shapes, in soft hues of pink and mauve silk, with the centre shape in yellow, representing the sun. On some of the flower centres, Kathie had ingeniously printed a photograph of varying aged men, women and children and pets, representing all the members of one family. An intricate English garden scene, with ornate shrubs, spring flowers and several types of birds, surrounded the flowers. The sides of the quilt were edged with perfectly fashioned oak leaves and in one corner were the embroidered words, 'Family Tree', with the initials KN, 2014.   It was truly exquisite. Kathie was overcome with pride and emotion as everyone applauded.   Even more so when it was unanimously agreed that this should take pride of place on their forthcoming stand.

Bowens' stand was the talk of the exhibition and enjoyed enormous success. As promised, Madeleine Colbert attended on the second day, drawing even more crowds. Reporters and press photographers were in abundance, anxious to get that special image, featuring the famous celebrity standing next to the beautiful young designer, for the morning papers. Josie and Kathie were kept busy round the clock, discussing the quilt with enthralled customers. Over the three days, they took in excess of a hundred orders for custom made versions. Kathie was horrified at first, fearing that she would be spending the rest of her life making them, but Josie, clearly amused, assured her that the commercial versions would have to be adapted to be made by machine and finished off by hand by the other girls.

As a big thank you to every member of staff, and to celebrate their huge success, Bowens' MD, Rupert Levick, known affectionately as 'Bear', announced that he had booked a table for the following evening at the newly opened Italian restaurant, 'Benji's, in Soho. Benji was currently appearing in his own TV programme, which meant his restaurant was receiving wide publicity and acclaim.

Everyone was enjoying the evening immensely. Wine was flowing, the food was delicious, and all twenty members of staff, from MD to junior clerk, were in high spirits. They had finished the main course and were noisily deliberating on which of the wickedly calorific desserts they would choose, when Josie looked up, nudged Kathie, and whispered, 'isn't that your ex over there?'

Kathie turned to see Max walking to a table with two of his fellow players, Stefano and Philippe, accompanied by three glamorous young women.

'She turned back quickly, before he could spot her.' 'Yes that's him,' she said, feeling familiar knots in her stomach. 'Don't look at him, please.'

Too late! All the girls were now gawking across at Max. He was looking resplendent and very fetching in his Armani suit. Sporting a new, shorter hair style, and the hint of a designer stubble, he was as ridiculously handsome as ever.

Comments from the females were making Kathie cringe:

'God, he's even more gorgeous than on the telly.'

'Isn't he just! Wouldn't throw him out on a dark night!'

'Cor! Even better looking than David Beckham.'

'Talk about sexy. I love his new hair style, don't you?'

Kathy was upset, and the comments from her female colleagues were making her feel even worse. Just looking at him again gave her butterflies. 'Well, looks can be deceptive,' she commented icily. 'Have we all made up our minds yet?' She waved the menu, as a clear signal that she didn't want to hear another word about the wonderful Max.

Josie could see how uncomfortable Kathie was and added, 'Yes, come on you lot. We're here to celebrate our success, not drawl over some cheating footballer type!' She winked at Kathie.

They were all enjoying their coffees and liqueurs, when Kathie felt a light tap on her shoulder. She turned and looked up into the smiling face of Max.

'Hi, Kathie. I thought that was you. I'd know that mop top anywhere!'

'Oh, hello, Max.' Kathie managed a weak smile and tried to sound surprised.

Max looked around the table. 'Good evening everyone. Are you celebrating something? We could hear you from over there.' He nodded towards his table.

Rupert replied politely. 'Good evening Mr. Rawlings. Sorry, I guess we have been a bit noisy, but we do indeed have something to celebrate. We had an excellent result at the Ideal Home Exhibition, thanks largely to young Kathie here.'

'Oh yes, and what has she been up to?' Max was looking at Kathie, who stared down at the table, picked up her glass and took a sip of wine.

Josie explained. 'She produced an exquisite piece of work, and we took an awful lot of orders as a result.'

Max looked back at Kathie. 'Oh, yes, I saw the pictures of you with that actress.'

Kathie just acknowledged his remark with something resembling a smile.

Rupert stood up and handed Max his business card. 'This is us. Interior designers. If ever you need our services, we will be extremely happy to oblige. Well, I imagine you can afford us now!', he joked. Everyone roared with laughter and cheered, holding up their glasses. All except Kathie, who wanted the ground to open up and was thinking it was reminiscent of the bloody Casablanca movie ... *Of all the bars in all the world*!

Max shook Rupert's hand and said, 'Thank you, I'll bear it in mind. Congratulations everyone; enjoy the rest of the evening. Well done Kathie, lovely to see you again.'

Kathie turned and said quietly, 'yes, you too.'

As he walked away, there was a buzz of chatter from everyone. Having met Max was exciting, but the prospect of getting a contract with him was a real bonus.

For Kathie, the evening had been marred. The same old yearning and ache in the pit of her stomach came back with a reminiscent pang, and she realised how desperately she still loved and yearned for Max.

Following the exhibition, everyone at Bowens was working full out, as orders flooded in from all over the UK and even from Europe. Kathie was grateful for the diversion. Seeing Max again had been a heart wrenching shock and she now felt as churned up as the day they parted.

At the end of a hard week, Kathie was looking forward to a weekend's relaxation. She and Josie had been planning the furnishing for an apartment in The City of London's Barbican complex. A wealthy banker had just bought the apartment as a pied-a-terre and had given them the assignment to furnish out the whole six rooms, as long as there was no pink, anywhere!

A smiling Rupert walked into their office at 6.30 pm. 'Just before you go, ladies, I have some very good news to impart. None other than Mr. Max Rawlings has been on the telephone and he would like us to undertake the assignment of entirely refurbishing his new house in Leeds! House, I say - it's a magnificent mansion. Huge!'

Josie gasped. Kathie went pale as she looked at Josie in despair.

'Well - aren't you going to say something?' Rupert was clearly disappointed that the two women hadn't responded as he'd expected, which prompted Josie to say quickly, 'well, that's absolutely fabulous, isn't it Kathie? We were just a bit taken aback, Bear. Great news!'

'Well, it's late now, you two get on home. It's been a hectic week. We'll discuss it on Monday. Well done girls. Good night, have a pleasant weekend.' As Rupert turned to leave the room, he added, 'Oh, yes, and he particularly asked for you, Kathie. See you on Monday, bright and early.'

'Well, that's not going to happen!', Kathie said crossly, when Rupert was out of earshot.

'Are you kidding?' We can't turn down a job like that, - it'll be worth thousands!', Josie barked.

'About me doing it, I mean! You know how it is, Josie. Besides, I'm not qualified to take on a project like that yet. I haven't done anything on my own.'

'Well, there's always a first time, girl! And cut the bullshit. You can do it with your eyes closed. I can't teach you anything you don't already know. You've either got it or you haven't in this business, and I know damned well, you've got what it takes.'

Josie could see Kathie was upset, so she said kindly, 'look love, don't worry about it - I'm always here to help and advise you, of course. No probs! We'll talk about it on Monday. Go home and have a good rest.'

Kathie spent a fractious weekend, wondering what was in store for her. Part of her wanted to see Max again if she was honest, but nonetheless, it was a daunting prospect. Why had he asked for her? Did he want to try to win her back, or was he just punishing her - getting his own back for dumping him? She had, after all, refused to even give him a chance to explain. She had gone over and over the whole episode in her mind and often regretted being so stubborn and unforgiving, but it got more and more impossible for her to give in as time went on.

There was no escaping it. Kathie was assigned to spearheading the Rawlings contract, no arguments. It promised great publicity for the firm as well as the financial rewards. An email from Max, forwarded from Rupert, hit Kathie's screen as soon as she booted up her laptop on Monday morning. Max had confirmed that he would like Bowens to undertake the project, and gave a few dates when he would be available for the first meeting at his new property. Kathie stared at the screen and gave a big sigh. Josie looked up. 'What's up Doc?'

'Confirmation from Max. Just what I needed to cheer me up on a Monday morning!'

'Just put personal feelings aside, young lady, and think of the commission! Get your finger out and arrange a date!'

Josie turned back to her computer with a little smile. She guessed there was more to Max's request for Kathie than meets the eye.

CHAPTER THIRTEEN

Reunion

Outside the railway station, Kathie hailed a taxi and told the cab driver the address. He looked at her, clearly very impressed. 'Going to see Max Rawlings are you? I've driven by his new place a few times - it looks fantastic. Must have cost a fortune!'

Kathie just smiled and nodded as the cabbie continued to chat. 'I'm not a Rangers fan myself, but you can't help admiring Rawlings. Best player we've had since Beckham, in my opinion!'

'God!', she thought. 'I wish people would stop their inane comparisons to ruddy David Beckham. He's nothing like him!'

The taxi drew up outside huge, black, wrought iron gates.

'Do you want me to take you down the drive?', the cabbie asked, hopefully.

'No thanks - I could do with a walk,' Kathie replied, eyeing the long driveway leading to the house. She paid the driver and turned to the gates. Below the house name 'Rangers Lodge', was the entry system. She pressed the one marked 'visitors' and moments later, one small gate at the side swung open and, with her heart now thumping, she made her way to the house. Before she could ring the doorbell, the huge door opened, and there stood Max, smiling widely.

'Hey, Kathie. Right on time! Well done, come in - it's good to see you!'

Kathie looked at him, stone-faced, as she stepped inside, into an ornate, spacious vestibule.

'Hello Max. Sorry, but what's all this about, eh? What do you think you're doing?', she asked, unable to contain herself a moment longer.

'That's charming! What do you mean? I thought I was doing you a big favour - you and your firm. It'll be a feather in your cap!'

'You arrogant sod! You might be Mr. Big and Mighty to all your sycophantic fans and airhead girls, but it's me you're talking to. I'm only doing this because I'm forced to, thanks to you!'

'Well, I can ring and cancel, if that's how you feel.' Max was peeved. 'And you can leave the fans out of it. In the main they're just decent people who love football - and they are very loyal!'

Kathie looked down and he could see she was biting her lip, on the verge of tears. 'More than I can say for you!'

'Look, Kathie. I'm sorry, I am, really. I guess I did get you here on false pretences. Well not really false, I do need the place professionally kitted out. I've been on-

172

line, and your lot look really good. Come and have a cup of coffee, please, and we can talk, properly.'

Kathie quickly wiped away a tear threatening to trickle down her cheek. 'Sorry, really unprofessional of me,' she said. She thought of Josie and took a deep breath to compose herself. 'Lead the way'.

Sitting in the enormous kitchen, Kathie was looking round, already visualising how it could be transformed. It was an old house and clearly hadn't been modernised for years. She sipped her coffee, then took out from her briefcase a laptop, camera and a few magazines.

She opened a copy of 'The World of Interiors' at a double page spread, illustrating a beautiful Clive Christian kitchen. 'Something like this would be gorgeous!', she ventured, pushing the magazine towards Max.

'Max looked at the picture and opened his eyes wide. 'Wow! That's really ace! And it's got an Aga like mine. I like what they've done with that, that ornate surround. And I like that central bit ....'

'The island. Yes, I love the oak finish on it. Well, it's only a suggestion. I'll give you a few alternatives before you make up your mind. This room is huge enough for a large rustic table and chairs.'

'I'm impressed, Kathie. You're good!'

She looked pleased with herself.

Max sensed he might be making headway.

'Before we get down to business,' he said, 'can we please clear the air.'

Kathie nodded. 'I suppose so.'

'This is bloody difficult. Look, first of all, I've said it a thousand times before, on voicemail, by text and email, but you've never answered any of them. You can't deny that, Kathie. You've never given me even a chance to explain, or apologise. I'm really so sorry Kathie, so sorry. Please say you'll forgive me.'

'It's water under the bridge now, I've moved on,' Kathie lied. 'There was nothing to say, was there? I gave myself to you, against everything I'd been brought up to do. You knew what a huge thing that was for me! But I truly thought that we would be together, forever, which made it okay in my tiny mind. Then I find out, from a filthy newspaper article, that you have slept with some horrible little slapper! I just wanted to die of shame. So humiliating! It was like everyone in the world knew what a pathetic idiot I was.' Kathie felt all the bitterness and hurt that she had tried so hard to put behind her, welling up inside her again.

'Kathie, it was a big mistake, God, don't I know it, but it happened ages before you and I got really serious. It didn't mean anything, honestly. I wish I could turn back the clock, but I can't, and I can't pretend it didn't happen, because it did. I've regretted it every single minute of every day. I've prayed that you will forgive me ever since. I've never stopped loving you, Kathie - never will! When I saw you that night at Benji's, it reminded me how much. It really hurt, like a knife going through me. I couldn't sleep that night.'

Max looked so sad, so sorrowful, that Kathie felt her heart beginning to melt. Her emotions were in turmoil. She just wanted to throw her arms around him and say that everything would be alright, that they could start again. Instead, she just shook her head.

They drank their coffee in silence for a moment or two, then Kathie took a deep breath and said softly, 'I know. It was such a shock seeing you there. It made me feel quite sick really. Especially seeing you with another woman.'

Max laughed. 'That wasn't another woman, sweetheart. That was Stefano's young sister, over from Italy. I was just there to make up the numbers. You can ring him and ask him if you don't believe me,' he added, earnestly.

Kathie felt relieved, but why? What was happening here? She allowed herself a little smile. 'I believe you. Oh well, that's out of the way. Shall we get down to business?'

'You still haven't said you've forgiven me.'

'Max, you broke my heart, you ruined me. What do you expect?'

'I expect you to be honest with me - and yourself. I'm sure you still love me, I can tell, no matter how much you try and hide it. Don't let your pride spoil our chance of happiness, Kathie. We belong to each other.'

Kathie could hold back no longer and began to cry.

Max leaped to his feet and pulled her up, enclosing her in his arms, as he began to sob too. 'I love you so much, Kathie.'

'I love you too, Max. I never stopped, not for a minute!'

Max kissed her, looked at her tear stained face, then kissed her again. It was an unspoken moment, when each knew they were destined to be together and the endless pain of heartache was over at last.

'I must look a fright!' Kathie sniffed and wiped her eyes.

'You look as beautiful as ever my darling! I'll show you the bathroom - er - one of the bathrooms, and you can freshen up. Kathie, I can't tell you what this means to me. You've made me the happiest man in the world - even more than when I turned pro with Rangers!!'

Kathie playfully punched his arm.

'You won't change your mind, will you?' Max looked anxious.

'No, I won't. Course not. But I will **never** forgive you, if you ever do anything else like that again, I promise you that!' she replied sternly.

Max led her upstairs and showed her into the master bedroom. 'You can use the en suite,' he said, pointing the way.

When Kathie came out, Max was perched at the foot of a huge four poster bed. 'What do you think of this then? Isn't it the dogs goolies! I thought I'd wait until the decor was decided, so that the curtain thingies on the bed will match,' he said proudly.

'I'm impressed! That's exactly right - not sure they're called curtain thingies though! We prefer drapes, or hangings.'

'Come and see what you think. It's really comfortable,' he said, patting the mattress, with a devilish grin on his face.

Kathie giggled. 'Déjà Vu or what!!'

She walked over and sat down, bouncing slightly beside him.

'It's lovely, Max. Good choice.'

'Just like you!' He turned and folded his arms around her. 'I love you so much. I can't believe you are actually here!

'I know. It's weird.'

'Weird and wonderful!'

The soft, sensual embrace became a passionate kiss, as the familiar, all consuming, desire engulfed them both. Neither spoke as Max held her tight for a while, and then he pulled away slightly to look at her.

'I want you so much, Kathie. You know that don't you! I always will.' Max's voice was low, breathless, as he pushed her gently back onto the bed and kissed her.

She didn't resist. She returned his kiss, passionately, pulling him closer, holding him tight, never wanting to let him go. Her longing for Max, painfully stifled for far too long, was now hopelessly rekindled, as he quickly undid her blouse and kissed her neck, then down, down to her breasts, his hands searching out every inch of that lovely body he'd missed and dreamed about so much.

He deftly unzipped her skirt and pulled it off, then holding her towards him he reached round and undid the fastening of her bra. He kissed each breast and then gently took each erect nipple into his mouth, until she gasped with pleasure.

The exquisite tingle of desire that she'd first experienced with Max, the thrill that only he could ever give her, could satisfy her, enveloped her now, as she ran her hands under his shirt, across his broad shoulders and arched her body to meet his. 'I've dreamed about this, so many times!', she whispered. 'You know, that awful aching - yearning. I've thought about you every day. It was agony!'

Max tore off his clothes and kneeled astride her, unashamedly rampant, as he removed her last little wisp of lacey garment and entered her gently. 'And this is the ecstasy!', he whispered, as their two bodies moved together, sating an urgent sexual and emotional need which coursed through each body and soul until they reached the pinnacle of their overwhelming love and physical desire for each other.

They lay together in silence for a few minutes afterwards, just holding each other in a loving embrace.

'I'm so happy, Kathie, darling!', Max said at last, kissing her forehead. 'Thank you for coming back to me. I hoped and prayed you would.'

Kathie's had laid her head on Max's chest, as she gently stroked his chest. She looked up into his eyes. 'You know, somewhere, deep in my heart, I always knew we'd be back together one day. I hoped so anyway, if I'm honest. There hasn't been anyone else Max.'

'Thank God! I'll never let you go again.'

Kathie looked at her watch and said, reluctantly, I think I'd better see the rest of the house!

'I guess so! But I'd rather stay here!'

They spent the rest of the day going from room to room. Kathie was making notes on her laptop and taking numerous photos. She was excited by the project now and couldn't wait to get started. She stood in the centre of the vast dining room. 'I know just what would go perfectly in here. A Christian Laigre dark Wenge-Wood table with a dozen matching chairs.'

'I'll take your word for it.'

'I've got a picture of it somewhere in my office - I can email it to you.'

'Can't wait!'

'Do you realise what this floor is?', she asked Max, as they perched on a sill of a bay window in one of the huge reception rooms.'

'Yes, wooden!'

Kathie laughed and bit into a sandwich. Max had thoughtfully bought a selection on his way to the house. 'Max, it's what's called wide oak planking, Louis XIII style. Must have cost a fortune.'

'Blimey! Who'd have thought it!', Max was still teasing.

'At least that's one excellent feature of this house we won't have to alter. But that awful fireplace needs replacing, without a doubt. I visualise something like a Regency period type. I'll have to think about that.'

'Sounds great. Well, I'm happy to leave it to you, darling. I'm sure it will be absolutely fabulous when you've finished. I just have to make sure I can afford it.'

'Are you kidding? You're forgetting I know what you top players earn - much more in one week than most people pay for a house! It's obscene really!'

'Well, I'm not complaining!'

They both laughed.

'Why would you? Neither am I.'

Kathie looked at her watch. 'I'd better be off. My train leaves at 5.40. I'll make a start on your project when I get home. I have some ideas already. It's a beautiful house, Max. So much character. I love it.'

'That's just as well, seeing you will be living here soon!', Max replied, with a huge grin.

'Whoa! Hold your horses. We've had this conversation before.'

'I know, but I can hope! Anyway, I won't push my luck. I'll run you to the station. I would offer to drive you back to London, but I've got training early tomorrow.

'No, that's fine, honestly. I wouldn't dream of it. I can look at my notes on the journey home, that's if I don't fall asleep. It's been quite a day. I was up at six this morning.'

'I can understand that. You couldn't wait to see me.'

'Actually Max, I was really nervous. Can you believe it?'

'So was I. Terrified!' He lifted her off the window sill and held her tight, kissing the top of her head. 'Just remember how much I love you.'

'I will! And I love you too, always did, always will!'

At the station, they kissed goodbye, a long, lingering kiss. With one last hug, Kathie jumped aboard the train. Max was still standing on the platform, smiling and waving, as the train disappeared from view.

The following months were hectic for Kathie. She and Josie worked long hours, designing decor, deciding on furniture, soft furnishings, floor covering, etc. for Max's house. There were meetings with suppliers, English and French, professional decorators in the Leeds area, and of course, Max was kept in the loop. Once he had approved all the designs, work began on ordering and installing every item. The finished result was breathtaking. Kathie had been at the helm, with Josie's valuable input. Max was delighted.

'I'm really proud of you, Irish!', he beamed, 'it's absolutely brilliant. We must celebrate soon. At your favourite restaurant, when I'm next in London.'

Kathie frowned. He hadn't called her that since when they first met. But nothing was going to take away the thrill of having undertaken such a huge, successful, assignment. 'Famous People's Houses' magazine had featured the newly furbished 'Rangers Lodge' with photographs of Max and Kathie. The young designer was the toast of Bowens once again.

'Kathie, you're so talented', Max said over dinner in London, a month after he moved into Rangers Lodge. 'You're wasted working for someone else. Haven't you thought of branching out on your own - start your own business, I mean? You can work from home - our home!' He smiled and raised his eyebrows as he looked hopefully at the girl he so desperately wanted to marry.

'Yes, it has crossed my mind, of course, but not yet. For one thing, I haven't got the capital behind me, and I can't throw in my job, just like that,' Kathie replied.

'Rubbish! You could if we got married.'

'Is this your cack-handed attempt at a proposal?' she giggled.

'Just testing the water.'

'How very romantic!'

'Just didn't want to spend a few grand on a ring, if you're going to turn me down!'

'Well, you'd better give it a try then!' Kathie was secretly thrilled.

'I love you so much, Irish! I can't wait to make an honest WAG out of you!', he teased.

'Don't call me that!'

'What, Irish or WAG?'

'Both - either, I mean!'

He reached across the table and squeezed her hand. 'You're my gorgeous girl, whatever you're called. I adore you.'

Two weeks later, moments after the whistle blew for half time at a home game, Max went down on one knee at the edge of the pitch. In full view of thousands of fans in the stadium and on television, he proposed to Kathie, who was seated in the VIP box. He had primed the rest of the team, so that every player stood in a semi circle around him. He cupped his hands around his mouth and shouted out, **'Kathie, will you marry me**?' Thousands of heads turned to see the beautiful redhead, her hand to her mouth in shock. Then the stadium erupted and fans were cheering at the tops of their voices and chanting, 'say yes, say yes,' until Kathie called back, **'Yes, I will**!', blushing to the roots of her hair. Overnight, she became almost as famous as Max, which she had to learn to contend with very quickly.

Leaving the football ground, the couple were confronted with a dozen members of the press. Flashlights were going off everywhere and reporters were shouting questions at them. It was the same thing for the next week. Pictures of the couple were featured in all the tabloids, together or apart. Once more, Bowens was in the spotlight, as Kathie was photographed arriving and leaving the premises.

The famous footballer and glamorous young designer were married the following year, in the full glare of global publicity which only the 'glitterati' could attract.

On a delightfully warm and sunny June day, the beautiful bride, wearing an exquisite, designer wedding gown, entered an enormous, lavishly decorated marquee in the grounds of 'Rangers Lodge'. By her side was a proud and beaming Margaret. Kathie had asked her mother to give her away and Margaret was thrilled and delighted. She had taken Kathie's hands and with a tear in her eye, replied, 'nothing would give me greater pleasure. I know your father would be pleased. In fact, he'd be thrilled skinny!'

Kathie hugged Margaret and kissed her cheek in a shared emotional moment of sadness and joy.

'Thanks, mum, there's no-one else in the world I'd rather have give me away'

Max, standing alongside his best man, Chris, had a lump in his throat as he turned to see the vision of loveliness, his beautiful Kathie, walk towards him, smiling radiantly. As she stopped at his side, he leaned towards her and whispered, 'you look so beautiful, I could cry. I love you.'

Kathie looked into his eyes and nodded, unable to speak. She too was overcome by emotion as they entered this ceremonious union together. Their marriage was to become one of the most cherished and publicised newsworthy stories in the following years, as they became the nation's favourite golden celebrity couple.

Kathie, at long last, was mistress of the famous house in Leeds, having reluctantly resigned from Bowens. Rupert and Josie were devastated that they were losing their star, but Kathie had decided that, after the honeymoon, she would embark on starting her own business. Besides, the thought of commuting to London from Leeds every day was not one she relished.

When their daughter was born two years later, the publicity was worldwide. A radiant Kathie, holding her little bundle wrapped in a white shawl, crocheted by an aunt in Ireland, made front page news as she emerged from hospital. Max, his arm proudly around Kathie, was smiling from ear to ear and answering the various questions being directed to him from the dozens of photographers and reporters. Later that day it was featured on every television news programme.

George Wallis was one of the few people unimpressed by the scenes as he watched the late night news. 'Anyone would thinks they're bleeding royalty!' he moaned to Susan.

'I think it's lovely. Shut up you miserable old sod!' she scolded.

The success of Kathie's new venture, 'Interior Motives', was an overwhelming success. Her fame, her beauty and her talent ensured that she was sought after from discerning, affluent clients, from day one.

Their new life together as part of the world of the mega rich, world-famous glitterati was sealed.

CHAPTER FOURTEEN

Confrontation

George swung round in his chair and stared out of his office window with a pained expression on his face. He gazed over the Rangers' pitch, just beginning to fade from view as darkness fell. He always felt how strangely spooky and desolate the pitch looked in the gloom after the fans had gone and the floodlights were turned off. Unusually for George, there was a glass of brandy in his hand. He was not a drinking man these days, but the warmth of the spirit sliding down his throat brought him a modicum of comfort. He was a worried man. He felt old and tired, with the troubles of the world on his shoulders. He sighed as he reflected on the diabolical turn of events over the past year; proving yet again how one's fortunes could change dramatically in a very short space of time.

The morning had begun with a meeting of Rangers' Board of Directors at which even the club's Greek owner, Costas Papapavlou, was present. This in itself was unusual.

George had been made to feel like the sacrificial lamb. There was a distinct air of discontent in the room. The Board members were not happy; indeed some were hinting that his very job hung in the balance.

Sunday's game against a second division club in the quarter finals of the FA cup had been a humiliating disaster. To a gambling man it was a certainty that Rangers would win, with odds at two-to-one on. No-one with a lick of sense would put money on a club like Newington Town FC beating Rangers. But beat them they did. Rangers was caught napping by a determined and hungry young team, with nothing to lose. The Premier team were outplayed and outclassed and, to add insult to injury, four of their players collected yellow cards. Max pulled off a stunning goal from a free kick and nearly saved the day, but Newington's one and only talented striker scored the winning goal in the last five minutes.

George had watched the game unfold in dismal disbelief, getting angrier and angrier at every decision by the referee that didn't go Rangers' way. He blamed himself for not taking steps to ensure his team won. He certainly had the wherewithal to do that! There was a small fortune riding on Rangers to win, and now he would have to face the backlash of his shady associate punters. But for Christ's sake, who would have dreamed that they, the near infallible Rangers, would not run rings round a poxy little provincial club! 'It comes to something when your own fucking fans boo you off the field!', he had shouted at his shell-shocked players afterwards in the dressing room.

'Give me bleedin' strength!', he grunted as he took another swig of his brandy, still seething at the onslaught he'd received from the Board that day. What was so outrageous, constantly causing George's blood pressure to reach new heights, was that, in his mind, 'they were to a man a bunch of ignorant prats, who knew sod all about the game.' They might well have their fingers on the pulse of high finance, three of them being senior executives in the hierarchy of the banking world, and two so-called captains of industry, but they never got involved in the day to day, nitty gritty of the business that is modern day football. To these fat cats it was just business, pure and simple; a commodity; a matter of profit, which only came as a result of success, affording them all massive payouts.

Bar one, that was. George's immediate boss, Bob Trevelyan, Rangers' Chief Executive, was the only man amongst them whose knowledge and understanding of the game was as great as George's. Probably even greater, George reflected. Bob had been at George's side for over ten years and his loyalty was unflinching. He had done his utmost to back George up at the meeting, but his efforts fell on stony ground. Costas was very animated and vocal. Under normal circumstances, that is to say, over the last few years when the club never seemed to put a foot wrong, Costas certainly did not deem it necessary, nor remotely important enough, to bother himself by getting physically involved with the day to day running of the club. As a junior director of his family's shipping company, Costas was already a multi millionaire when he decided to buy an English Premier League football club. His investment in Rangers was considered a fortune to followers of football, yet it was a mere spit in the ocean to a man of his immense wealth.

Affluent men such as Costas, members of vastly prosperous families, enjoy enviable trappings of untold wealth to the full. Their luxurious, hedonistic lifestyles are far beyond the imagination of ordinary folk. Such a surreal way of life was the norm for Costas and his exorbitantly privileged peers throughout the world. Yet, enormous wealth is often not enough for certain of these self-indulged individuals. They are forever searching for even more; craving stimulation and excitement beyond their world of commerce, glamour and excess.

Global notoriety was an added bonus to ego maniac Costas. Sport, especially football, was the attraction for this man. The monetary gain from owning Rangers was undoubtedly immense, but of no exceptional consequence to Costas. He was content to wallow in the social rewards that came with owning a successful, world-renowned Premier football club. The fame, kudos, publicity and glory, which Rangers afforded him, was greedily relished by the hardnosed Greek mogul. Being in the public glare, however, in the face of the club's recent and most unprecedented demise, that was quite another matter and could not, would not, be tolerated by him. He had gone against his father's wishes when he bought the club in the first place, and the prospect of having to confront the family and admit that his ill advised investment might be in danger was a situation to be avoided at all costs.

Costas faced George across the board table, the gold and diamond rings on his fingers glinting as he put his fat hands together in a steeple against his double chin. He was seething, but managed to address George in a cold, calculated manner, with a false little smile on his lips. 'Georgiou,' he began, which was what he always called him, to George's infuriation, 'this situation is not in the slightest way acceptable. My family have built an excellent reputation over many years, and I will not be humiliated in this way. I even have your English journalist scum outside my house in Kensington whenever I am over here. Every morning, every evening, always they are there!'

George wanted to hit him. 'It's not fucking personal Costas!', he barked. 'Do you think any one of us sitting round this table enjoy what's going on? This is not the first, and it won't be the last club to have a bad season. It's the name of the game. It happens. Get over it!' He glared back angrily at Costas. 'It's not like it's going to bankrupt you, for Christ's sake!'

Costas looked at him in disgust. His fury was evident. He opened his mouth to respond, but before he could speak, George carried on.

'Okay, you've all had your say, and yes, the buck stops with me. I appreciate that. But let's examine the facts shall we gentlemen? You have bloody short memories if you don't recall that we lost two of our top players, Marino and Courtney, last year. It was no-one's fault. You can't buy loyalty, and if a player wants out when his contract ends, what can we do to stop him? We can't afford to pay all our players three hundred grand a week like Real Madrid, or Munich, and so they vote with their feet. Who can blame them? Not only that, you have to understand that we're talking people here - you know, human beings, not just profit and loss!', he sneered sarcastically. 'The young footballers of today like to maximize their talent and push themselves forward. They want fame as well as fortune. Everyone wants to be a Ronaldo or a Messi and be worshipped as a bloody hero, like they are in Europe. They're treated like film stars over there! And if you also recall, I strongly advised buying young Sagnita from Preston when we had the opportunity.

He was well up for it too! I could see his potential, but, as usual, I was outvoted. Now look at him! He's scored more goals for City than any other player. Bob was the only one who backed me up.'

Bob Trevelyan nodded.

George was on a roll now. He stood up and put his hands on the table, becoming more agitated by the minute. 'I didn't agree with the signings to replace Marino and Courtney either, and you must agree I was right. Bloody useless the pair of them! Another thing, why the hell do we need millions in the bank, you tell me that! We need to invest in more top players. Never mind lining your own pockets - more to the point!'

George had overstepped the mark this time, he knew it. But 'fuck the lot of them', he thought. He was right and they knew it.

Bob Trevelyan spoke up quickly, aware of the exasperated reaction of the Board members, and Costas becoming red faced with rage.

'George, we appreciate you are doing your level best and have done a great job over the years. Gentlemen, can we calm down and proceed with the business in hand. This is getting us nowhere.'

There was a general buzz of murmurings, and a few members left to go to the Gents, which caused a welcome natural break in the tense atmosphere in the room.

The meeting continued on for another two hours. Discussions turned to the negotiations with the kit sponsor, Sportsattire, who had made noises to the effect that renewal of their five year contract at the end of next season was coming under review and it could not be taken for granted that they would renew it, given Rangers' recent form. Rangers had enjoyed four years of their exclusive sponsorship, amounting to a hundred million pounds, and to lose that would be a massive blow.

George was pretty certain he had convinced the Board that Sportsattire could be relied on for another term, though in truth he was bluffing. This high profile sports manufacturing company wanted to be seen as the sponsors of winners, not losers.

At last the meeting was drawing to a close. George was left in no uncertain doubt, through carefully crafted euphemisms, that his job as manager could be in jeopardy.

Rangers had got off to a dismal start at the beginning of the season. Their position in the Premier League had now plummeted to tenth, an all time low in the long history of the club. It was imperative that they somehow turn things around to achieve a place in the top four over the next few months, before the end of the season in April. This would give them at least a fighting chance to qualify for the UEFA Champions

League in Europe. In financial terms, this would mean millions of pounds to the club and certainly guarantee their chances of lucrative sponsorship and television deals, and more importantly to George, the chance to buy some quality players.

To compound this sorry state of affairs, Rangers had drawn Stampford away in the next round of the FA Cup, with the match fixed for the Saturday following the Board Meeting. For many reasons it was vital that Rangers win this match. Firstly it would ensure continuance of their chances to win the FA Cup and gain automatic entry into the Europa League. Secondly it would lift morale hugely for players, directors and fans. Lastly, and most importantly to George, he had been made aware from certain quarters that there would be enormous bets being placed on Rangers, and it was up to him to make sure they won!

'We *will* win against Stampford,' George promised the Board emphatically. 'I'll make sure of that – you can put your houses on it, or you can have my resignation on your desks the following day!'

Knowing looks passed between everyone, but no-one uttered a response. It was an unspoken understanding.

'Okay, let's move on to the last item - Max Rawlings,' George said quickly. 'You all know the proposal on the table, and I need a vote on it before you leave.'

Now, an hour later, as he turned back to face his desk and pick up the phone, George thought what an ungrateful load of shits they all were, with the exception of Bob, of course. How easily they overlooked what he had achieved in the twelve years he had managed Rangers. Three times FA Cup winners, in the top four of the Premier League for several years, having won the Premiership three times, plus the undisputed prestige of being UEFA Champions just two years ago for the second time. The club's record of trophies was formidable and unprecedented.

George checked his watch. He was expecting Max in fifteen minutes. 'Another bloody nightmare to deal with!', he was thinking. 'Christ! What have I done to deserve this? I should have taken my old man's advice and been a bookmaker!'

He dialled a number and waited for a reply. 'Chris — we need to talk. Tomorrow! I can't, no, not on the phone — do I need to spell it out? You're gonna have to work the oracle, sunshine. I'm in deep shit, and if I go down, take it from me, you and a few others will be going with me. Yeah, okay — see you there in the morning. Usual place. 10.30.' He put the phone down without even a 'goodbye' and blew out his cheeks, thumping the table gently several times with both fists.

Outside George's office door, waiting patiently to knock, stood a shocked Max. He had been summoned to an urgent meeting with George and Max's agent, Marcus Freeman. Max had been with Freeman Sports Management since he had joined Rangers as a teenager.

Max had a good idea that they wanted to talk to him to discuss his deal for next season. He was prepared mentally for them to suggest freezing his salary until the club's recent decline improved, and he was pretty relaxed about it. He had arrived early, and on reaching George's office, he put his ear close to the door before knocking, to make sure he wouldn't be interrupting a telephone conversation. George was inevitably on the phone and got extremely annoyed if anyone dared interrupt him. Max hated George's habit of waving his hand dismissively if you dared to approach him when he was talking on the phone. In fact, there wasn't much about George that Max actually liked. The two men had a history of massive run ins over Max's period with Rangers, some even reaching the ears of the press, and it was no secret that there was a mutual dislike.

Max was the undisputed golden boy and to George's huge chagrin, was an essential, if not the most important, part of the team. Had it not been so, he would have had no compunction in going all out to transfer Max long ago. He was a double edged sword. Brilliant, yes, but a thorn in George's side.

Max heard every word George had uttered into the phone, and stood stock still in shock and disbelief. Was it his Chris - Chris Faraday - George was speaking to? He got the gist of the one-way conversation and was appalled. His mind was working overtime. Knowing about the Board meeting, he guessed that the implications of the forthcoming match with Stampford would have been discussed. It must be Chris Faraday! Jees, what was the crazy little git up to now? He didn't even want to think it, but deep down, he knew. He had had his suspicions for some time now that George was bent, but hadn't allowed himself to pursue it, hoping against hope that he was mistaken. But Chris!

Max needed time to get his head round this, his mind was working overtime. What's more, he needed to calm down and control himself, enabling him to be able to speak with George without giving him a clue that he had heard the brief telephone conversation. He was well aware, and concerned, that Rangers would suffer financially and morally if they didn't start winning matches, but they'd hit bad patches before and come through on top.

There must be more to it than that, he thought. He figured there must be serious betting being laid on Rangers' winning their match against Stampford, and no doubt Billy's charmless band of East End crooks were expecting huge payouts.

He turned and hurried quietly through Susan's office, back down the stairs leading to the players' lounge. He waited for ten minutes, then walked back up to George's office, knocking loudly on the door. 'Come in Max,' George called.

While they waited for Marcus to arrive, George filled him in briefly about the Board meeting, but Max's mind was elsewhere. They discussed the order of play and strategy for Saturday's match against Stampford. Max made what he believed to be constructive suggestions, but knew George would do it his way anyway.

He figured it wouldn't be a good time to announce that he had been approached again by Turin Spartans, who had made no secret in the past that they were willing to buy Max Rawlings and would pay a hundred million pounds for the privilege! Max had assured George some months ago that he was not in the least bit interested.

There was a knock at the door and Marcus, a short, very overweight man in his fifties, entered the room. He was red faced and out of breath, having walked up just one flight of stairs.

'Ah, Marcus! Take a seat,' said George, as he and Max shook his hand.

Max relaxed back in his seat, hoping that this little charade of going through the motions of his contract renewal would not take long. Everyone knew he would never leave Rangers in a million years.

George looked at Marcus and then Max, shifting nervously in his seat. 'Max, we've known each other a long time,' he began.

Max, who had been sitting with his elbow on the chair arm, his chin in his hand, looking down at his shoes, was still reeling from what he'd heard George say on the phone. He looked up.

George continued. 'And I'm not going to beat around the bush. We - the Board - and Marcus here, have decided that we should accept the offer from Turin and transfer you. The time has come for you to make a fresh start - broaden your horizons so to speak.'

For the second time that afternoon, Max couldn't believe what he was hearing. He sat up straight and leaned towards George, as it dawned on him that Turin had been negotiating with George all along without his knowing.

'What the hell do you mean? Have you gone mad? You know bloody well I'll never do that! Broaden my bloody horizons! They couldn't be any broader if I could walk on water!' Max turned to Marcus. 'And you knew about this? How come you haven't mentioned it to me?'

Marcus took out his handkerchief and wiped his brow. 'Look Max, it's only just been decided. No-one wants you to leave Rangers, but let's face It, it's an offer we - I mean Rangers, er, and you of course - can't refuse.'

Max glared at him with a look of utter disbelief.

'Is that right! And what about me Marcus? Whose side are you on? You're my bloody agent! You're supposed to look out for me!' Max raised his voice angrily. 'Let's not forget you've built an empire for yourself and made a fortune out of me, for Christ's sake!'

George leaned over the desk to put his hand on Max's shoulder, who shook it away and fell heavily back in his chair. 'Calm down, calm down Max. Let's talk about this sensibly. Redthorn Rangers is not all about you, or me, or Marcus come to that. The club is bigger than all of us. When Man U's plane crashed in the fifties and a lot of players died, the club didn't die did it? It not only survived, it went on to produce one of the best teams in the world. You'll do well to think on that!'

Max was scowling at George but chose not to rise to the last comment.

George was trying not to show his annoyance with Max. 'Pompous bastard!', he was thinking as he continued to reason with the enraged player.

'The club desperately needs the revenue. Max, surely you can appreciate that. It's been a terrible season and we could be in danger of losing Sportsattire, one of our biggest sponsors. We can't afford to buy the kind of new players we need unless we sell someone, and you are obviously one of the most expensive players in the country - probably the world - aside from Ronaldo or Rooney I'd say. We've thought of it long and hard and the Board are behind me on this. Sometimes it's necessary to make harsh decisions.

'You are right George. It's not all about me, but it is about my family! Do you really think for one minute that I'd ask Kathie to move to Italy? She has a life as well you know. Her business is really taking off now. I couldn't do it to her - I wouldn't do it! And what about Becky? She's only six years old. We wouldn't dream of putting a kid of her age in a school where she doesn't even know the language. Forget it. Dream another dream, boss!'

Marcus began to say, 'Max, I'm sure there are schools for English children, and ....'

Max glared at him in distain, and before Marcus could say another word, he shouted, furiously, 'do you know something? I've never heard such a load of old bollocks in my life! Sponsorship problems? You must think I'm stupid! Credit me with a bit of savvy, please!'

George was beginning to lose patience. 'From where I'm sitting, you aint got a lot of choice, lad.

You're nearing the end of your contract, and, to be quite frank, you're not getting any younger are you? This is football we're talking about - you are at your peak now. Look Max, this deal is worth serious money. Ten per cent of a hundred million would be very nice in your bank account wouldn't it? Or possibly even more, we can talk about that. If you've got any sense, you'll grab the money with both hands. You won't get another offer like it, I'm sure of that!'

'None of this makes any sense!, Max spat. 'One minute you're saying Sportsattire might pull the plug, the next you want to get rid of your best player! It's me they want in the team, and you know it! It's Max Rawlings who gets all the publicity for them! And it might surprise you to know, boss, that I do have sense. Enough to know that this whole stinking set up is more to do with you two taking a massive backhander! You're very much mistaken if you think us players don't know about your big fat 'brown envelope' bonuses.'

Marcus was spluttering. 'How dare you!'

'Watch your mouth, Max!' George had turned puce with anger. 'That's slander, and there's two of us here to bear witness to it. I'd think very carefully about what you're saying if I were you. You don't know what you're talking about!'

'Don't I? So you're telling me that everyone in the game is squeaky clean - no corruption, no bribes, no backhanders, no bent refs - not to mention managers and agents on the take!' He glared at Marcus. 'I'm sure I don't have to remind either of you about the Grobellar affair a few years ago? An international goalkeeper caught taking bribes for all the world to see. There were a few arses twitching over that lot, as well you know!'

'That's all water under the bridge,' George said, waving his hand downward in a dismissive fashion.

But Max had the bit beneath his teeth now. 'I see it on the pitch, week after week. Deliberate fouls, right in front of the ref, who conveniently doesn't see it; linesmen turning a blind eye; keepers letting in soft goals; elbows and head butting, getting stamped on, it's so blatant. You two should try being on the end of a pair of studded boots taking your legs out! I don't know how anyone gets away with it, knowing the replay will be shown in slow motion on TV later. Even the commentators are joking about it. One said last night, 'it's the name of the game nowadays. If you see a player coming towards you to give you a kicking, you have to protect yourself and give the same back!' What's all that about? It makes me sick. Who named it the beautiful game? It should be the despicable game!'

George held up his hands. 'Max, this is getting us nowhere. We're here to talk about your transfer.'

Max glared at him angrily. This was unbelievable.

'There is no transfer George - nor will there ever be. I'll quit the game first,' he shouted.

'What, and cut off your nose to spite your face? That's just plain lunacy. You're turning down the prospect of millions of pounds!'

'Maybe so, but this certainly isn't about money, boss. I've got more than I know what to do with already. As Marcus knows, we're negotiating an offer from a TV network. That's still on the table, plus my numerous modelling and sponsorship contracts. Don't you get it? I don't need to play anymore!'

Marcus nodded his agreement to George, who was staring at Max in despair. Max was savouring George's discomfort, as he went on, 'several publishers have been hounding me for years to write my autobiography. That would be an eye-opener wouldn't it - I could let an unsuspecting world know my first hand experience about the corrupt side of the game. I'm sure the FA would be interested too!'

Finally, Max crossed his arms and said with a smile, 'apart from all that, I'd like to open my own youth academy one day. Something you're not familiar with boss - putting something back into the game!'

George and Marcus exchanged glances. This was far worse than they could ever have expected. Marcus was visibly shaken and becoming very agitated. He had visions of his lucrative lifestyle going down the drain if he lost his ten percent from his biggest client. He appealed to Max, placing a podgy hand on Max's arm.

'Of course, it's your decision Max.' 'I just went along with it because I could see it was an amazing offer, and made a lot of sense. You know I have always had your best interests at heart.'

'Do what?', Max exclaimed, pulling his arm from under Marcus's hand. 'Best for you, you mean, you blood-sucking creep! You can take it from me, pal, our partnership is at an end, as soon as legally possible. I'll be calling my solicitor first thing tomorrow. As for you!' He turned to George. 'You can tell your Board to stick their transfer where the sun don't shine! I'm out of here!' Max slammed his chair against the desk as he got up and strode out of the room.

George jumped up quickly and followed him. Outside his office, he closed the door and took Max's arm. 'Max, don't be a fool. Go home and think about this calmly. Talk to Kathie. Look, we've got an important match against United on Saturday. You need to be in a good frame of mind for that. You know it's vital that we win! We haven't got much time left to turn things round, but we can still make the top four.'

'Oh yes, I know that all right!' Max spat at him. 'And that's the only reason is it? Nothing to do with you and Marcus's cut? Or perhaps the massive bets riding on it? I know why, George, believe me. Don't worry, I won't let you down, even though apparently I'm nearly drawing my pension at twenty-nine!'

'See you at training then,' George said weakly. This had turned out to be a total disaster. 'What a fucking nightmare!', he mumbled to himself as he walked back into his office.

Marcus was sweating profusely. He looked up aghast at George, wiping his brow with a handkerchief. 'Do you think he knows anything George?'

'Nah! He's bluffing. Blowing it out his arse as usual!'

'I'm not so sure. He seemed pretty clued up to me! My God, if he started going public, can you imagine the consequences? Apart from Max, one of my biggest clients, I could lose all my other clients. I would be ruined! We could even go to prison!'

'Don't be ridiculous Marcus - for fuck's sake get a grip on yourself. He can think all he wants, but he knows nothing. He can't prove a thing.'

'I hope and pray you're right! I hope you're right!' Marcus was shaking his head.

George sat down and poured them both a stiff brandy.

'Just remember Marcus - he may be a big shot, the nation's wonder boy - but in certain quarters, he is just another face. I can deal with him, don't you worry!'

CHAPTER FIFTEEN

Marcus Freeman

Marcus Freeman was more than worried. He was terrified. His reputation as owner of one of the biggest, high profile, sports management agencies in the UK was at risk. Catastrophic consequences loomed, like the sword of Damocles, should this whole cesspit of corruption, in which he had become entangled all those years ago, be exposed. God knows he had spent every minute of his life regretting the day he ever got drawn into George's web of manipulation and illegal profiteering.

Marcus joined Fitzgerald Associates, a famous and thriving sports management agency, based in High Holborn, London, as an office junior when he left school at fifteen. He had scant qualifications to his name, but he was smart, shrewd, hardworking and willing to learn. Moreover, he could talk a good talk and had a certain charisma, despite his lack of physical attraction.

Marcus proved himself to be a valuable employee and by the time he turned eighteen, he had been promoted to junior account executive, with, as he would boast to his family, his own desk and phone.

He had the charm and gift of the gab when it came to recruiting up and coming sportsmen and women, and, more importantly, in finding them sponsors.

His first notable signing was a young amateur golfer, Clive Hammonds, who was making a name for himself in lesser known golf tournaments. Marcus followed Clive's progress with growing interest and decided he could be worth a punt. He cleared it with his director, then tracked down Clive and telephoned him one evening. Clive was based in Sheffield, where he was employed as a car salesman, and was very surprised and excited to receive a proposition from a well known sports agency. He agreed to meet Marcus for lunch in London on the Saturday following Marcus's call.

Marcus was impressed with the easy manner and confidence of the tall, good looking young man. Clive was eager to become a professional golfer, but he explained that he had recently married, had a mortgage, and was not yet willing to take a huge risk and quit his job. Marcus already had the solution up his sleeve.

He knew that Henbury Golf Club, an exclusive, members only club in Surrey, was looking for a new resident pro. Marcus had a good friend, a director of Henbury, who was well aware that Clive had won a recent tournament organised by the club. He agreed to see Clive and set up a meeting.

Within a week, Clive attended an interview for the position as resident pro, and landed the job with ease. For his part, Marcus got 5% commission from Henbury G.C. on Clive's first year's salary of £30k, plus another 5% of all private golf lessons which Clive would give to the rich, exclusive members of the club. The cherry on top was when Marcus negotiated with 'Samuel Separates', the internationally famous up market sports knitwear manufacturer, to sponsor Clive to the tune of £50k a year. Both men were equally delighted with the arrangement. Mark had taken his first step as a successful sports management executive and Clive went on to become one of the UK's most famous golfers. His meteoric success culminated in him becoming the youngest British Open champion to date. This, in no small way, was elevating Marcus in his own field, and he was quickly riding high as a successful executive and director of Fitzgerald Associates.

Just ten years after he had joined Fitzgerald as a wet behind the ears teenager, the ferociously ambitious and talented twenty-five year old Marcus Freeman embarked on his long awaited project to open his own agency. He had no trouble enticing most of his own clients onto his books, having had the foresight, and the means in his senior position, to ensure that they had not renewed their contracts with Fitzgerald the previous year. He was, however, falling significantly short of the enormous amount of cash needed for the kind of opulent set up required to attract high earning sports personalities.

Marcus had always envisaged a lush office in London's West End, with up to date computer and communications equipment, efficient administrative staff, and a couple of sports executives with proven experience and their own client list to bring to the table.

Marcus needed a backer and had approached several avenues to raise his much needed revenue, including banks and finance companies, who in his words, wanted his blood in interest for such a huge loan. 'No way, you thieving Shylock bloodsuckers!', he shouted down the phone to one bank in fury, as he was running out of options and coming to the end of his tether.

Britain, along with the rest of the world, was teetering on the brink of recession. As a last resort Marcus had appealed to his many Jewish friends and business associates, but not one was willing to take the risk. They were reluctant to put up the cash, invest, or even enter into a partnership with Marcus until the Economy looked like becoming strong again.   He turned in desperation to his parents but that was a definite no go area. They worked six days a week managing a dry cleaning business and would describe themselves as 'comfortable'. They hung on tightly to their precious savings and wouldn't dream of divulging their worth to Marcus. They were adamant that they had nowhere near enough to fund his venture, even if they were willing to risk it in such a hairbrained scheme!

'I should have married for money', Marcus thought ruefully, after yet another argument with his father. He reflected on how he had rejected Nancy, the daughter of a wealthy jeweller in Golders Green, Essex. From the age of nineteen, Marcus had courted the very unattractive, bordering on obese, Nancy for the best part of a year, when he made the decision to call it a day. He had tried, God knows he had tried, to hack it with the unfortunate Nancy. He knew full well that, should he marry her, he would be welcomed into the bosom of her affluent family, which would offer him all the financial trappings of a secure future with the means to fulfill his hopes and dreams. But, uncharacteristically, for the first and only time in his selfish, manically ambitious, money orientated life, the young Marcus followed his heart, and carnal cravings, rather than his head, and married the luscious Sophie.

Marcus encountered the nineteen year old Sophie in Morrie's, a popular salt beef restaurant, on the fringes of the City of London, where she worked as a waitress. The sexually promiscuous and attractive girl was lusted after by many rich City businessmen who frequented the restaurant, some of whom rewarded her favours with expensive gifts and cash. Sophie was grateful for the easily earned subsidy to her meager wages.

Marcus was one such businessman, but not content with the odd evening of debauchery with Sophie, he fell in love with her and offered her marriage, willing to overlook her loose morals. He suffered no delusions about her background, but he was hopelessly smitten. Sophie had nothing to offer him but her voluptuous body, devotion and sexual appetite, which he accepted gratefully. Marcus was no looker, with a fleshy face, piggy eyes and a large nose. His only redeeming features were his fast wit and charming manner, combined with a ready, friendly smile. Moreover, he was well endowed in the genital department, which was a bonus for Sophie. He stood just five feet five and was already showing signs of being overweight at the age of twenty.

Sophie hailed from a much poorer Jewish family, who for generations had lived and worked in the East End of London. Her father and two brothers were porters in the Borough Fruit and Vegetable market, near London Bridge. Sophie knew which way was up and saw a sweet future with Marcus. He didn't need to convince her that he was going places. She was a good, honest girl at heart, but was lacking in any form of social graces until she met Marcus. Over time he managed to transform her into a respectable, even classy, married lady. They had a son in the year following their wedding and moved into a modest semi detached house in Ilford, Essex. Marcus promised Sophie that one day they would own a detached house in Hampstead Garden Suburbs, London's affluent area inhabited largely by wealthy Jewish businessmen, and she never doubted for a minute that they would.

Marcus was now thinking back to those early days. He had reluctantly resigned himself to the fact that his dream would have to be put on the back burner for a year or two, when, out of the blue, he had received a telephone call from George Wallis. It came as a complete surprise and initial cause for concern to a wary Marcus.

Several of Rangers' players were represented by Fitzgerald Associates, and had already been approached by Marcus, who was cautiously testing the water. George had got wind of it and was calling to find out what Marcus was up to. Marcus had to come clean and explain that he was planning to open his own agency.

'Sounds an excellent idea', said George. 'What's stopping you?'

'Cash, would you believe! Okay, yes, sure, I know I could rent a little office somewhere in the suburbs, and work out of there to start with, but, you know as well as I do George, it would take bloody years to build it into anything as prestigious as Fitzgerald's. I'm not prepared to start at the bottom again. I've got big plans - I know I can make a success of it. Look, I've got the talent, the knowhow, and I'm working my balls off day in, day out for Fitzgerald's. It's me who's brought in some of the biggest names in sport over the past few years and I've made millions for that bloody company.'

'But you must be on a big wedge yourself, Marcus.'

'Not big enough my friend. I could be a multi millionaire if I ran my own outfit.'

'Let me think about it - maybe I can be of help. I'm interested. Speak to you soon.'

The line went dead. Marcus looked at the phone in his hand in astonishment. The call had come out of the blue and had given him quite a shock.

'Bloody hell - what a turn up!', he thought. This could be the break he was waiting for - but on the downside, he knew George Wallis was bad news. It was general knowledge within the closed ranks of the sporting fraternity that George's old man was crooked, and Marcus did not relish having anything to do with the 'mob', not even in a small way. On the other hand, his frustration and burning ambition to own his own agency was eating away at him like a cancer.

A few days later George called Marcus again.

'How much are we looking at?' George didn't waste time with small talk.

'I've got a hundred grand, but another one should do it.'

'Fuck me - what you got in mind, Kensington Palace?'

Marcus laughed. 'Not quite, but it needs to be in London, that's for sure - West End preferably. I'm not talking about small fry clients, George, I'm talking the Max Rawlings of this world! He's interested by the way, along with several other famous names, who I could mention. I've done my groundwork and for an office with all the facilities, the equipment, phones, staff, etcetera, two hundred should cover it. Like I say, I've got a dozen clients already, so there shouldn't be too much time before the cash flow kicks in. There's six months' rent in advance required, which is one of the biggest layouts.'

Marcus wiped his brow, waiting for a response.

'Okay. Let's meet,' George said after a few moments. Call my secretary and arrange something for next week, preferably evening.'

'Sure, will do. Thanks George. You won't regret it.'

The two men met in a private room at George's Club in Leeds City centre a week later. Marcus had brought along his detailed business projections and costings. He had already sourced suitable premises in London:

King Street, near Covent Garden. George was impressed as he scanned all the data spread out on the table before him. Marcus was visibly excited, enthusiastically answering any questions George directed at him.

'Okay, no need for the big sell Marcus,' George said, smiling slightly, when coffee and brandy on a silver tray was served by a waiter. 'I get the picture.'

'So, you'll invest then?'

'I will, yes, but obviously there are terms and conditions.'

'Naturally.'

'But not quite what you might be thinking.'

Marcus felt a constriction in his sphincter and a slight sense of alarm. 'Go on.'

'Me - well the backers - are willing to get involved, but in return you will have to do us a few favours now and then.'

'What, you mean like knock someone off?' Marcus laughed nervously.

George was not amused at Marcus's attempt at levity. He just closed his eyes and grimaced in annoyance.

'Here's the deal, Marcus, take it or leave it. For two hundred k, cash, I will go on the payroll as a sleeping partner for 10% of all profit. The loan is repayable in two years max, interest free.'

Marcus raised his eyebrows. 'Go on.'

'But it goes without saying that if the loan isn't repaid on time, your business will become our business, if you get my drift.'

Marcus gasped. He got the message loud and clear. George and his cronies would get their hands on his agency. Well, that was never going to happen, as long as he had breath in his body. He would make sure of that.

'I'm fine with you being a partner,' he said at last. 'Of course, after all, you will be able to introduce players as clients. I can see that as being a big plus. But ... but, no interest, that's incredibly generous. What's the catch?'

'Like I said, you will have to be willing to be a party to certain, what can I say, arrangements.'

Marcus was definitely getting the drift. 'Or putting it another way, fixing!', he said, beginning to feel very hot and uncomfortable as he pulled on his collar.

George looked round. 'Keep you voice down for Christ's sake man!' He lowered his voice and leaned closer to Marcus. 'Let's just say sometimes a match has to go a certain way in order for serious punters to make it worth their while. It's big business, all over the world my friend, no big deal. It happens. Not just football either. Look, you don't need to know the whys and wherefores. Running your own agency, you will have access to all the big names, footballers, tennis players, cricketers, jockeys, etcetera, even referees. A word from you .... need I say more? Not very often, I promise,' George added quickly, as he saw the look of concern on Marcus's face, 'and I will do my best to persuade all my players that you are the man to represent them, which is probably true from what I can see. You will also get a slice of the action on pay day! That should help with squaring the loan. As Brando said, it's an offer you can't refuse.' George winked and gave a sly grin.

Marcus was facing the biggest dilemma of his young life. He could envisage untold riches awaiting him, but the merest thought of any shady shenanigans with the likes of Billy Wallis and his villainous associates, whom he knew were the backers George referred to, was frightening the life out of him. He would effectively be as criminal as they were. He had two choices. Agree and become incredibly rich and live a life of luxury, or say 'no' and struggle on for God knows how many more years with no certainty of success at the end of it.

He gritted his teeth and held out his hand. 'You're on.'

'Well done Marcus. This is the beginning of a whole new life for you and your wife - Sophie isn't it? I'm sure she will be over the moon.'

'I don't think she will ever need to know!' Marcus replied hastily.

CHAPTER SIXTEEN

Blood Brothers

Max ran down the stairs from George's office and made his way through the exit and into the directors' car park. He jumped in his car and sat staring ahead, trying to take in everything that had happened in the short space of less than an hour. First the shocking situation with Chris, and then the smack between the eyes from George. What a lowdown, cheating scumbag that man was! He switched on the ignition and drove his Porsche swiftly out through the gates. He had a lot of thinking to do on the way home.

Sitting in his study, Max decided that he would not show his hand yet. He would not even discuss it with Kathie. That night he hardly slept. He mulled it over and over in his mind, trying to decide what was the best course of action.   First and foremost he had to ascertain without a shadow of a doubt that it was Chris Faraday George had been speaking to.   But where would the two men meet?   Where was the 'usual' venue?   Chris lived in Surrey and George in the Leeds suburbs.   It was fair to surmise that they had a meeting place halfway between them.   Max knew the route to London with his eyes closed, and it didn't take much working out that to get to a halfway point at 10.30 am, George would have to leave his house before 9 am. Max decided he would have to follow him. It was the only way. He lived just twenty minutes from George. There was, he realised, a problem with his plan. George knew every car Max and Kathie owned and would soon suss out that he was being followed and by whom. Max thought furiously. He must act quickly.

He reached for his I pad and Googled car hire firms. Bingo! There was one in the city centre. He phoned them immediately and within minutes was on his way to pick up a Ford Escort. The car hire firm's manager was ecstatic when he realized that it was THE Max Rawlings. Max had to swear him to secrecy by explaining that he was planning a surprise for his wife, but couldn't divulge any more at this stage. The manager was thrilled to be able to help, and assured Max that his Porsche would be kept safe and well hidden until Max returned the hired car. Boy, would he have a tale to tell his kids!

Driving home, Max felt a mixture of anger and despair when he thought about his friend, Chris. They had been good friends for many years, together through boyhood into manhood, sharing successes and failures, laughter and tears. If the mystery man was in fact Chris, he would have to have it out with him and find out what the hell was going on. If what he'd overheard today was what he dreaded, that Chris was somehow going to help fix the match, then he would somehow have to persuade him to change his mind.

Max was, sadly, only too aware that Chris was going through yet another bad patch. With his mounting debts and increasingly disappointing performances on the pitch, Chris had gone from bad to worse, both financially and emotionally. He had become very depressed and out of control.

The catalyst of his tortured life could be laid at the door of an ambitious young woman. At a crucial milestone in his early career, Chris had hooked up with the beautiful Francine, who delighted in spending his money as fast as he could earn it. It was obvious to everyone, except Chris, that Francine was a scheming little gold digger, and it would all end in tears. Kathie certainly had a low opinion of her. Chris had been coerced by Francine into buying a huge property in London's Holland Park, as well as an expensive sports car for her, together with an ever increasing wardrobe of designer clothes and shoes. The inevitable divorce settlement cost him dearly, emotionally and financially.

A few years later, when Chris married Beverley, everyone had breathed a sigh of relief. This time he had got it right it seemed. Their first few years of marriage appeared blissful, but the tragedy of losing their only child, and the dreadful business of the under aged girl, finally took its toll.   Beverley did her level best to save their rocky marriage but it was an uphill struggle.

Chris's drinking and gambling habits were reaching an all time high. But for Beverley's salary he would be facing the miserable state of bankruptcy.

Every aspect of the various ups and downs of Chris Faraday's chequered career and personal life had always been well covered by the media. True to form, they mercilessly reported the latest catalogue of disasters down to the last detail. Graphic pictures of him emerging from a night club, usually with young women in close proximity, in the early hours of the morning, weeping at the possible breakup of his marriage, or trying unconvincingly to assure some TV interviewer that he was back on track, were all too common.   To his credit, he had booked himself into a drying out clinic, and emerged, apparently cured, looking fit and more like his old self. He was taken off the subs bench he'd been occupying for months and was back in action, playing for his team, thrilling everyone with his weekly performances, which were as exciting as ever. Now, however, it seemed to Max that his friend was falling off the wagon once more.

Max and Kathie had been so concerned about the way things were going with Chris.   Max was praying that Chris wouldn't go the same way as the likes of

George Best and Paul Gascoigne, in his eyes two of England's finest players. It was all so distressing. Now it looked as if Chris was adding to his own decline by getting involved with match fixing.

'Poor, pathetic bastard,' Max thought. 'He must be so desperate, but I can't believe he would stoop so low. It must be another Chris – it must be!', he kept telling himself.

Still unable to sleep, Max decided to go downstairs for a drink and swung his legs out of bed. Kathie stirred and realised Max was getting up.

'What's up, darling? You've been tossing and turning all night.' She reached out and rubbed his back gently as he sat on the edge of the bed with his head in his hands. 'You're not still worrying about that meeting today are you? Listen, George is a big boy and can take care of himself – he's not worth worrying about!'

'Don't I know it, precious! No - I've just got a bit of a headache. Think I'll get a drink. Can I get you anything?' Max turned and looked at his wife: no makeup and her gorgeous hair splayed randomly on her pillow, yet she looked as ravishing as ever.

'No thanks, sweetheart, just a big cuddle when you get back in bed,' she smiled.

'I really love you, Kathie. I can't tell you how much. I don't know what I'd do if I lost you and Becky.' For some reason Max felt really emotional.

'Well you never will, darling. I love you too, more than anything in the world.' Kathie snuggled back down under the duvet. 'Hurry up and come back to bed and I'll show you how much!'

'There's an offer I can't refuse,' Max smiled tenderly, then with a heavy heart, wishing he could tell Kathie what was troubling him, he went downstairs and made himself a hot chocolate. He sat at the kitchen table, slowly sipping his drink, working out what he would say to Chris, if indeed it was he who was meeting George. When Max finally crept silently back into bed, he was thankful that Kathie was now sound asleep. Unusually for him, the last thing on his mind tonight was sex! The next morning he was up, showered, shaved and dressed when Kathie came downstairs holding Becky's hand.

'You're an early bird!' she said. 'Going somewhere nice?'

'Not really. I said I'd meet Chris for a coffee – he's up this way for a meeting. I haven't seen him for a while and I just want to make sure he's behaving himself and not getting into bad habits again!', he lied.

'What are you, his mother?', Kathie asked good naturedly, with a heavenwards flick of the eyes.

Max laughed. 'You know how it is!'

'Yes, I know how it is alright. Have you had some breakfast?'

'No, not yet. I thought I'd wait for my two favourite girls to get up.' Max grabbed Becky and pulled her onto his lap, giving her a big cuddle and kiss.

Becky giggled. 'Can you make me some porridge please Daddy?'

Max looked at his gorgeous little girl and felt his heart melt. 'I think I can manage that, sweetheart.' He mixed some instant oats with hot milk, poured on some honey, and gave the bowl to Becky. She looked at the bowl then up at Max.

'This isn't real porridge! You've cheated!', she pouted.

Max and Kathie laughed. 'No fooling her is there? Just like her mummy,' Max said.

He checked the time. 7.40 am. Time he was on his way. He grabbed a piece of toast, then kissed Kathie and Becky goodbye, and left the house. Twenty minutes was time enough to get to the car hire firm and pick up the Escort. He needed plenty of time to drive to George's and park up out of sight, just in case George decided to leave really early.

It wasn't difficult to park out of view. George's mansion, like his own, was set way back at the end of a long drive in a cul-de-sac, and the road itself was tree lined. Max parked in a turning off the cul-de-sac, so George would have to drive past him on his way out to the main road. Max sat watching intently. He could feel his heart beating loudly in his chest and his mouth was dry. This was all surreal – a bit James Bond, he thought, having to smile inwardly. He had put on his beaney hat and dark glasses while he waited. A few cars passed by in both directions and then, suddenly, George's familiar, silver Range Rover came into view and drove by. Max had kept his engine running and quickly pulled out. Luckily, there was a car behind the Range Rover, so Max could keep a safe distance. The next hour and a half were nerve wracking for Max, but he kept a constant tail on George, always with a vehicle or two in front, twice having to speed through the amber lights so as not to lose him. Finally, just after 10 am, he saw George's break lights come on and the left indicator was flashing. Max drove straight on, glancing left to see that George was pulling into the entrance of a long driveway to a huge, private house, as the security gates opened for him. Max drove on past a few houses, and then did a U turn and parked opposite the house, giving him a good view of the front entrance. There were a few other expensive cars parked in the driveway when George drew up, none of which, Max knew, belonged to Chris. He switched off the engine and slid down into the seat until he could just see over the dashboard, hoping against hope that one of the vehicles belonged to George's bent contact. Five minutes went by and Max was beginning to feel relieved, figuring that the mystery man was already in the house, when he glanced up to check his rear mirror and caught sight of a black Aston Martin approaching, its right indicator flashing. Max's heart sank as he recognised his friend's car. He quickly ducked down under the dashboard until Chris overtook his Escort, then braked, preparing to turn right.

Max watched, hand to his mouth, as Chris swung into the drive, parked and headed to the front porch. He rang the doorbell and a male figure, not George, opened the door. Max gasped in shock. He recognised the famous referee. Chris shot a quick look over his shoulder, and walked in. The door closed behind him.

Max felt sick. He sat up and just stared at the house. He was really shaken and then very angry. He punched the steering wheel. 'Fucking idiot! I can't believe he would do this!', he said aloud. He sat, motionless, for a few minutes, trying to take it all in. If he hadn't seen this scene with his own eyes, he wouldn't have believed it. He ran his fingers through his hair and blew out a deep breath. His mind was reeling; what to do next? He would have to wait for however long it took for Chris to come out of the house, and then follow him. Once a safe distance away he could call Chris on his car phone, so they could pull in somewhere and have a nice little chat! The crucial FA match was only a week away and he just had to put a stop to whatever George was hatching with Chris. But would it be that simple? This must be a really big deal. George was smart and knew every angle, every trick in the book, aside from having a father with dangerous allies.

Max had a good idea that Billy had his grubby fingers in numerous illegal pies, although miraculously nothing had ever been pinned on him. He was far too savvy for that. Possibly having powerful lawyers and certain members of the police force in his pocket helped! George must have something massive on Chris to get him involved in his sordid dealings. That was it – they must be blackmailing him. Max could think of no other logical reason. Chris was a prat, granted, a weak willed loser, but basically he was a good bloke. Certainly he wasn't bent; Max knew that for a fact – well he thought he did.

Max had just over an hour to sit in the car and think hard. He wasn't blind to the fact that any modern day sport is open to corruption. It made him sad to come to terms with the fact that there will always be huge temptation for aspiring athletes and team players, managers, coaches, gamblers, bent businessmen, and the like. The copious opportunities of making serious financial gain from illegal dealings within the sporting industry were too hard to resist for some. He had been ashamed and sick to the stomach to be part of such a profession when, just six months ago, every newspaper had carried headlines relating to a well known Premier League football manager. It was alleged that he was taking huge bribes for transfers from his own club. It wasn't proven, but everyone knew he was guilty, and it left a nasty taste in the mouth of every decent person connected with football, especially the thousands of loyal fans, who were left reeling with shock and disbelief. They paid good money out of their wages most weeks to sit on the terraces, cheering and singing themselves hoarse, as loyal supporters of a football club they trusted and players they worshipped.

Even now, after all the years he had been at the very top of the game, as one of England's most loved players, Max still couldn't get his head round how lucky and privileged he was.

On the heels of the transfer scandal, two weeks later, came the revelation that a goalkeeper, faced with damning evidence, had admitted taking an enormous payout for letting in a goal, causing his team to lose the match.

The media had eked the story out relentlessly and coverage of the scandal went on and on for days. It was the end of the keeper's footballing career, and cast a nasty slur on the whole game. The bad publicity caused deep concern to fellow players, even more so to fans.

Max hadn't been able to stop worrying about those two incidents. He knew it was just the tip of the iceberg and it weighed heavily on his mind. And now, even more astonishing, news was hitting the headlines that sent shockwaves throughout the whole world. Several high ranking members of football's governing body, FIFA, were being investigated for raqueteering and corruption.

He had watched the news, open mouthed, as it was reported that an international investigation was taking place into FIFA's possible fraudulent activities. The FBI and other governing bodies within the European football community were leading the enquiries. Allegations were being made of major corruption and bribery and it was suspected that millions of pounds had changed hands illegally over the last twenty years.

There had always been conjecture of skullduggery in high places within the sporting world, especially at some of the unlikely venues hosting the Football World Cup. The investigation now taking place was throwing suspicion on the 2010 World Cup venue, which it was alleged should rightly have gone to Morocco, but was in fact awarded to South Africa.

For many years these mumblings and rumours had gone unchallenged, as FIFA, the highest echelon of football, had the wherewithal to close ranks, ensuring that the iron ring of secrecy surrounding them was impenetrable by any lower authority. Max was as shocked and disgusted as everyone else hearing the news, but at the same time, he couldn't help feeling relieved, pleased even, that the truth was at last coming to light. Perhaps now the hornet's nest had been well and truly poked, things would start to change for the better.

As Max sat waiting in the car, he tried to fathom what on earth was going on with Chris. He made up his mind that he would move heaven and earth to get his mate out of whatever fix he was in, even if it meant paying off his debts.

He was rapidly coming to the conclusion that the recent disturbing turn of events with George and Chris could be the very catalyst he needed to quit the game himself. As the end of the season was a few months away, and with his contract nearing its end, he could now achieve his ambition – to establish a youth training academy like his hero Doug Masters did all those years ago! As Max had pointed out to George in no uncertain terms, his salary as a player didn't even come into the equation. He was beyond rich! He had more money than he could ever spend if he lived to be a hundred.

Apart from Max's enormous wealth, his first biography was on the horizon, he still featured in several advertisements, and companies were calling his agent every day wanting him for their products. He had also been approached by several television sporting networks to appear as a pundit on their programmes when important matches were being covered.

Then there was Kathie's new venture, "Interior Motives", which had taken off like a rocket and was exceeding all expectations. Admittedly, as the wife of one of the world's most famous celebrity players, Kathie commanded much media attention, and benefited from Max's reflected glory. But she had proved to the world that besides being glamorous, she was a very talented and innovative new designer. The public loved her, as did the media. Her photogenic looks meant that she was always in demand by the up market "House and Garden" type journals, as well as the popular everyday women's magazines. Kathie too was on the brink of signing a contract with a television channel, who were launching a new programme featuring interior design for vastly differing houses, from bedsits in Hackney to mansions in Mayfair.

With all these thoughts going round in his head, Max never once took his eyes off the front door of the house in which he knew George and Chris were hatching their plan. He wished he could be a fly on the wall. Suddenly the door opened, jerking him out of his reverie. He turned on the ignition and backed up a hundred yards or so, just in case Chris was on his guard and would notice the parked car opposite as he drove out. He needn't have worried. Chris jumped in his car and turned out of the house's driveway, and sped off without a sideways glance.

Max let a vehicle pass, then turned his car round and drove off in hot pursuit. Ten minutes down the road he slowed down and, checking no police were around, he found Chris's number on his mobile and called him. He knew Chris would have no problem answering his hands free phone.

Sure enough Chris answered immediately. 'Mate! You alright?'

'Chris, I'm behind you in a Ford Escort.'

'What?'

'Listen, I have to speak to you. It's really urgent, mate. Can you pull in at the nearest lay-by please.'

'Sure Max. What the hell's going on? You sound weird. Is it Kathie?'

'I'll explain everything. Just watch the road for a pull in.'

'Okay.'

It was another five miles before Max saw the lay-by approaching and Chris indicating to turn in. He pulled in behind him, parked and walked quickly to Chris's car, opened the passenger's door and slid in.

'Blimey Max! What the fuck are you up to? Why are you here?' Chris was looking at him in utter bewilderment, then began to grin. 'What's with the disguise? You like something out of Mission Impossible!'

'It's more a question of what are **you** up to Chris my old mate!' Max glared at him. 'And it bloody well feels like a mission impossible, I can tell you!'

'What are you on about? Have you gone mad?'

Max sighed and looked down at his hands, rubbing them up and down his thighs in agitation. 'Look Chris, I know you are in some sort of cahoots with George. I don't know why, but I bloody hope you're going to tell me. And before you waste your breath denying it, let me tell you I heard his conversation on the phone with you yesterday, and I followed him this morning. I saw you arrive, and I've been waiting outside ever since. Very interesting to see whose gaff it was!'

Chris was gob smacked. He just stared at Max in disbelief, then shook his head and bit his lip, desperately thinking what to say. Finally, he stammered, 'so, what about it? We had a bit of business, that's all! Look, Max, I love you like a brother, but you're not my bleeding keeper. What I do and who I see is my business – no offence, but what's it got to do with you?'

Max knew he had to bluff Chris into thinking he knew more than he did. 'It's everything to do with me Chris. First off, you're my best mate. Like you said, more like a brother to me, and I'm really worried about you. I know you must be in deep shit. Secondly, I care about the game. Ha!' He pulled a wry face. 'The beautiful game! What a laugh. The despicable game, as I told our mutual friend! Have you read the papers recently? Can you believe it? FIFA for God's sake!'

Chris nodded. 'I know, I can't believe it either. It's bloody shocking. But don't tell me you've driven all this way to talk about that!'

'Of course not, you plonker!' There were a few moments' silence between them, as Max took a deep breath. 'I told you, I was standing outside George's door when he called you and I heard him tell you that you had to work the oracle – no prizes for guessing he was talking about Saturday's match of course. What's more, I spoke to him afterwards and he told me about the Board meeting. Apparently they wanted his nuts on a plate if Rangers lost the match. So I decided to get to the bottom of it and I hired the Escort, knowing no-one would ever expect to see me in such a car, and I followed him to the house you just came out of. I saw you arrive.'

'Quite the fucking Sherlock aren't we!' Chris's face had turned a shade paler as he looked straight ahead. He couldn't face Max. 'That doesn't prove anything. You're just putting two and two together and making ten.'

'Chris.' Max turned to face Chris and grabbed his arm. 'Don't be a shit for brains all your life mate. This is me you're talking to!'

Chris raised his eyebrows but remained silent.

'Listen, you've had a really diabolical couple of years, but you've come through it. You're back playing well aren't you, on the pitch most weeks, and as far as I know still on the wagon, so there must be something really huge going down to make you get mixed up with the likes of Wallis – or even worse, his dad. Whatever it is, just tell me, and we can work it out. If it's money, I can help you out, you know that. I'm here for you mate!'

Chris hung his head and Max was shocked and hurt to see he was sobbing. He wiped the tears away with the back of his hand, sniffed and said, 'Christ, Max, I can't tell you how bad it really is.'

'Take your time mate. There's nothing that can't be solved.'

Chris's mouth tightened and he shook his head. 'Not this time. They've got me by the short and curlies alright.'

'What d'you mean – who have?'

'You're right Max. That shitehawk, George Wallis, wonder fucking manager of your Rangers, is as bent as a corkscrew.

Max nodded, encouraging Chris to continue.

'He's been on the take for donkey's years as far as I can see. But it's Billy Wallis who pulls the strings – him and his gangland friends.'

'First of all, I owe Billy mega bucks – you know, after losing little Jack, I went out of control with the gambling. Don't ask me how George gets to know these things, although you can't fart without some lowlife reporters hearing about it! George got in touch with me and said if I could help Stampford lose a match he would wipe off a hundred grand.'

'A hundred grand – Jesus, how much did you owe him?' Max was stunned. He gawped at Chris.'

'A lot more, believe me.'

'I can't get my head round this!'

'I know! Anyway, I agreed and deliberately caused a penalty when we were one-all in the second half, and we lost the game.'

Max was staring at Chris, mortified.

Chris took out a hanky and wiped his eyes and blew his nose. 'It gets worse! Do you remember when my lot were in Belgium last June for that friendly match? I got hammered and ended up banging the arse off some young tart who followed us up to our hotel rooms.'

Max rolled his eyes and looked upwards in disgust.

'Yeah, yeah, I know,' Chris nodded. 'That's me all over though. But I was out of it - wonder I got it up when you think of it!' He gave a wry smile. 'Then, the following week, Rick took a phone call from some French bloke who said he had photos of me and this girl, who by the way was only fifteen. He said she was going to sell her story to the papers if I didn't come up with a hundred grand.'

Max was listening in horror. 'Oh no, Chris, you stupid bastard!'

'I know, I know. Don't tell me! But I had to somehow pay them off didn't I? Can you imagine it all over the fucking papers? Not to mention the police! My career would be over – I could even go to prison. I've done some terrible stuff, but this was the biggest mistake of my life. Billy Wallis called me the next day and told me he knew all about this Belgian bitch - she's French actually - and her ponce. He offered to pay them off for me. I was going mental and didn't even ask him how he knew – but you know what, Max? I'm beginning to think now that he probably set the whole thing up to get his clutches on me even more. He and his cronies make millions out of fixing matches, now I'm just a pawn in their stinking game.'

Max put his head in his hands. 'Oh my God, Chris! I guessed it was bad - but this!'

The two men sat silently, staring ahead through the car windscreen, both lost for words. Max was thinking furiously. There had to be a way out of this, surely. He turned to face Chris.

'What if we turn the tables on them and threaten to expose the rotten lot of them? There must be a way – surely!'

'No, not a chance. They're bloody professionals mate. You can't take on a syndicate, both sides of the Channel by the look of it. We'll end up in concrete, holding up a motorway flyover, and I'm not being a drama queen! Do you remember years ago, when George got injured by that Scottish bloke – can't think of his name?'

'MacFarlane,' Max said.

'Yeah, that's him. I reckon it was Billy's mob who caused that accident, as it was called - put money on it! Last year I heard his name mentioned by Billy when he was mouthing it off at one of the charity do's. He'd had a lot to drink, and I was passing his table with some drinks. He was laughing and joking with his friends. It got me thinking afterwards, but it was so long ago.'

'You're right', Max said, 'there was a big stink over it, but all of a sudden the case was dropped. I expect the police were taking a bunger as well.' He grabbed Chris's arm. 'But that gives me an idea, Chris. I did an interview with Bernie Cummings – you know, the sports pundit - writes for the papers as well.'

'Yeah, course I know him.'

He's a really genuine bloke, and he knows the game inside out. The way he goes on, he sounds just like my old man – the game, the players, the fans – none of it like it used to be, ya di ya di. But come to think of it, he did say he hated how corruption in the game was rife now and he really wished he could do a big feature on it, but no editor would touch it. We spoke about it quite a lot in fact. Oh yeah – and we talked about the MacFarlane episode. He said it stunk of a hit job too. I wonder if he could help us?'

'You're playing with fire, Max. Don't even think about it. I'm just going to have to go along with their demands for the time being. Look, it's a fair chance that Rangers will beat us anyway. George just needed to make sure they do. Our normal keeper, Jonesey, is off injured, and his replacement is too new to be trusted with a bribe, plus I found out that the ref is not one on George's payroll, so it's all down to me to make sure Stampford lose. Absolute shite isn't it!'

Max shook his head in despair. With a sinking feeling, he had to admit that under the circumstances, there was nothing he could do right now. Helping Chris pay his debts was one thing, but the underage girl scandal was dynamite. It would be the end of Chris, no danger, and he was not indispensable as far as Billy's lot were concerned. If they did go ahead and shop Chris to the papers, it would serve as a warning to any other player who might qualify for an ex gratia payment for services rendered.

'Okay mate. Much as I despise all this, I agree I can't do anything now. It's too late. Anyway', he added with a grin, 'we'll beat your lot easy – never any doubt!'

They both managed a dry laugh.

'Thanks Max, you're the best. I'm really sorry you've got involved in all this. Can't you just forget the whole thing? It'll blow over, and I'll pay them off – and we'll get back to normal.'

'In your dreams, Chris. As you say, they've got you right where they want you now, mate, and will have until you quit the game unless we do something about it. I know I can't do anything now, but believe me, I will figure out a way to get the bastards exposed, if it's the last thing I do. You know I'm thinking of quitting the game anyway. I've got lots of irons in the fire now – plans for the future which don't include playing football!'

'As long as it **isn't** the last thing you do!' Chris said emphatically.

'Don't worry. Slowly, slowly, catchey monkey.' Max looked at his watch. 'I must get back with this Ferrari. See you on Saturday.' He held out his hand, which Chris took with both hands and warmly shook it. Then he put his arms around Max and have him a bear hug. 'Love you man! Thanks for everything and for worrying about me. I'm more trouble than I'm worth. A fucking nightmare!'

'Yup, no argument there!', replied Max. 'But for some reason, I just have to put up with you. 'Bye for now. Look after yourself – and drive carefully!'

Chris drove off and Max turned the car round and headed for home. He returned the hired car to find the manager had waited to personally hand over the Porsche, all smiles and pleasantries, getting a treasured autograph for his son in the process.

As he drew nearer to home, Max was still worrying about Chris. Like so many other players, enormous wealth and notoriety had come too quickly for a young man from a poor background. He had gone the way of many of his contemporaries who could not handle their sudden, totally alien, hedonistic lifestyle. Chris was not just Max's best friend, he was like the brother he'd never had. Max smiled as he recollected the day they had become 'blood brothers'. They had performed the deed when they were nine years old. Chris had nearly passed out when Max nicked his arm with a razor blade he'd taken from his dad's bathroom cabinet that morning. The sight of Max's blood trickling down his arm made Chris feel queasy, and the thought of having to do it himself was horrifying. Max had reassured him, 'Come on it don't hurt, honest. Do it quick.'

Chris took the blade and closed his eyes, then quickly nicked his own arm. He opened his eyes to check the blade had done its job, and seeing his own blood, looked up at Max and grinned. 'Come on then!'

They pressed their arms together and solemnly said aloud, 'We swear to be blood brothers and best friends from this day forward, forever!'

Max's present concern for his friend was well founded. Chris had been on a downward spiral of self-destruction for a few years, and he had even attempted suicide when he found himself at rock bottom less than eighteen months ago. With the help of Max and Kathie, and an expensive sports counsellor, paid for by Max, Chris had tried really hard and had managed to lay off the drink and beat the depression.

As Max approached the heavy gates of his driveway, he pressed the remote control on his console and they swung open. He surveyed the beautiful scene as his house came into view and his thoughts turned to his precious Kathie. She was never cut out to be just a footballer's wife - a 'WAG' - he mused. He had always encouraged her to be her own person and fulfill her ambitions. He loved her with a passion and admired her abilities – all part of why she was so special to him. Yes, he was a very fortunate man to have her and Becky. It seemed to him that he had everything a man could wish for.

But there was still the problem of Chris, George and Billy!

CHAPTER SEVENTEEN

Enter Beverley

Chris Faraday was still in a state of shock and disbelief as he drove home. He had tears in his eyes as he thought of Max - how lucky he was to have a friend like him. Max had always been there for him, through thick and thin. Chris was the first to admit that he had been a world class idiot at times and had wasted more money than most people make in their lives, and more importantly, put his livelihood and marriage in serious jeopardy. Things seemed to have gone from bad to disastrous lately. He had screwed up his life big time and he couldn't see a way out.

Sure, Max had enjoyed the benefit of a happy home life, with a father who was passionate about football. Brian had encouraged his son since he was a toddler, whilst Chris was the product of a broken home. His mother had been in several short relationships since Chris's father had walked out on them, leaving her to bring up their small son on her own. The subsequent series of 'uncles' only tolerated Chris for his mother's sake, as he was a difficult child, given to bouts of temper and sulking. Chris had received plenty of beatings at the hands of one particularly violent man.

Added to the boy's frustrations was the fact that his only real interest, indeed the only thing he excelled in, was football, which went ignored in his household.

Chris was what was known as a latch key kid. His mother worked full time in a supermarket, and he was left to his own devices after school. After making himself a bread and jam, he would go to the nearby park and kick a battered old football about for an hour or two, waiting for his mum to come home. He became resentful and rebellious, with a bad attitude towards other, more privileged, kids, dismissing them as spoilt wimps. He was disliked and shunned by his classmates, apart from Max, who was always to be found in the same park, with his own top of the range new football.

Max was the most popular boy in his class, but he felt sorry for Chris. It didn't matter to him that the other kids thought he was soft for giving two hoots about such a horrible boy. Max was a good natured lad, with a big heart, and he knew Chris had it rough at home. He could see that the boy was good at football, like himself, so one day he suggested that they practice together after school. Chris jumped at the chance, and although they were like chalk and cheese, they became best mates. Chris got great kudos from his friendship with Max and began to lose some of his aggression. He gradually changed his bad attitude and became more popular himself, especially when he was picked to join the school team.

Brian also took Chris under his wing and would often as not let the kid tag along with them when he and Max went to matches. Max's dedication and eagerness to improve his skills rubbed off on Chris, and they were thrilled and excited when they were both selected to join Hartley Rovers.

Chris was subsequently selected by Stampford United to attend the club's Youth Academy, and, like his friend, Max, went through the ranks to end up as a prominent player in their Premier League squad. The two men stayed in touch regularly and socialised together whenever possible.

Chris had met Melanie at a night club in Edmonton, North London, when he was nearly eighteen. She was just another in a long line of pretty girls as far as he was concerned, but poor Melanie deluded herself into thinking it was a lasting relationship. She fell for Chris in a big way and was thrilled when her best friend, Kathie, starting going steady with Max Rawlings. Melanie was proud that it was she who had introduced them by taking Kathie along to a match in which both boys were playing.

Melanie was heartbroken and inconsolable when Chris unceremoniously dumped her without so much as an explanation. She had naively thought that as she had willingly 'let him make love to her', or as was truly the case, have casual sex with her, they were a couple, in a serious relationship.

Kathie's words of wisdom and advice to her friend had fallen on deaf ears. 'Mel, are you stupid or what? As soon as he's had what he wants he'll dump you! You know what boys are like - especially footballers. They'll shag anything with a pair of boobs and a pretty face!'

'He's not like that!' Melanie retorted indignantly. 'He loves me, he says so all the time. And by the same token, I'll tell you something Kathie - you won't hold on to Max if you keep refusing him! They're used to getting their own way - you just have to look at all the girls throwing themselves at them whenever we are out. It's embarrassing.'

Kathie had to agree. It constantly crossed her mind that Max's patience would soon run out. He could have any girl he chose, and probably had, she realised that, but then again, she was well aware that she also had the outstanding looks and figure to have any boy she wanted! Kathie was determined to hold on to her virginity, and that was that!

As soon as he was receiving a sizeable income as a professional footballer, Chris left home and bought an apartment in Croydon. Having been brought up in a one-parent home, where money was always scarce, Chris wallowed in his new found wealth. He became one of Stampford's highest paid Premier League players, and now had more money than he could ever dream of. One week's wages was more than his poor old mum earned in years. He sold the flat and bought a huge house in Surrey, where he would regularly hold lavish parties, entertaining his new social circle of hangers-on and faux friends with champagne and food prepared by his cook. His celebrity lifestyle became notorious.

The only sensible thing he ever did in those early years, having been through a quick but costly divorce to the empty headed, gold digger, Francine, was to marry Beverley Crompton, a budding young actress. She was beautiful, talented and, unlike most of her peers, very unaffected and down to earth.

Chris had just turned twenty-four when he first caught site of Beverley at a BBC Sportsman of the Year Awards ceremony. He was at the bar drinking with Max and a few of his fellow players after the show. She was standing a few feet away, engrossed in conversation with a young man and several people he recognised as actors from a popular TV soap, "Town and Out". He had caught the show a few times, more by luck than intent, and he had noticed that one of the young female characters was, in his parlance, a very fit bird. Beverley was becoming well known and was appearing more and more in the newspapers' gossip columns, women's magazines and TV chat shows, as an up and coming star. The soap's producers were aware of her increasing following and were rapidly bigging up her part in the show. Her huge fan mail and proposals of marriage from sad male viewers highlighted her increasing popularity.

Beverley was laughing at something the young man had said when she looked in Chris's direction and saw him looking at her. She recognised him immediately, and slightly nodded, then turned back to face the young man.

Chris downed his drink and walked over to Beverley's group. 'Sorry, I know you must hear this a thousand times, but I think you're really brilliant in that soap - what's it called, Down and Out?'

Beverley and her fellow actors all squealed and laughed. 'Town and Out,' she said, 'as I'm sure you know!'

Chris laughed and offered his hand. 'Just my little joke! Chris Faraday by the way. Pleased to meet you.'

'I know who you are,' said Beverley, shaking his hand. 'Not that I follow football, heaven forbid, but I do recognise you. Hard not to with your ugly mug all over the papers every day!'

Chris grimaced. 'Not every day, surely.'

'Just my little joke,' grinned Beverley.

Her friends were tittering at the repartee.

'I like a girl with a sense of humour.' Chris was looking into Beverley's beautiful dark eyes. 'I could drown in those eyes.'

'Oh please! Not that old chestnut'.

Beverley's little crowd giggled, but they were intrigued and had stopped chatting as they looked from one to the other. This was becoming interesting.

Beverley, suddenly aware that she and Chris had become the centre of attention, quickly diffused the situation. She nodded dismissively and said, 'well, so nice to meet you Chris - good luck with your team - Stampford isn't it?'

'I'm impressed! Yes it is. Would you like to come and watch us playing some time?'

She laughed. 'I don't think so. For one thing, I'm not a big fan of football, and for another, I'm always busy rehearsing - I'm glad to say. You know how it is in show business, one minute you're up there, next you're a has-been.'

Chris smiled politely, hiding his frustration as best he could. He was not used to any kind of rejection. On the contrary, underdressed, underaged and over made up young women throwing themselves at him all the time had become the norm over the past few years. Now, unbelievably, he was finding that the whole adoring female scenario was becoming somewhat tiresome. It was great at first and he took advantage, wholeheartedly, of almost every available opportunity offered to him on a plate, but, before long he came to realise that the excitement, the anticipation and titillation, was sadly lost without at least some sort of chase.

This gorgeous creature was totally different! He had fancied her for some time, admittedly, from the other side of his 50" television screen, but he now found he actually liked her and was enormously attracted to her as a person, quite unlike the normal faceless bodies he took advantage of. Chris's respect for the numerous young women he had hitherto known intimately was nonexistent. 'Gagging for it!', he would boast to his fellow players.

Chris wanted Beverley and was not about to give up. His macho intuition was that she was playing hard to get for a reason. However slight, he gleaned from their exchange that the attraction was mutual. 'Can't imagine you ever being a has-been!', he gushed. 'I think you are going to be really famous. Soaps are just the beginning aren't they? Look at Catherine whatsername - who married Michael Douglas. She started out on TV and now she's a Hollywood superstar.'

'Catherine Zeta Jones! Yes, I agree. She's so beautiful.'

'So are you - just as beautiful - even more I'd say.'

As Chris gazed at her it was obvious to everyone witnessing the scene that this was not just a cheap chat up line. He meant it. The atmosphere was becoming slightly awkward.

'Please let me call you. I'm sure you can spare an hour or two to have dinner with me one evening.'

Beverley was about to reply, when the young man standing next to her said, 'Oh go on Bev, for goodness sake - you know you want to!'

They all laughed. Beverley said, 'Oh, okay, perhaps.'

'Give me your number then,' said an eager Chris.

'Just call my agent, and they'll get in touch with me. RST - they're in the book. I don't know the number offhand.'

'Bet your life I will! What's the agency again?'

'Rising Stars Theatrical - in Covent Garden.'

'Got it! 'Bye for now then, good luck with the show. What is it they say - break a leg?'

They all laughed, and Chris felt a bit stupid, as he took his leave, but he didn't care. What the hell, he was going to get this girl's number, and he was going to wine and dine her, and he was going to make love to her, of that he was sure.

Early next morning he looked up the agency and phoned the number.

A plummy female voice answered, 'RST Agency - how can I help you?'

'This is Chris Faraday. I met Beverley Crompton last night at the Sports Awards and she asked me to call you to fix a dinner date.'

'Really, that's most unusual. Not like her! Would you give me your contact number Mr. Faraday and I'll check with Miss Crompton and get back to you.'

Chris was making a face and miming the woman's words - adding under his breath, 'stuck up bitch!'

'Pardon?'

'I didn't say anything.'

He stifled a laugh and gave her his mobile phone number. 'Thanks for your help, miss, I look forward to hearing from you,'

'Goodbye,' came the curt reply.

A week went by and Chris was beginning to give up hope of ever hearing from Beverley, when he picked up a voicemail on his phone after training.

'Oh shit! Can you believe it?', he exclaimed as he recognised the soft female voice straight away. The other players looked up. 'Hang on though - YES! She's left her number. Get in there!'

There was a communal cheer in the changing room as Chris jumped up and punched the air. They were all sick of hearing about the amazing actress, Beverley, he'd been harping on about all week. Now was the perfect opportunity to pull his leg mercilessly, with the usual barrage of banter.

'What would that little cracker see in an ugly bugger like you?', was one of the many jibes. 'Oh yes, I forgot, you're loaded, and I don't mean in your pants!'

'Fuck off you tossers! Jealousy will get you nowhere!' Chris was elated as he committed Beverley's number to his contact list before dialling it. She answered immediately. 'Hello'.

'Hi Beverley, this is Chris. I got your message. Thanks for calling.'

'That's okay.'

'Does this mean you'll have dinner with me?'

A few of his colleagues looked over at him, grinning, some with thumbs up, some grabbing their crotches and thrusting suggestively.

'Yes, I guess so. Do you have a date in mind?'

'You tell me when you're not rehearsing.'

'I can do next Thursday.'

'You're on! Where can I pick you up?'

'Outside the studios - is that okay? Around 7.30.'

'Yes, that's fine. That's great! I know where they are. Been there a few times myself. I look forward to seeing you then.

'Same here.'

'How's it all going by the way? Have they found out who took the diaries? You see - I've been following the programme.' Chris was smiling smugly to himself as he threw in the last comment.

Beverley chuckled. 'I couldn't possibly divulge. I must go Chris. See you Thursday.'

'Yeah - see you then. Bye for now.'

A few boots and towels were thrown at Chris as several of the younger players mimicked him, with, 'Bye for now - see you soon,' in high pitched voices, then sticking fingers in their mouths.

A young player was opening his locker as he yelled out, 'no need to have a shower then, Chris.'

'What?'

'Well, you're gonna have your dick in a little bit of soap later.'

Everyone roared, including Chris. 'You can bet on it boys.'

Chris was waiting in Reception at the TV studios when Beverley walked out with two other actresses. She looked stunning. Just as beautiful, even more, he thought, as she appeared on screen. She smiled warmly as he got to his feet and kissed her lightly on the cheek.

'Where are we going?', she asked, as he put his arm around her and guided her through the swing doors into the street. He hailed a taxi.

'The Ivy' - hope you'll like it.'

'I love it.'

'Sorry - of course! Why wouldn't you have been there before'. Chris was annoyed with himself. He

257

wasn't with a footballer groupie for God's sake! This girl was an up and coming actress, already making a name for herself. She was just as likely to be recognised at the famous restaurant as he was. What a prize dick!

They had a wonderful evening and enjoyed each other's company more than either of them could have imagined. Throughout the meal, they talked and laughed endlessly, oblivious to the stares from other diners who recognised both of them. Beverley was politely expressing an interest in football, and Chris was intrigued with the goings on in her showbiz world. As they emerged from the restaurant, the inevitable paparazzi were waiting to pounce, but neither of the young couple cared. They were high on the first flush of mutual sexual attraction and the sheer excitement of being with each other.

For once, Chris surveyed the morning newspapers with pride. 'Not the usual slagging off by some know-it-all sports reporter', he muttered. Instead, there were several flattering pictures of him with the beautiful young actress, along with conjectures of romance, in nearly every tabloid - and not just the back page.

Chris and Beverley were already falling in love with each other after just one evening together. Simultaneously, their sensually conscious feelings were mutual. Despite his prediction to the other players in the changing room, Chris, quite out of character, did not attempt to seduce Beverley that night. Instead, he escorted her by taxi to her flat, and when she invited him in for a nightcap, he accepted, but played his hand well. After drinking his coffee, he kissed her tenderly goodnight, and said, 'thank you for such a great evening, Beverley. I think you're absolutely gorgeous and I hope we can do this again - that's if you want to of course.'

His ploy worked. Beverley couldn't make up her mind whether she was impressed or disappointed, but either way, she couldn't wait to see him again. She was pleasantly surprised that she had found him so attentive, intelligent and entertaining, as well as easy on the eye.

On the occasion of their next romantic dinner, after they had enjoyed delicious food and fine wine, they were equally aroused and highly expectant, each predicting that tonight was the night! Chris took Beverley home to his house and led her into his sumptuous bedroom, where they made love until the early hours.

Stripped of her clothes, Beverley was even more gorgeous than Chris could have imagined. He knew that she was the only one for him and proposed to her within weeks. To his utter amazement and delight, she said 'yes'.

It was a glorious, celebrity wedding in late August. Chris was on top of the world and Beverley, looking ravishing, was glowing with happiness. Their wedding photographs featured in every magazine and newspaper, although Beverley insisted they did not receive a penny from the various celebrity magazines that vied for their cover story, as so many celebrities did. 'It is so tacky', she told Chris, and wouldn't entertain the idea. 'It's not as if we need the money is it!'

'I don't know - how much is too much?', Chris wondered, but figured that to voice such a notion was not a good idea.

His footballing skills were at an all time high, and he was behaving himself with a hitherto unknown decorum off pitch. Beverley was the making of him, everyone agreed.

They had been married for almost two years when an excited Beverley broke the news to Chris that she was pregnant. They were both thrilled and hugged each other all night. The television studios agreed to write Beverley out of the current story line for a few months when the time came for her confinement. She gave birth to a beautiful baby boy whom they named Jack, after Beverley's father.

Chris adored the baby more than he thought he could love anything. He was besotted with his son and took every opportunity to look after him when he had free time. Beverley was anxious to return to her role in the 'Town and Out' show that was gaining a bigger audience than ever before, and was being tipped as the winner of the next Soap Awards. She was anxious to regain her pecking order in the casting as soon as possible. Conscious of the fickleness of show business, Beverley knew only too well that actors could be written out or replaced at the drop of a hat.

She and Chris interviewed several applicants for the post as nanny to Jack and finally settled on a 50 year old divorcee. Mary Botting lived nearby, with grown up children and grandchildren of her own. She became indispensible in the years to come, with her own room, should she need it, in their huge mansion. Not only was she wonderful with their little boy, but gradually she evolved into their housekeeper and became almost a family member.

During this happy period, Chris had, with Beverley's help, managed to reduce his alcoholic intake. He still enjoyed a drink, but confined it to one or two, only getting 'bladdered' on special occasions, or if he had a night out with his friends and co players. At last it seemed like the bad boy of football was emerging as a popular player, family man and all round good bloke! Unfortunately, this was a short lived conception.

CHAPTER EIGHTEEN

Despair

It has been well documented in the annals of sporting history over the years that, as well as enjoying a 'purple patch' in their career, even the most successful and talented sportsmen and women can go through a seriously bad period, either in their performance or private life, or both.

Chris Faraday was no exception. Emerging as a talented and exciting young player, he had, from the start of his footballing career, been in the media's glare, catapulted into a life changing status that he was far too immature and naive to handle; unlike his closest friend, Max, who became a worldwide, enormously respected icon. For Chris, not as strong minded and grounded as Max, it was a case of too much, too soon.

For a few years, following his marriage to Beverley and arrival of Jack, Chris was flying high both in his game and private life. In common with so many high profile showbiz or sporting celebrities, however, he began to experience the effects of enormous 'highs' when he was being revered by an adoring public and praised by the sporting media, followed by depressing 'lows', when the spotlights went out. Even more so when he'd had a bad game and was the subject of harsh criticism in the papers next day.

For some famous personalities, the consequences have proved to be disastrous. This phenomenon, which is a scourge of the modern game of football, was laid bare in a television documentary during the time of Chris's demise. A shocked television audience watched a famous ex-footballer admitting that, before he quit the game, he and several other players interviewed in the programme, at best had been left destitute by gambling and reckless investments, at worst had attempted suicide, once their playing career had ended.

Chris's massive earnings and subsequent wealth somehow did not outweigh his gradual loss of self worth and search for 'something more'. This missing factor eventually led to a wayward lifestyle which began to take preference over his football and his family. It was plain to see that his hitherto brilliant talent as one of Stampford's top players was now repeatedly showing flaws. He was constantly the butt of criticism levied by disappointed fans, who cruelly booed his lack luster performance from the stands. The media was scathing, and his coach and manager were desperately worried. The team's poor position in the Premier League was a real concern, especially for the club's Board of Directors. Stampford was being crucified on a weekly basis by the unrelenting sports writers, like wolves preying on an injured animal. Over three months, the team's position had fallen to eighth in the league, with little hope of regaining its usual form, let alone making the top four. Morale amongst the team began to wane, with discontent spreading like a virus, from the club's directors down. Chris found himself sitting on the subs bench more often than not and he became increasingly depressed and rebellious. He argued with his manager, his coach, even accusing his team mates for playing like tossers and putting the blame on him.

Beverley, meanwhile, was now the most important member of the television 'Soap' cast and was working full out, appearing in nearly every episode. This meant long hours away from home, leading to altercations with the frustrated and morose Chris. Their relationship was beginning to be tested. Beverley was usually too tired, or had to learn her lines, to make love, and Chris by now had taken to drinking heavily again and was often drunk and incapable.

Beverley would come home to find him slumped in an armchair, or flat out on a sofa, obviously the worse for wear due to excessive alcohol, or he would go on a bender with his team mates and stagger home in the early hours of the morning. Worse was to come when the newspapers got wind of it and began to hound him through their disparaging columns on the sports pages. It was history repeating itself.

During the very early years of his career, Chris's decline in performance and reports of his private life had landed him in serious trouble with Rick Wandsworth, his manager, more times than Rick was prepared to accept. Chris's fall from grace had come with a final warning, and he was informed in no uncertain terms that he was in danger of not having his contract renewed. Rick had warned Chris that he would be gracing the sub bench for the foreseeable future if he didn't get his act together.

After one embarrassing 3-0 defeat, which was due largely to Chris's ineffectual defending, Rick had finally erupted in the dressing room. Chris seemed unconcerned by his dismal performance, nor the resulting loss of the game.

'Who the hell to you think you are anyway, sonny?', Rick screamed at Chris. 'Do you think getting over a hundred grand every sodding week entitles you to act like a brainless, irresponsible moron! You are letting everyone down! You can't bother to turn up for training on time and your performance on the pitch lately, today especially, is absolutely abysmal. I despair of you! You're skating on very thin ice mister!'

He grabbed Chris's soiled strip from the floor and threw it at him, then turned and strode out of the room, banging the door almost off its hinges. This outburst had come, purposely, in the changing room, in front of the rest of the team, who stood, shocked and hushed, as they witnessed their manager almost bursting a blood vessel.

Chris looked sheepishly round at his team mates. 'Looks like someone got out of bed on the wrong side!'

The silence was deafening as some players simply ignored him whilst others looked at each other and shook their heads in disgust as they brushed past him on their way out. They too were losing patience with the young player.

Chris shrugged. 'Suit yourselves!'

Max had heard through the grapevine of this episode and took Chris to task the following Sunday. He and Kathie were visiting their families in London, so he took the opportunity to drive to Chris's house. His ring of the doorbell was answered by Mary, who was on her way out. She raised her eyes and gave a nod of the head upwards to indicate that Chris was still in bed.

Max climbed the stairs and opened the door to Chris's bedroom to find that he was dead to the world at one o'clock in the afternoon. He stank of alcohol and Max noticed, with horror, traces of white powder on the bedside table.

'For God's sake Chris, just look at yourself! And that's not bloody talcum powder is it!' Max was fuming as he shook Chris. He crossed the rooms, yanked open the drapes and opened a window.

Chris opened his eyes and blinked at the light, covering his eyes with both hands. 'Shit Max! What the fuck's your problem? I'm just having a lie in. I had a heavy night!' He pulled the sheet over his head. 'Give me a break, pal, and piss off. I'll give you a bell later.'

Max grabbed the sheet and pulled it off Chris, who had turned over and buried his head in the pillow. 'Oh no, sunshine. Not this time. I'm not baling you out any more, I mean it. You get your arse out of this bed and start doing some explaining. I've heard what happened last week in the changing room, and it sounds like Rick was well within his rights to bollock you. Christ, man, you're giving the game a bad name, as if it wasn't bad enough already! What sort of example are you setting for all those young kids who dream of having the chance you've had! What are you, only twenty, and already you're on the way to becoming a piss head - no, worse - a coke head!'

Chris gradually sat up and rubbed his eyes. 'Well, he's a knob head, a fucking nut case! How do you know anyway?'

'Do me a favour - everyone knows. It'll probably be in the Sunday's Sun! Have you got the papers?'

'No, course not. I don't read that garbage!'

Max sat down on the bed and put his head in his hands. 'Chris, for God's sake, pull yourself together man. Why are you doing this to yourself. You're gonna end up like Gazza! Think of what you're throwing down the drain.'

'I know, I know! I'm a waste of space!' Chris swung his legs out of bed and reached for his dressing gown. 'I need a shower. Do us a favour, mate and put the kettle on. I'll be down in a minute.'

Max went down to the kitchen, filled the kettle, and found the coffee. By the time Chris emerged, two steaming cups of black coffee were waiting on the table.

'Thanks mate, you're a star', Chris said as he slumped into a chair. 'Look, I know you're trying to help, but it's no big deal really. So, I like a drink, and I was late for training a few times. Christ, talk about over-react! He's only putting me on the subs bench! I'm one of his best players, and he bloody knows it!' He took a sip of his coffee and sniffed. 'He needs me more than I need him!', he said smugly.

Max sat down opposite him. 'I know what you're going through mate. It's the same for all of us. Overnight you've suddenly got everything, a lifestyle you could only dream of when you're a snotty nosed kid. Being out there on the pitch, hearing your name being sung out by the fans - the highs of winning the game! It's bloody fantastic. Then, you come down to earth and wonder what it's all about. You're not the first player to go off the rails, nor will you be the last, but you can put a stop to it right now.'

Chris looked across the table at Max, through bleary eyes. He was touched by his friend's concern.

'Yeah, you're not wrong, Max! I don't know what's happening to me. I'm a moron, I know. But you of all people know what it was like for me growing up. I wasn't mollycoddled like you, was I? And as for that bastard who used to beat me up! It was bloody hard. I remember I was always hungry and miserable! It's like all my Christmases came at once when I got signed up with Stampford, and I guess I couldn't handle it. I've never grown up! Yeah, like I said, I'm a waste of space.'

'No you're not Chris. You're a talented player with a wonderful future. You've just got to take yourself in hand, mate!'

Chris laughed. 'I love it when you talk dirty!'

'What am I gonna do with you!'

CHAPTER NINETEEN

The last straw

As many of Chris's envious peers often remarked, he was a very fortunate man. Life with Beverley had made a world of difference to him in the early years of their marriage. He did appreciate how lucky he was, of course, and that he now had more than anything he could ever have dreamed of when he was growing up. He would never forget his unhappy years as an underprivileged kid with a single, dysfunctional mother and Lord knows how many 'uncles' along the way.

So, why, in just a few years, had life become so bloody complicated?, he wondered. His marriage was falling apart, his game was suffering, he was drinking heavily again, and worse, losing enormous amounts of money on gambling.

To cap it all, what had started out with smoking the odd spliff, had led to experimenting with Speed and various other amphetamines.

A family Christmas with Beverley's parents was marred by Chris's drunken behaviour. After an upsetting row with Beverley, which caused her and little Jack to cry, Chris had stormed out of the house on Boxing Day and gone to the nearby pub to drown his sorrows. The following months saw an uneasy truce between the couple, and both were very miserable.

On a hot July afternoon, Beverley was working, the nanny had the day off, and Chris was relaxing in the garden, minding Jack. The toddler had just turned two and was playing happily in his sandpit. Chris was enjoying a beer and reading the sports pages of his newspaper in a lounger on the patio nearby, keeping one eye on the two workmen who were cleaning out the swimming pool to the side of the huge garden. When they had finished their work and refilled the pool, the younger of the two, who couldn't believe his luck at being in the famous player's garden, came over and sheepishly asked Chris for his autograph. The other man joked, 'yes please, on the bottom of the invoice!'

Chris laughed and obliged the young man, who said he was 'well chuffed' that he had a story to tell his mates in the years to come.

'You can leave the cover guys. I'll be having a dip later on. Can't believe how hot it is today,' Chris called out.

'Okay governor,' said the older man. Good luck on Saturday.'

'Thanks.'

The phone rang from inside the house. 'Dammit! Piss off, whoever you are!', Chris muttered, and ignored it. He heard the answer phone response then Beverley's voice.

'Oh God, she'll be flapping if I don't answer it.' He jumped up and ran inside to the hall, casting a look at Jack, who was busy throwing sand out of the pit and screaming with laughter. Chris picked up the phone. 'Hi babes, how's it going?'

'Oh, you know, same as ever! How is Jack? Did the pool men come? And switch your mobile on!'

'Fine, yes and okay, sorry. In fact I'm going in for a swim soon, so I'll let Jack have a splash in the shallow end with me. I've left him in the sand pit. Little bugger is chucking it everywhere. I'd better go. See you later.'

'Okay, give him a big kiss from me. 'Bye.'

Chris put down the phone, went to the toilet, then the kitchen, where he took another beer from the fridge, before going back into the garden. Jack was not in the sand pit. Chris looked round and started to call out. 'Jack, where are you? Jack!' He ran round searching the immediate vicinity, looking behind bushes, trees and flowerbeds.

'Come on out, wherever you are. Mummy will be very cross if I tell her you've been naughty.' Chris was becoming irritated. He scanned the huge garden, tool shed, summer house and greenhouse, but there was no sign of the little boy. Suddenly, with a terrible pang of fear coursing through his body, Chris thought of the pool, which was some ten yards from the patio. Jack was big for his age, and could run quite fast. 'Like his old man', Chris would say. 'He's gonna be a striker, no danger!'

Chris was at the poolside in moments, and there, to his excruciating horror, a scene met his eyes which would haunt him for the rest of his life. Jack was lying motionless in the middle of the pool, face down. His brightly coloured plastic ball was floating nearby. Chris dived in and swam furiously towards the child, lifted him out of the water onto his own chest, and swam backstroke towards the pool ladder. He hauled himself and Jack up the ladder, laid him on his back and began to administer resuscitation. After two or three minutes, with no reaction from the child, Chris picked him up and ran indoors, lying him on the sofa. He dialled 999, and managed to describe the incident. He was beside himself with shock and horror and had to hang on to a nearby table, feeling faint and nauseous. He put down the phone and went back to Jack, who was stock still, his skin turning blue. Chris fell to his knees and wrapped his arms around the cold, lifeless little body. 'Oh dear God. It's my fault, it's my fault,' he wept.

The ambulance arrived within ten minutes, and the paramedics confirmed what Chris already knew. Jack was dead, with no hope of resuscitation. Chris now knew he had to do the unthinkable and tell Beverley at the TV studio. When at last she came to the phone, he tried to soften the awful blow, at first by saying that there had been an incident and she should come home straight away. But Beverley was hysterical and insisted on knowing what was going on.

'Is it Jack? What's happened? Chris, for God's sake tell me!', she screamed down the phone.

Chris was shaking, his words hardly coherent as he sobbed, 'Bev, Jack fell in the pool. I only turned my back for a minute, you know, to answer your call and have a quick pee. He was in the sand pit. When I came back, he'd gone. He must have shot across the garden.'

'What do you mean - wasn't the cover on it?'

'No, no! The bloody men had just left, and I asked them to leave it off. I told you, I was going to have a dip. Bev, get someone to drive you home. The paramedics are with him but he looks dead. Jesus Christ, how can this happen? Hurry, Bev, please. I've got to go. I don't know what to do!'

The next few weeks were purgatory for Chris and Beverley. Their own personal grief was indescribable, and the publicity surrounding the incident was relentless. The papers and television coverage seemed inexhaustible, then there was the funeral. It should have been private, but it turned into a public circus, exacerbated by several 'exclusive' interviews with both the men who were servicing the pool not an hour before the accident.

The bereaved couple were inconsolable, their only small solace being in each other's shared grief. Max and Kathie were unstinting in their support and love and truly felt their friends' pain. Chris was suicidal with self blame and grief. He was diagnosed with clinical depression and was forced by his doctor and Rick Wandsworth to take compassionate leave for two months. To her enormous credit, Beverley did not once blame Chris for the tragic incident. Instead, she blamed herself for making the fateful phone call. She knew her husband's suffering was punishment enough.

Beverley threw herself back into her acting in a desperate effort to relieve her anguish. The reaction of her fellow actors and thousands of fans, who showered her with love and consolation was overwhelming and gave her both comfort and strength. It helped her through the following agonising months. Chris, however, was still struggling to come to terms with the stark reality of such a terrible tragedy, despite everyone's efforts. He was inconsolable.

Their marriage was being kept together by a thread. Beverley felt that, although her pain and grief were every bit as debilitating as Chris's, she was managing to stay strong, hold it together and try to get on with her life. She was beginning to lose patience with Chris's weakness and constant depression. Despite his attempts to hide it, she knew he was hitting the bottle again. She'd had more than enough experience to recognise the signs.

Rick Wandsworth and the Board had enormous sympathy for Chris, and when they thought the time was right, they encouraged him back to the squad. He commenced training again and was given short spells of playing time in a few matches, to wean him back as a full time player.

Chris was in the squad going to Anderlecht, in the June of the following year, to play a friendly before the qualifying rounds of the Europa Cup. He was on the bench for most of the game, and was brought on as a substitute for the last ten minutes. Stampford scraped by with a 1-0 win and the whole team hit the town that night, ending up in a strip club. Even Rick Wandsworth joined in the celebrations, as there were no league home games to worry about until the autumn, and he reckoned it was good for morale for the boys to let their hair down occasionally.

Some of the players, including Chris, moved on to a bar near their hotel and continued to drink and behave raucously. A group of young, scantily dressed, women were eyeing the boys up and whispering to each other. They recognised the English football players and were preparing to make their move when Angelino, the team's handsome Italian midfielder, called out, 'hey, girlies, come here - have a drink with us.'

The girls needed no second bidding. A diminutive blonde latched onto Chris straight away. 'We saw you today, on TV', she said with a heavy French accent. 'You are very good! We're glad you beat those Belgian creeps.'

Chris laughed out loud. 'Did you hear that boys? What are you then, French?'

'Yes. I moved here with my parents when I was little.'

'Oh well, drink up and enjoy tonight.' Chris refilled her glass with wine. 'What's your name?'

'Yvette.'

'That's a nice name. Drink up, Yvette!'

Eventually the whole group of six players and the four girls ended up in Agelino's hotel room, where they continued to drink and romp around with the girls. They switched on the television, and tuned into the music channel. They began to dance, hooting and singing loudly. Yvette stuck close to Chris all the while. He put his arms around her and started to move unsteadily to the music being played.

'Where is your room?', she whispered in his ear.

'Along the corridor, but forget that, sweetheart. Everyone will see us and it will be all round the club tomorrow. I'm in enough trouble as it is.'

'No-one needs to know. I will say I have to go home and you can stay for a while. I will wait for you at the end of the landing, near the toilets - no-one will see me.'

Chris nodded and laughed at her reference to the corridor. 'Got it all worked out haven't you!'

She smiled knowingly, then said out loud, 'I'm sorry to be, what you say? - a party pooper, but I must go home now.'

A few people looked round, with mild interest. Yvette was picking up her handbag. 'Don't break it up because of me, but I have to be up early tomorrow.'

Chris shrugged. 'What a shame. Nice meeting you anyway.'

Yvette said, 'goodnight everyone,' and left the room. Chris went to the bathroom. When he came out, Angelino and one of the girls was missing, but the rest of the group were still noisily singing along to the music and cavorting about. Chris joined in for over half an hour, then declared that he was shattered and too pissed to carry on any longer, so amidst shouts of 'lightweight', he left.

He saw Yvette leaning on the wall under a dim light at the end of the corridor. He made his way a few yards along and motioned to her. He unlocked the door to his room and ushered her in, looking up and down before following her.

'Shall I make you some coffee?', she offered.

'Good idea - I'm just going for a leak and freshen up,' he said as he ambled towards the bathroom. He sat down heavily on the toilet. His head was spinning and he was not sure what he was doing, or why he had agreed to let this young girl in his room. It was a hark back to his early days. 'Stupid twat', he muttered. He thought of Beverley. 'This is bad. I'll have to get rid of the girl.'

He relieved himself, washed his hands and then splashed cold water over his face and smoothed back his hair. He walked out to find Yvette had made them both a coffee. She handed him a cup and he sat on the edge of the bed, sipping the hot drink.

'Look, love, I'm sorry, you'll have to go. This was a big mistake, believe me. I don't know what I was thinking! I'll give you money for a cab.'

Yvette looked at him in surprise. 'No, you don't mean that.' She moved over to stand in front of him and took his face in her hands. 'You want me, don't pretend.'

Chris looked up into her pretty young face, reached up and fondled her long hair. 'Of course I do, but, it's wrong. I'm married.'

She laughed. 'Oh, really, quel surprise! And that makes a difference?'

'It's supposed to!'

After Chris took another gulp of his coffee, she gently took the cup from him and stood it on a nearby table. She sank to her knees and deftly unzipped his fly. Before he could say another word, he felt her soft, wet lips. He groaned and began to thrust himself gently, then urgently, into her mouth, until she drew back, stood up and pulled him onto his feet. He grabbed her buttocks and began to grind against her. 'Okay, what's this all about? How much do you want?'

She pulled away slightly, perfecting an insulted expression. 'I don't want your money, Chris. I like you very much. You are a very handsome English football player. I can be your girlfriend, yes?'

'You're forgetting already - I have a wife!'

'No, I do not forget.' She turned away from him. 'Undo my dress.'

Chris pulled down the zip and she stepped out of her dress, turning to face him once more. She was stark naked, with a completely smooth, hairless pubis.

'Christ, you dirty little bitch! Not even a G string,' he gasped.

As she began to step out of her high heeled shoes, Chris said, 'no, don't! Keep them on.' He was running his eyes over her. She was so tiny. He cussed under his breath as he wrestled with an inner turmoil of temptation and conscience. He knew, of course, that temptation would be the inevitable victor.

'You look like a bloody Barby doll!', he laughed, as he pulled her towards him and caressed her firm breasts. Your little boobs are like tennis balls!'

He picked her up and laid her on the huge bed, where her body looked even smaller and frailer. He ripped off his clothes and was on her in seconds, prising open her slim legs with his knees, then brutally thrusting himself into her, grunting and groaning loudly. He had not heard the door open gently, nor was he aware of a series of quiet clicks of a camera, before the door silently closed.

'Oh, God, Yvette. I'm sorry', he breathed heavily, as he rolled off her delicate, motionless body. 'It's been a while! I'm not usually as quick as that. Look, please stay with me tonight, and when I've had a little kip, we'll make love properly.'

The girl slid out of bed and began to walk towards the bathroom. 'Sure, no problem, I understand. You have a little sleep while I shower.'

Chris was already snoring.

She showered, hurriedly dressed, and quietly left the room. As she walked out of the lift in Reception, an expensively dressed, middle aged woman, got up from a sofa and walked towards her. 'Well done, Marianne. Any problems?'

'None whatsoever. Stupid English pig!' She laughed.

'Do you have my ...?'

'Yes, yes, of course. Outside.'

They left the hotel via the revolving doors. The older woman handed the girl an envelope, and they went their separate ways.

Chris woke at 4 am to answer the call of nature. He turned to see that the girl was not there. The bedside lamp was still on and he made his way quickly to the bathroom. He knocked the door. 'Are you in there? Sorry, it's urgent. I'm busting for a pee!'

There was no answer. He gently opened the door, then pulled back the shower curtain. 'Blimey, she's gone already. That's weird,' he said out loud, as he urinated. 'Oh well. C'est la vie!' He chuckled, got back into bed and went back to sleep.

Chris thought no more about this incident, other than occasional pangs of guilt at cheating on Beverley. He vowed it would not happen again, never! What concerned him more was that he hadn't used a condom, an absolute no no! What was he thinking of? Well he knew what he was thinking of - shagging that sexy little French tart. What man wouldn't? She was so up for it!

Within days of the squad's return, a puce faced Rick strode into the changing room after training. Chris was already dressed, sitting on a bench, reading a newspaper. The rest of the substitutes were chatting, whilst some of the players were getting dressed. Rick sat down beside Chris and said quietly, 'I want a word with you, so stay put when everyone else has gone.'

'What about boss - what's up?', asked a bemused Chris.

'You'll know soon enough, you stupid prick!', Rick hissed.

When they were alone at last, Rick shook his head and faced Chris. He handed him a large envelope. 'This is what's up, Chris!'

Chris opened the envelope and took out three photographs, each depicting him in all his natural glory astride and atop the young, naked girl, Yvette. He scanned each one quickly. He had gone deathly white and started to sweat. His mouth was dry. He was unable to say a word, just put his head in his free hand and took a deep breath. 'Where the fuck did these come from?', he asked eventually.

'Through the post, would you believe! Followed by a phone call from some French guy, who demanded a hundred thousand, or the photos would be sent to the French police and English newspapers. The girl is fifteen for fuck's sake! Are you completely off your rocker, Chris? It's bad enough you had to shag someone at all, but an under aged girl. You're finished Chris, unless you happen to have a hundred k to spare!'

'You know I haven't, Rick. I'm just getting back on my feet after - well you know, Jack. It's been a really hard year for me. I was out of control, before that even, I know that, and I've wasted so much money, but I'm getting back on track now.'

Rick glared at him. He was furious.

'Back on track! Is that what you call shagging a fifteen year old girl? You know you could go to prison for this, you irresponsible maniac? I only hope it was worth it!' He sat down heavily next to Chris.

'Look at the photos, Rick,' Chris said angrily. 'Does she look fifteen to you? She looked like a bleeding twenty year old hooker to me. Plus I was slightly hammered. But, no way would I have touched her if I'd known. I've been set up, it's obvious. That stinking little bitch has set me up. I bet she got a bloody good whack for her efforts! And no, it wasn't worth it, not by a long chalk. I fell asleep afterwards and she pissed off, so there were no second helpings.'

'Spare me the details, please! I **have** looked at the photos, Chris, believe me, anyone can see that she looks like a skinny little kid. Who can tell how old she is? You must have been out of your head, never mind a bit pissed!'

'What am I gonna do, that's more to the point?' Chris hung his head, on the verge of tears. He looked woefully at Rick. 'And what about the publicity for the club if it came out? Holy shit, what a mess. My life is one big catastrophe - a fucking train crash. In fact, that's a good idea - I might as well jump under one as soon as possible and put everyone out of their misery.'

Rick had to feel sorry for the poor fool. Chris was just of many celebrities to go astray. He was just unlucky to get caught!

'You can cut the drama queen bit for a start!' Rick stood up and shook his head, sighing deeply. 'I need time to think. This lot has only just been dumped on me this morning.'

'But even if I could raise the money, how do we know they'll destroy the pictures? Probably got several copies on discs by now. We're stuffed!, Chris wailed.

'Let's not panic. Leave it with me, and keep your head down. Don't forget blackmail is a crime as well, so whoever they are, they've got to watch their arses. Now, on your bike, and lay off the booze, please!'

Rick walked out, leaving a dazed and despondent Chris staring down at the floor. 'God, could life get any worse?', he sobbed.

He spent a troubled and miserable few days, not knowing where the money would come from or who he could possibly turn to for help. At all costs he had to keep this from Beverley. If he lost her now it would be the final curtain for him, he knew that.

A telephone call from George Wallis came as a bewildering surprise less than a week after the episode with Rick.

'I hear you're in trouble son,' were George's opening words.

'How do you know that?', was all the shocked Chris could reply.

'Does it matter? Is it true or not?'

'It depends what you've heard. How do I know what you're on about?'

'Let's cut the crap then. It's about Belgium.'

'Oh, right. Well, what about it?'

'Maybe I can be of assistance. You're a close friend of Max. Does he know anything?'

'No, and I don't want him to!'

'I understand. Well, we should meet. We're all in the same game, right? And the thought of a good player like you being manipulated by some foreign shit makes my blood boil.'

Chris couldn't make any sense of this at all. Why would Wallis, manager of their arch rival team want to help him? There had to be a hidden agenda. Wallis didn't do anyone a favour, unless there was something in it for him. But Chris was so desperate now, facing a certain end to his career and police investigation. He had no option but to grab at this straw George was offering. 'Sure. Tell me when.'

They met the following week when George was in London. Chris parked in the hotel car park and took the lift to George's room, feeling very apprehensive.

George opened the door and greeted Chris. He motioned to a sofa. 'Drink?' He held up a bottle of whisky.

'Please.'

George poured them both a generous glass and sat down opposite Chris. 'Look, lad', he began, 'you're not the first and you won't be the last to get caught by these lowlife bastards. It's so easy for them. They pray on twats like you, with more money than sense.' He sniggered. 'Although in your case, no money or sense it seems!'

Chris rankled at George's acerbic remark, but bit his tongue, still intrigued as to what was coming next. He was pinning his hopes on some kind of salvation.

'You are aware of course that my father has important connections in the commercial world?'

Chris smiled inwardly at George's euphemistic use of the word *commercial*. He nodded.

'I understand Billy's contacts have knowledge of the gang who done you up like a kipper, mate. They operate all over Europe, targeting the rich and famous. Blackmail is very lucrative.'

'As I know to my cost!' Chris took a good swig of his drink.

'Well, they're amateurs, believe me. Small time. And they made a big mistake by picking on one of our boys, this side of the Channel. They got paid off, as a matter of principle - you know what I mean, honour amongst .... and all that. But not the full amount.'

Chris looked at George in amazement.

'What - you mean ....? George was nodding. 'How much then?', Chris asked.

'It doesn't matter. Suffice to say that you are off the hook.'

'I don't know what to say. That's amazing! Jees - I owe you big time,' Chris exclaimed, putting out his hand to shake George's.

George shook his hand and smiled. 'Well that's the point, Chris. You do owe me, but not money. I just want your assistance, shall we say, when there's a lot of cash riding on a game.'

Chris was beginning to see the light and his heart sank. 'Oh, God no! You mean, you want me to help fix a match?'

'Well, that's putting it bluntly.'

'How else can you put it? Either you do or you don't!' Chris was beginning to get hot under the collar.

'Look, don't worry about it right now. Let things settle down and we'll talk about it when the occasion arises. But don't forget son, I still have those photos.'

'So, I'm still being blackmailed!'

'Not at all. It's just a precaution. If you keep your side of the bargain, I'll give them back to you, and no more will be said. All in good time.'

Chris got to his feet. His head was spinning and he his legs had gone weak. He was between a rock and a hard place, without a doubt. As he turned to go, he gave George a long, hard stare. 'Well, thanks a bunch!', he spat angrily. 'Not much more to say is there?'

'Wise up Chris! Think about it carefully. You've got a lot to lose, so just keep a lid on it. You may not appreciate it right now, but you're a lucky man. You could have been facing a prison sentence, let alone losing your career.'

Chris strode towards the door, hardly hearing George's last words as he opened it and walked out, slamming it loudly behind him.

CHAPTER TWENTY

Max 's plan

'This is all very cloak and dagger!', Bernie gave Max a quizzical look as he slid in beside him. Max was sitting in Kathie's red Mercedes sports car.

'Thought the Maserati would be a bit obvious!' Max grinned.

'This is not exactly discreet, old fruit!', Bernie smiled. 'What's on your mind?'

'This is difficult', Max began, 'but I know I can trust you, Bernie. You are about the only member of the media I know who is not willing to sell his own Grandmother up the river!'

Bernie smiled. 'Thanks for that!'

'It's about Chris Faraday. Well, not just him actually, but he's in deep trouble. I think he could be in danger. I can't do much about it for now, but what's more important is that because of him, I think I've uncovered something really big.'

'I'm all ears!'

'I'm talking about match fixing etcetera - real syndicate stuff! Huge money involved.'

'Tell me something I don't know! We're all aware it goes on, but proving it is something else.'

Bernie was intrigued. 'What's your angle Max? Do you know something?'

'Only that George Wallis and his old man are involved somehow.' He looked anxiously at Bernie. 'You're not taping this are you?'

Bernie laughed. 'Give me a break! You can frisk me if you like.'

Max laughed nervously. 'God Bernie, I can't afford to stick my neck out. Can you imagine! But I kinda thought maybe you could write one of your famous tell it like it is articles. If we could get some real evidence, we could expose them in the papers.'

'More like get a law suit slapped on us!'

'Yeah, yeah, I know! I'm clutching at straws, but I can't just sit back and do nothing. Chris is my best mate. And it's common knowledge that you're not exactly fond of George.'

'That's putting it mildly! I think it's true to say we hate each other's guts. If I could nail that lowlife and his excuse for a father, I would die a happy man.'

'That's what I thought. I loved the piece you wrote about George a while ago, by the way, 'though from what I heard from Susan, he was 'incandescent with rage!' I meant to thank you for that,' Max grinned.

'My pleasure!'

'Sorry Bernie, I haven't got a lot of time, but I just wanted to run this by you - just to get your reaction. I don't want to waste your time, but I'm getting desperate. Look, I'm trusting you not to breathe a word about this, but I'm not renewing my contract. This lot has finally helped me make up my mind.'

'You have my solemn word, Max', Bernie replied earnestly. 'That's a shame. Can't imagine watching the Reds without you! Anyway, let me think about it. We're on the same wavelength, Max. I've already done some digging on my own account, and I have a few useful contacts, but you know in this business we hacks have to be very careful. Libel suits can be very costly!'

Max nodded. 'Of course, that goes without saying - but what if I were to give you a statement, after I've quit the game I mean?' He hesitated for a moment. 'Like I said, if you've heard any rumours that I'm quitting Rangers, you can now believe them.'

'Not tempted by a spell in Italy then?'

'That's another story! I'll come to that later. First things first though. I've got to get the Chris problem sorted, then we can get on to the rest of the sordid stuff! Have I been naive all these years or what! If I did spill the beans - tell you what I've found out - you would only be reporting what you have been told, wouldn't you, and no-one could touch me for telling the truth, especially if I've quit the game.' A thought suddenly crossed his mind. 'Do you guys have to expose your source of information by the way? I didn't think you did ... always reading about reliable source, etcetera.'

Bernie chose not to answer that, but just raised his eyebrows and shrugged. 'Exactly what is the truth, Max?'

'Well it's no secret Chris has had his problems with the drink and gambling. The press have given him a really bad time, as well you know. He just went a bit wild, then his marriage suffered after that tragedy with his little boy, and he drank more and more. He's been dried out more times than his strip.'

Bernie chuckled.

'And you know he took an overdose once.' Max shook his head. 'The pro player's curse! One minute you're up there on cloud nine, then make a few wrong moves and you're in the gutter! To cut a very long story short, Bernie, he owes George, big time. He's wasted millions gambling over the years, apart from getting taken to the cleaners by that gold digger, Francine. I now find out that the stupid idiot got himself involved with an underage girl in Belgium, to put it politely, and was being blackmailed for thousands. It's a wonder Beverley is still with him!'

Bernie shook his head in disbelief. As a top media man, he always had his ear to the ground and knew Chris was in some sort of trouble, but this was all news to him. Bad news!

'I remember Francine - that didn't last long did it! I don't think the ink was dry on that celebrity magazine when they split!', he said. 'But this is a different kettle of fish by the sound of things! A bloody disaster!'

Max was shaking his head. 'Tell me about it! George bailed him out apparently, but now it's payback time and the bent swine is getting Chris to fix matches. Billy and his so called associates are cleaning up with the bookies of course. And it's not just here, not in England I mean. They've gone bloody international as far as I can make out. Chris and I both reckon they were all behind the Belgian scenario actually. It's really fishy. I know for a fact, Rick wouldn't have had anything to do with it. He's as straight as a die, and according to Chris, he genuinely went apeshit when he got the photos.'

Bernie was genuinely shocked. 'Well, how the hell did you get wind of all this?'

'Pure luck, if you can call it that. I've just found all this out because I happened to be standing outside George's office. I was waiting for him to come off the 'phone before knocking, and I overheard his conversation. When he said 'Chris' I couldn't believe my ears. I just hoped it wasn't Chris Faraday. George was asking him to meet him next day - so I made up my mind to get to the bottom of it, and I followed George the next day!' Max smirked proudly. 'Just call me Columbo!'

'Stone me, Max. You didn't! Bloody hell. This gets better by the minute!'

'Like I said, Bernie, this goes no further. Chris seems to think we could all end up brown bread if we grass.'

'I don't think he's wrong either!' Bernie was still reeling.

'And the upshot is, Chris has to make sure Stampford lose on Saturday. There's massive money riding on it. If by the second half it looks as if they could win, he's gonna have to cause a penalty, or get an own goal, or something.'

Bernie looked grave. All his suspicions over the last few years appeared to be founded. 'Look Max, I feel the same as you, but it's too late to do anything about Saturday, I agree with you. Rangers will win anyway - without a doubt!', he grinned.

'That's what I told him!'

'So, after the transfer window closes and you have definitely left Rangers, we can get together again and work something out. I can't say it gives me pleasure to expose the rotten goings on in the game to an unsuspecting public, but it's high time someone did. It's shameful. It comes at an opportune time though - on the back of what's going on with FIFA! What a turn up that's been.'

'I know, unbelievable! I admit we used to wonder about some of them, but it's still hard to swallow.'

Bernie said softly, 'you remember George getting injured back in the 60's, when he was a really great player - much like yourself - but not quite as brilliant!', he added, smiling. 'His career came to an abrupt end when Andy MacFarlane clattered him in a shocking two footed tackle and broke his leg in two places. MacFarlane got the red card, but it was the end of the road for George Wallis, and if that wasn't bad enough, Stampford lost the FA Cup. I remember we spoke about this some time ago.'

'Yeah, I remember. My dad used to go on about it as well, when I was a kid! Especially when MacFarlane had that car crash soon after. In fact, even Chris mentioned it when we had our little chat the other day. Whatever happened to him by the way - MacFarlane?'

'He ended up with permanent brain damage. Never worked again, let alone play. What's more, as we all know, the poor girl in the car with him lost her life. When I covered the story I wanted to write what a coincidence it was that the man who put Wallis out of the game came to a sticky end shortly after.'

He shook his head. 'But old Tom, my editor, was shit scared and wouldn't agree. I've always had my suspicions that Billy Wallis was behind it, but it couldn't be proved. The police mysteriously dropped the case like a hot potato. My guess is that someone got paid off.'

Max looked horrified. 'Chris wasn't exaggerating then!'

'Nope. We're dealing with the big boys here. Anyway, there's more than one way to skin a rabbit.'

Bernie made a move to get out of the car. 'I'll be in touch. Get yourself a pay-as-you-go phone and don't use it, or give the number to anyone in the world, not even Kathie, except me. Okay?'

Max nodded. 'Okay, Bernie. Thanks a million. 'Bye for now.' He switched on the ignition and watched Bernie walk to his own car. As he pulled out of the car park, he felt a sense of relief, having shared his problem.

Bernie drove home deep in thought. He was sad to hear Max's story, but really elated at the faint prospect of playing some part in exposing the cheats and crooks infiltrating the game he loved so much. He had been itching to do a big exposé for years on the corruption in sport, especially football. He was beginning to think this could be his big chance.

Reaching home, he made himself a strong coffee and took it into his office. He opened his laptop, read his emails, deleted most of them and quickly answered the important ones. He then logged onto Rangers' website and began scrolling down the familiar script he'd read many times before, until he reached Max's biography.

Max hadn't given too much away during their conversation earlier, but he had let slip in so many words that he knew a lot more that he was prepared to divulge at this stage.

Bernie Googled Max's agent, Freeman Sports Management, surveying the company history, list of clients, and the photo of Marcus Freeman. He then went into the Companies House site and scrutinised every word and figure therein on the agency. 'That's interesting!' he murmured to himself. He Googled George Wallis, and nodded. 'Yup, thought so! They go back a long way. Thick as thieves, as they say! Mmm!'

He picked up the phone and dialled a number. A woman's voice answered.

'Good afternoon, Reynolds and Son.'

'Hello, gorgeous!'

'Hello Bernie, love. How are you?'

'Never better Rosie, but very sad about Max Rawlings.'

'I know, isn't it tragic. I cried when I read about it.'

'Rosie, I want you to do something for me.   I wouldn't ask, but it's really important. It concerns Max actually.'

'Max? What can I do for you?'

'I've just looked at Freeman Sports Management site, and I need to get a look at their annual report for last year. Is that possible? I seem to remember you had a friend who was temping there as a secretary. Is she still there?'

'Really, Bernie, fancy you remembering that. No wonder you're such a bloody good hacker!'

'The word is hack dear! If I were a hacker, I'd be able to get in their bloody computer system myself!'

'Whatever! Anyway, I'll try, but no promises. You'll owe me a very large drink - no, a very expensive dinner, if I can do this.'

'Believe me, it will be very well worth it. And, Rosie, no kidding, you will be doing a very public spirited service to the sporting fraternity.'

'Leave it with me.'

Bernie was up early next morning. The journalistic juices of old were beginning to flow again.

'Nothing in this world will ever convince me that that boy took his own life. Nothing! And I'll prove it if it's the last thing I do.'

CHAPTER TWENTY-ONE

The Match

Max adjusted his headphones and selected a music track on his Iphone, in an attempt to block out the noisy banter around him. He gazed idly through the window of the team coach, which was speeding southwards on the motorway. A light blanket of snow covered acres of fields, which spread across endless miles of open countryside. The virgin snow sparkled in the morning sun, creating a scene of tranquility and softness. Max couldn't help thinking what a stark contrast it was to the impending scenario in London.

He had hardly slept a wink the night before, worrying about today's match against Stampford. He was beginning to wish he'd never confronted Chris. But, too late now! He'd pushed Chris into a confession, putting him in a hopeless position, and his friend had had no option but to unload his shocking baggage. Now Max was wrestling with the fact that he, himself, was party to the fiasco about to unfold on Stampford's famous pitch.

Earlier in the season, Rangers' form would have made them odds-on favourites to win today, but lately, Stampford were on a roll and had won their last four league matches. Max was praying that today's result would be a fair win for Rangers. He closed his eyes and tried not to think about it anymore.

The two famous teams filed side by side through Stampford ground's tunnel, emerging into bright daylight and onto the pitch, to a tumultuous and deafening roar from a pumped up crowd. The stadium was filled to capacity with 29,000 home team supporters and some 9,000 Rangers supporters, who had travelled by coach, train and car to watch the game. Chris shot a quick backwards glance to catch Max's eye. Max, looking straight ahead, moved his eyes slightly to meet Chris's and gave an almost undetectable nod. Then his heart sank, as he recognised the player in front of Chris. Juan Nunez, Stampford's formidable Spanish striker, who had been out of the game for a few weeks nursing a strained thigh muscle!

'Oh great, just our luck!', Max thought.

It was a tight first half. Both teams had played a nervous, defensive game, not wanting to open themselves up to a sudden attack. There had been a few missed chances of a goal from both teams.

When the half time whistle blew, there was still no score. In Rangers' changing room, their coach had already primed the monitor so that George could pinpoint areas of concern.

'Okay lads,' George began, 'settle down now. Right - the good news is, we haven't conceded a goal, and that's a bonus for a start! Well, more like a fucking miracle, the way you've all been fannying around out there!'

This caused a few sniggers and broke the tension.

George was one of the most successful football managers in the history of the game, as well as having the reputation as once being one of England's most talented players. He was respected and revered globally. His long and distinguished career with Rangers spanned over twenty years, an achievement not surpassed by any other club. Aggressive, controversial, blunt to a point of arrogance and tough on his players, George was an exceptional man. There was nothing anyone could teach him about the game. Moreover, he could instruct and motivate his players like no other.

He continued his half time onslaught and instructions for the second half, laced with his usual sarcastic humour, foul language and encouragement.

'Fortunately for us, they've been playing 'safety first' tactics, same as us. So no damage. But from where I've been sitting, it's more like a schoolboy friendly than an FA semi!

Emile, you've got to take out that little shit, Nunez. He's turned you over three times, and it's only a matter of time before he puts one in ..... and Jack, forget the Hollywood passes! I'm not sure if you were trying to brain someone in the back row of the terraces, or kill a fucking pigeon, but that last shot at goal was diabolical, at least ten feet over the crossbar. Mateo was in the box waiting for you to pass it to him for Christ's sake. Are you fucking blind or stupid? ..... Stefan, I thought you were waiting for a bus, standing there on the right wing, when the ball came over. Don't wait for something to happen, get up his arse and **make** it happen. He was three yards down the field before you woke up!.............'

Max was not really concentrating on George's diatribe. He was wondering how the hell Chris was going to turn this game around, should Stampford forge ahead. Players were getting to their feet, rousing him from his thoughts, as he heard George's final words.

'So go out there and get stuck in. I can assure you Rick is saying the same to his team. You know my motto - do unto them before they do unto you! Good luck! You can do it!'

The second half was far more intense and significantly more physical. The referee's whistle was constantly being blown, yellow cards being handed out to players of both teams, several players nursing kicked shins and ankles, and tempers beginning to fray. With fifteen minutes to the final whistle there was still no score. Both teams had several attempts at goal. Three of Rangers' shots had hit the goal frame, the last of which bounced off the right post and out of play. Stampford's keeper kicked the ball high and long. Berlovic, Rangers' giant full back, won the ball in the air and headed it onto Max's right foot. Max cleared another few yards before chipping the ball some twenty yards over the heads of Stampford's defenders, where it landed perfectly at the feet of Jack Fairbairn. Jack spun round in a nano second and drilled the ball into the back of the net, to a thunderous roar from the crowd. Jack and Max disappeared under a heap of bodies as their jubilant team mates jumped on them in euphoric relief, while their supporters were celebrating jubilantly on the terraces.

Stampford's reaction was fast and furious. Spurred on by the sudden realisation that they could now lose this important match, they resorted to an 'all or nothing' strategy and stepped up their attack, hoping to catch their opponents relaxing after their goal. A pass from Rangers' winger, Martinelli, fell short of its target and was quickly picked up by the formidable Nunez. He sped down the field, skillfully controlling the ball, wove audaciously through two defenders, and delivered his perfect trademark 'postage stamp' strike into the top right hand corner of the goal. Peguy made a brave attempt to stop the ball, almost got his fingers to it, but he didn't have a chance. It flew powerfully past him, high and accurate, to give Stampford the equaliser. The home crowd by this time were cheering hysterically.

Along with the thousands of Rangers' fans, Max and Chris were stunned. In a matter of minutes the game had turned round, and there was precious little time left for Rangers to score again. Both men glanced at the huge digital clock at the visitors' end of the ground, and saw that they had less than five minutes left, plus whatever extra time the referee gave.

Chris realised, with a sinking heart, that it was now up to him. Minutes after kick off, the ball was delivered yards outside Stampford's twelve yard box by an accurate pass from Rangers' winger, Van Gellis. Jack took possession and pelted towards goal. Two Stampford defenders were already in position, with more players piling into the box, as Jack prepared to take a shot at goal. He was spared the effort, as Chris sent him sprawling with a sliding tackle from behind, missing the ball completely. Jack landed on his face, grabbing his ankle in agony. Over 30,000 pairs of eyes in the stadium and millions of people at home, witnessed an undisputed penalty, in full view of the referee and his assistants. Stampford supporters suddenly stopped their singing and chanting.

Thunderous boos, then massive cheers, erupted from Rangers' end, as the referee issued Chris with a straight red card and signalled it would be a penalty.

Chris walked off the pitch, amidst a deafening outburst of boos and jeers. It was the worst feeling in the world, knowing that what he'd done was despicable - he had betrayed his own team and supporters, but what option did he have?

The stadium fell silent as Max placed the ball on the white spot, stepped back a few yards, then drilled it powerfully past the keeper into the back of the net, skillfully clearing the left post by inches. Never in his footballing career had he felt so sick at heart at having to take that penalty. It gave him no pleasure, other than knowing that it was to save Chris's bacon.

The return journey to Leeds was torturous for Max. He and Jack had been continuously congratulated and patted on the back by the rest of the team, Now they were all chatting loudly about their victory, making derogatory remarks about the Stampford team. Even more gut wrenching for Max was when George shook him warmly by the hand and said, 'well done lad. You were brilliant.'

It was all Max could do not to smack him in the face, but he merely clenched his fist in his lap and gritted his teeth. 'All in good time, pal, all in good time!', he thought.

Nearing Leeds, Max heard his phone bleep. It was a text from Chris. It simply read, 'Well done mate.'

CHAPTER TWENTY-TWO

Fatal Mistake

Max sat back in his favourite recliner, took a swig from a bottle of Fosters, and reached for the remote. It was Saturday night, a week after the Stampford Match. Kathie was out with the girls, Mary was off duty and Becky was fast asleep in bed. He had the house to himself. Perfect. Rangers had won at home earlier that day and he was looking forward to watching the highlights on TV.

Half an hour later, just as his awaited match was due to come on, the sound of the gate intercom buzzing caused him to look up, surprised. He checked his watch. 'Ten thirty - bloody hell, who could that be?'

It buzzed again.

Swearing under his breath, Max put the television on hold and went into the hall. He pressed the intercom and checked the CC screen. He could see a black saloon outside the gates.

'Who's that?'

He was taken by surprise when a voice he recognised answered. 'Max, I need to speak to you urgently. I apologise for the lateness of the hour, but it's about Chris.'

'Chris? What's he done now for God's sake?'

'I won't keep you long Max, but I have important information.'

Max pressed the button to open the gates. 'Okay. Come on then.' He checked the car had cleared the gates, and pressed the button to close them.

Minutes later Max opened the door, not to his caller, but to two men in balaclavas. He took in the scene in a flash and started to slam the door, but they were too quick and powerful for him. They pushed open the door with force, knocking Max backwards.

'What the hell is going on? Who are you - what do you want?', he stammered. 'The safe is locked and can't be opened until morning, I promise you! Everything is in there - cash, jewellery, everything.' His head was spinning. It was obvious that the person he had just spoken to on the intercom was neither of these men. Where was he then? Had they held him at gunpoint? Max's mind was working overtime.

One of the men, huge and powerfully built, pushed Max roughly towards the other, smaller man, who grabbed his arm and twisted it up his back. Max yelled out in pain.

'We don't want your money, you pathetic, rich fool,' the huge man hissed. 'You just need to be taught how to keep your big mouth shut!' He pushed Max in the chest. 'Where's the kid?'

Max was terrified. He knew that voice from somewhere - it was deep, with what he thought was an Eastern European accent. He and Kathleen had always dreaded the possibility of Becky being kidnapped. He was thinking furiously. They didn't want money, what then? What did that thug mean about keeping his mouth shut? In a flash it dawned on him. He had threatened to go to the press - someone needed to stop him, and kidnapping Becky was the answer. Blackmail - but not for money! The world knew how much he adored his little girl and he would never, ever, endanger her life.

'She's having a sleepover with a friend,' he lied.

The big man laughed and sneered at Max. 'Nice try.' He turned to his accomplice. 'Keep hold of him, I'll go upstairs and find the brat.'

Fired by pure adrenalin and fear for Becky's life, Max suddenly gave a mighty backwards kick into the crotch of his aggressor, and pulled himself free. The man let out a scream of pain and fell to the floor clutching his groin.

Max leaped at him and grabbed his balaclava, pulling it up to get a good look at his face. He gasped. 'You! Why - what the hell - where's............?'

Before Max could utter another word, the larger man took him down in a rugby tackle from behind and pinned him to the floor.

Max was winded and unable to move under the weight of the huge man, who was shouting, in his thick accent, to the man still writhing in agony on the floor.

'Get up, fool, he's seen you now! Do you realise what this means? We can't go through with this. Give me the stuff, and try one of those doors. One of them leads to the garage.' He was looking up and down the hallway as he grappled with the now struggling Max.

He banged Max's head even harder into the floor, causing him to groan in pain. Snarling and breathing heavily the brute addressed his terrified accomplice.

'What are you waiting for? Move!'

Still holding his groin, the injured man staggered to his feet. 'The garage? Why the garage? Let's get the fuck out of here.'

'Do what I say!', the huge man shouted angrily. 'This is a disaster! He can identify you now and he knows who sent us. Forget kidnapping, we'll be doing a stretch for GBH! With my form I'll be an old man before I get out - and you'll be deported. That's if we're lucky and the boss doesn't get us killed first! This all ends here, do you hear me? Just go and see if you find some car keys. Try the kitchen.'

Max's assailant snatched the small bottle from the hand of his groaning partner and grabbed Max's hair, roughly jerking his head upwards. Max tried to struggle as he became aware of a pungent smell, then felt a cloth being held over his nose and mouth, until he passed out and his body went limp and still.

The injured man hobbled painfully into the kitchen, finally found several bunches of keys in a small wall cupboard in the utility room and came back into the hall, as Max was beginning to stir.

The two men acted quickly. Max never regained consciousness.

CHAPTER TWENTY-THREE

Breaking News

'What is it Levi?' Bernie swung round in his chair to face his desk.

'God, Bernie, it was horrendous - a bloody nightmare! I'm still shook up. You'll never guess - Max Rawlings has topped himself!'

Bernie was stunned. He felt the blood drain from his face, He couldn't believe what he was hearing. He stubbed out his cigarette and grabbed a pen.

'What! How? You sure Levi? You sure it was him?'

'Course I'm bleedin' sure! I was there wasn't I! Me and Mick were called out last night - this morning I mean - at gone one o'clock. I couldn't ring you before Bernie, we didn't get back off duty till six.'

'That's alright, that's okay! Well done, son. Just give me the details.'

The young paramedic went through the night's ghastly events, as Bernie furiously wrote on his pad. When Levi had finished, Bernie sat back and ran a hand through his hair.

'Thanks Levi. Bloody hell, that's terrible, oh, my God, just unbelievable. So sorry you had to witness that. What a shock.' He was shaking his head and reaching for another cigarette. He could feel tears beginning to prick his eyes, and had to quickly end the conversation with Levi. He needed a drink.

'Thanks again, son. You did well. I'll sort out the fifty - usual way.'

'Thanks Bernie. Sorry to give you such bad news. I expect it's breaking as we speak. I know one of the coppers - he's got a big mouth!'

'Bye Levi. I'll be in touch.' Bernie was devastated. He lit the cigarette with a trembling hand and wiped the tears from his eyes as he leaned over to the cabinet behind him and grabbed a bottle of whisky. He poured a large measure into his empty coffee cup.

'Oh no, not Max!', he said aloud. He had often wished he'd been lucky enough to have had a son like Max. He loved the man - was a big fan, along with most of the population. Max stood for everything that was good about football; 'and God knows there wasn't a lot these days', he was thinking.

Over the years Bernie had attended most of the games Max had played in, and had interviewed him several times. He had written many a glowing article on the player's virtues. It was hard not to like and respect Max. Despite his wealth and fame, Max was modest and the epitome of decency. Bernie was not too ashamed to admit he was very fond of the young man, and liked to count himself as a friend, not just a sports pundit.   Max was such a wonderfully gifted player and ambassador of the game.

Bernie sighed deeply and turned to his laptop. His first job was to send his report down the wire before the whole world knew about it, although he suspected that the paparazzi were already alerted and heading towards Max's home. He took a swig of his drink and began to type:

MAX RAWLINGS FOUND DEAD AT HIS HOME:
SUSPECTED SUICIDE

'Suicide my arse!' he thought.' No way on God's earth would he kill himself. I'd put my own life on it! He's been murdered! And I've got a pretty good guess why!'

He thought about the last time he had spoken to Max. Just a few months before his death, Max had called Bernie out of the blue and asked if they could meet. Bernie was delighted and intrigued. This was certainly unprecedented, but he was thrilled to think he might be getting an exclusive from Max Rawlings. He didn't ask questions, just said, 'of course,' and they arranged to meet in the car park of a pub Max knew of in Bingley, on the outskirts of Leeds.

Bernie turned that meeting over and over in his mind as he struggled to find the right words for his article. He was wishing like hell he could put his thoughts, his suspicions, into print. Something was radically wrong, he knew it, and it all pointed to Max knowing more than was healthy for him. He'd been tetchy and obviously worried when they had spoken that day.

Bernie hadn't been at the sharp end of the media and the sporting world all his working life without recognising the stench of something rotten! The thrill of chasing down a good story flowed through his veins like his own blood. Now, it pained him bitterly to swallow the fact that he was obliged to simply stick to the facts, before adding his own personal condolences. But the time would come!

He added a brief summary of Max's career and emailed the article to all the TV networks and newspapers on his database, hoping he would get first pickings. He would be writing a full eulogy for his Sunday supplement column next.

He slumped back in his chair and drained the rest of his whisky. He wept for his own unhappiness, the cruel loss of his sporting hero and the shame of what was once the beautiful game.

CHAPTER TWENTY-FOUR

The funeral

Kathie pulled the collar of her fur coat tightly round her neck against the cold wind blowing across the cemetery, watching in deepest sorrow and horror as the coffin was lowered slowly into the open grave. She felt faint with grief and fatigue, having hardly eaten or slept properly for over a week. Her eyes were sore with days of endless tears. Her body was wracked with emotional pain. But now, as the dreaded moment had arrived, and the final act of this whole, indescribably sorrowful scene unfolded before her, she could not shed a single tear. She was drained, unable to speak or react to anything or anybody. Her body seemed to have taken over in a state of shock and her mind was a blank numbness.

Hardly hearing the priest's words, she felt an arm around her. It was her mother, Margaret, quietly urging her to take a handful of the earth from a silver pot being passed around the circle of mourners. Mechanically and slowly Kathie responded, taking one hand from her collar to lift a small handful of the carefully sifted earth from its box, and, still standing motionless, she closed her eyes and took a deep breath. Clenching the earth in her hand, she put her arms across her chest and began to rock gently backwards and forwards. She glanced sideways at Brian and Pauline, Max's parents, standing close to her. The grief and sorrow etched on their drawn faces echoed her own pain. She shook her head in despair several times, before looking back down at the coffin in the yawning grave. What could ever be more devastating than the stark realisation that this was her last goodbye to her beloved Max? The agony of his death was destined to dwell in her heart and mind for all time.

'This will always be the worst moment of my whole life!', she thought. 'Whatever happens to me until the day I die, could never, ever, be as harrowing and heartbreaking as this.'

She unfurled her hand and watched the earth sprinkle lightly onto the coffin. This part, at least was over at last; this unbelievably painful ordeal, the heartbreaking finale to the horror that was the loss of her darling Max. He was her first and only true love, and had become her friend, soul mate and her husband of only six years. Why, oh why did he do this to himself, to her? How could he? They were so happy! They were young, and they had everything: rich beyond compare, a beautiful daughter, fabulous houses and lifestyle, and a wonderful future. None of it made sense. No, no, it wasn't true – she still could not bring herself to believe that he had committed suicide. Since his death, these questions had gone round and round in her head, pervading every thought, every waking minute of every day.

She looked around at the huge crowd of mourners surrounding the intimate circle at the graveside. This strange mixture of family, friends, Max's manager, coach and fellow players. She knew that a mass of reporters, photographers and television crews were waiting at the gates of the cemetery and shuddered at the thought. 'Vile vultures!', she muttered under her breath. Then she looked down at the small child, her beautiful little girl, the image of her father, who was clutching her grandmother's hand, tears trickling down her lovely little face. Margaret bent and gently wiped her face with a tissue, then gathered her up in her arms and whispered, 'it's alright, sweetheart, time to go now'. She nodded to Kathie. 'Come on, love'. Let's get back to the house.'

With one last look at Max's grave, Kathie turned to walk away.

'Mummy, mummy'. Becky was wriggling in Margaret's arms, hands outstretched towards Kathie.

'OK, lovely – come here'. Kathie took her child in her arms and hugged her tight. 'I can't carry you, darling –

mummy is not feeling too well, but you're my big brave girl aren't you! It's only a little way to the car; you can walk that can't you? We're going home now, and you can have something nice to eat and then you can go to your room and play with your new doll's house. Anna will be there'.

Kathie put Becky down and took her hand. She slipped her arm through Margaret's and the three of them began to walk down the pathway, through the crowd that must have been in excess of three hundred people, who were standing in little groups talking quietly, most of them looking towards Kathie. At last the two women and child were approaching the waiting limousine at the cemetery's entrance.

'Just let the day end, just let it end!', she wanted to scream out loud. The thought of the ordeal yet to come back at the house was filling her with a sickening dread. Hundreds of so-called mourners, half of whom she didn't even know, and many of whom she despised and all they stood for. And as for the media reps, they could all go to hell!

As they reached the gates of the cemetery, a man broke away from a group of reporters and quickly approached them. Looking directly at Kathie he said, 'Mrs. Rawlings, may I have a quick word?' She shot a brief sideways look at him in disgust, then rolled her eyes upwards in disbelief.

'Are you kidding? Get lost you creep. Do you really think I'd speak to one of you lot, especially today!'

The man stepped aside as she brushed past him, but as he did so he said in a low voice, 'I think I know what happened to Max. I mean what *really* happened.'

Kathie stopped in her tracks and looked at him again briefly. He was a good looking man, with kindly eyes, in his late forties she guessed, about her mum's age, but he had a care-worn look about him which may have made him look older than he was. His hair was dishevelled and he obviously hadn't shaved for days. His clothes were good quality, but shabby. He had the air of a man who didn't take care of himself, yet his manner and well spoken voice indicated he was an educated man. Somewhere, in the back of her mind, Kathie thought she recognised him, but in her distressed state, she couldn't call him to mind. As much as she hated the press, this man seemed to have sincerity about him. She looked around her quickly. No-one was near enough to have heard him. Margaret was already in front of her, lifting up Becky to put her in the limo. Kathie sighed. 'What do you mean?,' she asked quietly, averting her eyes.

'Look, we can't talk here — not appropriate.' He pushed a small card into her hand. 'Call me please, when you are up to it. It's important, you have to believe me, I'm a friend of Max. Please call me.'

He stepped back as half a dozen reporters slipped through the police barrier, surrounded Kathie and began jostling for position. Cameras were clicking and shouts were coming from all directions.

'Come on Bernie you old git, give us a break – move over!' .... 'Condolences Mrs. Rawlings' ...... 'Do the police believe it was suicide ?'..... 'Was Max quitting the game?' ..... 'Is it true you were about to divorce?' ...... 'Kathie, over here!' etc. etc.

A flash went off in Kathie's face as she reached the limo. Becky began to cry. Margaret turned and, grabbing Kathie's arm she guided her firmly towards the car's open door. Standing behind Kathie with her arms outstretched sideways, creating a barrier between her and the milling paparazzi, she waited until Kathie was safely inside the car, and then said to the funeral attendant, 'Let's go!' He closed her door and, nodding to the driver, slipped quickly in beside him.

As the car took off, Kathie looked at the card the reporter had given her, which simply read: 'Bernard Cummings, Sports Correspondent', with a mobile telephone number.

'What was that all about, love?' Margaret was leaning over to look at the card.

'I haven't a clue', Kathie replied. 'I told him to get lost in no uncertain terms, but then he said he knew what had really happened to Max.' She pulled a quizzical face. 'I don't know why, but I feel I should know him.'

'You're not gonna fall for that old baloney I hope!' Margaret raised her eyebrows. 'It's a scam. He just wants to get a scoop for his crappy paper. They're all the same. Bloody scumbags, the lot of them.'

'Oh my God, I've just realised who he is! He's quite famous - always on the telly, you must have seen him, mum - he's one of those football pundits. Max often mentioned him too - he really liked him - said he was a good bloke,' Kathie explained, as she slipped the card into her bag. 'Don't worry, mum, I'm not an idiot'.

'I know that, darling, but you're so vulnerable right now and that lot know it! You've been to hell and back and don't know which way is up at the moment.'

Kathie gave a weak smile and reached for Margaret's hand. 'What would I do without you, Mum? You've been marvellous.'

'That's what mums are for. You and Becky are my world now. I only wish your dad was here with us. He always knew what to do. He was my rock. An old bugger mind you, but you know I loved him to bits'.

'I know, of course, so did I.'

They both gave a little smile, and looked down at Becky who was sitting opposite, eyes closing and her head beginning to droop. Margaret leaned across and adjusted her seat belt so that she could lie down.

They continued the rest of the journey in silence, each with their own thoughts. Kathie felt herself dozing off. The strain, medication, and sleepless nights had taken their toll. She was tired, so tired. Her head ached and the pain in the pit of her stomach would not go away. She closed her eyes, not opening them again until she heard Margaret's voice. 'We're here, love'.

The huge iron gates were swinging open and the limo made its way down the long driveway to the house. Kathie stared blankly out of the window at the magnificent gardens. It was a gloomy day, cold and dank. The trees were bereft of leaves now and their bare branches were swaying gently in the wind. Still the gardens were stunning. Evergreen shrubs abounded and the vast lawns were immaculate. The immense water feature in the middle of the main lawn was beautiful, the millions of cascading droplets being illuminated with soft coloured lights. She had always loved this feature – had in fact been the one to instigate its installation, but now she looked at it and felt nothing but emptiness. What did anything matter now that Max was gone? She would give it all up in an instant, live in a two-up, two-down somewhere and be more than happy, if only he were there with her, like it used to be, like it was when they were teenagers, before he became the famous Max Rawlings, the nation's favourite sportsman, not just her husband.

Max was adored by his millions of fans and young would-be footballers all over the world, propositioned by women wherever he went, sought after by the media, with television appearances and sponsorship offers pouring in nonstop. Over and above his football career and pop idol status, Max had become a well loved personality, a household name and a wonderful ambassador of the game. 'You could have made it as a model, never mind football!', Kathie used to tell him.

Kathie had shared their celebrity lifestyle, which oddly enough became the norm even to her after a few years. Yes, of course, she had embraced being a lotus eater. Who wouldn't? She had revelled in the glamour, the houses, the gorgeous designer clothes, the endless travel to beautiful places – everything was like a fairy tale come true. A far cry from the little house she once shared with her mother in Enfield!

Her gaze turned towards the fabulous house as they drew nearer. The mansion! Max's dream house, with its ten en suite bedrooms, three bathrooms, games room, gym, indoor and outdoor swimming pools, a kitchen you could fit a normal person's house in, a study for Max, her own office and beauty room. The whole interior of the house had been designed by Kathie, to a magnificent standard. And that was just here in the leafy suburbs of Leeds. There was also the villa in France, one in Barbados, their town house in

London and an apartment in New York. And the cars! Always new cars - a succession of Mercedes, BMWs, Porsches, Jaguars, a Ferrari, a Maserati Granturismo Sports, even a vintage MG, and above all others, Max's pride and joy, his customised Harley Davidson motor bike. Kathie's very own red Mercedes Sports car had been a 21st birthday surprise and she had simply loved it. It was a thrill for her just to sink into that beautiful soft, luxurious leather upholstery and take in the smell, the newness.

'Kathie, come on, pet, shake a leg!' Margaret was already out of the car holding Becky's hand. Reluctantly, with a heavy heart and a cloud of dread enveloping her, Kathie walked into the house. As they crossed the vast marble tiled hallway, the clicking of their high heeled boots breaking the silence, they were met at the dining room door by Anna, Becky's nanny, and the housekeeper, Dorothy – Dot as she liked to be called. Dot was a 60 year old woman from the neighbouring village. She was a treasure; honest, hardworking and totally reliable. One of Kathie's better choices! She had found out the hard way that good staff were difficult to find.

Anna, a young Irish woman, had been with Kathie and Max for over two years. She was the daughter of a cousin of Kathie's father and had come to England at Margaret's suggestion, to escape the rigours of life in

Ireland as the eldest child in a huge family. Margaret remembered too well what that was like! Anna loved her job, the house and all its trappings, and above all, she adored Becky.

'Hello poppet, come here and let me take your coat off. Let's go upstairs', Anna said to Becky in her soft Irish voice. She smiled down at the child as she took her by the hand and began to guide her gently towards the immense double staircase. 'I've got a lovely surprise for you in your room – your favourite lunch, and as you have been very good, some chocolate buttons. And I have something new for your doll's house.' She turned and winked at Kathie who was standing motionless, taking in this little scene.

'See you later, darling, she managed to say at last, as Becky released her hand from Anna's and ran up the staircase. 'Be good', Kathie called after her.

'Bye mummy', Becky called back.

Kathie now reluctantly turned her attention to the dining room. Dorothy had been standing patiently, waiting for Kathie to speak to her.

'Thanks, Dot – if you could greet guests at the front door and take their coats, that would be great,' Kathie said, as she walked through the double doors, now fully open to reveal the impressive spread of food laid out on the huge table. She was greeted by the manager of the catering firm she and Max had employed over the years for their many social events and dinners held in the house and garden.

A young man of Italian origin, immaculately dressed in a dark suit and tie, stepped towards her. 'Mrs. Rawlings, please may I offer my sincere condolences.' He bowed his head slightly. 'We are all so shocked about Max – er, Mr. Rawlings. He was always so kind to us – appreciated everything we did. So sad!' He looked very somber.

'Thanks Mario – I know, I know. It's a terrible shock to us all.' Kathie moved towards the table. Several catering staff, dressed in their smart blue uniforms, were busying themselves loading canapés onto large trays in the adjoining kitchen, while others were opening bottles and filling glasses.

'Everything looks wonderful, Mario – up to your usual high standard.' She managed a little smile, and Mario nodded his appreciation. Kathie looked at him. 'You remember what I said, no champagne!'

'Of course, of course! Just the wine, soft drinks, tea and coffee -- and brandy, at my discretion!', he added.

'That's good. Please greet people personally as they come through. Dot is manning the front door. I'm just going upstairs to freshen up. I'll be down in ten. I know I can leave it all in your capable hands.'

Kathie walked up the stairs with Margaret close behind. Pauline and Brian followed and headed towards their guest room in silence. Kathie had urged them to spend a few days with her and Becky after the funeral. Margaret had insisted she stay for a few weeks and Kathie willingly agreed. Margaret's room was next to Kathie's.

'See you in a mo,' Margaret whispered, as Kathie was turning the handle of her bedroom door. 'Don't be too long Kathie, love – the madding crowd will soon be here!'

'Don't I know it! No, I won't be long, mum. See you in about ten.' Kathie walked into her sumptuous bedroom. The lamps had been turned on by Dorothy and there was a welcoming glow of soft lighting all round the room. But how empty, how quiet! 'As it will always be from now on!', she thought sadly.

She took off her hat and coat and pulled the pins from her swept up hair, shaking her long auburn locks back into their usual, comfortable shoulder length style. She pulled off her boots and laid down on the four poster bed, closing her eyes, the horrific reality of it all sweeping over her once more. How could it be possible that Max would never share this bed with her again? Would she really never feel his arms around her when they cuddled up, never enjoy his sensual kisses – and he was a great kisser! Nor feel his hard toned body against her when they made love? In the midst of her terrible grief over the past days, she hadn't given a thought about missing the physical side of their relationship, and now, as she daydreamed about him lying there next to her, she felt slightly ashamed that such thoughts could even enter her head.

But then, why ever not? Why should she not remember and cherish what was an important part of their love and life together? It was never just 'sex' when they made love. They loved each other deeply: passionately and emotionally. For one thing, Max was not just a gorgeous man, he was an imaginative and skilled lover, unselfish and sensual, yet always adventurous! Often, after they had made love, they would talk long into the night, giggling over something silly that had happened to either of them that day. With Max it was usually about what that had happened in the changing room, or a joke one of the lads had told in the players' lounge afterwards. Kathie would tut in disapproval, but then laugh out loud. Or, she would be relating what Becky had said or done – or even the latest gossip about one of her circle of close friends, mostly footballers' wives and girlfriends.

Kathie shook her head to dispel the reverie, and took a deep breath. Coming to terms with losing her life partner at such an early age was simply too hard to bear. Max had been everything in the world to her, her whole being, her very life had revolved around him, and now he was no more. It was so cruel. She still couldn't believe it, and certainly could never, ever accept that Max took his own life. She was not going to settle for that!

She reluctantly braced herself to go downstairs and face the music. She went into her personal en suite, cleaned her face with a cosmetic wipe and splashed on a little cold water. She reapplied her makeup, skillfully concealing the dark circles under her eyes, brushed her hair and straightened her dress. She put on a pair of high heeled sling back shoes and took a small handkerchief from the top drawer of a dresser. Taking a last look in a massive, guilt edged, full length mirror, she walked out onto the circular landing above the hall, and began to walk down the stairs.

By now all the guests had arrived. Pauline and Brian were stoically greeting them. Most people had moved into the lounge, but a dozen or so were still congregated in the huge hall, having just left the dining room with their drinks. Kathie could see Margaret engaged in conversation with a couple of the players' wives. She grimaced at the thought of the ridiculous label the media chose to give these females. She was, after all, a footballer's wife herself! As she reached the foot of the stairs, all eyes turned towards her. Even on such a day, she noted, two of the young women who were talking in hushed tones to Beverley and Chris Faraday, drinks in their hands, looked as if they were going to step onto the red carpet any minute at a film premier. Their perfectly made up faces, false eyelashes, fascinators perched on their expensively styled hair, down to their six inch heel designer shoes, left no-one in any doubt as to who they were.

Ditsy Barbara, as her girlfriends good naturedly had named her, spoke first. She was a beautiful, tall blonde with surgically enhanced breasts and amazing legs, clad in glossy black tights, which were shown to maximum advantage by an inappropriately short dress. 'Oh, babe! How are you, darling?' Not waiting for a response, she continued, 'it was a lovely service, everyone said so.'

'Thanks Barbara. I'm doing okay,' Kathie replied, as Barbara planted a kiss on her cheek. 'Thank you so much for coming.'

Beverley gave Kathie a big hug and a peck on the cheek. She bit her lip, her eyes beginning to fill with tears. 'Kathie, we can't tell you how sad we are. Chris is really taking it badly. You know, don't you, if there's anything at all we can do to help, we will.'

'Thanks Beverley.'

Kathie turned to Chris. She was shocked at his appearance. He had lost weight, his face looked drawn and pale and she could swear his left hand was shaking slightly. He saw her glance at his hand and self consciously tucked it under his right armpit.

She knew Max and Chris's history.   They were at school together and were eight years old when they both first played for their local team, Hartley Rangers. Max was always the star player, repeatedly winning the Player of the Year Award, but just once, over all the years they played for the club, Chris beat him and took the award, and he never let Max forget it!   Max had often spoken of Chris to Kathie, recounting little adventures the two boys had shared, the laughs they had, the scrapes they had got into as boys. The two men remained firm friends, close as brothers, until the day Max died.

Kathie had never really taken to Chris, which was a small bone of contention between herself and Max. For one thing, he had broken her best friend Mel's heart when they were teenagers, and had suddenly dumped her when he got bored, to move on to pastures new.

Kathie and Max were at odds over Chris from the outset. 'He's so flash', she would say. 'I hate what he did to Mel, and what he puts poor Beverley through is terrible. I'm sure he's been unfaithful to her.   Mind you, at least she's got a career of her own. She's a damned good actress.'

Max wouldn't have any of it. 'Listen to yourself Kath! He's a good bloke – been a bloody good friend to me. You don't know him like I do, darling. Honest, he's a diamond. I know he comes over a bit lairy, but that's just the way he is. He's got a heart of gold really.'

'We'll see,' Kathie had said. After all, Max was right. Given, she didn't know Chris as well as Max did, but, apart from the Mel scenario, it was purely a gut feeling she had about him which she couldn't explain to Max. Kathie came to the conclusion that it was not worth falling out over, and it was a waste of energy and emotion.

As far as Kathie was concerned, the lovely Beverley was not just typical footballer's wife material. She was an intelligent and talented actress, and she had stuck by Chris through thick and thin. There were a handful of women in Kathie's circle of players' wives who had achieved a modicum of success in an enterprising venture of their own, albeit on the back of their husbands' fame. Beverley, however, wasn't one of them! She had done it on her own merit, and Kathie applauded that.

It was a well known fact, enjoyed by the chattering classes and endorsed by the media, that most footballers' wives had achieved their sole ambition of hunting down a rich, high profile player, trading their glamour and sex appeal in return for an enviable lifestyle. A popular television serial depicting such scheming females was enjoyed by huge audiences and amused Kathie no end. She consoled herself by knowing that she and Max were an item long before he became the famous Premier League icon. She had known him since she was sixteen.

Now, at her dear husband's funeral, she was staring at his best friend, and had the most compelling feeling of contempt. Chris, who had been looking down into his drink, now faced Kathie with a pained expression.

'Kathie, I'm so sorry, so sorry', was all he could say. He shook his head and she could see the tears in his eyes. He looked absolutely wretched, and Kathie sensed, very, very uncomfortable. His distress seemed to go deeper than normal grief for a friend. She dismissed it for the time being, but knew that it was a notion she would be returning to when all this was over and done with.

'Thanks Chris – I'll catch up with you later,' Kathie said coldly, and turned away, avoiding any form of contact with him. Thankfully he was holding a drink with his free hand.

She moved away from Chris and walked into the lounge. Looking around the room, she was relieved to see that her dear friend, Melanie, was trying to catch her eye.

'Thank goodness' she thought, as Melanie and her husband, Anton Peguy, Rangers' French goalkeeper, made their way towards her. Max used to tease him and call him Mr. Piggy.

'Non, non – No, Max!' Anton would say, in his delightful French accent. 'It's pronounced Pegeee!', which Max knew perfectly well, but it would really amuse him to wind Anton up.

All three hugged for a few moments. Finally, Melanie pulled gently away, and put her arm through Kathie's. 'I can't begin to imagine how you're feeling my darling!', she said. 'At least the worst bit of all is over now. You're doing really well, isn't she, Anton?'

Anton nodded. His English was very good, but he was feeling emotional and finding it hard to say anything. He simply put his arm around Kathie's shoulder and gave her a big squeeze. 'She's been brilliant!', he said at last. Kathie looked from one to the other, suddenly feeling very tearful, with an overwhelming love for Melanie.

Melanie bit her lip, trying to contain her emotions.

'We're always here for you Kathie, you know that don't you? Anything you want, just give us a call. Promise!'

Melanie had been at Kathie's side since Max's death, along with Margaret, making calls, helping to organise the funeral, making sure Kathie ate, sharing glasses of wine, just being there for her best friend when she poured her heart out and cried incessantly.

Kathie nodded. 'I promise, Mel. Thanks you two for all your love and support. You've been brilliant yourselves.' She looked round. 'I guess I'd better mingle. I'll catch you later.' Kissing them both on their cheeks, and with another big hug with Melanie, she turned to walk away and came face to face with George Wallis. She jerked back momentarily at the sudden confrontation.

'Oh, George,' she gasped, 'you gave me a start!'

'Kathie!', he said, in his familiar Cockney accent, arms opening theatrically. He gave her a huge bear hug, patting her on the back all the while. Kathie shuddered as she heard his words.

'I wish I could say something, anything, to make you feel better, but I know it's useless. Been there myself, when my Ruthie passed away. What a devastating loss, what a bloody waste. He was like a son to me, Kathie.'

'I know, George. What can <u>anyone</u> say? Nothing changes the fact that he's gone does is?' Her lip trembled and, for the second time, she felt close to tears. Perhaps because she knew that this horrible man's words were so insincere. He wasn't fit to breathe the same air as her Max!

There was a brief, embarrassing silence.

'Have you had something to eat?', she asked quickly, noticing that he just had a drink in his hand.

'I'm fine thanks, love. Susan's getting it for me.' He looked around and smiled weakly. 'Great turn out,

Kathie. Max would be proud to know so many people cared about him'.

'If only that were true, George!' Kathie snapped back, surprising herself at her own vitriol, but nonetheless she continued pointedly, 'if only everyone really <u>did</u> care for him! Someone obviously didn't!' She realised she had said this in quite a loud voice and looked round to see if anyone was listening to their conversation. Fortunately everyone was occupied, either drinking, helping themselves to more food, or talking.

Kathie looked back at George with a scowl. She lowered her voice. 'You know as well as I do, there are some people here who couldn't give a toss about him – or me for that matter! They've just come to rubber neck or get a free drink. Like those two over there,' she said, pointing to two foreign looking men she had never seen in her life before. They were standing near the window, locked in conversation with Billie Wallis and Costas.

George looked quite uncomfortable as he glanced in the direction of the small group of men. He made an exaggerated face of shock horror. 'That's not true Kathie, love, not true at all! Max was one of the most popular players I've ever known. We all loved him – he was a good lad, one of the best. I would be proud to have a son like him!'

Kathie eyed George closely. What was it about him that made her feel uneasy? He was Max's manager. His father figure. Hadn't he always been Max's guide and mentor and given him the opportunity to become the famous footballer that he was? Certainly, George never stopped reminding them of that fact!

'I know, George – sorry, I don't know what's going on in my head lately. I'm all over the place.'

'Don't worry gal – it's only natural. Grief is a terrible thing. Once you get over the shock, the pain sets in. But it does get better in time, believe me. It sounds like a cliché but it's true. Not that you ever really get over losing your loved one.' He took a sip of his drink and looked down at his feet, shifting them uncomfortably.

'Not that it took you long to find yourself a young replacement!' Kathie thought, but managed to stop herself voicing it. She had caught sight of George's wife, Susan, who was standing a few yards away talking to a group of Rangers' young players. Susan was an attractive, voluptuous woman, some twenty years George's junior. She had worked as his secretary for many years, and no-one really knew whether they had been carrying on before his wife Ruthie had died a few years ago. Susan was well spoken, intelligent and witty. She was attractive, not beautiful, but had ample, very eye catching, curves. She also possessed a sense of style which was like a breath of fresh air to Kathie. Susan obviously adored George. 'Lord knows why!', Kathie often thought. He was a rough diamond and no mistake.

Kathie looked back at George, who was speaking to her. 'Sorry George – what were you saying?'

'Just saying I hope we'll still be seeing something of you. Don't be a stranger.'

She winced inwardly at the inane platitude and then replied, 'I'll catch up with you soon, honest. In any case, we have a lot to sort out. My solicitor is dealing with Max's estate - the insurance etcetera. I expect he'll be in touch with you soon.'

'Sure, sure. Speak soon Kathie. Take care – and anything I can do, you know ......'

'Thanks a lot, George.' Kathie intercepted. She turned away and smiled at Susan, who had looked round and was making her way towards them. Kathie was genuinely fond of Susan, but just couldn't cope with talking to her at length today. Susan had a reputation for being a real chatterbox. 'Verbal diarrhoea!' Max used to call it. Kathie quickly made her escape by waving to a young woman looking in her direction from across the room, as she walked towards a group of friends from her health club.

She spent the next hour circulating, politely accepting condolences and making small talk, and at last, relieved to see people begin to leave, she found Margaret.

'Mum, I must go and lie down', she said, 'my head is splitting. Can I leave it to you and Dot to see to things? And will you see Brian and Pauline are alright, please? They look shattered. Mario has everything under control in the kitchen, and I think people are starting to go home now. Thank goodness,' she added.

Margaret nodded. 'Of course, my lovely. No probs! You go and have a long soak and get to bed. I'll pop in later to see if you need anything. God Bless!'

Kathie spent a few obligatory minutes with Costas, so dramatic in his sympathy and condolences, then she bid her goodbyes to the few remaining guests and went upstairs. She took off her shoes, and walked along the landing, relishing the feel of the plush carpet on her stockinged feet. Reaching Becky's room, she opened the door. Anna was quietly putting toys away and gathering up clothes as she looked up.

'She was tired out, poor lamb!', Anna said, as they both looked towards the bed where Becky was sleeping peacefully. 'It's been quite a day for such a little one. But she ate her supper and seemed a lot perkier after she'd had a bath and played with her doll's house.'

'That's good.' Kathie looked down at Becky, then back at Anna. 'I know you didn't really approve of me taking her to the funeral Anna, you and other people

I'm sure, but it was just something I felt I had to do — I mean, I wanted her to be part of it and to understand what was happening. Max thought the world of her, and she loved him so much. As it happens, she was really brave, apart from a few tears at the end.'

Anna looked down, clearly embarrassed. She had indeed considered it unwise to subject a small child to such an ordeal, and had tactfully suggested this to Kathie and Margaret, but they were both of the same opinion that Becky should be there. 'Well, I'm sure you were right, Kathie. She seems to have coped with it very well. She's such a darling child, and can be so grown up. She's going to have a wise head on her shoulders one day — just like you!'

Kathie smiled. 'Sometimes, Anna, but not always! What did you buy for the doll's house by the way?' Kathie tried to lift the conversation.

'Ah! You won't believe what they make now — only a flat screen television set for the lounge!'

Kathie smiled. 'Good grief, whatever next? Thanks, Anna, you've been a rock. Make sure you go down and get some food now.'

'Thanks Kathie, I will. Good night now. I hope you can get some sleep - It's been a long day!' Anna's eyes filled with tears and she sniffed loudly and blinked, brushing them away as they began to trickle down her cheeks. She rushed towards Kathie and gave her a huge hug. She was by now unable to stop herself weeping uncontrollably.

Kathie clung to her and suddenly, without warning, all the hurt, the pain, the pent up emotion, came flooding out of her. She, too, began to cry, sobbing into Anna's shoulder as though she would never stop, her whole body shaking with emotion.

She pulled herself away at last, and wiping her eyes with her little handkerchief, she turned and walked out of the room. 'Night Anna,' she whispered as she opened the door, 'thanks for everything.'

'God Bless you Kathie.'

CHAPTER TWENTY-FIVE

Evidence

Kathie closed the bedroom door behind her and leaned back against it, letting out a huge sigh as she closed her eyes. 'That's it, then,' she said to herself. 'That's over, and now I have to move on, as they say,' although how she was ever going to move on, or where to, she couldn't begin to guess. She went into her en suite and turned on the gold taps to run a bath, pouring in a generous amount of bath essence until it foamed, filling the room with a delightful smell of lavender. She undressed and took off her makeup.

The image staring back at her from the mirror was drawn and pale. Her skin looked grey, lifeless, accentuating the dark circles under her eyes. Certainly no resemblance to the usual perfectly beautiful features so admired by men and envied by women. Max told her almost every day how gorgeous she was.

'Don't think the magazines would want this ugly mug all over the front page now!', she grimaced. But she had to face the inevitable; it would be a different story where newspapers were concerned. Without a doubt, as Max's widow, and a celebrity in her own right, she would be caught up in all the publicity and conjecture surrounding Max's death. Judging from the media's reaction so far, she would have to face the paparazzi every time she stepped out of her front door for a while yet! And if she dared to be seen in public talking to – heaven forbid – another man, even if it was her solicitor or father-in-law, she would be splashed all over the papers the next morning. They would be watching her like hawks.

Her only small consolation was, once the media had sucked out every atom of newsworthy minutiae they possibly could from the story, it would eventually become yesterday's news. Until then, the 'suicide' of one of the nation's favourite celebrities was the juiciest piece of news for ages, and speculation as to the whys and wherefores of this enigma was rife.

She took a packet of paracetamols from the medicine cabinet and swallowed two with a glass of spring water taken from one of the several bottles always kept nearby. Her eyes were so sore, and she noticed with alarm that her hands were actually shaking. She rubbed them together, and shook her head. 'Get a grip!', she scolded herself. She lowered herself into the large sunken bath, welcoming the foamy water, which enveloped her with its comforting, warmth and aroma.

'I wish I could just stay here forever', she murmured as she closed her eyes and felt herself dozing off. She woke with a start and realised that the water was by now very cool. She climbed out, dried herself briskly and walked into Max's en suite, where she took his bath robe from its hook. She pulled it on and wrapped it around her, the size of it swamping her slight body. She could smell him – his cologne – it was eerie and comforting at the same time. In bed, still wearing Max's robe, Kathie sat propped up on the pillows and stared at the ceiling. 'To quote those famous words, tomorrow is another day!,' she thought. 'But nothing will have changed for me!'

She closed her eyes, hoping that she would at last be able to sleep without the prescribed sleeping tablets. The pain killers and alcohol should do the trick, she guessed, her mind reflecting on the day's events. Suddenly, she remembered the man at the cemetery. She opened her eyes. 'Oh my God, what did he mean? He said he knew the truth about Max! But, as Margaret had pointed out, it was probably a clever scam – no doubt he was trying to get an exclusive. Still, it was something to think about, something to focus on. And then there was Chris. Something wasn't right.

The bedroom door opened quietly and Margaret popped her head round. 'You alright, love?'

'Yes thanks, mum. I feel quite tired now, and I've taken some pills for my headache.'

'That's good.'

'Mum – I was thinking about that chap, you know, Bernard, at the cemetery. I can't help wondering what he knows.'

'Kathie, for goodness sake, will you listen to yourself!' Margaret's Irish brogue was at its most pronounced when she was making a point. 'I told you! Don't take a blind bit of notice. He's just a reporter, and you know to your cost what they're like. Haven't they given Max and you a terrible time over the years, printing all sorts of rubbish, most of it made up! I honestly don't know how they get away with it!'

'I know, mum, but, don't ask me why, I think he's kosher!'

'Kosher? What sort of language is that? Where do you get these expressions?'

'You know what I mean, mum. I think he's genuine. There was something about him.'

'Well, if I had my way, he'd have got a kick up the backside – that's what they all deserve if you ask me!'

'I've got it!', Kathie suddenly exclaimed. She tapped her fingers on the side of her head. 'How bloody stupid can I be? Mum, I think I must be losing it!'

Margaret looked alarmed. 'I hardly think so. What is it?'

'Well, fancy me not realising who Bernard was! I've never met the man myself, but Max did lots of times, and often mentioned him. Oh my God, and I was ever so rude to him! But he looked different somehow. Not as I remember him on TV - he looked a bit scruffy.'

'Well, he's probably just like the rest. I wouldn't trust any of them as far as I could throw them, and that's a fact,' Margaret retorted.

Kathie couldn't help but smile. 'G'night Mum. Thanks for looking in. We'll talk about it in the morning. Love you.

'Goodnight m'darling! I love you too. Sleep tight. See you in the morning.'

Margaret closed the door quietly behind her, and, before long, Kathie fell into a restless sleep. She opened her eyes and was surprised to see that the room was no longer dark. Even the heavy drapes could not blot out the bright sunlight of this winter's morning. She looked at the bedside clock.

'Ten-thirty! Good grief. I must have slept like a log!' She put out her arm to feel where Max would have been lying and stroked the pillow. Looking round the room, now so devoid of his presence, she thought with deep sadness and an ache in the pit of her stomach that this was how it would be every morning when she awoke. A few fleeting moments when everything seemed normal, then the grim realisation that Max was gone - forever!

As Kathie lay there, reflecting on the past few weeks, and yesterday's funeral, she thought about

Bernard Cummings. It might be nothing, Margaret could be right, but there was a slim chance that he knew something. Besides, it was something she could focus on, a distraction, something other than wall to wall grief. At least she would be doing something practical! She had already vowed that she would not rest until she could prove what really happened to Max.

She put on Max's dressing gown and went down to find Margaret in the kitchen.

'Morning, mum.' Kathie kissed Margaret on the cheek.

'Oh, you're up, love! Did you have a good sleep?'

'I did thanks. I can't believe you didn't call me. Look at the time. Where's Becky?'

'Hush girl! You were worn out for goodness sake! She's out with Anna - gone to the park. Now what will you have for breakfast? - and I won't take no for an answer. Look at you, all skin and bones!'

Kathy suddenly realised she felt hungry. She hadn't eaten properly for days. 'Just cereal - and I think I'll have a boiled egg.'

'You sit down, girl. I'll see to it. There's some tea in the pot.'

'Okay captain!' Kathie smiled, as she obeyed Kathleen's command. She sat down and poured herself a cup of tea. 'I'm going to ring that Bernard Cummings, mum. I've been thinking about it, and I honestly think he knows something.'

Kathleen pulled a disapproving face, as she popped an egg into a saucepan. 'Well, it's up to you, of course. It'll do no harm I suppose.'

After breakfast, Kathie took Bernard's card from her handbag and entered the number in her mobile phone before calling it. He answered straight away.

'Hello, Bernard Cummings.'

'Mr. Cummings, this is Kathie Rawlings.'

Bernie was slightly surprised - it was only the day after Max's funeral, and he certainly wasn't expecting to hear from Kathie for a while, if ever.

'Mrs. Rawlings. Thanks for calling. How are you, if that's not a stupid question?'

'Well, at least I had a good night's sleep for a change. But, as well as can be expected I suppose.'

'Of course! It must be absolute hell for you. I can't imagine what you're going through. I am so sorry, Mrs. Rawlings. I haven't got over it myself. I loved that man, he was one of the best. I'm Bernie by the way.'

'Call me Kathie.'

'Thanks. It was real bun fight at the cemetery. I wasn't sure you even understood what I was saying above all that commotion!

'Yes I did, that's why I'm calling.'

'That's great, Kathie.'

'My pleasure. I'm intrigued.'

'Well, to cut to the chase, I need to meet you, as soon as possible. What I have to say is not safe over the phone. Kathie, I have reason to believe that, sorry to put this so bluntly my dear, well I believe he was murdered.' He heard a little gasp from Kathie at the other end of the phone.

'I know,' she said, 'so do I.'

Bernie was looking at his calendar on his laptop as he spoke. 'What about next week, say Thursday morning, after ten?'

'That's fine. I look forward to seeing you. Come to the house.'

CHAPTER TWENTY-SIX

Confession time

It was gone nine o'clock at night when Beverley came home after a long day's rehearsal, to find Chris sprawled in an armchair, drink in hand and a half empty bottle of vodka on the coffee table. He had been desperately trying to obscure the images of Max's funeral the previous day.

'Hello, love, she said, switching on the light. 'What are you doing sitting here in the dark?'

There was no reply.

She sat down in a chair opposite him, kicking off her shoes. 'Chris, you look terrible! And that's not a good idea is it?' She pointed to the drink.

Chris looked a very sorry sight; pale, unshaven, with red, swollen eyes.

Beverley was alarmed to notice that his hand was shaking slightly.

'What's wrong, sweetheart?', she asked, leaning across to take his hand.

'Bev, I can't do this anymore, I just can't. Max was the last straw. I loved him all the world - he was my best friend, my blood brother. It's all my fault, Bev, it's all my fault.'

He put down his drink and, putting his head in his hands, he let out a wail and began to weep, sobbing loudly.

Beverley kneeled down in front of him.

'Chris, what's your fault? What's wrong? Tell me please. You're freaking me out!'

'It's my fault he died! He didn't kill himself, Bev.'

'What do you mean - you had a fight?'

'No, no, course not. Nothing like that.' Chris reached for a tissue on the table and wiped his eyes. 'Bev, I don't know where to start, darling. My life is a total mess. If it weren't for you, I'd top myself.'

'Don't you dare say that, Chris, just don't! It can't be as bad as all that. Just tell me, for Heaven's sake!'

'I will, Bev, but promise you won't leave me when I do. There are things I hoped you would never have to hear.'

Beverley by this time was becoming really concerned. She steeled herself to hear what he had to say. 'Calm down, love, and take your time,' she encouraged.

'When I met you Beverley, my life changed. I got dried out, my game improved, we were so happy. I love you so much, you know that.'

'I know, of course I know, and I love you too.'

'Then ... then, poor little Jack.' He started to cry again.

Tears sprung into Beverley's eyes. The pain, the terrible heartache, was never far away.

Chris wiped his eyes and took a deep breath. 'I went downhill, lost my mojo, got into all sorts of trouble and my game suffered. Everyone blamed me for the team's bad season. Well, I don't need to tell you how I was. I'll never get over losing our lovely little boy. Anyway, you and me nearly broke up over it all, didn't we? It was a really bad time. I was convinced you were going to leave me. Anyway,' he braced himself for what he had to confess to next, 'do you remember when I went to Belgium for a match that year?'

Beverley nodded. 'Of course.'

'I was so depressed, I got hammered. Well, we all did. To cut a long story short, a few of us went to Angel's room with some girls who'd latched onto us. I didn't want to know, honest, but this little tart followed me to my room.'

Beverley stiffened. She was looking at him aghast, her hand to her mouth, already picturing the scene.

'I don't remember too much about it. Like I said, I'd had a lot to drink, but we ended up in bed. When I woke up, she had gone.'

'But you must remember if you shagged her or not!', Beverley shouted angrily.

'Yes, I did, but it was nothing, just a meaningless quickie, and I wasn't myself. I was so depressed.'

354

'That's what everyone says. *It didn't mean anything*! Of course it meant something. It meant you cheated on me, your wife, and had sex with someone else, that's what it meant!' Beverley was incensed and shocked to the core. 'How could you do it, after everything we've been through?'

'Don't be angry Bev. It was a one off, and never, never will happen again. I am so sorry, darling. I was a king size, stupid, downright twat! I've regretted it ever since.'

Beverley sat, her head in her hands, tears beginning to fall. Chris steeled himself to continue.

'But that's not the worst bit! Rick got sent some photos of me and this girl. Christ knows how that happened! I didn't hear or see anyone.'

'Not surprising, seeing you were banging her at the time!'

Chris looked away from her in shame. 'Then, some French geezer phoned him and said they wanted a hundred grand, or they would go to the police and newspapers. They said she was fifteen, but I don't believe it.'

'A hundred grand? Good grief, where did you get the money from. I can't believe what I'm hearing,' she sobbed.

'I didn't! That's the whole point. I didn't have anything like it at that time. I'd lost a lot on gambling -

well you know. But, out of the blue, George Wallis contacted me and offered to bail me out.'

'George Wallis? Why would he do that? He's not even your manager.'

'He and his old man's contacts needed someone to help fix matches, and he said if I would help him on a couple of occasions - that's what he said, only a couple, the lying shit - he said they would pay the blackmailers - not the full amount, but enough to satisfy them, apparently. He said Billy's contacts knew who the French gang were and would put the frighteners on them - you know, threaten to expose them, or beat them up. Who knows?'

'So, have you helped fix matches?'

Chris hung his head. 'I had to. But I'm not doing it any more. I've made up my mind, and they can do what they like to me. I've paid my dues as far as I'm concerned.'

'But what has this got to do with Max?'

'It's a nightmare, Bev. Max overheard George on the phone, fixing a meeting with me before the match with Rangers, and he only bloody well followed George in a rented car to the house where we met!'

Chris had to smile through his tears. 'Can you believe it? It was Ray Stafford's gaff - he's one of the top refs. He's as bent as a corkscrew himself. He takes bungers from all and sundry. Strange how no-one questions why he's got a mansion getting on for a million quid - and a place in France. And I'm bloody sure no-one knows about his tax free Swiss account! I feel sorry for the fans, you know, poor buggers. We spend more on drink than they earn in a week. That bastard gives penalties when he shouldn't, totally ignores blatant fouls - and have you ever noticed how much extra time he gives to a certain losing side, for no reason whatsoever?'

'Can't say I have,' replied Beverley, drily.

'Anyway, then Max tailed **me** and called me on his mobile and told me to pull over. He caught me on the hop, and I confessed everything to him. In a way it was a huge relief to get it off my chest. He knew about the fixing anyway. He was always a smart cookie. He told me he was quitting the game and then he was going to do a big exposé to the press - with the help of Bernie Cummings.'

Beverley was sitting with her mouth open, gawping at Chris while he regaled her with this tirade of information. 'So, you still haven't told me about Max - how he died I mean.'

'That's it, Bev. I don't bloody know, but I do know he didn't do it himself. Someone has done him in, that's for sure!'

'God, that's terrible.' 'Poor Kathie. Does she know any of this?'

Beverley was so shocked and upset, she even managed to overlook Chris's infidelity for a while.

'No, but she will do. I've done a lot of thinking lately, and I've made up my mind what to do. I owe it to Max. He'd still be alive if it wasn't for me.'

'You don't know that, Chris. If he was already on to George, he would have gone ahead and done what he wanted to do anyway.'

'Probably, but when he found out about my blackmailing episode, he really got the bit between the teeth. Anyway, I'm quitting the game myself, Bev. I mean it. I'm going to take up where Max left off. I'm going to speak to Bernie and Kathie and blow everything sky high, just what Max would have wanted.'

'But, you'll be putting **yourself** in danger then!', Beverley exclaimed.

'That's a risk I'll have to take. They can't kill all of us, can they! We'll have to play it carefully. What we need to know is, who's behind all this? If some thug did away with Max, he had to be working for someone. Someone with power, and money!'

Beverley was devastated as she listened to Chris's revelations. The past year had been a testing time for both of them, and yes, they had drifted apart for a while. Her acting career had taken off and she had thrown herself a hundred percent into it. Now she wondered if she had not been there for Chris, not seen the signs, or not wanting to see them! Suddenly, she felt pangs of guilt herself.

'Do you want to hear something really ironic, Chris? I came home tonight, full of the joys of Spring. Couldn't wait to tell you my news!'

'What's that then?', Chris asked, blowing his nose.

'I've been offered to audition for a part in a film - in the USA! It's not a huge part, but it's a good one, and the movie is going to be a blockbuster apparently. A famous actor has the leading part. Not sure who yet. Could even be Brad Pitt for all I know! My agent called me this afternoon. I have to be auditioned, of course, but she says they are really keen to have me.'

'Bev, that's brilliant. Congratulations! But what about the Soap? Do you think they'll let you do it - you know, you've got a contract I mean.'

'I know, that's the fly in the ointment. But I can't turn down a movie, can I? We're talking about global cinema - not an English TV Soap! I'll talk to my producer tomorrow. They can always write me out for six months if need be.'

'Is that how long it'll take? Blimey. You'll have to be in the States for six months?'

'No, Chris. **We** will be. I was wondering how on earth you would take it, but after this little lot, if you do quit football, it would be perfect for you to get away.

Don't you see? Perhaps you could do some coaching, or something? I don't know. That's if I decide to forgive you for the Belgium thing, that is!'

Quite unexpectedly, Chris could see a glimmer of light at the end of his very long, dark tunnel.

'Please, Bev. It's over and done with. I've been punished enough, believe me. I promise that I will never let you down again. I know we can make a real go of it!'

'We'll see!'

CHAPTER TWENTY-SEVEN

Promising liaisons

Kathie showed Bernie into the kitchen. He looked around and gave a low whistle of admiration.

'Wow, this is beautiful.'

'Thanks. Please sit down. 'Would you like some coffee?'

'Love one. Black, no sugar please.'

Kathie was filling the coffee machine, when Margaret walked in.

'Oh, mum, this is Bernie - I told you about him - and this is Margaret, my mother.'

Bernie stood up. 'I can see where Kathie gets her good looks,' he said, shaking Margaret warmly by the hand, holding on to it rather longer than necessary, Kathie observed.

'Pleased to meet you,' Margaret said, returning Bernie's appreciative look. 'Sit down, Kathie. I'll make the coffee and leave you two to get on with it - whatever that is.'

Kathie looked at Bernie and raised her eyebrows, trying to suppress a grin.

Bernie's eyes were following Margaret as she left the room. When she had gone, he winked at Kathie.

'Your mother's really something!', he said.

'I know, she's amazing!' Kathie nodded. 'She's staying with me for a while, which is really lovely. I don't know how I'd have got through all this without her.'

'Your father died when you were quite young, didn't he?'

'Yes, I was eleven.'

'I'm surprised she never married again - I mean, she was so young when she lost her husband. And she's a lovely looking woman.'

'I know, but she's never looked at another man. She loved my dad so much. We both did. He was a wonderful man, Irish as they come. Mum says I'm the image of him - that's where I get my colouring from!'

'Lucky you! It's gorgeous.'

'Are you married, Bernie?'

'I was, but divorced now. Veronica is a big cheese for a fashion magazine. We met at uni. Unfortunately, our careers got in the way in the end.'

'Do you have any children?'

'Sadly, no. Sore point! I always wanted a family, but Vonnie thought otherwise.

Kathie noticed his despondent look, so didn't pursue that line of conversation. 'More coffee?', she offered.

'No, I'm fine thanks. 'Guess we'd better get down to business.'

'Good idea. You said you know something. I'm intrigued.' Kathie sipped her coffee and looked at Bernie expectantly, anxious to hear what he had to say.

'Kathie, what I have to tell you will come as a bit of a shock. I don't want to upset you - God knows you're going through enough already.'

'That's okay, I can handle it. All I care about right now is what really happened to my Max.'

'Well, I'm with you there! That's why I'm doing this. Not just the reporter in me - which is how I started out - but I loved Max - really. He was a good man, one of the most genuine people I've ever met, and his talent! Well - he was a modern day one-off wasn't he. We've had a few over the years. Stanley Matthews, Bobby Charlton, Georgie Best - you'll have heard of them!'

Kathie nodded. 'Of course.'

'Then along came David Beckham, who's still a mega celebrity even though he doesn't play anymore. He did for football what Mohammed Ali did for boxing, in my opinion. If Beckham's on the red carpet, he gets more attention than Tom Cruise! So when your Max arrived on the scene, it was like football had been reborn! I've covered loads of Rangers' matches and met Max quite a few times. We became friends actually.' Bernie paused, obviously getting a little emotional. He shook his head. 'I still can't believe it! Anyway, to get to the point. This is all very confidential, and very sensitive. I'm afraid I have to ask you to promise you won't breathe a word to anyone about this conversation - or even that we've met. For now, anyway.'

'Of course,' Kathie said, 'I understand.'

'It concerns Chris Faraday, among others.'

'I might have known! He's always been a pain in the proverbial - nothing but trouble. I don't know why Max thought so much of him!'

'They were boyhood friends, Kathie. Chris isn't such a bad lad - he just went the way a lot of young players go these days. The money they get is preposterous. They just can't handle it. Chris is a really good player, but his private life has been shambolic sometimes. That business when his little boy drowned was tragic.'

'I know, it was so sad. I can't imagine what I'd do if anything like that happened to Becky.'

'Well, to cut a long story short, Max came to see me before the match against Stampford a few weeks back. He told me that he knew Chris was somehow mixed up with George Wallis. He was really concerned about Chris, who was in a right old state apparently. Wallis had somehow managed to pay off some French low lives who were blackmailing Chris.'

Kathie was wide eyed. 'What for?'

'Well, he had been photographed in let's say a compromising position, to put it politely, with an

364

underaged girl in Belgium, and Rick got a phone call demanding a hundred grand. Personally, I think it stinks! Chris had been set up, good and proper, but I can't help wondering if it was an ingenious plan by Billy Wallis's conglomerate. It's no secret that George's father is not exactly squeaky clean.'

'Good grief!' Kathie was hanging on every word. All this was shocking news to her.

Bernie continued. 'There's huge money at stake for professional gamblers, and they stand to make thousands - shed loads! Trouble is, they don't like losing, and it's worth paying someone like Chris, or a referee, or even a manager, to make sure the team they have backed wins - or loses - whatever. Not just football - the horses, dogs, boxing, you name it. Even athletics has been called in to question lately regarding performance enhancing drugs.'

'I know, it's outrageous!', Kathie said.

'Tell me about it! Even a snooker player recently got struck off because he colluded to fix games to skin the bookies. I won't go into details, but Max had good reason to suspect that George was up to something, and he got a confession out of Chris, who told him all about the blackmail, etcetera. He owned up to having to fix the Rangers/Stampford match the following Saturday.'

Kathie gasped.

'I don't suppose you watched the match, Kathie, but Chris caused a clear penalty with minutes to go, and Rangers won.'

'Sorry, no, but I do remember Max talking about it. I rarely watch football on TV, I'm always so busy, but I did go to watch him sometimes, when Rangers were playing at home. That's where he proposed to me - what a surprise that was!'

'So, that's where I'm up to. It's a bit of a coincidence, don't you think? Soon after Max refuses to be transferred to an Italian club, accuses George of duplicity and threatens to go to the press, he is found dead in suspicious circumstances. And that's without the Chris factor.'

'Oh my God!' Kathie began to cry. 'I knew it, I knew it. But how on earth will we ever be able to prove it?'

'It won't be easy, that's for sure. I'm surprised the police haven't investigated this case with a fine toothed comb. I mean, this lack of evidence crap. How long were they in the house after the incident?'

'A few days. We stayed with my friend, Melanie. She was with me the night we found Max.'

'And what about the CC system? If someone did get in the house, it would be recorded wouldn't it?'

'Yes, but the detective took the tape - for forensic purposes he said.'

'So, you never saw it?'

'No. He called me to say there was nothing untoward on it. I still haven't had that back, by the way.'

'Do me a favour, Kathie. Get on to - do you know his name?'

'D.I. Hackett.'

'Good, get on to him and make sure you get that tape back asap. We can go through it, frame by frame, and see if they missed anything. Just a long shot.'

'Yes, that's an idea! I just can't sit back and do nothing. Anything's worth a try.'

'Meanwhile,' Bernie continued, 'I aim to do a feature article in my Sunday column, hinting that some sort of skullduggery might be behind Max's unexplained death. That should stir things up a bit. Might even flush out the perpetrators. You never know!'

'But, Bernie, isn't that dangerous? You'll be asking for trouble. Whoever it was might come after you! I don't think I can handle another - well you know!'

Bernie shrugged. 'Don't worry. I'll have to watch my back!' He checked his watch. 'I'd better be going, but we'll speak soon. If you can think of anything, anything at all, please call me.'

'I will, of course. There is one thing I meant to mention, not sure if it's important, but when Mel and I came in that night, the TV was still on. Max had been watching football highlights, and had paused it. And there was a bottle of lager on the table by his chair - still had over a half still in it.'

'What!! First I've heard of it. What did the police say?'

'Nothing really. The detective said people did the most weird things when they were depressed. Max may have gone to the loo and forgotten about the TV.'

'That's bullshit! Sorry! But Max wasn't depressed, was he?'

'Of course not, I told them that, over and over again. They didn't want to know.'

'Kathie, that's brilliant! Now we have at least a small thread of something to go on.' Bernie got up to leave.

Kathie called out to Margaret, 'mum, Bernie's off now.'

Margaret put down her magazine and came into the kitchen. 'I'll show him out, Kathie,' she said, smiling at Bernie.

When they reached the front door, she said, 'thanks so much for coming. We really appreciate what you're doing - Kathie and me. It's been so nice to meet you.'

Bernie took her hand once more, holding it gently.

'It's my pleasure. I've enjoyed meeting you both. I'll see you again soon. Look after her.'

Margaret smiled and nodded, as she closed the door behind him. She turned to face Kathie, who was standing a few yards down the hallway, a grin on her face.

'What?' Margaret gave a little sniff, which Kathie knew was a sign that she was a tad embarrassed.

'You fancy him!'

'Don't be ridiculous! But I have to say, he's not what I expected. You said he was scruffy.'

'Well he was when I saw him at the funeral. He scrubs up well though, must admit! Quite a good looking chap - and around your age too.'

'Behave! Away with you girl.' Margaret followed Kathie into the kitchen with a smile on her face.

'Now, what do you have in mind for lunch?'

CHAPTER TWENTY-EIGHT

Collusion

Chris stood looking down at the phone on the hall table. Finally, he picked up the receiver and dialled a number. He heard the ringing tone at the other end for a few moments, then he quickly put the receiver down. He took a deep breath, picked it up and dialled again. This time he waited until he heard the answerphone click in.

'Oh shit!', he muttered under his breath. He didn't want to leave a message, no way! He'd heard enough about phone tapping and recorded messages being used for all sorts of reasons. He walked into the TV lounge and sat down.

He was flicking through the hundreds of channels, when he heard the phone ring. He looked over at the handset on a small table near the window. Whoever it was, could wait. Probably for Bev anyway. The phone continued to ring. He heard Beverley's voicemail message, then, 'Hello, this is Bernie Cummings. You called this number ....'

Chris leaped to his feet and grabbed the phone before Bernie could continue.

'Bernie, it's Chris Faraday.'

'Chris! What can I do for you?'

'I need to talk to you, urgently. Not over the phone though.'

'I see. Where would you like to meet?'

'I don't know, it's difficult. You got any ideas?' Chris was feeling nervous. He could feel his heart beginning to pound, now that he had taken the first step.

'My house? Your house? Somewhere in between?'

'No, no. I can't be seen with you - anywhere.'

'I understand! Leave it with me, I might have the answer. I'll get back to you shortly.' Bernie grinned broadly and thumped his desk. He had a good idea what this was all about. He made a call straight away.

Chris had broken out in a cold sweat. He wiped his clammy hands down his jumper. He was nervous, afraid even, but somehow relieved. He had done it!

Less than ten minutes later, Bernie phoned him back. 'Got the answer. We can meet at Kathie's house?'

'Kathie's?'

'Yes. She's having a few visitors, naturally after she's lost her husband, so, if anyone makes it their business to see either of us there, what can they deduct from that? You're his best mate, and I'm a friendly sports writer. We go back quite a way.'

'Shame she's not Jewish - you know they have those Sitting Shivers don't they - go on for ages. I've been to one myself. But I'm not exactly her favourite person, Bernie. You sure she's okay with me coming there?'

Bernie tutted. 'Of course! It's the best I could come up with anyway. You got any better ideas?'

'No, s'pose not. When?'

'I've spoken to Kathie and next Monday looks OK. I've checked your schedule with your Club Secretary, and you are free too.'

'Cor, you don't hang about do you!', exclaimed Chris. 'Who are you, Bernie the Bolt?'

'Oh, I haven't heard that one before! I'd have thought that was before your time! Well, I can't afford to waste time in my business - so, see you next week then. I've made it 11.30 am - I know you've got quite a drive from London.'

'Thanks a lot. I'll be there.'

Chris was up, ready to go, at 7am the following Monday. Beverley looked at him in surprise. 'Get you! What are you up to?'

'Bev, I'm going to meet Bernie Cummings.'

'You never said.'

'I know, I wasn't sure I wouldn't bottle it! But remember I told you I was going to make a clean breast of everything?   Well, I am, and he's the man. If he can't help, no-one can.'

'Chris, are you sure you know what you're getting in to? It sounds dodgy to me.'

'You don't have to tell me that! We're meeting at a safe house - I can't say where yet.' He grinned. 'Or I might have to kill you!'

'Don't even joke about it Chris. It's not funny. I'm worrying already.'

Chris gave her a big hug and a kiss. 'Don't worry, darling. I'm doing the right thing at last. Wipe the slate clean and start all over again. It will be great, I promise you, especially if you land that movie part! Imagine it - my wife on the big screen!'

'Well, don't count your chickens. Am I allowed to know which part of the country you are going to for this clandestine meeting?'

'No, love - but it's quite a hike, so I'm going to get on the road. I'll grab some breakfast at a service station.' He kissed her goodbye, picked up his car keys, and was gone.

Shortly before 11.30 am, Chris pulled up outside the familiar gates, hopped out and keyed in the security code. The gates remained shut. He tried again, but they still didn't open. He pressed the buzzer. Kathie answered.

'Kathie, it's me, Chris. The gates wouldn't open.'

'I know, I've had the combination changed.'

'Oh, okay. Will you let me in then?'

'Course!'

The huge gates began to swing silently open.

Chris drove his Aston Martin, the last remaining vestige of his affluent lifestyle, down the long drive. He pulled up alongside a Volvo Estate, which he guessed belonged to Bernie.

Once inside, Kathie showed him into Max's study, where Bernie was already seated. They shook hands and Bernie pointed to a chair.

'Glad you made it, Chris. We wondered if you would change your mind.'

As he sat, Chris noticed that there was a pot of coffee on the table, with three mugs and some biscuits. Kathie sat down in the Chesterfield leather swivel chair behind the huge mahogany desk.

Chris looked at Bernie in surprise, then at Kathie. 'Sorry, Kathie, not being rude, but this is a confidential meeting.'

Bernie leaned over and put his hand on Chris's arm. 'She knows everything, Chris. We wouldn't be here otherwise.'

Chris looked from one to the other. 'What? I don't follow.'

Bernie explained. 'You see, Chris, we're aware of your predicament. We know all about the young girl and the match fixing. It's clear you were stitched up, my friend, and we know what you've been up to.'

'What - you mean, was it Max ....?

Bernie nodded.

'Jesus, what a bloody nightmare! Why did he have to get involved? I never wanted him to know any of it. I'm so ashamed, but I was scared shitless. Can't believe I've been such a gutless idiot!'

'You're only human, Chris. We all make mistakes,' Bernie said.

'I made one stupid mistake - well one disastrous one amongst quite a few - and they've nailed me to the wall ever since. When Max died, that was the final straw for me. I know you don't have a very high opinion of me, Kathie, but I loved Max like a brother. He was an absolute diamond; my only true friend. I'd never do anything to endanger his life, believe me!'

'I do know that,' Kathie assured him. 'And so did Max', she said kindly, as she saw Chris's eyes begin to fill with tears.

'I miss him so much,' he said, 'there'll never be anyone like him.'

Kathie poured them all some coffee. Chris took a sip from his cup, wishing it was a large brandy, but grateful for a moment's respite.

'So, what's on your mind, Chris?', Bernie asked. He glanced across at Kathie who was staring intently at Chris.

Chris blew his nose and took a deep breath. 'My life has been one disaster after another. My own fault, I know that, most of the time anyway, but, what with the blackmail episode, then Jack, and now Max. It's just too much, too much! I just can't take any more, simple as that!' His voice was breaking with emotion.

The other two were silent. Chris was such a pathetic sight. He was evidently in a bad way.

'Go on,' Bernie said softly. 'You didn't come all this way just to tell me that.'

'No, you're right. I want to fess up, let the whole bloody world know what happened to me - why I'm quitting. I want everyone to know that it's my fault Max died. Not directly of course, but he got involved in it all and tried to help me. I know he was going to ask you to do an article on corruption in the game. I think he threatened George and then he got silenced - big time!'

Bernie and Kathie exchanged glances.

'Chris, Max did talk to me,' Bernie explained. 'He told me about his suspicions, but I sussed he wasn't ready to divulge the truth and nothing but. He had to be careful, I understood that. Upshot was, I agreed that after he'd definitely quit, we'd get together and I would write a bit of a blockbuster. Controversial, but not libelous, of course! Enough journalistic power of suggestion to make a few arses twitch! Give an unsuspecting and naive public a taste of what really goes on. Especially the fans! They deserve more. Max did let on about the game against Stampford, though.

It was obvious to all and sundry that you committed that foul on purpose, by the way.'

'Don't remind me.' Chris shook his head, remembering that terrible day. He had felt he was the biggest lowlife in the world! 'I got slaughtered by Rick and the rest of the team afterwards! Nearly led to a punch up between me and our keeper. Have you seen the size of him? He's even bigger close up! Well, anyway,' he went on, 'not long after Max cornered me and told me about his bust up with George, he was found dead. It don't take a genius to work out why, does it!'

Kathie burst out, 'Exactly! I know he didn't kill himself, Chris. Bernie thinks the same.'

Bernie took a tape recorder from his brief case.

'I need to get this all down, Chris. Don't worry, I'll keep the tape in the safe in my office, in my house. I propose to do that article soon. We'll see where that takes us. My guess is that it might entice a few worms out of the woodwork. In the meantime, with Kathie's help, I'm going to go over everything surrounding Max's death, and see if we can find anything the police might have missed - accidentally on purpose probably!'

Chris's face brightened up. 'I'll do anything I can to help, Bernie, and you of course, Kathie. Look, this is strictly confidential too, but Bev is in the running for a part in a movie. Well, she's got an audition, and her agent really thinks she'll get it. If she does, we will be in the States for six months, out of the way! Maybe even move there, who knows?'

'That's wonderful, Chris,' Kathie said, sincerely. 'I do hope she gets it. She's so talented, and she's really good in Town and Out.'

Bernie was amused. He'd never watched a 'Soap' in his life, couldn't see the point, but he was aware how popular they were and he knew that Beverley was a famous television actress.

Chris drove through the open gates to head home, feeling elated.   He sensed a huge burden was beginning to be lifted off his shoulders and he could see a brighter future for him and Bev at last.   He checked the road before pulling out. Looking to the left he noticed a large black saloon, parked some twenty yards away, outside the gates of a house, on the opposite side of the road. He sat there for a minute, studying the car. All the magnificent houses in this exclusive cul de sac were owned by seriously wealthy people - bankers, brokers, actors, sports people and a well known politician. Each magnificent property was protected by electronic gates and a security entry system, fronting a huge drive with space to park half a dozen vehicles.   A parked car in the road was rarely seen, except maybe a delivery van, waiting to be let through the gates.

The executive saloon's dark tinted windows prevented Chris from seeing if there was anyone inside. 'Strange,' he thought, but it didn't seem the kind of car a burglar would use; it looked like a BMW. And it was the middle of the day. He checked to his right again and pulled out, thinking no more about it. He couldn't wait to get home. Maybe he could find a nice florist and buy Bev a huge bouquet!

Two men, one of Mediterranean appearance, the other, smaller, Eastern European, were sitting in the car watching Chris' car pull out. The larger of the two was speaking into the car phone. 'Yes, he's still in the house, but the player, what you call him, Faraday? - he just left.'

A voice at the other end said, 'okay, when he does come out, let me know where he goes. Keep a close tail on him.'

It was another half hour before Bernie left Rangers Lodge. Kathie had made some fresh coffee, and Margaret had joined them as they moved into the lounge. 'How did it go?', she asked.

'I think we are making some progress,' Bernie replied. 'Quite a turn up with Chris, though. Can't believe our luck!'

He smiled at Margaret as she took a seat near him. 'You're looking very glamorous today, if I may say so,' he said.

'Thanks,' she replied, casting a quick look at Kathie, 'not sure about that!'

Kathie was grinning. She was amused to see Margaret had made a special effort with her hair and makeup, and was wearing one of her favourite dresses, which flattered her trim figure. Kathie was pleased. Bernie was a really nice man, and she hoped that something might come of this mutual appreciation society!

CHAPTER TWENTY-NINE

The article

Back in his office, Bernie read through the article he had written:

HOW DID MAX RAWLINGS REALLY DIE?

"The mystery surrounding the tragic death of Max Rawlings is no nearer being solved. Police appear to be satisfied that it was suicide, due to lack of evidence proving otherwise. The Coroner's verdict endorsed this. I for one cannot, do not, believe that this young man took his own life.

Along with millions of his fans all over the world, I learned of Max Rawlings' death with feelings of shock, deep sadness and loss.

Shock, because he died long before his time. He was just twenty-nine, a brilliant player at the top of his game and adored by his family and millions of fans. He was a truly remarkable ambassador of our national game, and a credit to us all. He had everything to live for.

Sadness, because of how unbelievably painful it must be for his family. Their grief and sorrow is compounded by doubt and suspicion. My heart goes out to them. There will be no hope of closure for his wife and parents until they know, without a shadow of doubt, how Max really left this world.

Loss, because I doubt that, in my lifetime, I will ever see the like of this talented player again. More than that, I counted Max as a friend.

Those who knew Max intimately are convinced that he would never have taken his own life. We must ask ourselves, why would a young, talented footballer, at the height of his career, with an enviable millionaire lifestyle, suddenly decide to end it all, leaving a beautiful wife and daughter? Nor did he leave a suicide note. It just doesn't add up!

Another factor is shortly before his death, Max was enjoying a beer, watching match highlights on TV. When his wife, Kathie, and her friend Melanie Peguy, returned from an evening out, in the early hours of the morning, the television was still on, having been put on hold! A half drunken bottle of lager stood on the table.

So, what happened to make Max put the TV on hold and get up? Did he decide to go and get a snack? Did he go to the toilet? Did he have to answer the telephone?

Whatever the reason, did he then take it into his head to suddenly go into the garage and end it all? I find that very unlikely. Or could it be that someone buzzed to open the electronic gates at the end of the drive?

If the last option is true, Max must have known the person, yet there is nothing on the tape taken from the Closed Circuit Television system to indicate that anyone entered the house at that time. Is it possible that the system was tampered with? If so, by whom? Not the intruder, surely, as such a technical task would need an expert, with special equipment installed in their workplace.

I realise the implications of making my thoughts and observations public, but I qualify my actions, as I can reveal that I have been made aware of certain facts that the police seem to have conveniently 'overlooked'. Shocking revelations came to my knowledge from Max himself, shortly before he died, corroborated recently from another reliable source. This crucial information leads me to wonder whether Max's sudden death is as a consequence of his threats to expose those involved.

Max had discovered evidence of corruption involving certain influential people in Premier League football, who were benefitting hugely. He had threatened to expose them through the press. When he came to me with the proposition, I agreed that I would be more than happy to cooperate.

The police have simply put down my account of this as conjecture or hearsay, with no hard evidence. Lack *of proof has determined the verdict of suicide and the case is consequently closed.*

I find this wholly unacceptable! I will continue my crusade to get to the truth, which, hopefully, will eventually come to light for all to see."

Bernie sat back in his chair and re-read his article. 'That aint half bad at all, Bernie old boy! Let's hope it has the desired effect! Shit or bust! The worst that can happen is they bump me off too!'

He wondered how it would go down with his editor. Fortunately he loved the piece. Controversial and sure to sell many more papers! He gave the thumbs up and it went to press.

Along with several other interested parties, and thousands of football lovers up and down the country, George Wallis couldn't believe what he was reading in his Sunday newspaper.

'God alive! Is that man completely fucking bonkers, or has he got a death wish? I just don't believe this load of bollocks!'

Minutes later his phone rang. It was the first of a dozen calls. Marcus was the first, followed by Ray Stafford, the referee, and then Costas and some of the Rangers' players. Costas was spluttering with rage.

George did his level best to calm him down and reassure him that it was a storm in a teacup, knowing full well that tomorrow's dailies would also be carrying the story.

'Costas, I haven't got the slightest idea who his reliable source is. For all I know he's making it all up for sensationalism and to sell more copies of that rag he works for! You know yourself how unscrupulous reporters are!'

'He's more than a mere reporter, George, as well you know! He's a famous media correspondent and TV pundit. He'll be shooting his mouth off on breakfast television before we know it! I want you to get hold of him and find out what he knows!' He slammed down the phone.

'Yeah, like he's going to tell me!', scowled George, putting his phone down. He looked out of the window and spotted a couple of reporters. By midday, a full complement of paparazzi and television cameras were camped outside for the duration. Experience told him that he had no option but to face them and get it over with, so he drafted a brief statement. He finished the whisky he had been drinking and took a deep breath.

He opened the door to a barrage of blinding flashes and approached the milling throng. Ignoring the chorus of questions being thrown at him, he held up his hands and began, in a loud voice:

'Good afternoon, ladies and gentlemen. I wish to state how shocked and saddened we are at the loss of

Max Rawlings. As far as I am concerned, until proved otherwise, there was no foul play involved with his tragic death and I know no more than you do. It's very, very sad and I am as devastated as the rest of the world, believe me. He was my best player, and a wonderful person - he was like a son to me.

Despite the unfounded accusations of one disillusioned, attention seeking sports writer, the facts remain that the police are satisfied with the verdict and will not take any further action. I hope you will have the decency to give Mrs. Rawlings and her family the privacy they deserve at this sad time. Good afternoon.'

He turned, went in and closed the door.

Susan was very concerned and was waiting in the hall as he came in.

'Don't worry, love,' he put his arm around her. 'It'll pass.' Despite his assurances to Costas, George had a good idea who the 'reliable source' was. 'If that little shit is responsible for this, he'll wish he'd never been born!', he swore to himself.

Bernie was delighted that his article had made the dailies, as he had hoped. As Costas had predicted, Bernie appeared for about five minutes on most of the TV news channels, and on an ITV breakfast programme. The dreadful news was on everyone's lips, not just football enthusiasts. Max had plenty of women admirers, who were really sad to hear of his death.

'It's like when Diana died!', many tearful women were commiserating with their friends.

Bernie was expecting George's call, so was not surprised when he phoned early the next morning. 'George, what can I do for you?', he said innocently.

'I think you know, Bernie - your article verges on total fiction! It's nothing more than a load of unsubstantiated crap and speculation on your part, but it seems to have caused quite a stir.'

'Thank you, I think.'

'Obviously your accusations are casting doubt over everyone connected with Max. Let me make it very clear to you that it was nothing to do with me. If I hear one word which suggests otherwise, I'll hit you with the biggest lawsuit you could imagine!'

'George, don't take me for a fool. You were at an awards dinner that night with Susan. It was on TV for Christ's sake, and the cameras picked up your ugly mug!'

'Well, there you are then!'

'It's not you I'm worried about George. It's certain people you might know.'

'If you are implying that it could be my old man, you're not as well informed as you think you are. He's in a hospice. He's got stomach cancer.'

'Oh, no! I'm sorry to hear that. I knew he was ill, but that's bad news.'

'He's known about it for over six months, but he didn't want to go public, apart from close family and his legitimate business associates. He hasn't had any contact with anyone else for months, so you can forget putting any of them in the frame. They have bigger fish to fry than worrying about some star struck player shooting his mouth off. Look, between you and me, Billy cottoned on that some of his business associates were getting into drugs, and he wanted nothing to do with it. He was getting on anyway, then he found out about the cancer, so he made that his excuse to bail out. So, take it from me, you can count out anyone to do with me or Billy. My advice is, keep your nose out. It could be bad for your health!'

'Is that a threat?'

'No, just good advice. Think on it.'

Bernie heard the phone go down at the other end. He smiled. 'He's worried!' But he knew George of old. He couldn't be ruled out, nor Billy, cancer or not! But, there were a few others who would want to do away with Max to stop him going public. He could think of a few bent refs besides Stafford, and other players, plus there was Marcus of course. He had a lot to lose if the shit hit the fan. Bernie had discovered from Freeman Agency's accounts, thanks to Rosie, that 10% of its annual income went to a certain George Wallis, a silent partner. It was easy to figure out what this was in recompense for! Two days later he received a call from Kathie.

'Bernie, I've got the tape back. I've run it through and must admit I can't find anything suspicious. I've looked at it twice!'

'Okay, I'll come over later and take a look myself, if that's okay with you.'

'Yes, fine. See you then.'

He sat back and closed his eyes. It was crazy! Someone must have got into the house, but how? Cameras covered the front and rear of the property. If the CC tape had been tampered with, who did it? Certainly not the intruder - it would have taken an expert, with sophisticated equipment, as he'd pointed out in his newspaper article. And there were no finger prints, other than Max's, Kathie's and Anna's, according to the police.

Later, in the study at Rangers Lodge, Kathie loaded the CC tape and they watched it play. There was Max leaving early in the morning en route to the home game, Anna and Becky going out and coming back in, Max returning home and, finally, Kathie going out alone in the evening, returning at 1 am with Melanie.

Bernie was as frustrated as ever.

'See, I told you,' Kathie said. She adjusted the speed to minimum and they watched it, frame by frame. After nearly an hour they were both beginning to flag.

Suddenly Bernie put his hand on Kathie's arm. 'Hold it!' he exclaimed. 'What's that in the bushes?'

Kathie peered closely at the screen. It was dark, and the outside lights threw shadows onto the gardens verging the driveway. In the shadow of a rhododendron bush was a small black shape. 'I'm not sure,' she said.

Bernie was squinting at the image, trying to focus more clearly. 'Can you blow up that frame?'

'Yes, of course.' She enlarged the image.

'It looks like a cat. Have you got a cat, Kathie?'

Kathie examined the area Bernie was pointing to. 'No, but it looks like Mrs. Beseler's black cat. She's our closest neighbour - I think she's got about three of them, but this one is a ruddy nuisance. Always pooing in our garden!'

Bernie was examining the frame again. 'Yes, you're right. Talk about a black cat in a coalhole!' He wrote down the time on the frame, 22.23. Move it on to the next frame. Look, he's suddenly disappeared - just like the Cheshire cat in Alice! Even if he'd run like a greyhound he should still be in the next frame. Keep going, Kathie.'

'I see what you mean,' Kathie said excitedly. She moved the recording on, frame by frame.

Bernie was peering closely at each one, until at frame marked 22.46 he said, 'Stop there! Look, our puss has suddenly appeared again! Where has he been

390

for - er - twenty-three minutes? I think a chunk of this tape has been removed, or erased!'

Kathie gasped. 'Oh, yes - you're right But did he go back under the bush perhaps?'

'No, look, he's facing down the drive, and in the first frame he is beginning to walk towards the house.'

'That's right! I've seen him do that before, then he goes back in the garden, round by the fountain. I think he finds mice or something there, because he sits there for ages. But, the times on the tape are consecutive aren't they! I mean, if some had been cut out, there would be a big gap, and there isn't. It looks perfectly normal.'

'No, good point, but whoever did this must be bloody good! They've somehow managed to alter the times to fit. If you gave it to the D.I. , and you haven't touched it at all until it was returned to you, then either he, or more likely someone in the police lab must have done it. Curiouser and curiouser!'

'Oh, dear God!', Kathie exclaimed. 'You mean someone's been paid to do this!'

'Absolutely! For a lot of money, I'm guessing!' Bernie was doing some calculations on his notepad.

'Let's see. The time of death by monoxide poisoning was given as eleven to eleven-thirty pm, by police forensics. If a car arrived at the gates at 10.25 and Max answered the buzzer, let's say he opened the door three minutes later at 10.28. Whoever it was must have rendered Max unconscious somehow, found the keys, carried him into the garage and put him into the Porsche. Then they had to cut the length of pipe from your hosepipe, commit their foul deed, then get out of the house and drive away. They must have opened the gates from inside of course. I take it they close automatically once the vehicle is clear of the gates?'

'Yes,' Kathie confirmed.

'So, add another couple of minutes to get in the car and clear the drive. I reckon they could have been in and out within fifteen to sixteen minutes. So …. that would all have been on the tape - the outside activity I mean, which would have to be erased of course. That would account for the missing twenty minutes when old Blackie disappeared into thin air!'

'Good grief! You're brilliant! You should have been a detective!' Kathie was patting Bernie on the back. 'But, what do we do now?'

Bernie was thinking hard. This had to be handled carefully. 'Well, we can't go storming in accusing the police, that's for sure. They'll just close ranks. Hackett might be totally innocent and unaware that it was tampered with, but if he did have something to do with it, we can't alert him, yet!'

'That's true,' Kathie agreed, 'but you know, thinking about it now, he was so adamant that none of us should touch the tape that night. I was almost hysterical at the time, didn't think anything of it, but, wouldn't it have made sense for him to have run it back to look at it there and then?'

Bernie nodded. 'It stinks, doesn't it!'

'It does! If there was anything on it, the police could have acted straight away to track down the intruders.'

'Of course. I think the first thing we do is get a copy made, with a signed receipt of date and authenticity. Then, if we do make an official complaint to the police - and we'll have to go over Hackett's head - we will always have back up. Evidence has been known to 'disappear' before now from police possession. We'll have to go to the Chief Superintendent. I know C.S. Barton. I'm pretty sure he's straight.'

'You're not giving me much confidence in our police force!' Kathie was shocked to hear Bernie's blasé comment on a senior police officer.

'There's always a rotten apple, I'm afraid my dear. I've been around too long to think all policemen are clean as the driven snow. Shocking I know, but true!'

'I think we deserve a cup of tea!', Kathie said.

'Good idea. Then I'll head off home and make a start. I'm thinking of my old mate, Ron Brownley. He was on the Herald with me back in the day. We used to drink together. I remember he was a whizz kid with computers - rubbish as a journalist though! I'll have to track him down. I know when he left the Herald he went on to be an IT consultant. If he can confirm that the tape has been tampered with, and better still, make a duplicate for us, we're in business!'

CHAPTER THIRTY

Vital evidence

Chris spent a nervous few days after Bernie's article had been published. He expected George Wallis to call him any time now and had rehearsed in his mind what he would say. He hoped when push came to shove, he would have the guts to man up and tell George where to go! Chris and Beverley had just sat down to eat dinner when the phone rang. They both looked at each other.

'You get it,' Chris said.

'What if it's George?'

'He usually calls me on my mobile.'

Beverley got up and answered the phone. 'Hi, Jenny. No, it's okay.'

Chris looked up to see Beverley with her mouth open, then smiling, then shrieking. 'Oh my God!! Really? I can't believe it! Hang on a minute.' She put her hand over the receiver and looked at Chris. 'I've got the part! In the film!' Then, back to her agent, 'Thanks so much Jenny, for all you've done. It's just wonderful isn't it? Okay, speak to you tomorrow. 'Bye for now. And thanks again.' She put the phone down and shrieked, 'Yes!'

Chris was up with his arms around Beverley. She was overcome and crying with excitement. 'Bev, that's bloody amazing! Well done! The answer to all our prayers. Let's open a bottle of fizz!'

'She's going to call me tomorrow with all the details, but she did say it would be within three to six months. Oh Chris, I'm so excited. Honestly, I can't believe it.'

They hugged and jumped up and down like a couple of players celebrating a goal, drank champagne, ate their meal and talked until the early hours, making plans for their future. Then they made love, for the first time in months. Chris had never been happier. 'I love you so much, Bev. Thanks for putting up with me!', he whispered as they drifted off to sleep.

When George did ring the following day, Chris was ready for him. 'Hi, George. How you doing?'

'Never mind me, what have you been up to?' George was obviously ruffled.

'What do you mean?', asked Chris, innocently.

'Let's cut the crap. Have you been talking to Cummings?'

'What if I have?'

'Then you're more stupid than I thought, playing a dangerous game, that's what!'

'George, listen to me. I've had it with you and your lot. I've paid my dues, and as far as I'm concerned, that's the end of it. You can do what you like, but I have made sure that if anything happens to me, my solicitor has a full statement, chapter and verse, of everything that has gone on Every sordid little detail!' This last statement came from nowhere. Chris was amazed at his own quick thinking. He made a mental note that he must call his brief first thing tomorrow morning.

George's attitude became more friendly. 'Well, not sure what you're referring to Chris, but all I'm concerned is that you don't end up in Court facing a libel charge!'

'No danger, George. It's only libel if it's not true. Anyway, I'll be in the States soon. I'm quitting as a player over here, so you won't be able to touch me. I think you've bled me dry enough anyway. Just do one! Leave me alone, now, do us both a favour.'

'Well, I wish you all the best, I'm sure. I hope things work out for you in the States.'

'Thanks, 'bye now.' Chris put the phone down and breathed a deep sigh of relief. He hoped he was off the hook, but he knew George too well to think he would was going to let this one go. Bernie's article had stung George badly, casting doubt on his supposed integrity.

'Perhaps it would be Bernie in danger now?', Chris was thinking. He was well aware that George had despised the journalist for years.   He called Bernie straight away and told him of the conversation he's just had with George. 'You've really got up his nose this time, Bernie,' he said.

'Well, that was the intention. If he's got nothing to hide, he's got nothing to worry about has he?'

'S'pose not, but he's a cunning little shit. I'm worried that I gave the game away. I didn't actually deny that I was your informant. He'll do anything to stop you going ahead with your crusade to prove Max was murdered - if he is involved I mean.'

'I know, but I'm afraid there are a few other people who wouldn't want Max to go public about corruption in the game. I'm not even convinced whoever it was intended to kill him, you know. Maybe they just wanted to frighten him off, shut him up, and it all went wrong. Think about it. It's taking a huge risk to bump off such a famous celebrity, knowing the whole world will be reading about and following it on TV news. A lot of pressure on the police too! I don't put George down as callous or stupid enough to get one of his players killed, somehow.'

'All the same, he'll be gunning for you if he thinks you're smearing his name. If not him - whoever killed Max. Just watch yourself, Bernie.'

'I will, thanks.'

'By the way, I'm coming up to Leeds in a couple of days. Max has left me something in his Will, bless him. I think I might know what it is, but I'll wait and see.

Kathie's solicitor will be at the house at 2 pm, so I'll pop round to you first and leave you a tape I've recorded, just in case anything happens to me. I've made a copy to lodge with my solicitor as well. Can't be too careful.'

'Good thinking!', Bernie agreed.

'And now the good news! Bev has got the part she was hoping for - you know in the film. We will be off to the Big Apple in a few months and I can put all this behind me, hopefully.'

'Chris, that's great news. Give my best to Beverley. I look forward to seeing you on Friday then. 'Bye for now.'

Bernie lit a cigarette and thought about his conversation with Chris. His article had got the ball rolling, without a doubt, and it seemed to be having the desired effect. He guessed there would be a few worried people right now. The discrepancy on the CC tape that he had discovered with Kathie was an added bonus. Now for plan B.

He went through an old address book, which he was still loathe to throw out, despite having everything stored digitally now. Bernie didn't trust computers! He found Ron Browning's number and dialled it. To his delight, and relief, Ron answered.

'Ron, it's Bernie! How the devil are you?'

'Not **the** Bernard Cummings surely?', Ron said, with a hint of sarcasm. He heard Bernie chuckle.

'Yup, the very same!'

'Blimey Oh Riley! Not heard from you in bloody years. Well - of course, now that you're such a big celebrity and all that!'

'Leave it out Ron! Life just flashes by doesn't it. I've been meaning to catch up with you for ages, wondering what you're up to these days. I know you went into business on your own.'

'Yeah, I did. I'm doing okay as it happens. I teach horrible teenagers part time as well, at a local college.'

'That's great! That's what I want to talk to you about actually.'

'Oh yes? What, teenagers? Surely not computer lessons. You were always bleeding hopeless!'

Bernie laughed. 'Not any better now! What it is, Ron, I need confirmation that a CC tape had been tampered with, and I would also need a duplicate.'

'I see', replied Ron, intrigued.

'But, Ron, please don't be offended, I can't emphasise enough how important this must be in the utmost confidence. My career - perhaps my life! - could depend on it. I'm not kidding!'

'Blimey! Sounds serious. Bring it over and I'll take a look.'

Bernie arranged to meet the following morning at Ron's house, which turned out to be less than an hour's drive away. The two old friends were pleased to see each other after such a long time and greeted each other warmly.

'I've followed your column for years, and often seen your mug on TV', Ron commented. 'You've done really well for yourself. Well, I always knew you would. You were a bloody good journalist even back then!'

'Yes, I've been lucky I suppose,' Bernie replied.

After going over old times and filling in the intervening years with the events of each other's lives, Bernie explained the reason for his visit.

'What a terrible thing!' Ron shook his head. 'So sad. I'm not a big football fan, but even I know Max was an amazing player, and he came over as a real smashing man. Proper genuine! He was a credit to this country, and there aren't many overpaid, moronic football players who can say that!'

'They're not all like that!', Bernie said defensively, 'but I know what you mean.'

Ron had read Bernie's recent article and was only too pleased to be able to play a small part. It was quite an exciting interlude during his otherwise humdrum day.

Bernie waited anxiously as Ron used his state of the art equipment to scrutinise the tape.

'I'm surprised that someone like Max Rawlings is using this old CC system,' Ron said as he took the tape from Bernie. 'It's all digital and memory cards now!'

'I know - even I figured that out,' Bernie replied, 'but Kathie said it was there when Max bought the house and he didn't see any reason to change it as it worked perfectly. He said it might be bad luck! Strange.'

'Typical sportsman. They've all got their little idiosyncrasies. Have you noticed that tennis player - Nadal? He has to touch everything on his head twice before he serves. I find it really amusing.'

Finally, Ron swung round in his chair and said, 'Yup, you're perfectly right! It's an expert job, I agree the moggie is the clue.' He grinned. 'The cat's out of the bag now! I won't go into detail, but it's been tampered with, deffo! Quite a serious bit of kit they've got, whoever did it. The missing footage has just been cloned in from a period when nothing was being recorded, so it looks like a continuous period of inactivity. Very clever - almost undetectable, and I might never have spotted it, except, look at the times on the bottom of each frame, there's a second missing. The timing's been reset from 10.20, but there's no 10.19. They've missed it out. Very sloppy!'

Bernie banged his fist on the table in a gesture of triumph. 'Yes! I knew it! Brilliant! Well done Ron - How come I didn't notice that? I was too interested in the moggie, I guess. I owe you one. Are you able to put that in writing for me, and make a duplicate copy? I don't want the police saying I did it. As if!'

Ron chuckled. 'They don't know you very well if they thought you could do that! Of course I can make you a copy, but it'll cost you twenty quid. I've still got a living to earn!'

'That's fine! Nothing changes does it!'

With the two tapes in his brief case, and eager to get back to his own office, Bernie shook Ron's hand warmly. 'I can't tell you how important this is, Ron. Thank you so much my friend. We'll meet up again when this is all over and I'll buy you a drink!'

'I look forward to that,' Ron said, 'it's about bleeding time! Good luck, and watch your back, mate.'

Bernie drove home singing away to the radio. Things were looking up! Time for plan C. Reaching home, he had a coffee and a quick sandwich, and then called D.I. Hackett.

'Yes, Mr. Cummings. How can I help you?'

'It's about Max Rawlings,' Bernie began.

'Oh really! I think I know everything you have to say about that particular subject, from your version, if misleading, piece in several papers!', Hackett interjected irritably. 'It amazes me that an old snoop like you is more informed than the police who investigated the unfortunate occurrence and the Coroner. You must enlighten me as to how you achieve it - one day when I've got nothing better to do!'

Bernie smiled to himself. Hackett was rattled.

'Well, that's exactly it, Inspector. I have indisputable evidence about the tape you took from the CC system.'

There was a brief silence. Bernie was enjoying the fact that Hackett was obviously taken aback by this. He wished he could see his face!

'Oh yes, and what might that be?'

'It would appear that it has actually been tampered with! I've had this verified by a computer expert. Not casting any aspersions, don't get me wrong, but it wasn't easy to spot. It took hours and hours.'

'Are you having a laugh? I can assure you that our equipment is the most sophisticated in the world. If there was anything suspicious on the recording, our technician would have certainly picked that up. The image can be magnified enormously on screen. I looked at it myself. There was nothing untoward.'

'I know that! But you would have been looking for a person, or persons, who should not have been there, wouldn't you? I'm talking about a very small thing indeed. I think you need to take a look at it.'

'I certainly will. Thank you for pointing this out. It could put a whole new complexion on things. Can you drop it round to me, or would you like me to pick it up?', Hackett asked casually.

Bernie was grinning to himself, thinking, 'pretending he doesn't care - who is he kidding?' Then aloud, 'well, I'm out tonight, but I could pop it in to you tomorrow.'

'Thanks. Make sure you give it to me personally. I don't want anyone else touching it. Keep it under lock and key overnight. Just a minute.' He looked at the calendar on his p.c. screen. 'Is ten thirty hours okay?'

'Fine. I'll see you then. It'll be safely locked in my desk drawer, don't worry. Goodbye.'

Bernie sat back in his chair and rested his chin on his crossed fingers. Hackett had sounded surprised, but not, as he'd hoped, worried, or even slightly perturbed. He was either a good actor, or totally innocent.

Either way, the first part of Bernie's plan was now in place. He sealed the duplicate tape in a plain envelope and put it in the drawer, under an A-Z of Leeds, locked the drawer and put the key in his pocket. He took down a ring binder from the bookshelf next to the door. Inside was a special camera he'd bought from a retired store detective. Once set, it reacted to any movement in front of it and took a photograph. The lens was located behind the finger hole at the front of the binder, which was marked 'Invoices'. Bernie positioned the binder directly behind his desk then stepped in front of it. He heard an almost inaudible click, grinned and gave a thumbs up sign as he left the room.

At 8 o'clock that evening Bernie left his house. As he reversed his car out into the road, he was watched by the two occupants of a black saloon car, parked in a side street opposite his road. Bernie headed off in the direction of town. He'd booked a table at his favourite Italian restaurant. After his meal, he went into a pub to kill an hour. If anyone was intending to break in his house, he didn't want to be anywhere near the place!

He arrived back home at 10.30 pm, surprised to find that there was no sign of a break in. He was part relieved, part disappointed. Walking through to the kitchen, however, he saw immediately that the back door had been jemmied open. He rushed into his office to find that the desk drawer had also been forced. The tape had gone!

Bernie quickly grabbed the file with the hidden camera and looked at the last few images. There were three photos of the back of a large man facing the desk and two, when he had turned sideways as if he'd heard something, giving a perfect profile shot of his swarthy features. Despite the damaged desk and door, Bernie was delighted. He quickly called the police to report a break in. D.I. Hackett was off duty, so a uniformed policeman arrived to take down all the details. Bernie also showed him the evidence on his hidden camera.

'May I take the camera card, sir?' the P.C. asked.

'Afraid not officer, but I can print you some copies. They will have the date and time on them. Will that do?'

'That will be fine, sir, thank you.'

Bernie took out the card and printed off a couple of copies of the photos, then handed one set to the P.C.'

'Thank you sir. We'll be in touch as soon as possible. Make sure you secure your back door and get a new lock fixed tomorrow.' He wrote down a number on his notepad, tore out the page and handed it to Bernie. 'This is a firm we use - someone will come and board up the door for you tonight.'

'Will do. Thanks officer.' He showed the P.C. out, then went to get a large brandy. Wheels were beginning to turn!

Even before Bernie had finished his drink, D.I. Hackett was making a call on his mobile phone.

'It's done!' I've got the tape and I'm going to burn it...........I don't know do I? Christ knows what he's talking about. I ran the tape through again and I still can't find anything wrong with it. He must have been bluffing, he's getting desperate! ....Yes of course I did! It was Amir who did it, one of our top I.T. guys. He hasn't got a clue either...........No, he won't. He knows better than to open his mouth. He's got a thousand reasons to keep quiet!...............Okay, don't panic. There's no evidence now. Cummings is stuffed.'

Hackett put down the phone and breathed a sigh of relief. He thought it was all over!

CHAPTER THIRTY-ONE

Caught out

Early the following morning, as soon as he'd called a locksmith and his insurance company, Bernie phoned D.I. Hackett.

'Bernie, hi! I thought I was seeing you at 10.30 this morning?' Hackett sounded surprised.

'That was the plan, but I had visitors last night.'

'So, you've got a hangover?'

'No, I've got a damaged door and desk, and no tape!'

'Good Lord! You've been burgled?'

'You're quick! Yes, I've been burgled, and funnily enough, you were the only person who knew about the tape. Quite a coincidence!'

Hackett smiled smugly. 'What are you suggesting Bernie? Surely you don't think I had anything to do with it! Are you accusing a senior police officer? Not my style to go breaking in to people's houses.'

'No, but you know a man who does. Sorry to disappoint you, Hackett, but not only have I got the original tape, I've got a photo of the man breaking into my desk. Check with your uniformed department.'

There was no response for a few moments. Hackett had gone pale, his mouth dry. He took a deep breath.

'Don't you even think about suggesting I had anything to do with it!', he shouted. 'I'll have you up for slander. You haven't got a leg to stand on, mister. Where's your evidence?'

'I'm sure your Chief Superintendent will be very interested to know that you were the only person on the planet who knew where that tape was. I recorded our conversation by the way.'

Bernie waited for a reply from the other end, but nothing was forthcoming. He was loving every minute of this, trying to imagine Hackett's face at the other end of the phone. 'Oh, and another thing,' he continued, 'in case you were thinking of arranging an encore of last night's performance, think again. The original tape is in a safe place, not in my house!'

'I've had enough of this!', Hackett shouted angrily. 'Do your worst! You can't prove a thing, because I had nothing to do with it!' He slammed down the phone.

'That should do it!', Bernie said softly. 'My little trap is set!' He now had no doubt that D.I. Hackett was in cahoots with whoever murdered Max. He must have paid a techy to fix the tape, he figured, probably someone in the police I.T. department.

He called Kathie and brought her up to speed about the visit to Ron, then the burglary and his call to Hackett.

She couldn't believe her ears.

'Oh, well done Bernie!', she exclaimed. 'I can't believe it! I can't believe the D.I. would do such a thing! It's shocking!'

'I know, but there's no doubt he's involved. Someone's paid him a huge lump. We just need to find out who. Look, I have to put the tape and photos in your safe, okay? Then I'm going to call his C.S.'

'C.S.?'

'Chief Superintendent.'

'Oh, of course! Then what?'

'Not sure. Hackett will deny, deny, till he's blue in the face. Any copper will tell you that. Unless there is concrete evidence, I don't stand a chance of pressing charges. It's my word against his. He'll just say I must have told someone else about the tape. And we all know who the police will believe, don't we!'

'But, the tape is proof that it was tampered with, and it has to be someone in the police who did it. Hackett was the one who touched it that night.'

'That's true. My guess is, he's sitting there right now trying to figure out what to do. He thinks I am going to spill my guts to his Super, and let's not forget, if the shit hits the fan, whoever is behind all this is in danger of being exposed. Can't see Hackett taking the whole rap, can you?'

'I don't know Bernie, it's all like a bad dream. I'm worried that something awful will happen to you now.'

'Don't worry, petal, I'm a big boy. How's that gorgeous mother of yours?'

'She's fine, thanks. I think she's taken a shine to you!'

Bernie raised his eyebrows and grinned from ear to ear. 'When this is all over, I'm going to take you two lovely ladies out for a slap up dinner - with champagne!'

'I look forward to that - and I know my mum will too! Anyway, I'd better go, Becky is calling me. I'll see you later today, yes?'

'Yes, see you soon.'

Margaret had been ear wigging from behind the newspaper she'd been reading. 'What was that all about? Did you tell Bernie I had taken a shine to him? For goodness sake, girl, have you lost your senses?'

Kathie laughed. 'Come on mother, you know it's true. You go all unnecessary when he's around.'

Margaret gave one of her disapproving sniffs and tutted. Kathie went over to her and bent down to kiss her head. 'You're still a very attractive woman, mum. There's nothing wrong in seeing someone of the opposite sex. You won't burn in hell!'

Margaret just shook her head and hid her smile behind the newspaper.

Bernie drove over to Kathie's and put the tape, memory card and photos in her safe, then went back to his office to catch up on his work. He hadn't even looked at his emails that day. Before that, however, there was yet one more important call to make.

Chief Superintendent Barton picked up his phone.

'Hello, Bernard! What can I do for you? Long time no hear.'

'Harry, I need to speak to you in private. Any chance we can meet?'

'What's this about Bernard? I'm a busy man.'

'I know that, but this can't wait and it's very, very sensitive. It concerns one of your officers, plus information I have regarding a recent high profile case. That's all I can say right now.'

Barton raised his eyebrows in surprise. 'One of my officers?'

'Yes. I must speak to you in person.'

Barton checked his diary. 'It'll have to be tonight. I'm not available for a few days. Conference in Halifax.'

'That's fine by me. Where do you suggest?'

'You know my address. Make it around eight.'

'Thanks, that's great. See you later. Oh, by the way, forgive me for saying this, but don't breathe a word will you.'

Barton tutted. 'Please, Bernard, it's me you're talking to!'

'Sorry, but you can probably gather I'm slightly jumpy!'

'Point taken. See you later.'

Bernie couldn't believe that had been so easy. He had known Harry Barton since he was a uniformed police sergeant, some twenty years ago. Their paths had crossed professionally several times, and they had become friends over the years. Barton and his wife had dined with Bernie and Veronica on numerous occasions.

The two men sat in Barton's study, each with a glass of his finest brandy. The Chief Superintendent was anxious to find out what Bernie had to say.

'What's this all about then, Bernard? Spill the beans.' Barton relaxed back into his chair, listening intently, as Bernie related every detail to him, right up to that morning's conversation he'd had with Hackett.

Barton looked dismayed. 'He's one of my best officers, Bernard. I can't believe he would be so bloody mindless. He's got an impeccable record.'

'I'm aware of that. I've known him for years, but the facts are there, for all to see.'

'Quite! He must be held responsible, one way or the other. He says he looked at the tape and could see nothing wrong. Is he lying? Or didn't he bother to check it out, which I find totally inconceivable. Knowing his reputation, and his excellent record, he wouldn't have been able to wait to take a look at it. If he didn't check it, he's guilty of negligence. If he did, then he's guilty of getting a third party to fix it. The whole thing is very worrying. In all my years, I've never had to deal with anything so damning. Another kick in the balls for the force when this goes public.' He looked at Bernie, his lips tightening. 'Your lot will have a field day!'

'We just want the truth, Harry. Justice for Max! That boy didn't kill himself. I'd put my own life on it.'

'You'll have to leave it with me until I get back from the conference. I'll take a formal statement from you, with a police witness, and then I'll interview Hackett. In the meantime, just keep your head down and say nothing to anyone. You've got the two items in Mrs. Rawlings' safe you say?'

'Yes.'

'That's good. Okay then. I'll give you a bell in a couple of days and we'll go from there. I'll make it my personal business, rest assured.'

'Thanks, Harry. I can't tell you what a relief it's been to get this lot off my chest.'

'I can imagine. You've done a good job, Bernard.'

Bernie got up and shook Barton's hand. 'Goodnight, and thanks again.'

'Can't say it's my pleasure! Goodnight.'

Within the hour, a shocked D.I. Hackett heard the news that Bernie Cummings had visited C.S. Barton. The driver of the black saloon had been tailing Bernie and now the caller on Hackett's mobile phone was insisting that action would have to be taken to silence the troublemaking journalist once and for all.

How on earth he'd had allowed himself to get involved in this unholy mess Hackett couldn't begin to fathom. As a senior officer with years of exemplary service, nearing retirement, he realised he must have been stone bonkers!

When he was first approached with the proposition, he was told it would be a simple kidnapping plot, to get Rawlings to keep his mouth shut. He was assured no-one would get hurt, and as long as Rawlings did as he was asked, the child would be returned unharmed. A payment equal to a year's salary was a massive temptation to Hackett, and he had allowed himself to play a small part in the plan. For the first time in his long career, he was swayed by the huge monetary reward offered him. Enough to seriously swell his retirement package! All he had to do was sort out the tape, that was all. Then it had become the unthinkable - murder - Max Rawlings of all people - and he was up to his neck in it all, big time. It was nothing short of a catastrophe!

Hackett had been home for less than an hour when he'd taken the call on his mobile phone and learned Cummings had gone to his Chief Superintendent's house. He went outside for a smoke, his hands trembling as he lit a cigarette. Clutching at straws, he reasoned it would be his word against Cummings, and surely C.S. Barton would want to protect his own officer. But that was a long shot. He saw his job, his retirement - and God, yes, his pension, in fact his whole future, going down the pan. Even worse, he could go to prison. He was terrified. With sinking heart and feeling like a cornered rat, he had to face the fact that the only solution was for Cummings to be dealt with, permanently.

He felt sick to his stomach, but what was the alternative? The final deed would not be of his doing, granted, but should his implication in Rawlings' death come to light - that would be curtains for himself. There was nothing he could do now anyway. He just had to wait it out and hope that it had all been dealt with before the Super came back from his conference.

CHAPTER THIRTY-TWO

Chris to the rescue

Chris was driving up the motorway towards Leeds, feeling happier than he had felt in years. Now he had given his 'confessions of a footballer' story to Bernie, the truth would be out at last and he would be free of the burden of guilt and worry he had been shouldering for years.

There was a new life to look forward to in the States, and he and Bev were back on track. Life was beginning to look good again. Apart from the deep sadness of losing his best pal, Max, of course. He wondered what Max had left him in his Will. Whatever it was, he would treasure it forever.

He arrived at Bernie's house mid morning, and was about to swing into the driveway when he saw a black saloon parked alongside Bernie's Volvo. He parked up kerbside and got out to walk down the short drive. He stopped and stared at the black BMW. Something was registering in his brain. A warning. Why? Suddenly, he realised what it was. He was sure it was the same car he'd seen the day he pulled out of Kathie's drive, after the meeting with her and Bernie. He rummaged through his pockets, finally finding an old betting shop biro in his top pocket. He quickly wrote the registration number down on the inside of his wrist.

As he was deciding whether to get back in his car and wait, or just go and ring the doorbell, the front door burst open. Two men rushed out and jumped in the car. Chris heard the engine start up, and saw the car begin to move off. He stood his ground, waving his hands. The car sped towards him. He tried to jump out of the way, but it was too late. The impact knocked him sideways into the flowerbed, where he lay dazed and bleeding as the car disappeared out of the drive. He groaned in agony as he looked at his left leg, which was lying in a grotesque angle to his body, obviously broken. There was a gash on the side of his head where he had hit a stone garden ornament as he crashed down and blood was dripping down his face. Supporting his thigh with his hand, he struggled to get up. He managed to get his phone out of his jacket pocket and he rang Bernie. It rang for a while and then went to voicemail. He had to somehow get to the house. The two thugs must have been up to no good - maybe even hurt Bernie, or worse! Sheer adrenalin gave Chris the strength to hop to the front door of the house, holding his left leg.

The door was locked. He rang the bell and banged furiously on the door. There was no answer. He hopped to the bay window and peered through. The room was empty. He slowly and painfully made his way around to the back of the house. He tried the kitchen door. Miraculously it was unlocked. He went in and shouted, 'Bernie - are you here mate?' There was no answer, so he made his way across the kitchen to the door leading to the hallway. As he opened it, he smelt smoke and could hear the sound of a fire coming from the small room off the hallway, which was Bernie's study. He closed the door, looking round frantically for a towel to wrap round his face. He found a tea towel near the sink, which he soaked under the tap.

'Oh my God - the fire brigade!', he shouted to himself. 'And I should've called the police straight away as well - what a moron!' Leaning on a wall for support, he took his phone from his pocket and dialled 999. He gave the address then added, 'I think someone is trapped in the fire, so please send an ambulance - and the police! Please hurry, I've broken my leg and I don't know if I can get him out on my own.'

Chris wrapped the towel around his mouth and opened the door again. The smoke was becoming thick and acrid. He hopped to the study door and touched the doorknob. It was warm, but not hot. He turned it and opened the door a few inches. The sudden blast caused by the back draught nearly knocked him over and he heard the roar of the flames increase. He grabbed the wall and hopped into the room, which was full of smoke. He could see the curtains and some of the furniture were ablaze, but there was no sign of Bernie. He got on all fours and began to crawl towards the desk, dragging his painfully broken leg with one hand. As he approached the desk, he saw two feet and then as he crawled closer, realised Bernie was lying unconscious on the floor.

Chris managed to manoeuvre himself so that he could reach Bernie's arm and began shaking him and shouting as best he could through the tea towel, 'Bernie, wake up, wake up!' He felt Bernie's pulse. He was still alive. 'Thank God!', he whispered. He crawled back to position himself at Bernie's feet and sat on the floor. He gently placed his broken left leg and positioned his right leg in a V shape, either side of Bernie's legs, grabbed both his feet and began to shuffle backwards, pulling with all his might. The pain in his leg was excruciating. The flames were getting bigger and Chris could feel the increasing heat as he inched himself and Bernie towards the open door. He was almost out of breath and exhausted as he reached the hallway with his precious cargo. With one last mighty pull, he and Bernie were free from the room. Chris leaned over and pulled the door shut, then collapsed on his back. There was a loud banging on the front door.

Through a haze of semi consciousness and exhaustion, Chris could hear loud voices shouting.

'It's locked - round the back!'

Suddenly the kitchen door was flung open and three firefighters were through the kitchen and into the hall. They immediately started to pull Chris to his feet.

'My leg! Mind my leg. It's broken,' he screamed.

'Sorry, sir. We've got to get you and your friend out of here.' The burly firefighter hoisted Chris onto his shoulder as gently as he could and carried him to safety out through the kitchen, whilst a colleague did the same with Bernie. Other firefighters already had hoses in place and began their work.

An ambulance arrived within another few minutes, followed by the police.

Lying flat on his back, Bernie was beginning to open his eyes. He looked up at the paramedic, who was kneeling over him, holding an oxygen mask to his face. He could just make out a uniformed policeman standing next to the paramedic. Chris, who was being attended to by the other paramedic, grinned at Bernie and said, 'you've just had a bad dream mate. Go back to sleep!'

Bernie gradually came to his senses. He pulled off the mask. 'Kathie!', he croaked, between coughing. 'Kathie is in danger. They know she's got them in her safe!'

'What's in the safe, sir? Who's Kathie?' The police officer took out his notebook.

'Kathie Rawlings - Max's wife. Oh, dear God. Please officer, I'll explain later, but I think Hackett probably worked it out that I've put the tape and photos in her safe. They must be on their way to her house now. You've got to act quickly!' Bernie began to cough violently and the paramedic put the oxygen mask back over his face.

Chris was looking on in horror. He suddenly realised what Bernie was saying. 'He's right officer, and I've got their reg number here. The thugs who did this to Bernie ran over me in their car, the vile scumbags!' He pulled up his sleeve. 'Look, here's the number. It's a black BMW!'

The police officer took down the number and transmitted it straightaway to his station. He quickly described the situation and warned that the two men were dangerous and possibly had guns, so armed backup would be needed. 'Well done, sir, did you get a look at them?', he asked Chris.

'Not really - it all happened so quickly, and the windscreen was tinted glass, but I don't think they were English. I don't know why, but I got the impression they were foreign. They won't be able to get through the security gates anyway, not in their car, but if they are desperate enough, I guess they could climb over.'

'Don't worry, sir, our officers will be there in no time,' the police officer assured him. 'Now, let's get you two to hospital. Well done, Mr. Faraday. You've saved your friend's life, without a doubt. That was a very brave thing to do - especially for a London club player!', he joked.

The paramedics had put Chris's broken leg in splints and given him a pain killing injection. He was now being gently lifted onto a stretcher. Bernie was already in the ambulance.

'Thanks officer. Please don't tell me, you're a Rangers fan!' Chris was wincing in pain, but managed a weak smile. 'Talk about adding insult to injury!'

'No, Man U, sorry to disappoint you!', he joked. Rangers are only second best - your lot have come on well this season though.'

Chris grimaced at the reference to Manchester United. 'Yeah! We did alright in the end. They'll have to do without me from now on, I think. Even if I wasn't leaving the country, the foot on this leg will never kick a football in anger again!'

'I'm sorry to hear that. Good luck for the future anyway.' He shook Chris's hand. 'We'll catch up with you both soon to take statements.'

Bernie was lying on the opposite bunk to Chris in the ambulance as it sped off towards the hospital. He pulled the mask to one side and turned to face Chris.

The paramedic looked concerned and made a move to replace the mask. Bernie said, 'just a minute or two, I'm okay, honestly.'

The paramedic nodded his consent.

'What can I say, Chris?' Bernie said. ' Thank you isn't ever going to be enough. You're a bloody hero, and I'll make sure the whole world knows about it when I get back to normal.'

'There's a small matter of your burned out office, mate.'

'I only need a laptop!'

'Christ, I've just thought about Bev. She hasn't got a clue about all this. I'd better give her a ring. She'll be thrilled to bits to hear I've got in more trouble, I don't think!'

'She'll just be glad you are safe and well, believe me,' Bernie assured him, as the mask was firmly replaced by his attendant.

Beverley, Kathie and Margaret sat between the two hospital beds that evening. Chris had six stitches in his head and his leg in plaster, while Bernie was superficially unscathed other than suffering from smoke inhalation. He was enjoying the attention of Margaret, who was gently stroking his hand.

Kathie looked on in amusement, then began to relate the events that had taken place at Rangers Lodge earlier in the day.

'There I was, fixing our lunch, when the phone rang, and a man saying he was Inspector Wetherill. 'We have reason to believe that you may be in danger', he said. 'Mr. Bernard Cummings has been attacked and his house set on fire and he is sure the perpetrators could be on their way to your house'. I said, 'WHAT? Is this a joke?' 'No, madam', he says, 'please make sure all your doors and windows are locked, and don't open the security gates to anyone'. As if I would! I was terrified! First thing mum and I did was make sure everything was locked, then I checked the CC camera - and then I saw a black car pull up outside the gates. Oh, my God! I felt my knees go week! This huge guy got out of his car and started pressing the button to get the gates open. Then another man got out and they began looking around - I suppose to see how they could get in. I have never been so frightened in my life! I really thought they were going to climb over! Then, thank God, I could hear sirens and three police cars screeched up. The two thugs jumped back in the car, but the police cars surrounded them. They put up a good fight, but they were outnumbered and the police put handcuffs on them and shoved each one into a separate police car. It was like something you see at the movies! I had to let one of the policemen in, and he came and took a statement. I was shaking, I can tell you. I was just grateful Becky was at school.'

Margaret put her arm around Kathie. 'Yes, it was really frightening. But thank goodness we are all safe and sound. You were very brave, Chris, by all accounts. Bernie tells me you saved his life. Can you imagine if you hadn't turned up when you did? He would have died in that fire. It doesn't bear thinking about.' She turned back to look at Bernie. 'I'm so pleased you didn't!'

'So am I as it happens!', said Bernie.

They all laughed.

'But, we still don't know who these thugs are,' said Chris. 'I've been wracking my brains to work out who's behind it all. It could be something to do with Billy Wallis of course.'

'No, he's a dying man,' Bernie said. 'Cancer! He might even have passed away for all I know. Last time I spoke to George, his dad had only weeks to live.'

'I didn't know that,' said Chris. 'Well, I won't be sending a sympathy card! But the police will certainly know who the two guys are, because they will have checked the reg number straight away.'

The others nodded in agreement.

'And they've got the photos I gave them. We should know soon,' Bernie said. 'The cops will be here any minute to take statements from us two.'

'Well, that's enough excitement for everybody for one day,' Margaret said, standing up. 'I think we should let these two brave soldiers get some rest before the police get here.'

'Yes,' agreed Beverley. She kissed Chris tenderly. 'Goodbye, darling. Well done, I'm very proud of you. 'Bye for now, see you tomorrow. Love you.'

Chris grabbed her hand. 'I love you too, Bev. You'll never know how much.'

Kathie suddenly felt very emotional and felt tears pricking her eyes. She took out her hanky and blew her nose. 'Bye you two. We'll drop in tomorrow, won't we mum?'

'Sure thing!' Margaret was nodding. 'That's if they haven't let you out by then.' She leaned over and kissed Bernie on the cheek. Kathie raised her eyebrows as Bernie winked at her - a huge smile on his face.

'Oh my goodness', she suddenly exclaimed. I haven't told you about the Will, Chris! That was what you were coming up for - until you decided to act as Superman!'

Chris opened his eyes wide. 'Of course! I'd forgotten all about that, with all the excitement.'

'Well, he left you his Harley! He knew how much you coveted it.'

'Oh, no! Oh, bless his heart!' Chris buried his head in his hands to hide the tears springing to his eyes. He looked up at Kathie. 'He must have written his Will ages ago. Who'd have thought it?'

427

Beverley quickly put her arms around him and hugged him tight. 'It's okay, love. We all feel emotional.' She was close to tears herself.

Outside in the car park the three women noticed a police car pull up in front of the entrance.

'Well, they can forget about a rest now!', tutted Margaret.

Kathie and Beverley smiled.

'Come on, mum.' Kathie was opening the car door. 'I think our two heroes are too psyched up right now to worry about resting. It's been a crazy day one way and another. I bet they'll be chin-wagging in there nine to the dozen!'

Chris and Bernie were going over the events of the past few weeks and comparing notes, when a detective and a uniformed policeman were shown into the ward by a nurse, pointing in the direction of their two beds.

The officer in plain clothes addressed them. 'Good evening gentlemen. I'm Detective Chief Inspector Goodwin, and this is P.C. Woodcock.'

Bernie and Chris said in unison, 'good evening.'

'Well,' added Chris impatiently, 'who are they? Are you going to tell us who killed Max?'

'All in good time gentlemen,' D.C.I. Goodwin replied. 'First we have to take statements from you both.'

He took a seat.

Chris tutted impatiently and raised his eyebrows.

Bernie breathed an audible sigh.

The two men answered D.C.I. Goodwin's questions and signed their statements, which the uniformed policeman had written down.

'To answer your question, yes, we have arrested the two men, but you will both have to identify them of course.' The D.C.I. addressed Chris. 'To confirm that they deliberately ran you over'. He turned to Bernie, 'and attacked you and set fire to your house.'

Both men nodded.

'One of them is well known to the Greek police.' He looked at his notebook. 'Mr. Balios Dimitri. A very fruity customer, with form for GBH. The other one is a young Croatian, Lukas Radic. He's an illegal immigrant, we've discovered. You will be interested to know that the black BMW they drove is registered in the name of Parthenon Ocean Liners.'

Bernie gasped. 'That's Papapavlou's company!'

Chris looked at Bernie. 'Yeah - Costas! Rangers' owner. Bloody hellfire! I don't believe it!'

'It's true,' D.C.I. Goodwin confirmed. 'But unfortunately, we can't question him, as he appears to be out of the country.'

'How bloody convenient!' Chris was fuming. 'If he arranged to have Max killed ..... the bastard! Well -- I wish he could bloody well hang!'

D.C.I. Goodwin stood up, ready to leave.

'Well, it's only a matter of time before we catch up with him, with the aid of the Greek police. We have an officer booked on a flight to Athens as we speak. Unfortunately for Mr. Papapavlou, Mr. Radic has made a full confession. He didn't need a lot of convincing that we had the authority to help keep him in the country legally, so he sang his heart out! He's signed a formal statement that his boss, Mr. P, gave the instructions to kidnap Max Rawlings' daughter. Apparently, Max put up a fight and pulled off Radic's balaclava, so he must have recognised his attacker. Dimitri is apparently Papapavlou's right hand men and he wasn't prepared to take the risk of Max exposing the two felons and their boss, so they made it look like suicide. Radic insists he was threatened by Dimitri and had no choice.'

'I've always had a feeling it was something that had gone badly wrong. It's an absolute tragedy. Poor Max,' Bernie said. 'But what about D.I. Hackett? What will happen to him?'

'I can't comment on that, sir, but I can tell you that he has been suspended, pending enquiries. I wouldn't like to be in his shoes, I know that!' D.C.I. Goodwin shook hands with both men, then turned to go. 'Thank you for your assistance. I'll be in touch very soon.'

The uniformed police officer stepped up to Chris's bedside, clearly thrilled to be in the presence of the famous player. He offered his hand. 'Good luck Chris - Mr. Faraday. All the best. I'd hate to think we won't be seeing you on our TV screens anymore.'

Chris shook his hand. 'What's your name?'

'Peter.'

'Thanks Peter, I appreciate that. ' Bye now.'

After the police officers had left, the two men were silent for a while, each pondering the significance of the detective's revelations.

Chris spoke first. 'Can you believe it Bernie? Can you actually believe that Costas is responsible for Max's death? It's absolutely insane! The last person in the world I'd have thought! '

'I know. I've gone over and over in my mind how Max described everything to me that day. It got me thinking. There must have been so many people who couldn't afford the truth to come out about all the corruption in the game. Take Marcus for example. He's in it up to his neck. It could ruin him. Who's going to want to have him as an agent after this lot? And then there's George of course, plus certain referees. But Costas - well, think about it, he's a high profile figure and as such he has a huge reputation to protect. His father's company is prestigious - world renowned. I guess Costas couldn't hack the possibility of it becoming public knowledge that he owns a football club with proven dodgy dealings. On top of that, he's got ex cons and illegal immigrants on the payroll! It don't get much worse than that but, who knows what else he has to hide? The shareholders in his shipping company would not be too impressed with any form of culpability, I'm thinking.'

'But murder! That's just crazy, so fucking unnecessary! They must've really panicked.'

'I know, Chris. Unbelievable. Hindsight is a wonderful thing, but I did consider it was a kidnapping plot that went wrong. Max told me it was one of their greatest fears that someone would get hold of little Becky. There had been an attempt once before, a few years ago, apparently. So, Costas figured Max would have to keep his mouth shut rather than have his little girl hurt. He wouldn't have wanted Max killed though! What puzzles me is how those two thugs got into the house in the first place. Max opened the door, so therefore he must have known them.'

'Unless it wasn't who he expected.'

'What do you mean?', asked Bernie.

'Well, what if he recognised the car when he checked the CCTV, and was expecting Costas, but instead those two barged in when he opened the door?'

'I see. You mean, Costas would have spoken to him, but stayed in the car.'

'Exactly.'

'Well done, Poirot! You could well be right. It's beginning to make some sort of sense. I'd like to have been a fly on the wall when those two morons broke the news to Costas that they'd killed Max. He must have been shitting himself for weeks!'

'But, what I don't get, Bernie is this. How come a mega rich and powerful man like Costas felt threatened by a bloody footballer? Fair dues, Max was one of the most famous players in the world, but all Costas and George had to do was pooh pooh everything and put it all down to sour grapes on Max's part. Do you see what I mean? They could just say they had a fall out with Max, 'cause he didn't want to transfer to Italy, and he made it all up to get back at them. Everyone knows that George and Max hated each other's guts.' Chris was shaking his head. 'I can't make head or tail of it.'

'You are absolutely right, Chris, and you won't be the only one to work that out. In fact, I can't believe how bloody slow I've been. Must be getting old! It's been staring me in the face all this time!'

'What do you mean, what has?'

'Well, I know nearly everything there is to know about Mr. Pava...Papapavlou - except how to pronounce his name!' He smiled. 'As a matter of fact, I have been building a dossier for a few months now, and before all this lot kicked off, I was in the throes of putting together a really juicy article for my Sunday columns. It's what we columnists often do as a standby when there's not a lot of gossip to write about. There's much more to old Costas and his family problems than you'd think.'

'Yeah? Tell me more!'

'Well, for a start off, he is not the blood son of the senior Papapavlou - Nicodemeus. Nico's first wife died quite young, leaving two boys of thirteen and eleven without a mother. Nico then remarried a woman with a ten year old son, our Costas, and legally adopted the boy, but the kid turned out to be a vile little brat.

'No change there then!'

'He didn't get on with his stepbrothers and caused problems and heartache from the word go. They detested him. Probably still do! When he grew up and joined the family shipping business as a director, he proved to be even more of a liability. His stepbrothers complained bitterly that he was a waste of space, womanising, gambling and strutting his stuff all over Europe, spending company money like it was going out of style. He made Omar Sharif look like a vicar! There were incessant family disputes and infighting. Poor old Nico was getting on in years and took it all very badly, plus he was vastly overweight and had a heart condition - not surprising I suppose, the size of him.'

'Blimey!' Chris was wide eyed. 'How do you know all this? I've never read anything about it.'

Bernie tapped his nose. 'That's what I do, son! It's called keeping your ear to the ground - besides which, I have contacts all over Europe. They pass on all their latest gossip to me and I do the same for them! It's just journalistic networking. Anyway, aside from Costas, things were looking pretty bad for the Parthenon Ocean Liners company a few years ago. Firstly there was that terrible accident off the coast of Tenerife. One of their biggest liners was almost sunk and over a hundred people lost their lives.'

Oh, yes, of course, I do remember that. God, the pictures on TV were shocking. I didn't realise that was anything to do with Costas though.'

'Nor did a lot of people! The family must have greased a few palms big time to keep its name out of the press as much as possible. By the time the truth started to leak out, it was yesterday's news. There was a lot kicking off about the IS in Syria at the time, which naturally took precedence.' Bernie tutted. 'I missed the opportunity for a bloody good story there!

'You still can, surely,' Chris said.

'Of course, don't think I won't! It will dovetail nicely into my account of Max's story when I write it.' Bernie saw Chris's head drop at the mention of his friend, so he continued quickly. 'The insurance company wouldn't cover all the massive compensations the company had to pay out, because it was down to the negligence of the captain. The wrangling went on for over a year. It cost Parthenon bloody millions! And as if that wasn't bad enough, Costas bought Redthorn Rangers, against the express wishes of his father.

'Cor, just shows you doesn't it!' Chris exclaimed. 'Surely Rangers' Board - and George - knew all this!'

'Probably! And another thing, let's not forget the Greek Economy was looking in a really bad way. As it turned out, the rumours were well founded. The disastrous Greek financial meltdown was to take its toll on the whole country eventually, banks, companies and shareholders.' Bernie took a sip of his fruit juice. 'Well, they're still at loggerheads with the European Community aren't they.'

'You reckon his dad's company took a pounding, then?'

'Of course. You know, Greeks are paranoid about upholding their respect and their good name, and above all, family loyalty. Costas was doing his arrogant level best to shatter it all and cast shame on the family. Apparently, he was coming close to being kicked out of the business. As I see it, if the truth came out about Rangers being involved with corruption, you know, if Max carried out his threat to expose everything he knew, Costas would be dead in the water. It would be the straw that broke the camel's back as far as his father and stepbrothers were concerned.'

'So, he had to do something to make sure Max didn't spill the beans?'

'Looks like it!

Chris was shaking his head in dismay.

Bernie looked sideways at Chris and caught the look of despair on his face. 'I know, it's so tragic. But I still think Costas arranged for those two thugs to put the frighteners on him, that's all, and it all went disastrously wrong.'

Chris sank back on his pillow. The recurring image of his dear friend being murdered by two vile thugs was just too horrific for words.

'Oh, my dear God, poor Max - he didn't deserve any of it.' He sniffed and turned his face away from Bernie. 'I can't believe Max has left me his Harley Davidson. I'll keep that until the day I die, and I swear I'll make it all up to him - somehow!'

CHAPTER THIRTY-THREE

Closure

Chris, Beverley and Bernie had joined Kathie and Margaret for tea in the conservatory at Rangers Lodge. The little group was enjoying the last of the afternoon sunshine on what had been an unexpectedly warm day at the beginning of March. Everyone was anxiously awaiting the arrival of D.C.I. Goodwin, with news of Costas Papapavlou's arrest, subsequent hearing and the date of the Court case.

Kathie let the Chief Inspector in and he followed her into the conservatory. 'Please sit down, Inspector. Would you like some tea?', Kathie offered.

'Yes please.' He took a seat.

'Well, you'll all be pleased to know that as a result of the hearing, Mr. Papapavlou has been charged with complicity to kidnapping, but he has been granted bail, awaiting trial. His two accomplices have been charged with first degree murder and will remain in police custody.

Chris said angrily, 'You're joking!! So Costas gets away with murder!'

'I understand how you feel, sir,' D.C.I. Goodwin replied, 'but, although he was instrumental in the attempted kidnapping, according to Mr. Radic's statement, it was never Costas' intention to have Max killed. He cannot, therefore, be charged as an accessory.' He glanced at Kathie, as he heard her little intake of breath. She was holding her hand to her mouth. He quickly continued. 'The case is set for 10th August. A man like Costas can afford the best legal defence of course, so we'll just have to hope the outcome is in the Prosecution's favour. But I'm pretty sure the evidence, plus Radic's confession, will get him convicted.'

'Blimey - August! That's a long way off,' exclaimed Chris. 'I might still be in the USA.'

'Well, you'll have to fly back, I'm afraid, sir.'

'What about Hackett - and Amir isn't it?', Bernie asked.

'Hackett will be kicked out of the force, with no pension, and I'd say he will be facing prison. Amir is a civilian. He's also been charged with perverting the course of justice by tampering with police evidence.'

'Serves them right! That crooked detective deserves everything he gets, if you ask me!', Margaret said.'

Kathie closed her eyes and sank back in her chair.

'Oh, thank the Lord!', she sighed, wiping away a tear. 'I can't tell you what this means to me. I just had to prove to the world that Max would never have done that. I've never had a single doubt, not for a minute.'

'Well, you certainly managed that, Mrs. Rawlings,' said D.C.I Goodwin, with a smile. I have to say, you've all played your part. Well done everyone. They might all have gone unpunished without your intervention. I just can't wait to read your book, Mr. Cummings. How's it coming along - it's a biography on Max isn't it?'

'Yes, it is. I'm getting there,' replied Bernie. 'I've already had confirmation from the publishers. They're really anxious to print the book. Plus my Sunday supplement is going to serialise it. I'm hoping it will raise a few eyebrows and cause quite a stir in the sporting world. I did try to get an interview from George Wallis after he was sacked, but for some reason he didn't want to know!'

Everyone laughed and cheered.

'Well, I hope I can get a signed copy when it comes out.' D.C.I Goodwin shook Bernie's hand first, then everyone else's. 'I'll say goodbye for now. I wish you all the best. Thanks for the tea Mrs. Rawlings.'

Kathie showed him out and came back with a tray of glasses and a bottle of champagne. 'I think this calls for a celebration,' she smiled. 'Isn't that what they say?'

When she had charged their glasses, Bernie proposed a toast: 'Here's to our Max: a dearly loved husband, father, son and true friend, and one of England's greatest footballers. A genuine sportsman! We will always have a place in our hearts for him.'

'To Max', they all chorused as they clinked glasses. Bernie raised his glass in Kathie's direction. 'And to his amazing wife. She never gave up hope.'

'Hear hear. And to Kathie!'

CHAPTER THIRTY-FOUR

One year later

Becky reached for her mummy's hand. Kathie gave it a gentle squeeze and looked down at her little daughter, giving her a warm smile. They were sitting at the front of a few rows of gold framed chairs with red velvet seats in a lavishly furnished and decorated room. Beautiful floral displays adorned every corner of the room.

Kathie and Becky were part of a small, select gathering of family and friends. The room was a licensed registry office in one of Yorkshire's finest five star hostelries, Berkeley Hall Country Hotel, near Whitby, with a wonderful of the ocean.

In front of Kathie and Becky, being addressed by a lady Registrar, stood Margaret and Bernie. As the couple made their vows, Kathie bit her lip, trying really hard not to cry. Margaret, her beloved mother, looked stunning in a cream lace dress and jacket, her glossy black hair complemented by a stylish pale green hat and matching shoes.

'I have to wear something green, for Irish luck,' she had insisted, when she and Kathie were choosing their outfits.

'Absolutely!', Kathie agreed.

Bernie looked handsome in his dark grey suit, as he stood tall and proud and so happy, looking down lovingly at the smiling woman, now minutes away from becoming his wife.

Kathie glanced across at Chris, who was holding his wife's hand. Both were engrossed by the scene they were witnessing.

When Beverley's filming had finished, early reviews of her performance had been glowing and the movie promised to be a box office success. She and Chris had enjoyed over six months in Los Angeles, but both agreed that England was the place they would rather be. Beverley was surprised how homesick she was, and Chris had to admit that he really missed his family and friends.

'More beautiful than ever,' Kathie observed, looking at the radiantly pregnant Beverley. Her thoughts drifted away from the marriage ceremony for a few moments ....

A few weeks earlier she had invited Chris and Beverley to join her at Rangers Lodge for dinner. She had a proposition to put to them, now that they were back in the UK.

Margaret and Bernie were also guests at what Kathie hoped would be a very happy evening.

After the meal, everyone moved into the lounge with their coffees.

'Chris, I have been thinking hard about what to do as a memorial to Max,' Kathie began. 'You know he always wanted to set up his own football academy?'

'Yes, of course, he spoke to me about it. Fantastic idea. I only wish he'd lived to fulfill his dream!' Chris shook his head sadly.

'Well, maybe we can make his wish come true. If I were to fund it, would you be prepared to take on the project? I think you'd be perfect. It would be an excellent salary, with benefits - nothing like a premiership footballer's of course, but we can discuss the finer details later, if you are interested.'

'Kathie! If I am interested! Are you kidding? It would make me the happiest man on earth. You are an absolute star. Wow!' Chris jumped up and hugged her, giving her a kiss on the cheek. 'Bev, can you believe this?'

Beverley was smiling. 'Kathie, thank you so much. That's really wonderful.'

Bernie stood to shake Chris's hand. 'Well done mate. You deserve it!'

Margaret was clapping her hands. 'Absolutely! Congratulations Chris,' she said, as he bent to give her a peck on the cheek.

Chris picked up his glass. This deserves a toast!

Kathie was delighted. As they clinked their glasses, she said, 'that's good news, I'm so pleased. I know it's what Max would have wanted. I'll call my accountant and solicitor after the wedding, and we can get the ball rolling - so to speak! Meanwhile, here's to the future.'

.... Kathie heard the Registrar's words, 'I now pronounce you man and wife. You may kiss the bride.' She joined the small congregation as they stood and applauded.

'Mummy.' Kathie realised Becky was whispering to her.

'Yes, darling?'

'I wish daddy was here.'

So do I, sweetie, so do I.'

'Do you think he can see us?'

'I'm sure he can. He knows how much we love and miss him, but he will always be in our hearts, won't he?'

Becky was nodding. 'Yes, that's good. Is it over now? I'm really hungry!'

THE END

Other books from Penskills Publishing

From Author, David J Colane

WHOOSH! 'Miranda Don't Open Your Eyes!'
A children's time adventure, introducing a new superhero,
Miranda Knight.

ON MY LIFE
Hilarious biography, based on the life and times of Barry (The
Charity) Coombs.
Forthcoming:

SOUTH HARBOUR
Erotic, romantic mystery novel, based in a sleepy Cornish Village.

FOR PUCKSAKE
Hilarious antics and adventures of the residents of Puckingell, an
East Anglian village.